PRAISE FOR *THE HUNT FOR BIGFOOT*
Book One in the Human Origins Series

Another good addition to the cryptofiction library...For those that want to complete their Bigfoot fiction library, pick this book up.
Loren Coleman, author of

Bigfoot! The True Story of Apes in America The characters were well done and I found myself wanting to learn more about them. The action is well thought out and written with real dialog...I might add that having passed through Yoho National Park many times I was impressed with the accuracy of the descriptions [in this book]...So, did I enjoy this book? Do I recommend it? Yes to both.
Dan Fabian, Bard's Ink

A lively, exciting and gripping piece of fiction...If you are even remotely interested in cryptozoology, ancient cosmic visitors, the legends of Atlantis, human evolution and more, then grab a copy of [this book] as soon as possible.
Nick Redfern, *Phenomena* Magazine

An exciting, well researched rollercoaster ride of a novel...[I] enjoyed every last page.
Paul Vella, Center for Fortean Zoology

I encourage everyone who enjoys mysteries to read this book. You can also astound your friends by the knowledge you acquired concerning human evolution or the lack thereof.
Andrew Grgurich, *Marquette (Mich.) Mining Journal*

A good read for an evening-campfire setting gathered around in front of pitched tents near a lake.
Independent Publishing Review

PRAISE FOR *LORD OF THE DEAD*
Book Two in the Human Origins Series

Shiel uses her extensive knowledge of archaeology, anthropology, and Bigfoot to write a very rich story....I would highly recommend this book.

Paige Lovitt, Reader Views

Incredible high adventure...The pace is frenetic and the story lends plausibility to an number of evolution theories. We rated this book a solid four hearts.

Bob Spear, Heartland Reviews

[This book] immerses the reader in the strange and murky worlds of human origins, archaeological secrecy, and ancient cultures. With believable characters, a fast-paced plot, and a fantastic premise at its heart, Shiel's book is one not to be missed by anyone with an interest in the mysteries of this world and beyond.

Nick Redfern, author of *Body Snatchers in the Deser*

You end up just going along for the ride...This is a great adventure story.

Andrew Grgurich, *Marquette (Mich.) Mining Journal*

PRAISE FOR *BACKYARD BIGFOOT*
The True Story of Stick Signs, UFOs & the Sasquatch

Absolutely one of the best types of investigative reporting I've seen.

Beverly Pechin, Reader Views

[Shiel is] a skillful and accomplished writer...[This book is] as informative as it is entertaining.

Midwest Book Review

A skillfully written combination of field observations, academic perspectives, and discussions of other paranormal mysteries.

Thom Powell, author of *The Locals: A Contemporary Investigation of the Bigfoot/Sasquatch Phenomenon*

THE HUNT FOR BIGFOOT

Other Books by Lisa A. Shiel

Fiction

From Slipdown Mountain Publicatons
> Lord of the Dead (Book Two in the Human Origins Series)

Nonfiction

From Slipdown Mountain Publicatons
> The Evolution Conspiracy, Vol. 1
> Backyard Bigfoot

From The History Press
> Forgotten Tales of Michigan's Upper Peninsula

From Trails Books
> Strange Michigan (co-written by Linda S. Godfrey)

THE HUNT FOR BIGFOOT

Book One in the Human Origins Series

LISA A. SHIEL

Slipdown Mountain Publications
Lake Linden, Michigan
Toll-Free: 1-866-341-3705

THE HUNT FOR BIGFOOT: A NOVEL
© 2003, 2011 by Lisa A. Shiel
All rights reserved.
First edition published 2003. Second edition published 2011.

Cover Art & Interior Drawings by Kerrie Shiel
Used by permission

ISBN-13: 978-0-9746553-0-7
ISBN-10: 0-9746553-0-9
LCCN: 2004559553

Manufactured in the United States.

Slipdown Mountain Publications
www.SlipdownMountain.com
1-866-341-3705

Publisher's Cataloging-in-Publication Data

Shiel, Lisa A.
    The hunt for Bigfoot : a novel.—2nd ed. / Lisa A. Shiel.
    p. cm.
    ISBN-13: 978-0-9746553-0-7
    ISBN-10: 0-9746553-0-9
    1. Sasquatch—Fiction. 2. Michigan—Fiction. 3. Unidentified flying objects—Fiction.   I. Shiel, Kerrie, ill. II. Title. III. Series: Human origins series.
PS3619.H53 H86 2011
813'.6—dc22

                                                    2004559553

For Mom,
for saying "Write a book about Bigfoot!"

and

For Dad,
for all the help

PROLOGUE

HE STUMBLED TOWARD THE EDGE OF THE CLIFF. THE BEER BOTTLE CHILLED his hand. Leaning forward, he peered over the edge. Shoot, it was only a six-foot drop.

The night whirled around him. Jim swerved closer to the edge, collapsed onto his knees. As his vision blurred for the tenth time, he squinted at the beer bottle. Two beers. Hit him like a twelve pack. He struggled to his feet, shuffled in a half circle, and baby-stepped in the direction from which he had come, homing in on the flickering of the campfire.

"Buddy," he slurred, "wuz this stuff you're feeding me? Tastes like beer, feels like gasoline."

The man seated by the fire chuckled. He sat close enough that the fire warmed him, yet far enough that its light didn't reveal his features.

"Yah," Buddy said. "Beer."

Jim lifted the bottle to his lips and swigged more beer. Jeez, the stuff burned going down. Looked like beer. Tasted like beer. Felt like 200-proof vodka. "You sure izz beer?"

Buddy chuckled again.

Jim shook his head. "You're a weird one, Buddy."

Jim turned toward the cliff. Beyond the edge, over the tops of the birch trees and evergreens below, the stars glimmered. The moon smiled at him. He waved at the silvery disk.

"Want some beer, Mister Moon?"

He scuffled closer to the edge. The moon looked so pretty. So peaceful. He wanted to share his celebration with the moon, his folks, Annabelle, everybody.

Over his shoulder, he said, "Wanna see the body again?"

"I've seen enough, Jim. An amazing find."

"You get a look at the head? Those eyes, man, they're...unreal."

"I saw them." Buddy's voice sounded right behind him. "I like you, Jim. Wish you had never found that thing. I'm sorry it has to end this way, very sorry."

Something pressed against his back. Jim lurched forward.

"Hey what you do—"

Buddy shoved him over the cliff.

He let go of the bottle. As his body hit the water, he knew he was dying. And he knew why.

For the truth.

1

Dinosaur Valley State Park
Glen Rose, Texas
Tuesday, October 15

THE LUKEWARM WATER OF THE PALUXY RIVER TRICKLED OVER HER BARE feet as she tiptoed across the rocks. Her heel slipped. She threw her arms out to the sides. Her boots, which she clutched by their laces, flopped below her hands. As her balance returned, she leaped the last few feet onto the bank of the river.

Katy Gallagher dropped onto the ground and swiped her hand across her forehead. Sweat seeped from beneath the sweatband of her straw hat, dribbling down her forehead into her eyes and drooling down her chest. The air pressed against her like a wet blanket. The sun, though sinking below the tree line, boiled the atmosphere.

While she waited for her feet to air-dry, she studied the little valley the Paluxy River had carved for itself over the eons. Twenty yards north, the river made a hard right, a ways after that it twisted right again, forming a U bend that surrounded the parking lots of the state park. South of her position, past where the Opossum Branch emptied into the main river, the Paluxy widened into the Blue Hole before vanishing in the shadows of trees that overhung its banks. Even now, in the midst of a drought, the Blue Hole held as much water as a swimming pool.

Her feet dry, she yanked her socks and boots on and tied the laces. When she stood, she straightened her shorts and sleeveless shirt, the *only* clothes a human could wear in Texas in the summer. She was a Northerner, not an armadillo. So why had she dragged herself here?

For the truth, she reminded herself. Those three words had become her mantra this afternoon, her comfort as she slogged through briars, careened down near-vertical slopes, and battled minivans for a parking spot.

She pulled the official park map out of her pocket. The sheet was wrinkled and damp from the humidity. Since she got the map from the park office at the main entrance, she had no hope it would point her to her quarry. No, the Texas Parks & Wildlife Department had no interest in the truth.

Thanks to Jim Van Owen, she had a general idea of where the quarry might be. Jim found a site on the Internet that claimed the quarry lay on the north bank across from the northwest parking lot, near the U bend, on a ledge one yard above the river level. The website, however, was updated three years ago. She hoped the information was still right.

The truth tended to disappear if left alone too long.

The map showed theropod and sauropod tracks on either side of the river at that spot. Her quarry should await her alongside those dinosaur tracks. If the website was right. If the quarry ever existed.

Adjusting the straps of her backpack, she strode up the north shore toward the bend.

A child screamed.

Katy froze. Her heart hammered.

Just past the U bend, on the opposite bank, a toddler and her parents waded in the river. Katy relaxed. A knot lingered in her gut.

Maybe the tension stemmed from the fact that park rangers had been trailing her all afternoon. Although she saw neither of the uniformed men now, she felt gazes fixated on her back. Ridiculous. Why on earth would two park rangers stalk her? They knew nothing of her intentions. They knew nothing about her at all.

But she had seen them. Following.

Coincidence. Park rangers patrolled the park. It was their job.

She tromped over a pockmarked patch of stone. The river bottom was solid limestone and here the drought had revealed more of it. She hopped over a theropod print—a triangular, rounded depression with toes splaying outward from the widest end.

The park, named for the dinosaur footprints fossilized into the riverbed, held dozens of the tracks. The best and most famous tracks, discovered in the 1920s, had been removed to a museum in New York. Other holes marred the rock where time and water had eroded out depressions. Sometimes you needed to look closely to tell the dinosaur prints from the erosional depressions.

At the U bend, she stopped. No ledge. Either the website lied, or the ledge no longer existed. A flash flood might have torn it asunder. It might have crumbled away on its own.

Someone could have hacked it out of the earth.

There she went again, diving headfirst into paranoia.

Katy slipped off her backpack and dropped it onto the ground. She stared at the rock around her. Too bad she wasn't searching for erosional depressions, because she'd found a goldmine of them.

Wait. A depression caught her attention as surely as a whale flopping in the desert would. The depression was oblong, narrower at one end. Water filled the hole. She kneeled beside the hole.

Shoving her hand into the water, she felt along the edges of the depression. At the wider end, she probed the bottom. Her fingers bumped ridges in the rock.

Ridges.

Water, she had to get the water out!

She ripped open the zipper of her backpack. Spotting the water bottle, a plastic jug with a big straw sticking out the top, she yanked the straw out of the cap. With the straw she sucked the water out of the depression one mouthful at a time. She spit the mouthfuls of stagnant water into the river.

When she finished, she shoved five TicTacs in her mouth.

She studied the depression. Silt veiled the bottom. She shoveled the silt out with her hands. Shapes emerged, the ridges she had felt and a depression with a mound just behind it. The hole was an inch deep, about eight inches long.

That was no erosional depression.

Yes.

Her hat slipped off her head. As the breeze tumbled it away, she snatched her camera from her backpack. Snapping photographs from every side while standing, kneeling, lying on the rock, she imagined how Charlie and Jim would react to the news. Jump and yell? Get blind drunk and dance on the tables?

No. Charlie would rub his chin, nod, and say, "Good job, Katy."

Jim would get blind drunk and dance on the tables. Hell, she might join him.

Using the tape measure she had stuffed in her hip pocket, she measured the print—9 inches long, 3.1 inches wide across the ball of the foot. Oh yes, this was no mere consequence of erosion.

It was a 100-million-year-old human footprint.

2

FIFTEEN MINUTES LATER, SHE FINISHED CASTING THE PRINT. SHE USED SPRAY foam instead of plaster of paris because it dried faster, was easier to transport, and formed a lightweight cast. She tucked the cast inside her backpack.

In her journal, she made field notes. Size of print, location of site, type of surface, estimated age of print. Her hands trembled as she scribbled the information. She had done it, really done it. Those footprints don't exist, everyone said, it's a hoax. Modern humans evolved 200,000 years ago, not in the age of dinosaurs.

Garbage. She had the proof here, in solid rock. Erosion by the river smoothed the sharp edges of the print, proof that no one carved it. Erosion took centuries. Even if someone carved a footprint forty years ago, the print could not have eroded this much in so short a time. In geological time, forty years was like a millionth of a second. Besides, no one could have carved the delicate upswelling of the push-off mound, the lump behind the ball of the foot created as the foot pushed off from the step.

No one could've carved the footprint here, in a state park, where visitors moseyed along the river in summer and winter, rain and sun. Someone would have seen. Or heard. To carve a footprint in rock required more than a hammer and chisel.

No matter, the skeptics would deny the truth. They always did. People uncovered fossilized human footprints before and the scientists dismissed them. Erosional depressions, they said. Misidentified dinosaur tracks.

She wasn't a scientist. She had no advanced degrees, no internship at the Smithsonian. Who would believe Katy Gallagher, website designer?

The butterflies in her gut mutated into pebbles.

She kneeled beside the print, sat back on her heels. Damn.

A hand thrust her hat in her face.

Taking her hat, she looked up at the park ranger looming over her. The sun, glaring behind him between the trees, obscured his face.

She shoved her hat onto her head. "Thanks."

"You best be leaving, missy."

"Why?"

"Messin' with state property is a crime."

"Don't know what you mean."

A voice behind her said, "We saw."

She glanced over her shoulder.

The other ranger. Hands on hips. Squinting at her.

Her gut tightened. She zipped her backpack shut. The sun had dipped halfway below the horizon. Dark would come soon.

The rangers couldn't hurt her, someone would see. She glanced at the spot where the family of three frolicked earlier. Vacant.

Sweat dribbled down her spine.

Rising, she said, "Guess I'm done."

The ranger nearest her seized her backpack. He tore open the flap. Thrusting his hand inside the bag, he tossed out the cast and her journal. The journal plopped into the river. The cast clattered on the rock. The ranger nabbed her camera. He popped open the back and, ripping the film out, stuffed it in his pocket. He dropped the camera in her backpack.

As he handed her the pack, he drawled, "Have a nice day now."

The night descended like a great blind drawn over the window of earth.

The second ranger raised his hand. An object glinted in the waning light, a wedge of metal protruding from a wooden handle. An axe.

She floundered into the river, her boots slipping on the rock. Her knee smacked into the bottom. Pain ricocheted through her leg. She stumbled to the far bank and raced toward the stone staircase that led up the hill into the parking lot.

Behind her, blows echoed through the valley.

A voice shouted. "This ain't working, we need the jackhammer."

Katy ran up the stairs. Her legs burned, her chest ached, sweat drenched her clothes. At the top of the stairs, she paused to suck in a breath. Voices echoed along the river.

She hurried toward her car, a rental parked at the south end of the lot. Inside the car, she locked the doors and gunned the engine.

The tires screeched as she swerved the car backward out of the space, slammed the gear shift lever into drive, jammed the accelerator down. The headlights flashed on huge figures beside the road. She yelped.

The dinosaur models. In the headlights, the fiberglass versions of *T. rex* and *Apatosaurus* towered overhead from within their pen.

The car rocketed through the park entrance.

A light, reflected in the rearview mirror, flashed in her eyes. She checked the side mirror. A round, bright light hovered above the trees. Its size remained the same, even as she swerved onto the highway and sped away from the park.

She rammed her foot on the accelerator until the pedal hit the floorboard. The speedometer registered forty, then sixty, then seventy miles per hour.

The light stayed behind her. She slowed the car.

The light maintained its distance. A whirring sound grew louder, nearer.

Standing on the brake, she veered the car off the road onto the shoulder.

The whirring segued into thwop-thwop-thwop. The light zoomed closer. Daylight filled the interior of the car.

The thwopping deafened her. Outside, the trees swayed.

She rolled down the window and poked her head outside. A gale smacked her in the face, embedding dirt in her eyes. She bent her neck backward. The light, attached to a helicopter, passed overhead, continuing down the road for a hundred yards before banking east.

The thwopping faded into whirring. The light disappeared in a moment, carrying the whirring away with it into the night.

Katy withdrew her head and rolled up the window. The helicopter might have been chasing her. The moon might also be chasing her, but she doubted either was the case.

A creature warbled.

She yelped, her butt bouncing off the seat. On the passenger seat, her cell phone rang a second time. While it rang a third time, she took a deep breath.

She grabbed the phone. "Yes."

"Katherine."

"Dr. Spiegel." She leaned back, shutting her eyes. "Can this wait?"

"Dr. Bergren has not shown up for his classes."

"I'm not his mother."

Spiegel sighed. "Charles missed his classes yesterday *and* today. He doesn't answer his cell phone or pager. It's spring semester all over again."

"If he went on a hunt, I can't reach him either. Cell phones don't work in the wilderness and I am not telepathic."

"This is the last straw, Katherine. Someone must be here in the morning to answer for him or he can kiss his chances at tenure goodbye, not to mention his professorship."

"I don't work for you."

"You're his…*business* partner. Do you want him to lose his job?"

She gritted her teeth. Her knuckles ached as she tightened her grip on the phone. Spiegel always had a calming effect on her.

"I'll catch a red eye tonight," she said.

"There's more. It's about your little friend, Jim Van Owen."

"What now."

"He's dead."

Anameka, Michigan
Wednesday, October 16

Fingers of pink, orange, and red tantalized the sky with a promise of daylight. Katy shivered as she unlocked the front door of her cabin. A cold front swept through overnight, dropping the temperatures and spattering rain on the earth. She glanced at the sunrise.

The serenity that usually enveloped her when she witnessed the glory of sunrise, the stars, or the forest surrounding her home failed her this morning. Jim was dead. She'd lost a friend, a colleague, a nice guy who volunteered for the project she and Charlie started—the Human Origins Project. Jim's wife humored his interest in the project, even when he went off on three-day treks through the wilderness in search of hairy wild men or, as Katy called them, hairy hominids.

Katy flung the door inward and tromped through the screened-in porch to the inner door. Unlocking that door, she shuffled into the living room. The fire in the wood stove had long since died. Her breath plumed from her mouth.

Her home, a log cabin on ten wooded acres, had two rooms—the bathroom and the rest of the house. The kitchen, living room, and dining area opened onto each other like sections of one big room, so she never thought of them as separate rooms. The bar between the kitchen and the living room acted as the sole barrier between the sections. Along the right wall, a staircase led up to the loft, where she slept, and down into the basement. The basement housed her laundry room, a store room, and a door that opened into a half-underground wood shed.

The cabin sat on the side of a hill. The back door, beside the bathroom, opened onto a small, roofless porch that overlooked the upslope of the hill. Pines and birch trees loomed on all sides of the little cabin. Through the window of the front porch she could see, across the front acreage, the country bungalow owned by a couple from Chicago whose names she forgot, having met them just once. As it was a summer house, the bungalow stood vacant now, like a turtle shell after the animal has died. Smoke drifted out of the bungalow's chimney. Even summer houses were heated all winter.

Katy pushed her luggage, a wheeled carry-on suitcase, against the bar. The answering machine sat atop the bar beside the phone. The message light wasn't blinking. No messages. Gone for six days and no messages? If Charlie went out on a hunt, he would've let her know.

Unless he got so caught up in the excitement that he forgot. He and Jim could get so eager about a sighting that they forgot about eating.

She collapsed onto a stool at the bar. Jim. Dead. It seemed impossible.

Hopping off the stool, she faced the living room.

The hairs at the nape of her neck stiffened.

The drawers of her desk, in the corner of the living room behind the staircase, hung ajar. Each one was open a little more or less than the others, as if someone pulled the drawers out then shoved them back in a hurry. A paper stuck out of one drawer. On the desktop, her file folders were fanned out across one corner. Her day planner, which she kept in a cubbyhole of the desk, lay on the desktop.

When she surveyed the living room, incongruities popped out at her. Sofa cushions misaligned. The rug askew. Dried mud on the hardwood floor.

Her home. Her office. Ransacked.

Trotting to her desk, she reached for the power button on her computer. She froze. The green light glowed above the button, indicating the computer was on. The power light on the monitor, however, was dark. She pressed the button on the monitor. The monitor powered up with a buzz.

Her computer held all the files for the websites she designed and maintained for her clients. She kept backups of the web pages. That wasn't what bothered her. Her computer also contained all the passwords for clients' sites.

On the screen, the file manager window had been left open. It displayed the contents of the Human Origins Project directory—the files for the HOP website and other information about the project. The intruder perused her hard drive in search of…something. She closed the file manager. Another window came into view as the file manager closed.

A photo editing program. An image stared back at her from the screen. Red letters at the top of the image declared "Hairy Hominid Sightings—Past Six Months." Below the heading, red dots marked locations on a map of northern lower Michigan. Green areas delineated forests. Blue lines etched the courses of rivers and streams. Blue splotches showed lakes. Although the dots that marked sightings appeared all over the map, they concentrated in a ten-mile radius around the eastern side of Anameka.

The intruder didn't care about her clients' sites. He cared about the site she maintained for Charlie and the project. Why?

Thunk.

Katy turned her head toward the basement stairs, where the sound originated. The basement was dark. She slipped a hand under the desk, feeling for the holster she kept secured underneath the desktop. Finding it, she grasped the Taurus .357 revolver hidden there and pulled out the gun.

Click. The sound of a door unlatching. Sunlight, still wan at this hour, filtered up the stairs from the door to the wood shed.

The Taurus clasped in her right hand, she tiptoed down the stairs.

Crunch-crunch. Shoes on dead grass and leaves.

She raised the gun in front of her, arms outstretched, elbows bent. When she stepped on the last stair, the wood squeaked. She stopped, afraid to breathe, sure her heartbeat would give her away.

When no one surged out of the basement wielding an axe, she moved off the stairs and through the entranceway into the corridor that acted as a laundry room. To the right, a doorway led into the storage room. To the left, the wood shed door hung open, swinging on its hinges in the breeze. Outside, sunrise cast its fiery glow on the wood stacked in the shed.

Katy eased across the threshold into the shed.

The smell of damp earth filled her nostrils. An overnight rainstorm had muddied the ground and dampened the leaves that littered the earth. The shed had three walls, one of which it shared with the house, plus a roof. Through the unenclosed front, she could see the driveway, the storage shed, and the front acreage. The driveway encircled the storage shed, branching off toward the road. The front acreage, four treeless acres, sloped down to abut the road. From her viewpoint, she saw no one.

Stepping out of the shed, she studied the ground. Though the mud was drying and therefore no longer reproduced shoe prints like a mimeograph, the surface took the prints of her soles well enough. She kneeled a few feet outside the shed. Superficially, the ground looked undisturbed. Yet every creature left sign—evidence of its passing, whether a footprint, a broken branch, or disturbed vegetation. She must look for it. Sign could camouflage itself.

A patch of leaves grabbed her attention. She scuttled closer. The leaves were depressed in the outline of a shoe. *Bingo.*

She found another shoe print in the mud ahead and to the left of the first print. Drawing a mental line through the middle of the track she visually traced it across the inner curve of the driveway, where bricks lined the drive. She trotted across the driveway. At the brick border she discovered one brick jarred a finger's width out of line.

Estimating the intruder's path, she moved down the driveway toward the road. No tracks alongside the drive, no disturbances in the grass that she could detect. Gravel in the driveway had been kicked onto the grass, though, suggesting the intruder sprinted down the driveway. But she lost the track at the end of the drive. Backtracking didn't help. The road was gravel, so she could have searched for sign there, but why bother? The intruder was probably a rich kid who got bored with the majesty of nature and decided breaking and entering sounded exciting. Last summer, a boy whose family rented a cottage nearby thought rearranging the brick border of her driveway to spell "suck" was funny. Go figure.

Back in the cabin, she checked the clock above her desk—7:40. She had an eight o'clock meeting with Dr. Spiegel at the college. Forget breakfast.

She grabbed her keys and left.

NORTHERN MICHIGAN COLLEGE SQUATTED ON THE OUTSKIRTS OF ANAMEKA, A town of five thousand about ten miles from Katy's cabin. The town hunkered in a low spot between the hills. In the winter the big hill, known as Hunter's Hill because of the herds of deer that inhabited its woods, became a ski and sled slope.

Stomach growling, eyes gritty, Katy shuffled into the office of Dr. Jeremiah Spiegel. The plaque on the door declared him "Dean of Humanities." Though Katy usually laughed when she saw the sign, today she felt no mirth at the misnomer bestowed on Spiegel. She kept seeing Jim in her mind, hearing his voice greeting her as he had so many times before.

Mornin', Katy matey.

Spiegel sat behind his oak desk, straight as a statue in his leather chair, his rimless glasses balanced above the bulb of his nose. The acid frothing inside him had burned the hair off the crown of his head and left the remainder gray. His navy suit looked fresh from the cleaners. His loafers tapped a drum roll on the vinyl floor. He focused on a sheet of paper he held in one hand.

Katy cleared her throat.

Spiegel frowned at her. "You're late."

The clock on the wall gave the time as 8:01. Rolling her eyes, she settled into one of two high-backed chairs. "Anal retentive, as usual, Spiegel."

"Are you prepared to answer for Dr. Bergren?"

"I suppose."

"He's a history professor, you know, aside from his dalliances with you."

Her nostrils flared. She gripped the arms of the chair so hard her nails dug into the leather.

She leaned forward. "Pardon me, perhaps I misheard you. His *what* with me?"

"Everyone knows about you two. Your…closeness."

She wanted to punch him in the head. Spiegel wasn't worth it, though.

"Anyway," he said, "I thought I might persuade you to speak with Charles. Tell him to come back or he's fired."

Katy glared at Spiegel. She was used to his way of speaking without saying what he meant. Today she had no stomach for it. She slept all of two hours on the airplane. Park rangers stole her evidence of humanity's antiquity. One of her friends died and she still didn't know how or why. Another friend had taken off.

"What are you getting at?" she said.

He locked his fingers under his chin. A smile tugged at his lips. "When you see Charles, do tell him to stop all this nonsense. Jim's dead because of it. He needs to give up this ridiculous quest and be a respectable member of academia again."

"You think he's hiding at my place."

Spiegel shrugged.

Katy jumped out of the chair. Jabbing a finger in the air at him, she said, "First, Charlie is old enough to be my father. Second, it's none of your damn business what we do together and, third, I have neither seen nor spoken to Charlie since I left for Texas six days ago."

She slapped both palms down flat on Spiegel's desk and leaned over him, eyes squinted. "I'm tired, hungry, and confused. I have no time for your games."

"Yes, I can see how you seduced Charles with your charm and femininity."

"When did you last speak to him?"

"Can't recall." Spiegel sat back in his chair. "My secretary saw him Friday evening at the grocery store. Said he was buying the entire stock of granola bars and juice boxes."

"Did you call his son?"

"Yes, of course. He knows less than I."

"Your concern for Charlie's safety is touching." She whirled toward the door.

"Katherine," Spiegel said.

Although she halted, she kept her back to him. "What now?"

"Do the right thing. Break it off with Charles."

"Go to hell, Spiegel."

KATY STOOD AT THE DOOR. THE WORDS ENGRAVED ON THE PLAQUE MOUNTED on the door hypnotized her. It read, "Dr. Charles Bergren, History Department."

Where did he go? Why didn't he tell her? Was he coming back?

Of course he would come back. He had a son, friends, a job he loved. He knew Spiegel would fire him if he played hooky too long. In the spring he took off for two days mid-week, not once but three times, and missed the first day of finals. His graduate assistant administered the exams, but the girl transferred to the University of Michigan over the summer because she couldn't take Charlie's unpredictability.

Katy knew Charlie was obsessed with the project. When he received news of a sighting, he'd rush out to investigate, at two in the afternoon or four in the morning, whether he had a class to teach or had the day off. He wanted the truth more than his job, more than the respect of his peers, more than life.

Hairy hominids, wild men, Sasquatch, Bigfoot. Whatever you called them, strange creatures existed in the wilderness. Charlie started investigating the sightings six years earlier, first as a hobby, then as a full-fledged scientific project funded with his own money. Two years ago, Katy joined him after responding to an ad in the paper. She still remembered what the ad said:

WANTED: assistant for grossly underpaid work in ridiculed field of research. Must be willing to endure mud, rain, sleet, snow, and the attention of huge hairy creatures.

Katy called the phone number listed in the ad because she wondered who the hell would place such an ad in the newspaper. Besides, she needed a hobby for her spare time, something to do besides stare at a computer monitor until her eyes crossed. Charlie gave her more than a hobby. He gave her a mission.

According to half the town, she got the job based on her "openness" rather than her intelligence.

And they weren't referring to her open mind.

Jerking the knob, she thrust the door inward. Sunlight streamed through the mini blinds. Charlie's desk butted against the windows, which offered a view of Anameka and the hills and woods outside the city limits. Over a low hill, Lake Anameka glistened like liquefied sapphire.

Katy approached the desk. Ungraded exams overflowed their wire basket on one corner, while a photo of Charlie and his son, both dressed in waders and holding fish, balanced on the opposite corner. Settling onto the chair, she studied the photo. Charlie's gray hair, wrinkles, and pale blue eyes reminded her of Santa Claus, which made her having an affair with him all the more ridiculous. She might sit on his knee and rattle off a list of toys she wanted for Christmas, but carry on an affair? With Santa Claus? Please.

He looked a bit like Sean Connery, if Sean Connery ever played Santa. No matter, she wouldn't have an affair with Sean Connery either. Both he and Charlie were too old for her. She liked men who didn't have a driver's license yet the year she was born.

Charlie's son, Rick, smiled at her from the photo. The smile that made her stomach flutter. She fingered a lock of her chestnut hair, winding the spiral curl around her index finger.

She met Rick half a dozen times when he visited Charlie and, despite his derision of the Human Origins Project, she liked him. The way he towered over her, at least seven inches taller than her five-foot-six, made her feel small yet safe. He looked around thirty, though he grinned and changed the subject when she asked his age. He had eyes bluer than his father's, hair the color of milk chocolate streaked with gold, a physique neither too muscular nor too thin.

After seeing him, she often found herself skipping back to her car. *Skipping.* A grown woman approaching thirty bounding like a five-year-old.

"Get a grip," she said, releasing her hair and straightening in the chair.

Jim had died. Charlie had vanished. She ought to think about them, not Rick Bergren.

In the center of the desk, a clear mat covered a desk calendar. Charlie made no notes on the calendar, and didn't bother marking off the days. The page was wrinkled under the word "October." No. Not wrinkled. Lifting the mat, she touched the calendar. The page was torn out below the month name. She pushed the tattered page up, revealing the page for November beneath it.

Someone ripped October out of Charlie's calendar. Someone also broke into her cabin and scanned her files.

Nothing else seemed amiss in the office. She checked his computer. Nothing there. If he left a clue as to his whereabouts, someone eliminated it. She felt ridiculous for considering such a conspiracy, still…

She must know how Jim died.

After a quick call to her answering machine in case Charlie had called, she rushed outside into the parking lot. As she rounded a corner onto the row where she'd parked, she noticed a van cruising down the next row parallel to her. The van, an older model, had no windows in the back. The sunlight obscured the front windows and windshield.

She slowed her pace.

The van slowed.

She burst into a run.

The van matched her speed.

At her vehicle, a fifteen-year-old Ford pickup, she dug her keys out of her pocket. She dropped the keys, snatched them up, and shoved the key into the door. The van hesitated in line of sight of her.

The door lock disengaged. She yanked the door open, jumped inside, slammed the door, started the engine. While she backed out of the space, the van crept down the next row. When she swung out of the parking lot into the street, the van rolled out of the lot behind her. The van maintained a distance of three or four car lengths behind her. She slowed at a stop sign, easing into the right turn lane. After a car crossed the intersection in front of her, she veered across the left lane, swerving left onto the cross street. The van followed.

She punched the accelerator. The pickup surged down the street.

The van shrank in her rearview mirror. She loosened her fingers around the steering wheel.

Oh yeah. She had a grip all right.

THE DOORBELL CHIMED INSIDE, MUTED BY THE DOOR. THE VAN OWENS LIVED about twenty feet past the city limit in a double-wide trailer plunked on the edge of five acres. Jim bricked in the trailer, giving it the look of a home built into a concrete foundation. An American flag rippled in the breeze atop a pole sunk into a concrete island in the front yard. The mailbox was decorated like a black-and-white cow, complete with an udder.

Annabelle Van Owen answered the door after a moment. When she saw Katy, her lips quivered. Tear tracks stained her cheeks. Her eyes were bloodshot. She clamped a tissue in one hand, the door knob in the other. Her red hair accentuated the pallor of her skin.

"Katy, thank God," Annabelle said. Straightening, she lifted her chin. "I mean, come on in."

Nodding, Katy walked through the door. Annabelle guided her into the dining room, where they took seats on opposite sides of the birchwood table. Voices drifted in from the living room—*Good Morning, America* on television.

Annabelle bit her lip. "You heard. 'Bout Jim."

Katy knew Annabelle well enough to understand the woman hated pity, whether self-inflicted or poured on by another. She knew Katy empathized. No need for I'm-so-sorry or please-accept-my-condolences.

"Yes," Katy said. "What happened?"

"Somebody murdered him, that's what happened."

"Are you sure?"

"Damn sure." Annabelle tore a wad off the tissue. "They say he got drunk and drowned in the lake. Sure, Jim drank sometimes. But he'd never risk his life that way."

"What did the police say?"

"Impossible to prove his drowning was murder. Besides, his blood alcohol was above the limit and they found six beer cans and a bottle of whiskey near his campsite." Annabelle caressed the polished surface of the table. "Jim made this table for our anniversary last year. Worked on it every morning before I got up so it'd be a surprise."

"It's beautiful."

"Yeah." Tears welled in her eyes. She looked straight at Katy, lips twisted. "Jim hated whiskey. So why in hell would he drink a whole bottle of the stuff? And he didn't take beer into the woods with him. Where'd he get it?"

"Maybe he bought some—"

Annabelle slammed her palm on the table. "No!"

"I was thinking out loud," Katy said. "Didn't mean anything by it."

"I'm sorry, Katy, it's just the damn cops won't listen and I *know* Jim was on his way home. He called me Friday night, said he found a type specimen and he was bringing it back right away. The cell phone was working so he couldn't have been far into the woods. That was the last I heard until yesterday morning when some hikers found his body floating in the lake."

Katy gazed out the window at the woods behind the house. Jim found a type specimen. That meant a carcass. Somehow he discover the body of a hairy hominid. He wouldn't shoot one. The three of them agreed the creatures seemed too human to kill, despite realizing only a type specimen would satisfy the scientists. She had yet to see one herself, but the sightings painted a picture more vivid than a Rembrandt.

"You knew him best, Annabelle," Katy said. "Do you believe he had a type specimen?"

"Absolutely."

"When did he leave on the hunt?" Katy asked.

"Thursday morning."

Katy watched a squirrel skitter up a tree. "He must've met someone, had a beer or two, told that person about the specimen..."

"Knowing Jim, he woulda wanted to share the moment with anybody who passed by." Annabelle's chin trembled. "He was so trusting."

Tears streaked down Annabelle's cheeks. She mashed the tissue into the corner of her eye.

Katy stood. Meeting Annabelle's gaze, she said, "I will find out who killed him. I promise you that."

Annabelle nodded.

Katy strode out of the house and climbed into her pickup. Shoving a hand under the seat, she retrieved the Taurus revolver which she tucked there on her way out of the cabin earlier. Her stomach gurgled. She checked her watch. It was after 11:00, at least fourteen hours since her last real meal, nine hours since the pretzels and Pepsi on the airplane.

Food could wait.

She needed to see Charlie's place. He might have left a note there, some clue about his activities, if the shadows pursuing her hadn't gotten there first.

Christ, now she feared shadows.

She set the revolver on the seat.

THE FRONT DOOR HUNG OPEN. MUD SMEARED THE WELCOME MAT, A WOVEN rectangle emblazoned with a cartoon of Bigfoot and the phrase "Wipe your big feet here."

Rick Bergren stepped over the mat into the house. Dad left the door unlocked most of the time, but not open. The sinking he felt in his gut during the flight from Boston and the hour's drive from the airport intensified. Now it felt like a vacuum cleaner sucking out his insides.

What had his father gotten into this time?

The living room of the log house gave Rick the willies every time he walked into it. His father bought the house cheap from a guy with "legal problems," which meant he was evading alimony and needed to expunge as many assets as possible for as little money as possible. If he made a profit, his wife got half. So Charles Bergren, ever the humanitarian, snapped up the log house for a pittance. It was a nice house. A big, nice house.

Still, it gave Rick the willies.

The house, constructed from logs the color of blanched almonds, had two floors, the second a loft that comprised the master bedroom and bath. At 3,000 square feet, the house was huge. The cavernous living room and the woven-stick staircase created the sensation of standing inside a whale carcass. Sliding glass doors accessed the deck, which hung over the edge of a hill with a view of the river below.

Rick strolled through the living room. A sofa cushion lay on the floor.

He bent down and looked at the cushion. Strange.

Tossing the cushion onto the sofa, he proceeded up the stairs into the loft.

The bed was made. In the bathroom, the toothbrush and razor were gone.

He went to the closet. Several hangers hung empty. Dad's shoes lined the length of the closet, set out in pairs with business shoes at one end, outdoors shoes at the other. One pair was missing. Judging from the position, possibly hiking boots or sneakers.

Downstairs, he headed for the office at the rear of the house. As he reached the door, he hesitated. The door, though shut, was unlatched.

Rustling came from inside the room.

Should've grabbed one of Dad's guns. Oh well.

He kicked the door inward, surging across the threshold at the man hunched over the desk.

The man dropped a stack of papers.

Rick rushed at him. The man grabbed a chair and flung it at him.

The chair hit Rick in the chest, knocking him off balance. The man raced out of the office, his footsteps clattering on the wood floor as he careened out of the house.

Rick ran down the hallway to the front door. The man was gone.

While he contemplated searching for the man, the sh-shunk of the deck doors opening and closing changed his mind. Someone else had entered the house.

His father kept the guns in the basement. The living room was between him and the basement stairs. Rick hurried down the hallway with his back against the wall, careful that his shoes made no sound on the wood floor. Footsteps echoed down the hall from the living room. About ten feet from the living room doorway, he paused. The sounds stopped.

He eased forward. *Around the corner, he's around the corner.*

Rick leaped through the doorway, swinging his body toward the kitchen. The .357 revolver's muzzle bumped his chest.

He threw his fists up in front of him.

Katy sighed. She lowered the revolver.

Breathing hard, Rick stared at her. "I could've killed you."

"With what, your breath?"

He looked at his hands. Lethal weapons? Hardly. What a ridiculous thing to say, *I could've killed you.*

Shaking his head, he ran a hand through his hair. His heart pounded. His jaw muscle throbbed. He tried relaxing. It didn't work.

Someone other than Katy broke into his father's house, and he had no idea who or why. College professors, even ones who dabbled in silliness like Bigfoot research, didn't have enemies.

Hairy hominids, Dad called them. Occasionally mystery or wild men, but never Bigfoot.

"What are you doing here?" Katy asked.

"I should ask you that." He rested a palm on the wall, leaning against it. "This is my father's house."

"I was looking for Charlie."

"Spiegel thinks you know where he is."

Katy tucked the gun inside her waistband. She wore a tan pantsuit with more wrinkles than an elephant and sneakers smudged with mud. Strands of hair fell around her face, escapees from the puffy elastic thing that secured her hair behind her head. Dark circles discolored the skin beneath her eyes.

She still looked beautiful.

He frowned. "There was a guy in Dad's office. Going through his papers. The creep got away."

"Should've stopped him."

"He threw a chair at me."

She rubbed her forehead. "This is crazy."

In the living room, the cuckoo clock announced the hour. He watched Katy and waited for an explanation, which she might or might not give depending on her mood. If she did explain, he might not understand anyway. They spoke different languages, his based on reality, hers based on fantasies about hairy creatures in the wilderness and humans living during the age of dinosaurs. His father spoke her language. Sometimes he envied their relationship, the closeness that everyone in town thought signified a romantic relationship. Maybe Dad was sleeping with her. He didn't know. Maybe the doubt explained why he hadn't seen or spoken to his father since Christmas.

God, he felt like a jerk.

Katy folded her arms over her chest. "Jim Van Owen was murdered Friday. He found evidence someone wanted hushed up. And now Charlie's missing, his office at the college ransacked, his office here ransacked, my home broken into… and I think someone's following me."

Jaw set, she glared into his eyes. "Suppose you think that's nonsense."

The green of her eyes, deep as the sea, transfixed him. He looked away. "I don't know what to think. I have to find my father, that's all I know."

"We will find him."

He arched an eyebrow. "We?"

She smiled. "Afraid of being alone with me?"

He returned the smile. "I might get in trouble."

"You wish."

She strolled past him down the hallway. He turned to watch her march toward the office.

Glancing over her shoulder, she said, "Coming?"

IN THE OFFICE, KATY RIGHTED THE CHAIR. SHE SAT DOWN, WHEELING THE CHAIR closer to the desk. The intruder had left papers strewn across the desktop, the floor, and the file cabinet. Sorting through the mess would take hours. If strangers wanted Charlie dead, he might not have hours.

If they wanted her dead, she might not have hours either.

Yet if they wanted her dead, the intruder at her cabin or the people in the white van could've killed her. They could've shot her from half a mile away if they wanted. Thus far they seemed interested in eliminating evidence rather than humans. So far.

Rick clomped into the office. At first seeing him, she had gone numb. Her stomach did a gymnastics routine inside her belly, her pulse thundered through her veins, thoughts foundered in her mind. The moment, however, passed. For now.

"Forget this mess," she said. "We don't have time to go through it."

"What now then?"

"Back to my cabin." She hopped out of the chair. "I'll check the website in case Charlie uploaded his itinerary before he left."

Rick's expression blanked. "Whatever you say."

"I parked around back. You can follow me in your car."

She rushed past him down the hallway, through the living room, out the glass doors onto the deck. The sight of papers tossed about, drawers yanked open, it unsettled her. Three times today she discovered such a scene, and twice she avoided thinking about what it meant. She no longer had the luxury of denial. Someone murdered Jim. Charlie had vanished. Intruders stole all evidence of his activities before his disappearance. She wanted to scream. Cry. Hit someone.

Instead she sped down Charlie's driveway, gravel spraying up around her pickup, with Rick's rented Chevy two feet off her bumper. Swerving onto the paved road, she floored the accelerator.

Five minutes later, they turned onto the highway.

No white van.

That knowledge didn't relax her.

THE MODEM BUZZED AND BEEPED AS THE COMPUTER CONNECTED TO THE INTERNET. Katy drummed her fingers on the desk. Clanks and thumps emanated from the kitchen where Rick was making lunch. He insisted, ignoring her assurances a cup of yogurt would suffice. No, he said, sandwiches. Meat. Protein.

Maybe he liked playing servant. Maybe she looked so god-awful he figured she'd pass out without nutrition.

She smoothed her blouse. It still looked rumpled and dirty.

The computer finished connecting. In the web browser, she typed the address for the project website. If Charlie took sightings reports, he would've jotted the information on a report form during the interview, then transferred the information onto the website using an online form she created for him. Anyone could access the form, so individuals could post their own sightings if they chose. Charlie would also post his itinerary for the day in a private section of the site. Accessing that section required a password.

Katy navigated to the sightings section. A CGI program automatically posted the sighting information from the report form into a database, after omitting any foul language. A contents page listed the location, date, and classification of the sightings with a link to the witness account. The newest sightings appeared at the top of the page.

The sightings fell into one of five categories: exceptional, average, borderline, trace, and historical. Exceptional denoted sightings where a witness gave a firsthand account of a clear, visual encounter accompanied by physical evidence such as footprints or hair. Average referred to sightings where the witness gave a firsthand account of a clear sighting without physical evidence, while borderline meant either an unclear sighting of a creature or an experience involving only noises such as grunts or whoops. Accounts related by someone other than the witness, or accounts where the source was unknown, fell into the historical category. Everything else—footprint events, discoveries of hair or feces—belonged to the trace category.

Exceptional and average sightings could have equal importance, depending on the circumstances and the credibility of the witness. The classifications simply helped organize the information.

To date, the project had acquired over a thousand sightings. Over half fell into the average category.

Katy scanned the sightings. For the first two reports the letters "CB" in parentheses followed the location and date, indicating Charlie entered them into the database. The third sighting had her initials in parentheses. She interviewed a witness the day before she left for Texas.

Rick plopped a plate on the desk. Potato chips encircled a ham sandwich, sliced into quarters diagonally. Her mother sliced sandwiches that way. He set down a glass of milk.

She looked up at him. "Thanks, Mom."

"I'm not moving until you eat."

They exchanged stares for a moment until she gave in and took a bite of sandwich. He stayed there, leaning over her shoulder, while she chewed and clicked the link for the first sighting report. Anameka, Michigan, October 11.

While the page loaded, she crunched a potato chip.

"What is that?" Rick asked.

"A deep-fried slice of potato."

"No," he said, pointing at the screen. "That."

"A sighting report Charlie uploaded before he disappeared. It's dated Friday, which seems to be the last time anyone saw him."

The first report, designated average, related a mother and daughter's encounter with a hairy creature on their way home last Wednesday. The second report, a borderline encounter, told of a man who discovered a deer kill stash and heard strange noises.

Rick grunted.

"This all seems pretty silly to you, doesn't it?" Katy said.

"Screams in the woods. Hairy hands coming through car windows." He leaned against the wall beside the desk. "How does this help find Dad?"

"We need to retrace his steps leading up to his disappearance. Talking to these people might give us an idea of where he went."

"Those reports don't give names."

"The names are in the database, but not for public viewing. I'll have to log into the private part of the site for the names."

"Right, of course." He looked at his shoes.

She logged into the private area of the site, navigating to the database query page. Searching on October 11 returned the two reports Charlie submitted. This time, though, the reports listed names and addresses, plus directions to the locations where the sightings occurred. At the bottom of each report, Charlie included his notes.

For the first sighting, by the mother and daughter, he wrote, "Interesting that sighting occurred less than a mile from Pete Kryszka's deer kill discovery. Pattern emerging?"

Katy printed out the reports. Next, she checked the "Itinerary of Investigative Actions" page. Charlie updated it on Saturday, October 12, at 6:08 AM. The page contained one entry.

6:30 AM—Leave for hunt. Location undisclosed. THEY ARE WATCHING.

Rick squinted at the screen. "Who's watching?"

"I don't know."

"Dad wrote this?"

"Yes. The day he disappeared."

O'Hare International Airport
Chicago, Illinois

A FEMALE VOICE ANNOUNCED, "NOW BOARDING ALL PASSENGERS FOR FLIGHT 1093 to Pittsburgh."

Errando Warner shifted in the seat. An hour layover had progressed into two and a half hours of sitting in a hard chair between an elderly man who sniffled and a teenage girl who played her CD Walkman so loud he could understand the words to the songs. His flight, now scheduled for a 12:45 departure, had yet to board. He checked his watch. 12:30.

The teenager jabbed her elbow into his gut. He gritted his teeth.

His cell phone rang.

Withdrawing the phone from the inside pocket of his suit jacket, he flipped it open. "Yes."

"Warner?"

"Of course. This is my cell phone you called, Norman."

"Oh." Norman paused. "About the girl we've been watching."

"Tell me."

"I think she's onto us. We were tailing her at the college and she tried to get away. Now she's with Bergren's son at her cabin. What should we do?"

Warner sighed. "Keep watching her, obviously."

"Sir, I'm getting static on this end. Did you say keep watching her?"

"*Ja, ja,*" Warner said, his voice hard. Realizing he had slipped into German, he translated, "Yes, yes."

"Another thing, sir. They found Van Owen floating in the lake."

"I understand."

Warner disconnected. As he slipped the phone back into his pocket, he thought about his last talk with Charles Bergren. Warner offered him a great deal of money in return for his cooperation but he refused. During his nineteen years in America, he learned greenbacks could induce amnesia in most people. Not Bergren, though, and that made the professor dangerous.

He suspected Katherine Gallagher posed an equal threat. She might also lead him to Bergren. But if she found Bergren first…

The voice announced, "Now boarding those passengers with special needs for Flight 1580 to New York."

His flight. Soon general boarding would begin. First class would board first. He should gather his overcoat and move toward the gate.

The elderly man rose and headed for the gate.

Warner, grabbing his coat, approached the ticket counter.

"Change my reservation," he said. "I must go to Michigan. Immediately."

Anameka, Michigan

THE HARDENS LIVED ON A DIRT TRACK EIGHT MILES OUTSIDE OF TOWN. THEIR house, nestled in a clearing among forty-foot-high evergreens, was invisible from the road. A green mailbox marked their drive, its red flag raised.

Katy steered her pickup down the driveway. Gravel pecked the vehicle's body. Rick, seated beside her, gazed out the window, chin propped on his fist. He'd said little since leaving the cabin. If he'd gone into shock, he didn't show it.

A call to Liza Harden made certain the family would remain at home until she and Rick arrived. Liza and her daughter Mary reported the hairy-hominid-on-the-car-roof incident, the first of two reports Charlie took before he disappeared.

Katy hoped the women could enlighten her about his state of mind or at least where he might have gone. Something happened, something that convinced him he should undertake a hunt for the creatures in a specific location, perhaps the area where Jim found a carcass. But Charlie couldn't have known about the carcass.

Unless Jim called him Friday night too.

The pickup topped a low rise, the trees parted, and the house came into view. A Lexus and a Chevy Suburban occupied the two-car garage, whose doors were raised. A man walked out of the garage tossing a key ring between his hands.

Katy parked in front of the garage. She and Rick climbed out of her pickup.

The man stopped several yards away. "You the Bigfoot people?"

"Investigators, yes."

"Girls are inside." Turning on his heels, he marched back toward the garage. He mumbled, "Oughta keep their stupid mouths shut."

Katy glanced at Rick. A frown etched itself into his features. In his white shirt, gray slacks, and shiny black loafers, he looked professional. Whereas she, in clothes so rumpled they belonged on display in the Museum of Wrinkles, looked ready for the homeless shelter.

Screw clothes. She had a mystery to solve. Lives to save.

One of them possibly her own.

At the front door, she rang the bell. The door burst inward. A plump, blonde woman smiled at Katy, eyes gleaming.

Her voice mellifluous as a saxophone, she said, "Ms. Gallagher, I'm so glad you came. I'm Liza."

She spoke with a slight accent, Polish maybe.

"Call me Katy." She waved at Rick, who had shuffled up behind her. "This is Rick Bergren, Charlie's son."

Liza ushered them inside, shutting the door. She threw her arms around Rick. "You poor dear," she said.

Rick aimed a confused look at Katy.

She shrugged.

Liza released him and stepped back. "I was so sorry to hear about your papa."

Rick opened and closed his mouth, brow furrowed.

Katy bit her lip to suppress a laugh.

Liza herded them into the living room, a space larger than all of Katy's cabin. An entertainment center filled one wall. At its center, a 52-inch high-definition television gaped at them. Liza motioned them onto one leg of the L-shaped sofa. She settled onto the other leg.

"How long you two been married?"

Finally, Rick spoke. "We're not married."

"Whoops." Liza giggled. "The way you look at each other, I—never mind."

"About Charlie," Katy said. "We'd like to know about your meeting with him. What you told him. What he said. How he acted. Anything you can remember would be a great help."

"I'll try."

Liza studied her hands for a moment, fingering the hem of her blouse.

Rick fidgeted beside Katy. Seated at an angle, he had inched closer until his knee brushed against her thigh. Her gut tightened. She squished into the bend of the sofa. He was watching Liza, no doubt unaware of his movements.

"Of course," Liza said, "I told him of the creature that grabbed Mary. He asked a lot of questions about where it happened, what time of day and such. I said ten o'clock at night, about a quarter-mile north on this road, where the road curves west a bit and there's a fallen birch alongside. I remember the creature jumped over the tree into the road. It was huge, seven feet at least, and hairy all over like a gorilla. But it was no gorilla. I saw its face when it hit the roof because its head sort of slipped onto the windshield for a moment. It had a human face with a wide nose, thick lips. And the eyes, my God. They were red and glowing. Mary was driving and I screamed don't stop, don't stop, it will kill us.

"But when the thing grabbed her, its hand got stuck. The fingers were stubby and thick and it thrashed about trying to get free. Mary hit her head and passed out. I grabbed the wheel and kept steering. The thing sort of fell off into the road and ran away. Just then Mary came to and she drove back to the house, I was too scared to stop and change places. When we came inside, into the light, we saw her arm and hair were covered with this…goop. Like saliva."

A girl of about nineteen crept into the doorway. She hugged herself, eyes wide and locked on her mother.

Liza extended a hand to her. "Mary, come and speak to Ms. Gallagher."

Mary Harden grabbed her mother's hand. She crawled over the back of the sofa and curled up beside her mother. Liza wrapped an arm around her shoulders.

"This thing really upset her," Liza said. "She won't go out at night anymore. Three or four nights a week, when she hears a noise, she sleeps with me and her father takes the sofa. He doesn't believe us, of course, thinks it was a bear or a man in a fur coat. Tim's a skeptic about everything except the importance of football to civilization."

Rick's knee bumped Katy's leg. She scooted across the sofa.

Katy asked, "What did Charlie seem most interested in about your story?"

"Where it happened. He got out a map and I pointed out the spot. He drew an X there. Said something about a hunter who found dead deer near that spot. Then he went to the bathroom for fifteen minutes and when he came back he was so excited, like a kid on Christmas morning. He left a minute later."

Went to the bathroom for *fifteen minutes*?

"Speaking of the bathroom," Katy said, "could I use your facilities?"

Liza pointed through the doorway. "Down the hall, second door on the right."

When she reached the bathroom doorway, Katy hesitated. Charlie could've used the bathroom as an excuse for a moment alone so he could think about what Liza told him. He saw a connection between hers and Mary's encounter and the experiences of a man named Pete Kryszka. But he met with Kryszka after the Hardens. And he could've done his cogitating on the way to Kryszka's house. Why the bathroom? For fifteen minutes?

"Psst."

Katy glanced toward the sound. A girl, perhaps sixteen, peeked around a half-closed door at her. The girl crooked a finger, swinging the door inward and ducking behind it.

Through the doorway, Katy could see a bedroom. Posters of teen pop singers decorated the walls. Katy moved through the doorway.

The girl shut the door. "I heard you talking to Mama and Mary. About that man who came here last week."

"Did you talk to Charlie?"

"Yeah."

"What's your name?"

"Marta." She met Katy's gaze. "I saw those hairy things too."

"Your mother didn't mention it."

Marta averted her gaze. "Didn't tell her. I told Mr. Bergren, though, 'cause he reminded me of Grampa and he promised not to tell Mama."

"Tell me what you saw."

"Last time was Monday a week ago. Me and Billy—my boyfriend—we were parked in a clearing alongside the road not far from where Mama and Mary got attacked. This was before that happened. Billy and me, we were…"

Marta lowered her head. She rolled her shoulders forward.

"Studying?" Katy suggested.

"Yeah." Marta lifted her head. "All of a sudden, the car starts shaking so bad I thought it was gonna roll over. Just as sudden, it stops. Me and Billy looked at each other. Right then the thing screamed, this awful sound like you never heard, so loud I covered my ears. Out of nowhere, this hairy thing leaps onto the hood of the car. It was huge. Its eyes were red and flickering like candles. It screamed again and jumped down, took off into the woods. Never saw Billy get his car in gear so fast. That's it."

Katy reached for the door knob. As Marta's words replayed in her mind, she stopped.

Looking back at the girl, she said, "You called that the last time. You've seen these creatures before?"

"Yeah. Mr. Bergren asked me the same thing. I told him I see those hairy things a couple times a week when I go for walks near where Billy and me parked. But I haven't seen them since the one jumped on Billy's car. I drew a X on Mr. Bergen's map where I used to see them. Told him Mr. Van Owen knew about it too, 'cause I told him the day after Billy and me got attacked. He works for Papa at the factory and used to talk to me about weird stuff nobody else believes in, like UFOs and Bigfoot.

"That's when Mr. Bergren got all hyper and left."

5

BACKING THE PICKUP OUT OF THE HARDENS' DRIVEWAY, KATY SWUNG THE
back end around to head down the road.

Rick glanced at her sideways. "You were in the bathroom a long time."

"That's because I've discovered the allure of the Harden bathroom."

"And?"

She told Rick about her chat with Marta Harden.

"Great," he said. "My father gets worked up over hairy creatures that prey on teenagers."

"He gets excited about leads."

"Leads." He shook his head. "Where in tarnation is this one taking us?"

"Here."

Katy stopped the pickup. A birch tree lay on its trunk beside the dirt track. About fifty feet ahead, she spotted the roadside clearing where Marta and Billy "studied." The forest loomed all around, broken by the one-lane road and the clearing, spreading outward from those points. Birds chirped somewhere above.

Shoving the door open, she hopped out of the pickup.

"Where are you going?" Rick asked. "I thought you wanted to see Pete what's-his-name."

"Kryszka," she said as she shut the door. Through the open window, she added, "His place is past here. Might as well have a look."

Grumbling, Rick got out of the pickup.

Though he'd resumed speaking, Katy thought maybe she preferred him quiet and sullen rather than vocal and sullen. The Human Origins Project was an embarrassment for him—his own father investigating hairy hominids and Cretaceous humans, both of which science and dogma said could not exist. She tried convincing him before. Now she had given up. Her head throbbed, her back ached, and if he uttered one more wisecrack about "Bigfoot" she'd slug him. He could go home and wait for the cops to find his father.

They wouldn't look, of course. Locating a history professor who dabbled in alternative science with a girl half his age, whom everyone assumed was his girlfriend, ranked low on their to-do list. Since Charlie took off before, everyone assumed he'd done it again.

Katy stomped off the road into the grass at the perimeter of the woods. At the fallen tree, she paused, analyzing the ground. Charlie must've come here to search for sign, as she did now. If he found any, he left that information out of his report. Since he omitted Marta Harden's story, he might've left out other facts. They are watching, he wrote. She felt a gaze scrutinizing her movements too.

Aside from Rick's.

He tromped up behind her. "Katy—"

She slapped a hand on his chest, thrusting him backward. He stumbled, grabbed a sapling, steadied.

"What are you doing?" he asked.

"You were about to obliterate the evidence."

He bent over, squinting at the ground. "What evidence?"

"Don't know. But if there is any, you were about to cream it."

"Sorry, wouldn't want to mess up any bear tracks you could misidentify as Bigfoot prints."

She clamped her jaw shut to restrain a nasty response. He was worried about his father. He didn't mean it.

The tree lay five feet from her. She tiptoed closer. If a hairy hominid came through here, the creature should have left sign. Even after the rainstorm last night, some sign could remain.

Katy kneeled beside the tree. A branch, suspended from the trunk, dipped within an inch of the ground. Leaning closer, her nose brushing the branch, she noticed a hole where an object punctured the ground. Mud partially filled in the hole yet the lip was visible, rounded by the rainfall. A hole directly below the branch. Some force drove the branch into the earth.

Liza Harden said the creature she saw leaped over the tree. If it used the tree as a push-off point for clearing the ditch along this side of the road, the pressure could've driven the branch into the ground. Hardly conclusive sign, but a starting point.

Around the other side of the tree, the rainwater had carved a mini-channel as it drained toward the roadside ditch. Any sign there wash away with the rains.

She started for the road. Rick had already gone back to the pickup, standing beside it with one arm on the roof. Fingers tapping. Lips scrunched.

A shape on the ground popped out at her.

She halted, one foot in the air. A shoe print. She set her foot down beside the print. The shoe that made the print was two inches longer and one inch wider than hers. Ridges swirled across the print. The lines faded into a worn spot where the ball of the foot would be, while another line cut across the heel vertically where something sharp sliced the sole. It was almost as good as a signature. If she saw the print again, she would know.

She stood.

The brush rustled, leaves crackled.

A wild turkey raced out of the brush, gobbling and flapping its wings. The bird rushed across the road into the forest on the other side.

Overhead, birds squawked. Pairs of them evacuated the treetops.

What startled the birds? She canted her head toward the brush out of which the turkey bounded. A sound…what was it? A whisper like a breeze, except no breeze tickled her skin.

Moving only her eyes, she surveyed the woods. Nothing. If someone spied from within the foliage, he'd devised a darn good cover.

Of course, she could be paranoid.

No. Not anymore.

She strode toward the pickup.

By the time they reached Pete Kryszka's hunting cabin, Katy had lost her certainty about the shoe print. Probably nothing. Maybe something. She'd lost her bearings in reality. The sea of paranoia frothed all around her. She could no longer trust that her eyes told the truth or that she knew in which direction solid ground lay.

Kryszka's driveway, pocked and rutted, wound through the forest in twilight. Beyond the trees, the sun burned low in the sky as it sank through late afternoon toward sunset, but the trees dissipated the light. Branches scraped at Katy's pickup as she steered it into the shadows. Finally, the trees spread.

Pete Kryszka's cabin shared more in common with an outhouse than a home. The size of a storage shed, the cabin squatted in a clearing carved out of the hillside. The shingle roof and aluminum siding looked older than Earth. When Katy parked and climbed out of her pickup, a hound dog woo-wooed at her, straining against its line. The line tied the dog to a tree alongside the cabin.

The cabin's door creaked open. A man of seventy, bald and sporting bifocals, waved them inside. Katy and Rick entered the cabin.

The cabin had two rooms, one a bath. The main room housed a rollaway bed, folded and tucked into the corner, a black-and-white TV on a wheeled cart, a toaster oven balanced on a small refrigerator, one wooden chair, and two make-shift chairs fashioned from plastic crates and pillows. On the TV, Oprah Winfrey chatted with a psychologist about low self-esteem.

Pete Kryszka plopped onto the folding chair. "Sit."

Katy perched atop the nearest crate chair. The contraption wobbled. Rick stood near the door, both hands jammed in his pockets, shoulders slumped. She wanted to hug him. Instead she focused her attention on their host. "Mr. Kryszka—"

"Pete."

"Okay, Pete." She introduced herself and Rick, then said, "We'd like to talk to you about the day Charlie visited you."

Pete nodded.

"He visited you Friday, right?"

"Yup."

"What did you talk about?"

"Cryptography."

Katy scrunched her brow. "Cryptography?"

"Yup."

No wonder Charlie vanish after interviewing Pete Kryszka. He went insane from trying to get a complete sentence out of the man.

Katy took two long breaths. "Why did you talk about decoding encrypted messages?"

"Didn't."

"What did you talk about then?"

"Cryptography."

Holy God, it was like pricking porcupine quills from her eyeballs. She dug her fingernails into her knees. The pain kept her from leaping across the room to strangle Pete Kryszka.

"Cryptography," she said, "is the process of decoding encrypted messages."

"That's what he called it."

She thought for a moment. "Could Charlie have used the word cryptozoology, not cryptography?"

Pete scratched his chin. "S'pose."

Time for a new tactic. "Why don't you tell me everything you talked about, as much as you can recall. Anything is a help."

"Well…" Pete reclined in the chair, tipping its front legs off the floor. "Told him about the deers and the screaming in the woods. See, I went out hunt—uh, looking for deer. I like to take pictures of animals, ya know."

He almost admitted to hunting deer out of season. She cared little if Pete hunted out of season, as long as he *talked*.

Pete clasped his hands behind his head. "I was over on the north side of my property when I saw the deer. It was dead and its gut was sliced open neat as one of dem oh-topsies."

She assumed he meant autopsies. She didn't ask how he knew what an autopsy incision looked like. Some knowledge she had no desire to learn.

Pete continued. "I thought its innards looked funny, so I came back and called my friend Denny, he's a vet. He came out and looked at the deer, said its liver was cut out. We had some beers and talked about it but couldn't figure why anybody'd do that. Next day I went back out to see the deer again, thinking maybe I'd haul it home to show the cops.

"It weren't there. I started searchin' the area. All of a sudden there was this screeching, like a bomb dropped on my head. Only it weren't no bomb. This monster went tearing through the woods making a huge racket. Never saw it, but I knew what it was. One of dem hair enids."

"You mean hairy hominids."

"Sure."

"What did Charlie say to you?"

Pete shoved his thumbs under his suspenders. "Asked me to take him where I found the deer. I did. His eyes 'bout popped out their sockets."

"Why?"

"What he saw."

Katy bit the inside of her cheek. "Which was?"

"Pile of deer parts." He let the legs of his chair smack down on the floor. "Said it was a stash and got so worked up he almost run over my dog pulling his car out the driveway."

Katy rose. "Take me there."

Dark fell before they reached the clearing. Pete Kryszka clicked on his flashlight, a three-cell MagLite that lit up the woods like a spotlight. Katy followed Pete.

Rick followed Katy. He wasn't dressed for a nature hike. He wanted dinner, not deer parts, whatever that meant. He had a feeling after he saw the deer parts he wouldn't want dinner anymore.

The day had fallen into a sinkhole. He could see the sky above, but could find no way out of the hole. And it might collapse further anytime. The situation was crazy. His father managed to disappear while investigating Bigfoot. He got excited about a pile of deer parts. Sure, Rick had grown away from Dad lately, but had he let them become so separated they became strangers? But another question bothered him more.

What if Dad was dead?

He let the fear smolder inside him until he had no nerves left. He insulted Katy. She deserved better. She was the one person on earth, besides him, who cared about his father's safety.

Pete halted. He shined the flashlight on a pile of sticks. "Here."

The pile stood three feet high and at least as thick. A hole in the front gaped mouth-like. Katy edged nearer the pile. Picking up a few sticks, tossing them aside, she leaned into the pile.

Rick grabbed her arm. "Careful. You don't know what's in there."

Pete aimed the flashlight over Katy's shoulder. "Better?"

Katy murmured. She leaned deeper inside, planting a hand on the top of the pile. A breeze wafted the stench of decaying flesh over Rick. He moved closer to Katy.

"What's in there?" he said.

"Legs. Hooves. A breast maybe. Couple heads and some chunks of meat."

"Seen enough?"

Clack.

"You hear that?" he asked Pete.

Pete cupped a hand over one ear.

Clack.

"Yup," Pete said, lowering his hand. "Dat's dem."

"Them?" Rick searched the darkness for whatever or whoever Pete meant. He saw the outlines of trees and bushes backlit by the moon above, its rays glistening on the pine needles and Katy's hair.

The clacking sounded like wood hitting wood.

"The hairy ho-mo-nids," Pete said. "They're watching. And they won't like us messing with their stash."

Katy stepped back from the pile. "Turn off the light."

Pete obliged. The darkness deepened.

Clack. *Clack.*

The hairs on Rick's arms stiffened. While his eyes adjusted to the dark, he turned his head left and right, staring into the woods. The trees looked like men, the shadows like trees. Right then he wished he'd bought the night-vision binoculars he saw in a catalog last month. On sale. What did he need with night vision in the city, he'd asked himself, and thrown the catalog in the trash.

Clack-clack-clack.

Closer. He started forward. Katy laid a hand on his arm. He stopped.

Across the clearing, the clacking erupted in machine-gun bursts.

What was that?

Clack-clack-*clack.*

Behind them. He looked at Katy. Head tilted, eyes half closed, she stood motionless.

Clack!

The percussion rang in his ears. It came from across the clearing.

Vegetation shooshed and crackled.

Katy seized his sleeve. "On the count of three, run."

"What?"

She released his sleeve. "One—"

CLACK!

A shiver sidled up his spine.

"Two—"

A shriek ululated through the clearing.

"Three!"

Katy exploded past him. Pete scrambled after her.

Cursing, Rick bolted after them.

Another shriek, high and undulating, rattled his eardrums. Saplings cracked, twigs snapped behind him. He could barely see Pete, much less Katy, though their footsteps pounded ahead of him. He followed the sound, praying he hadn't slipped into the track of one of *them* by mistake.

The crashing resounded closer and closer.

His foot smacked into a tree stump. He bit off the cry that welled in his throat.

Crashing. Grunting.

Too close.

He vaulted over the stump, racing in the direction of Katy's and Pete's footfalls. He'd lost sight of them. Oh hell, he didn't know these woods—

"Uh-uh-uh."

What the blazes?

Never mind.

A flash of white up ahead alerted him to Pete's position and he veered toward it. Thank God for the old coot's shirt, it was the one clean thing the guy owned.

A hand nabbed at his shoulder.

Rick pumped his legs faster. His muscles burned but he pushed harder, harder, until he the pain melted into the background.

A hand seized his hair, jerking him back. He jabbed his elbow backward.

"Uh!"

The hand released his hair. He ran.

THE LIGHT OF PETE'S CABIN GLOWED AHEAD. KATY SEGUED FROM A SPRINT into a jog. Her chest heaved with each breath. A dozen feet from the cabin, she collapsed onto her knees. Sweat flooded over her face, down her back, between her breasts. Every muscle hurt.

Pete hurried into the cabin.

Rick.

She spun on her knees, facing the woods from which she had come. She could hear nothing through the rush of blood in her body, the jackhammering of her heart.

A figure wove through the trees toward her. *Let it be him, please let it be him.*

Rick stumbled into the clearing. He toppled onto the ground, landing flat on his back.

She crawled over to him. His eyes were open, his breathing fast and shallow. He looked pale, but everybody looked pale in the moonlight. She bent over him.

"You okay?" she asked.

"Sure," he said, shoving his hand through his hair. "Sure, I was attacked by some grunting monster but I'm fine."

"Are you hurt?"

He palpated the back of his head. "No."

She sat back on her heels. They disturbed the creatures' stash of deer meat, so the hairy hominids chased them away. If the creatures really wanted to kill the three of them, they could easily have done it. If a seven-foot-tall, half-ton monster wanted you dead, good luck getting away. Numerous sightings mentioned the creatures' great speed and strength.

"They let us get away," she said. "It was a warning."

"Warning!" Rick pushed up onto his elbows. "Whatever that thing was, it wanted my scalp."

"It was a hairy hominid."

"Bigfoot." He dropped onto the ground again. "For all I know, that was a crazy hunter in a fur suit. Or maybe a bear."

"Bears. Banging sticks together to signal each other."

Rick got up. With a grunt, he strode into the cabin.

Katy sat in the dark, alone, watching the night.

A distant clack reverberated through the forest.

She hopped up and trotted into the cabin.

THE DRIVE HOME PASSED IN SILENCE AS RICK STUDIED THE STARS AND KATY guided the pickup down dirt roads and highways back to her cabin.

Back at her cabin, she curled up on the sofa while he sat at the bar, his back facing her. Enough. She couldn't handle this mess alone. And she couldn't handle it with him if he acted this way.

"Turn around," she said, "we have to talk."

He rose, hurled the stool around, and dropped onto it. His expression betrayed nothing, which was worse than a scowl or a smirk.

"You're mad," she said.

"No."

"So you're normally a jerk."

His shoulders slumped. He lowered his head.

Katy rested her head on the arm of the sofa. If he needed a minute, she could give him that much. His father vanished. Both an intruder and a hairy hominid attacked him today. He'd earned some slack.

A chill had crept into the cabin. On her way to the wood stove, she grabbed matches from the bar and a log and kindling from the box beside the stove. In a few minutes, she started a fire. The flames crackled. Soon warmth radiated from the stove. She shut the stove's door. The vent on the door, open halfway, let the warmth spread throughout the room. Rick had moved onto the sofa. She sat beside him.

"I'm not mad," he said. "At you."

"I see."

He slouched into the sofa.

"It's not your fault," she said. "Charlie took his own risks."

"I should've called. E-mailed him. Anything. I haven't spoken to my own father in almost a year."

"You're busy, Charlie understands." She rested her arm on top of the sofa behind him. "He says geniuses like you are in high demand and have no time for calling their parents."

"I'm no genius. I'm an accountant."

She watched his face, the twitch of his lip when he said "accountant," the little jump as he tensed his jaw muscles.

He turned his head toward her. "What if he's dead?"

"Impossible."

"I don't know what impossible means anymore." He thrust his head back against the sofa and her arm. "I used to think I did. Now everything's shot to hell and I don't know what to believe. Some *thing* attacked me in the woods and nearly took my scalp off. You say it was a Bigfoot. I can't even say for sure it wasn't."

She stroked his hair. "The unknown is frightening. Especially for someone like you who expects everything should fit into neat boxes. This is new for me too. I've never had my house broken into or been followed by strangers. We both have to adapt."

He shifted his gaze toward the corner. She moved her fingers over the area behind his ear.

He winced. "The thing grabbed me there."

"Poor baby." She swept a lock of hair from his forehead. "Would blueberry pancakes make you feel better?"

"Maybe."

She hopped onto her feet. "I'll make dinner."

In the kitchen, she stopped. "Where are you staying?"

"Nowhere. I threw some clothes in a suitcase and flew here, then I drove straight from the airport to Dad's house."

"Stay here then." She gestured at the loft. "You take the loft, I'll sleep on the sofa bed. You're exhausted, you need the comfy mattress."

"I will not take your bed."

"We can talk about it later."

She got the frying pan and mixing bowl out of the cupboard. As she cracked eggs into the bowl, Rick turned on the television.

The evening might have felt normal, if not for the sensation of someone watching. If she turned around to see a pair of eyeballs peering at her through the window, the sight would not surprise her. The hairs on her neck seemed stuck at attention.

She pulled down the window shade.

Rick slid his plate across the bar. Katy grabbed the empty dish and put it in the sink. Dishes could wait.

"We should talk to the police," he said.

"And tell them what? Police deal in facts. We have no evidence. Someone broke into my house and Charlie's house, but that proves nothing. Charlie has taken off before. We can't prove he didn't do it again."

"He didn't."

"I know." She folded her arms over her chest. "But we have no proof. Jim's death looks accidental. He got drunk sometimes. Never at work, never on a hunt, but try convincing the police of that. His own wife couldn't convince them. To the police, we look like an estranged son and his father's concubine. Why should they believe us?"

Rick said nothing.

Her words sounded harsh, yet she must convince him of the truth. No one would believe them. They were on their own. Unless he accepted that, they would never find Charlie or unmask Jim's killer.

"What do we do?" Rick asked.

"Find Charlie."

"How?"

"From what we learned today and the previous sightings data, I think I can estimate where Charlie went into the woods. With any luck, we can find his sign." When Rick's forehead crinkled, she explained, "Sign is evidence left behind when an animal or human moves through an area. It can be tracks, hair, disturbed vegetation, trash, anything. If we find his truck, that would be conclusive sign."

"So…what," he said, "we traipse through the wilderness until we see him?"

"It's more involved than that."

"Sounds too hard."

She moved around the bar and stopped in front of him. Meeting his gaze, she said, "You have to trust me. I've been tracking animals in these woods since I was ten. I can find him. But I need your help, I can't be watching for bad guys at the same time."

He sat up, squaring his shoulders. "Okay."

"If you plan on arguing and snapping at me, stay here."

"I won't."

"Good." She walked toward the sofa.

"By the way," he said, "what is cryptozoology?"

Pulling the cushions off the sofa, she said, "Cryptozoology is the study of unknown animals."

She stacked the cushions by the desk. When she reached for the handle of the sofa bed, Rick stepped in front of her, grabbing the handle. He pulled out the bed.

"You take the loft," he said.

They stared at each other for a moment.

"Fine," she said, and trotted up the stairs.

In the loft, she retrieved the spare sheets from her trunk. Leaning over the railing, she tossed the sheets at Rick. The pile bounced off his shoulder and landed on the sofa bed.

He glanced up at her. "Thanks."

Ten minutes later, she lay in bed, in the dark, gazing out the windows that covered the wall of the loft. Beyond the window, the hill sloped upward into the trees at its peak. Above the tree line, stars glimmered. So beautiful. So peaceful.

So misleading.

"Katy."

"What?"

"When do we leave?"

"At dawn."

Smoke drifted up from the chimney of Katy Gallagher's cabin in ghostly wisps lit by moonbeams.

The bedroom window, situated on the second floor of the bungalow, offered a view of Gallagher's cabin. Warner stood in the dark room, arms crossed, leaning against the window frame. He smoothed the cap covering his clean-shaven head. If he thought his future included a trek into the wilds, he would have grown out his hair. No matter, he preferred the baldness. It distracted his enemies.

Behind him, voices emanated from the radio.

"When is dawn?"

"Go to sleep, Rick."

The children had gone to bed. Together? Not that it mattered with which Bergren Katy Gallagher shared her bed. Her mistake was the choice of hobbies, not the choice of lovers. If she would forget about Charles Bergren and accept Jim Van Owen's death as accidental, he could leave her alone.

From overhearing her conversation with Rick Bergren, through the device Norman planted that morning, he knew she would not forget. The woman had determination. Unfortunate.

Norman clomped into the room. "Well?"

"I leave at dawn," Warner said.

"You mean we leave at dawn."

"You and Young have caused enough problems."

"What?"

"He told me about the incident in the parking lot. She knows we are watching her. Following her will be much more difficult now, especially in the woods. I must go alone."

"But—"

"Go."

Norman went.

Warner turned off the radio. They would say no more tonight.

In the morning, he would follow them into the wilderness and—once he determined their destination—jump ahead to find Bergren first. If the professor had discovered evidence, Warner would give him one last chance at changing his mind. Perhaps a few more zeros on the check would sway him. Perhaps he required greater enticement. Whatever it took, Warner would change Bergren's mind. If Katy Gallagher interfered, he would change her mind as well.

He touched the windowpane. "Sleep well, *meine Kinder.*"

6

Thursday, October 17

Rick looked out the porch windows at the darkness. Though he hated clichés, it really did seem darkest before dawn. The moon had set. Unlike in the city, no glow blotted out the horizon. Here, night reigned.

Or morning. Whichever it was. His watch read 6:40. The sun would rise in a little over an hour. Katy had woken him up at 5:45 AM. When he asked how complete darkness qualified as dawn, she chuckled and said "rise and shine." By the time he walked out of the bathroom fifteen minutes later, she had a bowl of oatmeal waiting for him. Though he hated oatmeal, he ate it.

A light glanced in the distance.

Across the field, he could make out the silhouette of a house. Katy said it was empty. But the light had come from inside that house. Must have imagined it.

He walked back into the cabin. Sleeping bags, rolled tight, sat beside dirt-colored backpacks near the sofa. Katy must've packed while he took a shower. A small knife in a leather sheath stuck out of an unzipped pocket of one pack. He poked the knife with his foot.

"It's not alive," Katy said, marching up the stairs from the basement.

"If the bad guys get that close, we're in trouble."

She tossed what looked like a radio at him. He caught it. An Audiovox two-way radio with an LCD display.

"Your GPS radio," Katy said. "It uses Family Radio, which has a range of two miles. I assume, being a guy, you know what GPS is."

"Global Positioning System. You can track your position and plan your route using satellites."

"This one also has buddy tracking. So, if we get separated you can find me using the GPS, assuming mine is turned on." She tucked her radio into a fanny pack she had positioned over her abdomen. "Once we get out there, we might also be able to track Charlie, or at least his GPS signal. Assuming the battery hasn't died and he left it on. The radio part is for emergency use only."

"If he took one, why do you have two?"

"One was for Jim. He forgot it." Ducking her head, she veered into the kitchen. "Better grab some snacks."

While she rummaged in the kitchen, he took in her appearance. She had become the exact opposite of herself yesterday, in the rumpled suit and mussed hair. She wore a pine green jacket and black jeans with brown hiking boots. Her hair, tied back in an elastic band the color of her hair, curled around her face in spirals. A pinkness colored her cheeks. The green clothes enhanced the luster of her green eyes.

He cleared his throat.

Katy hurled two plastic bags at him. They hit the floor and he nabbed them. Freezer bags full of granola bars.

"Is this all we're eating today?" he asked.

"No." She walked into the living room. "The rest we catch."

"You mean hunt?" He hadn't hunted in three years. He hadn't caught anything in even longer. Why should they hunt when they could just come home every night to eat food somebody else skinned and gutted?

Snatching a piece of paper off the bar, she handed it to him. The paper was a map of what looked like the area around Anameka.

Katy said, "I cross-referenced the information from our database about hairy hominid sightings and deer kills in the last six months with the location where Jim's body was found." She jabbed a finger at an X drawn in marker on the map. "This is the most likely spot for Charlie to have started."

"Not far from where Pete what's-his-face lives."

"Exactly. Sightings have taken a disturbing trend lately. I believe that's why Charlie went on a hunt. He thought he figured out why."

"Why what?"

"Why the creatures have become violent. Attacking cars. Grabbing people." Taking the map, she traced a triangle with her finger. "The sightings have concentrated in this area near Anameka for about six months now. Something is happening here. Unfortunately, Charlie didn't write down his theory because he felt someone was watching him. He was right."

Rick scrutinized the map. The red dots marked sightings. Of what? He still could not accept that hairy, manlike creatures existed. It all seemed crazy.

Yet *something* grabbed him in the woods yesterday.

His hair stiffened as if an electric current surged through him. He looked out the window, through the porch, into the yard. Nothing.

Jesus, he'd gotten nervous.

Katy bent down beside her backpack. "I checked the weather. No severe cold spells expected but there's a chance of rain Saturday."

"Saturday! This is Thursday. How long are we staying out there?"

"Long as it takes."

After zipping her pack, she went to the desk in the corner. From a drawer, she withdrew two guns—the Taurus .357 with a short barrel and concealed hammer that she thrust in his face at Dad's house, and a service issue .45 auto. She held her hands palm up, a gun lying on each palm.

"You know how to use a gun?" she asked.

"Of course."

"Sorry, I wasn't insulting your manliness. But you are an urban dweller."

An urban dweller. So that was how Katy thought of him. No wonder she treated him like a twelve-year-old on his first camping trip. To her, an urban dweller must rank lower than an anthropologist. The way his father talked about anthropologists—"those scum-sucking, tree-hugging, descent-of-man bigots"—he wondered how long she might put up with him. Unless he proved he could handle himself.

"I live there," he said, "but I grew up out here. I was handling guns before I drove cars."

"Fine then." She handed him the .45. "Take the big one."

The .45 fit nicely in his hand. Her Taurus, as he could tell from glancing at it, would've cramped his hand in its small grip. The .45 weighed nearly three pounds, but he liked the weight. It felt...manly.

Better not tell Katy that.

He looked at the backpacks, the .45, the backpacks. "Not sure where I should stash this."

She dashed into the basement. When she came back, she tossed him a belt holster. Hooking the black nylon holster onto his belt, he slid the .45 into it.

Katy nodded approvingly.

He squared his shoulders. "I'm ready."

Katy tucked the Taurus .357 into its holster, which she had attached to the inside of her fanny pack.

When she bent down, the fanny pack slumped on her thigh. The Taurus weighed down on her leg. The GPS radio, in the pack with the gun, shifted among the two speed loaders she had dropped in there. A box of hydra-shock ammo, the same kind she had inserted into the speed loaders, was zipped into a side pocket of the backpack. Ammo designed for killing. Though she hoped she never needed it, she liked feeling prepared for anything.

Especially when that sensation of being watched kept tickling her skin.

Rick stood a few feet away, transfixed by the map. He kept touching the .45 holstered on his belt. In his gray jacket, blue jeans, green flannel shirt, and leather hiking boots, he looked as if he'd spent a lifetime in the woods. Charlie told her of their camping trips, fishing vacations, and the like. But Rick spent the past eight years in Boston. As an accountant.

Not that she had anything against accountants. On a hunt, though, you needed to feel comfortable in the wilderness. Did Rick still feel comfortable out here? Or had he become an urban dweller?

She would find out.

On dozens of hunts over the span of two years, she developed a routine for packing and knew what to take. While Rick was in the bathroom, she had finished the packing. If he saw some of the items she packed, he might get nervous. The emergency blanket, for one, might make him wonder what kind of dangers they would face. She assured him no bad weather was forecasted but forecasts changed. No reason he should worry about that, though.

She could worry for both of them.

When she handed Rick his GPS radio, she'd left out one fact. She turned hers on earlier, trying to locate Charlie's signal. Nothing. Either Charlie turned it off or the battery had run down. He would've taken extra batteries, though, so…she avoided finishing that thought.

Squatting in front of her pack, she slipped the straps over her shoulders. The metal frame curved around behind her head and back, holding the pack away from her body. A section of padding also shielded her from the pack.

After fastening the chest and waist straps, she stood. "Ready?"

"Guess so." Rick hefted his pack onto his back. "What's in here, lead?"

"Necessities. Can you handle it?"

Rick stared at her for a second, then stepped toward the front door.

"This way," Katy said as she tromped to the back door.

"But the car's out front."

"No car. We're being followed, remember?"

"So how do we get there?"

She pointed at her feet.

"Great," he said, as he followed her out the back door. "More walking in the woods in the dark. I remember how that went last time."

NORMAN BURST THROUGH THE DOOR, PANTING. WARNER, LOADING HIS GEAR into a backpack, said, "What did you see?"

"They packed a bunch of junk and left the back way. Saw a map."

"Were you careful this time?"

"Yeah, I peeked through the front windows. Nobody saw."

Warner zipped his pack. "What did the map show?"

"Got out my binoculars. Still could hardly see it. The woman pointed at a spot somewhere around here, probably where we thought."

"Then I must get there first." He slung the soft-frame backpack over his shoulders. The straps pressed against his shoulder holster. "You and Young will wait here until I return."

Though Norman protested, Warner quieted him with a glance.

Norman still believed he should go too. Warner had no room for errors now, and Norman had developed a sloppiness of late that made him a liability. When Warner returned, he would get rid of Norman. For now, he must settle for leaving the man behind.

Warner walked out the front door.

"There you are," a female voice chirped.

Diane Frasier and Ivan Thaw waited outside the garage. Diane, a woman of thirty-nine who told everyone she was thirty, leaned against the garage, her khaki pants and brown parka looking five minutes out of the store. Her feet, clad in canvas boots, tapped on the pavement. She had both hands shoved in her pockets. A ski cap with a frizzy ball on top adorned her head, strands of red hair hanging out from beneath it.

Ivan Thaw dressed all in gray, though his clothes looked as if they came from the same store as Diane's. He wore a Stetson hat instead of a ski cap, Wellingtons rather than hiking boots. The cigarette stuffed between his lips dribbled ashes.

Warner stopped. Adjusting the straps of his pack, he slipped a hand under his jacket and shifted the Glock 9mm pistol in its holster. He could have kept the Glock in a belt holster, but he preferred the shoulder variety. The discomfort would keep him alert.

Diane trotted closer. "We should hurry, Errie, they're getting ahead of us."

"I go alone."

"Sorry, Warner," Ivan said, "can't let you do that. We made a pact."

"We made an agreement. I lead, you follow."

"So we're following you out."

"I thought you were going to the distillery today."

Ivan dropped the cigarette and squelched it with his boot heel. "Moved that up because Diane's brother had to go out of town this week. We went last Thursday."

"Then at least you are sober today."

He had made one mistake in this affair. He let Diane and Ivan take part. Tracking Gallagher would take stealth and patience, both of which Diane and Ivan lacked. He could not take them.

Warner strode into the garage. His Land Rover was parked inside. Since Gallagher and Bergren left the back way ten minutes ago, he had no need of worrying they would see his vehicle leaving.

Ivan clomped after him. When Warner reached for the Rover's door, Ivan slapped his hand on Warner's chest.

"If you leave us behind," Ivan said, "we might get loose-lipped around the cops. Wouldn't they like to know about your private collection."

Warner exhaled.

Ivan smirked. "Time for a decision, boss."

"Get in the car." Warner grabbed Ivan's hand, flipped him around, and pinned him against the car, wrenching the man's arm behind his back. "But if you interfere, I will make you regret it."

Warner let go.

Ivan rubbed his shoulder. He scowled at Warner as he climbed into the back seat. Diane rushed around the car to the front passenger door.

Opening the door, she winked at Warner. "You're so strong, Errie."

He ducked into the car and slammed the door.

THE FLASHLIGHT BATHED THE GROUND IN RED LIGHT. KATY AIMED THE BEAM ahead a bit. The red filter provided light without ruining her night vision. Although the sun would soon poke its head above the horizon, she wanted to maintain her night vision as long as possible. Never knew when she might need it.

No one followed them, so far as she could tell, yet her nerves remained electric. If the bad guys used the map, which they viewed on the computer, they might realize where she and Rick would go. They might wait there. Armed. Hiding.

She must be careful.

They reached a fence. Bent and drooping, the fence was less than three feet high. Katy clambered over it. Her watch, a digital model she stowed in her pocket to keep its reflective face from betraying their position, told her they had left the cabin twenty minutes ago. The first hint of sunrise glowed along the eastern horizon. The site she marked on the map couldn't be far.

Rick stepped over the fence like walking over a stick.

Her worries about his fitness in the woods seemed silly now. He stayed right behind her and could've overtaken her if he wanted. That he stayed behind comforted her. She had glimpsed him surveying the woods as they moved, doing as she asked, watching for the bad guys.

What those bad guys wanted, she could not guess. Killing Jim made no sense. If someone wanted the hairy hominids kept secret, they need only get Jim drunk and steal the type specimen he collected. Sure, he could've told people how he found a carcass, but who would believe him? He regaled everyone with his stories of face-to-face encounters with hairy hominids and no one believed. Without the specimen, he could never prove his story.

So why kill him?

He saw too much. Knew too much. Or the sicko who killed him simply enjoyed taking a life. Get him drunk, push him off a cliff. A perfect, diabolical plan. Yet one question was unanswered. How had the killer gotten Jim drunk? He stayed sober at work and on hunts. Especially on hunts, since he took the research more seriously than anything else in life.

Except his family. He wouldn't have risked hurting his family by getting drunk in the woods, where anything could happen if you weren't alert. If he found a specimen, he would've rushed home to show Annabelle. Nothing made sense.

The gurgling of water up ahead interrupted her thoughts. They had arrived. She halted at the edge of the trees. In the first glow of sunrise, the sands on the beach appeared gray. The ripples where a creek emptied into Lake Anameka shimmered as ghosts.

By cross-referencing all the data, she had illustrated that the sightings and discoveries of deer kills concentrated in a rough triangle around the eastern side of Anameka. At first, she thought the sightings concentrated in a circular area, but including the location of Jim's body and the sightings of Pete Kryszka and the Hardens narrowed that area into a triangle whose legs measured roughly twenty miles apiece. Two points of the triangle lay in the woods, far from roads and known settlements. The third point lay smack on this spot: Lake Anameka State Park.

The police found Jim's body across the lake, floating face down. Bloated. Discolored. Murdered. *Bastards.*

She tramped across the beach toward the parking lot. One car sat in the lot, parked at the far corner beneath a maple whose branches hung low over the vehicle. From a distance, the black Dodge Ram blended into the shadows.

Which was probably why Charlie parked it there.

"Dad's car," Rick said, coming up beside her.

The Ram, less than two months old, would stick out if anyone came by here in the daylight. No one did, though, because summer had ended and winter had yet to begin. The tourists would wait until the snows came before visiting the area again. Right now, a few locals might stop by for a walk or a swim, but the odds of someone noticing Charlie's truck were low.

Katy opened the driver's door.

"He left it unlocked," Rick said, "and nobody stole it?"

"This is Michigan, not Boston."

She leaned into the truck. Charlie left nothing inside the vehicle except a Snickers wrapper crumpled on the floor. She checked the glove compartment. A tire pressure gauge, nothing else.

Shutting the door, she strolled around the truck, studying the ground for any sign. Since it rained after Charlie left, she held little hope of finding anything.

"Look at this," Rick said.

He had gone around the back of the truck into the trees. When she reached him, he pointed at a sapling several yards ahead.

"It's bent," he said.

And it was. One branch had snapped off and rested on the ground, while the trunk of the sapling canted away from where the branch fell. Katy crept toward the sapling. As she neared it, she noticed a hole next to the tree. Dead leaves surrounded and filled the hole. She kneeled. Some of the leaves were darker than the others, scattered this side of the hole. She picked up a darker leaf. The underside showed lighter. Underside. No.

The dark was the underside. The leaves had flipped over to show their backsides. A scenario played through her mind. Charlie leaving his truck. Heading into the woods. He trips in the hole, kicking leaves backward, grabbing the sapling for support.

She crawled forward. Most of the trees retained their leaves, as fall had barely begun. The leaves had turned on most trees yet stayed green on others. Dead leaves covered patches of ground. She stopped near one patch of leaves. One leaf, darker than the others, protruded from under its brethren. She lifted the leaves one by one, piling them on the ground alongside the hole.

A shape emerged from the mess. She removed a few more leaves. Lines and circles etched in the ground. The edges had blurred, yet the outline was unmistakable.

The print of a boot.

She glanced back at the bent sapling about a yard behind. Charlie tripped in the hole and grabbed the sapling. As he regained his footing, he stomped a few steps, depositing an overturned leaf that stuck to his boot. The print, protected by leaves that fell after he left, had endured the weather.

The rain obliterated any tracks. She might find more sign, though, anything else that would prove Charlie might have come this way. As she moved forward crab-like, the tree cover grew more dense. Overhead, the pines and birches formed a canopy, while lower down the saplings created a mesh of vegetation. A gust sprinkled leaves onto the ground.

Rick edged past the sapling. "Well?"

"He was here." She nodded at the print. "That's his print."

"You can't be sure."

"I know his shoes."

Rick gave her a funny look. She couldn't decide what it meant.

An engine grumbled.

"Get over here and get down," she said.

He hopped closer. While she ducked behind a sapling, he stooped behind the trunk of a pine. Through the trees she could see the parking lot. A forest green Land Rover had parked halfway across the lot. Three people exited the vehicle.

Katy got her binoculars out of her pack. The zipping noise, although loud from her perspective, couldn't break through the whoosh of the wind. The strangers wouldn't hear it.

As she raised the binoculars, she propped her elbows on low branches of the sapling. She focused on the trio exiting the Land Rover.

The first person, a man, gesticulated at the others as if ordering them around. Bald and muscular, he dressed in earth tones and wore black boots. He was attractive, his nose narrow but not too narrow, his lips full but not swollen, his physique imposing yet average in height.

The other two, a man and a woman, reminded her of the summer people. They dressed in expensive "outdoorswear," the kind peddled in gift shops that appealed to tourists and the wealthy who lived in the area. The woman smiled incessantly. The man alternated frowning and smirking.

Katy unfastened her pack. She pushed it between two saplings so the foliage disguised it. As she set the binoculars on the ground, she tiptoed forward.

Rick clasped her arm. He shook his head.

She mouthed, "I have to see."

He squinted. Maybe he misunderstood. If he had understood, he still might disapprove.

Shaking off his hand, she inched past the sapling, rolling her steps to avoid crunching on leaves. At the curb, she stopped behind a bush.

The trio approached Charlie's truck. They were fifteen feet away at most.

The bald man opened the driver's door. "Nothing."

He spoke with a faint yet recognizable accent. German.

The other man smirked. "Really think he'd leave a note telling us where he went? Get real, Warner."

Warner slammed the door shut. The Ram rocked. The woman danced on her toes.

"I should tie you both to a tree," Warner said.

"Diane and me," the other man said, "we got a stake in this. Like I said, you ditch us and we might get chatty. Way I figure it, you need us anyway. When you find them, what are you gonna do? Two against one. Not good odds."

"It is still two against one." Warner pushed past the other man. "Imbeciles don't count."

Warner strolled behind the truck. At the curb he stopped. He gazed into the woods with one foot braced against the curb.

Diane and the other man moved in front of the truck, further from Warner but nearer Katy. Heads together, they whispered.

Katy cupped a hand behind her ear. Tilting her head, she made out their words.

"—think he'll ditch us," the man said. "We can't trust him."

"I know, Ivan, but he can find them. We can't."

"We'll see."

Warner stepped off the curb into the trees. He stared straight ahead.

He saw the sapling. Did he know what it meant?

"Warner," Ivan said.

Warner raised a hand. Ivan silenced. Warner crept toward the sapling.

Crap, he knew what it meant.

She couldn't see Rick, which was good because it meant Warner couldn't see him either, but it also meant she had no idea whether Rick saw Warner coming for him. If she made any sound, Warner would hear. Without speaking, she had no way of warning Rick. She must move. The best trackers could move through the environment without a sound and sneak up on their quarry. She had tracked animals—deer, squirrels, bears—not humans. Her parents taught her about tracking and hunting because they thought anyone who lived in the woods should know how to survive alone, by catching food and avoiding dangers. They left out the part about evading crazies.

Use the same tactics. It's not that different.

Yeah right. One snapped twig or crunched leaf and she was dead. Black bears, while dangerous, rarely attacked unless you got between them and their cubs. Warner, whoever he was, might require no reason for killing her. Or Rick.

She lowered onto her belly, flat on the ground. Arms stretched in front, feet turned sideways, she did her best imitation of a centipede. Hands forward. Pull the body along. Every movement slow. When she encountered twigs or trees, she inched around them or moved them aside, all the while scanning the area. She kept her head forward and low to the ground. *Please let this work.*

Warner passed the sapling. He crept deeper into the woods, lifting his feet and setting them down again in slow motion.

Still no sign of Rick. Warner passed the tree behind which Rick had hidden when she left him. As she crawled parallel to Warner, she searched the woods. Through the leaves and branches she could barely see anything.

A gust of wind rattled through the treetops. Pine needles and leaves sizzled against one another. Warner stood still. He cocked his head in her direction, mouth open.

She froze. The wind gusted. Leaves hissed.

Warner closed his mouth, looked away. Spinning on his heels, he marched back toward Charlie's truck. After exchanging words and gestures with his pals, he led them across the parking lot to the Land Rover. Ivan opened the rear hatch. He and Warner exchanged more gestures.

They were arguing. Good. That should distract them for awhile.

Ivan and Diane didn't bother her. They acted like city people on a nature hike. Warner, however, posed a threat. He seemed comfortable in the woods, knowledgeable about tracking. He might know more than she did. From his appearance and manner, she suspected he'd stalked many people. What he did with those people once he found them, she avoided imagining.

Raising onto hands and knees, she crawled forward. Beyond where she found Charlie's boot print, a natural pathway led further into the woods. Charlie could've used that path. Since he left his truck in the parking lot—conclusive sign, for sure—he must've thought no one was pursuing him at that point. He knew someone was watching, but did he guess they would track him into the woods? Then again, she had no proof anyone tracked him into the woods. Warner was tracking her, which hinted he had no clue about Charlie's location.

So, if Charlie felt safe as he headed out on his hunt, he might've forsaken covering his tracks. Concentrated on tracking his quarry, the hairy hominids.

She stopped alongside the natural pathway. Half standing, she could see into the parking lot. Warner and his friends lingered near the Land Rover. Each carried a backpack slung over one shoulder.

Warner snatched Ivan's pack away. He ripped it open and dug inside. Ivan grabbed for the pack but Warner shoved him backward.

Katy sneaked behind the sapling where she'd hidden her pack. Grabbing the binoculars, she focused on Warner and Ivan.

Warner held a long, narrow box in his hand. He waved it at Ivan, his eyes narrowed, his expression sharp. Ivan looked at Warner with the indifference of a teenager sitting through his father's lecture on coming home late. She zoomed in on the box. The word "Marlboro" was printed in large letters across the top.

They were arguing over cigarettes. Even better.

As she tucked the binoculars inside her pack, she ducked down again. Poking her head through the vegetation into the pathway, she scanned the ground. Here, the thick cover sheltered the earth. The rain had pockmarked the ground rather than soaking it.

A shape popped out at her. She scanned back over the area. Charlie's boot print.

She scanned further down the pathway. The track continued as far as she could see. Good for tracking Charlie. Bad for shaking Warner. Ducking back behind the saplings, she chewed her lip. There must be a way.

Scritch-scratch. Someone was approaching from behind. She slipped a hand inside her fanny pack and gripped the Taurus.

A hand covered her mouth. She yanked out the gun, aimed the muzzle behind her head.

"It's me," Rick said.

He dropped his hand onto her shoulder.

Katy scowled at him. Keeping her voice low, she asked, "What the hell are you doing?"

"I didn't want to scare you."

"So you slap your hand over my mouth? Yeah, that keeps me calm." She holstered the Taurus. "I almost shot you. Again."

"I know, I'm developing a close relationship with your gun."

She popped out of the vegetation to check that Warner and his gang were still in the parking lot. Warner and Ivan were arguing over a rifle now.

Plunging into the leafage once more, she said, "We have to brush the track."

Rick stared at her.

She said, "Take a branch or something and wipe away the tracks. Dig them out if we have to, just *get rid* of them. Okay?"

"Gotcha."

If they could plant a false trail, one that led Warner in the opposite direction, they might gain some time and distance over him. Warner might recognize the deception. Of course, distracted by bickering with his companions, he could fail to notice. If she had Charlie's boots, she could fake it better. Sure, she could conjure a pair of boots, no problem.

Rick sidled past her, feeling the ground for fallen branches. He had shed his backpack. Katy watched his feet clomp past her.

She grabbed his ankle.

"Do you mind?" he said.

The soles of his boots were identical to the soles of Charlie's boots. While a different design decorated the leather upper, the soles matched. She read a book about military tracking once. A line from the book came back to her.

Take risks early.

"Where did you get these boots?" she asked.

"Dad gave them to me."

Rick's feet were larger than his father's. But, distracted by bickering, Warner might overlook that fact. Time for a risk.

Katy moved alongside Rick. She whispered in his ear, "I need you to lay a false track. Your boot prints are identical to Charlie's."

She glanced up the pathway. Four or five strides ahead, on the left, she spotted a break in the trees. Brush the track beyond that point, get Rick to plant a false track off into the trees far enough Warner would assume Charlie went that way, and sneak back here. Crazy. But plausible.

"No!"

The exclamation echoed from the parking lot. She poked her head out to check on the gang. Ivan was waving the rifle at Warner. Diane had retreated into the background. Warner stood immobile. Stiff. Silent. Arms straight at his sides. Bad news for Ivan.

"Here's how it works," she told Rick. "You match Charlie's stride length and go off into the woods right there." She pointed at the break in the trees. "Go as far as you think is necessary, but make it convincing. They must think Charlie went that way and they *cannot* see you. Got it?"

He saluted. "Yes, sir."

"You'll have to sneak back here. I'll wait a few yards past the break."

Together they found broken branches and brushed the track. Because the dirt was dry, wiping away the tracks took little effort. On two deeper tracks Rick dug the marks out with his fingers. Katy gathered leaves which she scattered over the brushed track, making certain the leaves landed lighter side up. A couple minutes after they started, she and Rick completed the task. Ten yards of earth, beginning at the break, no longer preserved signs of Charlie's passage.

Rick stepped into the break in the trees.

"Remember the stride length," she said.

"I know."

He took a step.

She grabbed his arm. "Be careful."

Head low, he strode into the trees.

A MINUTE TICKED BY BEFORE WARNER AND HIS GANG ENTERED THE WOODS. Katy crouched behind a pair of six-foot pines. Their branches, thick with needles, camouflaged her body while allowing her to view the enemy through a window between the branches.

Warner's gang passed within fifteen feet of her position. She stayed close to the break in the trees where Rick had gone, afraid he might walk right past her if she ventured too far.

Warner and his companions each carried a soft-frame backpack on their shoulders. Diane's pack was smallest, Ivan's largest. Diane gripped the shoulder straps of her pack, while Ivan swung his arms as he walked. Warner kept his arms straight at his sides, his strides long, his movements silent. Ivan carried no rifle. Apparently, he lost that battle.

Warner stopped where she and Rick had brushed the track. Kneeling, he touched the ground. The wood handle of a knife jutted out of the sheath covering its blade. The sheath clipped onto Warner's belt.

Ivan grunted.

"Shh," Warner said.

"What are you looking for, magic dirt?"

Warner sprang to his feet. As he swung around, he slipped the knife out of its sheath and jammed the tip under Ivan's chin.

Quietly, he said, "Speak again and I will silence you. We move in silence, we stop in silence, we live in silence from this moment on. Blink if you understand."

Ivan blinked.

Slipping the knife into its sheath, Warner backed away from Ivan. He turned his head left and right. When his gaze crossed the break in the trees, he paused.

Katy held her breath. He advanced into the break. There he halted, kneeled and touched the ground, straightened. From his pocket, he brought out a knit cap. As he pulled it down over his head, he started in the direction Rick had gone.

Her pulse quickened.

Ivan and Diane traipsed after him.

Katy scooted sideways in a crouch, her gaze fixed on Warner.

A few strides past the break, he hesitated. Moving only his eyes, he inspected the woods, the ground, the track ahead.

Katy held rock-still.

Warner followed the track through a stand of saplings and vanished behind their cover.

Katy tilted her head toward where he disappeared. She opened her mouth a little. She read once how opening your mouth helped your ears work better. She had yet to decide if it helped, but it couldn't hurt.

She listened as the footfalls of Warner, Ivan, and Diane faded.

After a moment of just-in-case time, she hurried back to the track. While she crept, she lifted branches out of the way, settling them back into their original positions before moving on, hopping over twigs and leaves that might crunch if she stepped on them. She monitored her breathing as well, lest she huff or wheeze her way into the trajectory of a bullet or the blade of Warner's knife.

At the end of the brushed track, she waited.

What felt like an hour but was probably five minutes elapsed before Rick scurried out of the trees thirty feet from the false track.

Katy sighed. She slumped her shoulders.

Rick started to speak.

She held a finger against her lips and he stopped. Motioning for him to follow, she headed down the track. They retrieved their packs.

Katy located another of Charlie's boot prints a few yards down the path.

She tracked his sign.

THEY TROD THROUGH THE WOODS IN SILENCE. NOW AND THEN A LEAF CRACKLED under a boot. Twice the metal frame of Katy's pack scraped against a branch. Although she considered each step before taking it, and lifted branches out of the way before settling them back into place, she wasn't used to the size of the pack on her back. On every hunt, settling into the feel of the pack and becoming attuned to its size and position took awhile. Never before had it mattered so much how long acclimating took.

Rick had no trouble acclimating, despite his lack of experience. She felt totally incompetent and useless. The stress affected her. That was all.

Charlie's track had gone off into the thickest part of the woods thirty yards after they latched onto it. Maybe Charlie finally realized he might have a tail.

Maybe it was instinct. Traveling through the thickest woods was the best way to avoid and/or confuse a tracker. But if Warner or one of his friends tracked Charlie, they should've known which way to go.

They are watching. If not Warner, who? And why?

Katy concentrated on the trek. Her mind had no room for questions now.

Although the woods had thickened, the trees and saplings and bushes still provided enough space for walking. The foliage hid Katy and Rick from view, and also hid anyone else from their view. The wind had died. Now every sound transmitted for miles. Including theirs.

As she crossed a patch of leaves, she slowed. Stepping down on the balls of her feet, she rolled each step backward into the heel. No leaves crackled.

Across the patch, she stopped for a rest. The sun had risen above the horizon. When she checked her watch, she found they'd been walking for an hour.

Rick halted beside her. He locked his eyes on hers.

She pulled the GPS radio out of her fanny pack. Flipping it on, she switched the GPS into buddy tracking mode. Nothing. She couldn't expect a signal. Charlie left four days earlier. Even if he survived until Monday, the batteries would have run down long ago.

Survived. Why did she use that word? He was alive. He was okay. They would find him and he'd have a great story about tracking hairy hominids and getting so wrapped up in the search he forgot what day it was. He had done that before.

But not for *four days.*

"Something wrong?" Rick asked.

"No." She shut off the GPS, slipping it into her fanny pack. "Nothing at all."

THE TRACK BECAME FAINT. KATY HAD STOPPED LOOKING FOR FOOTPRINTS, switching to signs in the vegetation. An overturned rock here. A displaced leaf there.

She couldn't say for sure she had the right track anymore. She could've been following a raccoon for the past forty minutes.

Charlie grew more careful the farther out he traveled. Just as she and Rick avoided leaving footprints, so had he. He must've lifted each branch up and replaced it after moving through the same way she did now. Why not, he taught her as much about tracking as her parents had.

But if he got excited because he found a hairy hominid track or perhaps even saw a creature, he might've disregarded safety and taken off after the quarry. Part of her hoped he hadn't because he was safer if his track vanished. Part of her hoped he had, though, because she would find him faster.

Her stomach growled. She pulled the granola bars out of her pack. They ate in silence, watching the woods around them, listening for sounds of Warner and his friends.

Friends seemed an inappropriate term for Diane and Ivan. She could think of no better word to describe their apparent relationship with Warner. He looked at the pair as if he despised yet needed them. Strange. Ivan said something about "getting chatty" if Warner ditched them, which could mean talking to the police or some enemy of Warner's about his activities.

Was Warner a mobster? She'd never heard of German mobsters, and besides, he acted like no mobster she ever saw on the TV news. He struck her more as a businessman. Crazy. He was out here tracking her and Rick in hopes of finding Charlie. Then he would probably kill all three of them. He knew about tracking and sign. He hired men to break into her cabin, as well as Charlie's house and office. Still, she had trouble visualizing Warner as the head of a crime syndicate. She had no trouble visualizing him killing. But not for sport or money.

She saw the man for all of five minutes. How could she know anything about him?

Bellies satiated, she and Rick headed out again. Ten minutes later, she checked the GPS again. No signal. Ahead, the trees spread around a clearing. She halted at the perimeter of the clearing. It was about five yards across.

"Maybe we should rest here," Rick said.

"Not here." Katy sneaked into the clearing. "Too obvious. We can rest a little further on where there's more cover."

A pine guarded one corner of the clearing, its trunk two feet thick, its roots snaking out from the base. The moss on the trunk had fallen off partway down.

She hopped closer. The moss hadn't fallen off the tree. Something rubbed it off. She touched the area. Looking down, she spotted indentations in the dirt. The indentations were round at one end, squared off at the other. The round end dug deeper into the earth.

Boot heels. Someone leaned against the tree. His boot heels dug into the dirt and his backpack scraped the moss off the tree. When she bent down, the outline of a sole became obvious. The elements coupled with the passage of time had degraded the print, yet she could trace the outline in her mind. Charlie had stood here.

Rick kneeled beside her.

"He was here," she said. "He leaned against this tree. We're on the right track."

"You weren't sure until now?"

She looked at Rick. With his brow crinkled, he regarded her as if begging for assurance. He trusted her to guide him through the wilderness. She promised him she could do it. If he lost faith, if he started thinking maybe he should've called the police instead, they were both in trouble.

"Of course I was sure," she said. "But this confirms it."

She walked across the clearing into the trees.

She stopped. Warner might find the clearing as well.

Turning around, she said, "Time for some track maintenance."

Ivan slapped his cheek. "Damn fly."

Warner shot a knife-sharp look at him.

Ivan slapped a hand over his own mouth, eyes wide. Lowering his hand, he grinned. In his other hand he held his Desert Eagle .50 Magnum pistol. Its polished finish of titanium gold glittered along the length of its ten-inch barrel.

"Keep that monstrosity hidden," Warner said.

"I need it out. What if that chick shoots at us?"

"Then you will shoot the tree a half mile south of her."

"You saying I can't handle this gun? Let me tell you, I know how to shoot."

Ivan could no more handle the grossly oversized gun than he could handle his own emotions. Both would kick back in his face and miss the target.

"Put that thing away," Warner said.

Ivan hesitated before shoving the weapon in its hip holster.

Warner focused on the trail once more. Perhaps he should tape Ivan's mouth shut. Duct tape might become the only way of silencing the idiot.

They had followed the wrong trail for ten minutes. Yes, he let Ivan and Diane distract him such that he misidentified the trail as genuine when, in fact, Gallagher and Bergren had laid a false trail for him. An amateur effort, but it worked.

Temporarily.

Warner searched for half an hour before he located the real trail. Gallagher had brushed the track. Smart. Not smart enough, though. He was behind them now, following their sign instead of Charles Bergren's, which simplified the task for him. Their sign was fresh.

Yet they seemed aware of the problem. Their footprints rarely showed, and disturbances to vegetation were scant. He could neither hear nor see them. Still, they left enough sign for him to follow—and that was all that mattered.

At first he thought Charles Bergren must have gone deep into the woods. Now he realized one need not travel far to become lost or invisible. The woods, though not thick with brush or briars as in some forests, provided enough leafage to ensure one saw little beyond the immediate area. Sounds traveled far in the calm, but disintegrated in the wind.

The task might take less time than he estimated.

They came upon a small clearing. Gallagher and Bergren had left footprints in the earth. The prints circled the clearing, spiraling inward. Deeper prints crisscrossed the spiral. Hmm.

The prints led nowhere. Warner backtracked to the edge of the clearing where he had entered. He may have underestimated Gallagher's shrewdness.

Ivan tromped into the clearing. He paused in the center and glanced around. Diane tarried behind Warner, hands in pockets, shoulders hunched. Lines and shadows replaced her smile.

Wheeling around, Ivan threw his arms in the air. He shook his head as he hissed out a breath.

Warner walked straight across the clearing. No footprints led into the woods, no sign at all. They had not gone this way. He turned in a circle. They would choose the least obvious exit.

A large pine stood to his right. He approached the tree. The smaller prints, obviously Gallagher's, ran across the tree's roots in three directions. Bergren's prints overlapped and underlay them. Bits had chipped off the roots where their boots clomped over the growth. Too obvious.

And yet...

The tree represented the largest obstacle in the clearing. No one would exit the clearing around the pine.

Warner smiled. He had them. As he moved past the pine, he waved at Diane and Ivan. They hustled after him out of the clearing.

Soon he would overtake Gallagher and Bergren.

Very soon.

K ATY KEPT WALKING AS SHE CHECKED THE GPS AGAIN. NO SIGNAL. SHE SHOULD give up on finding Charlie with the buddy tracker. She should give up on finding him at all.

Her throat tightened. She glanced behind her.

Rick half smiled.

She looked ahead. For the last ten minutes she had sensed Warner was right behind them. When she looked behind, she detected no sign of anyone besides Rick. The feeling teased her senses like a feather dangling in front of her nose.

Get a grip, nobody's back there.

Warner could've gained on them, especially when they took time to stomp around the clearing and scrape the rest of the moss off the pine tree. If he had gained on them, they should up their pace.

Glancing at Rick, she mouthed, "Go faster."

He nodded.

She accelerated into a fast walk. Although the temperature stayed cool, sweat broke out on her forehead and neck. Taking off her jacket would help. She had no time for the task. Stopping, or even pausing, gave Warner the advantage of time.

The ground became drier. The rain Monday night hadn't reached this area. Pine needles and leaves littered the ground. A breeze rattled the trees once in awhile, drowning out any sounds of Warner's gang approaching.

Her right foot dropped into a hole. As she toppled backward, she grasped at a branch. *Do not disturb the vegetation.* She yanked her hand away and, instead, thrust both hands behind her to retard the fall.

Rick caught her. He lifted her onto her feet.

Straightening her jacket, she looked down at the hole. It was four inches deep, twice as long, and masked by leaves. At the edge of the hole, an outline etched in the earth extended outward from it. Her heart thumped.

A footprint.

Not a shoe print, rather the impression of a bare foot. The print measured twice as long as her own and much wider. The foot had sunk an inch into the earth. The toes spread across the top of the print in an almost straight line, with a push-off mound at mid print. No arch showed in the print.

She dropped onto her hands and knees. With her cheek almost touching the ground, she studied the print. The ball of the foot had depressed deeper into the ground than the rest of the foot, as had the innermost toe. Hairy hominids didn't have a big toe in the manner humans did. All their toes were roughly the same size and shape, although the innermost toe was a bit larger and longer.

She retrieved her magnifying glass from a side pocket of her pack and held it over the print. Imprinted on one toe and a section of the ball, parallel lines swirled and curved. When she examined the walls of the print, she found more lines.

Rick kneeled next to her. "What is it?"

"Dermal ridges."

"Der-whats?"

"Dermal ridges. Fingerprints, except these were on a foot." She sniffed the dirt inside the print. "Smells recent."

"How can you tell?"

"Freshly exposed dirt smells different."

"You're kidding me."

"Nope." Lifting her head, she scanned the area. "Might be more around here."

"We should keep moving, we're looking for Dad, not...not..."

"Hairy hominids." She jumped up. "And we're looking for both. Wherever the hairy hominids went, Charlie followed them."

"But you said this is fresh. Dad came out here four days ago."

"Yes, but if the creatures have a nest he might've followed them to it."

"A nest. Sure."

She hopped forward a few steps. A broken twig lay about six feet away, at a diagonal from the print. She picked up the twig. The flesh was still pale and soft. The twig broke recently. She looked up into the trees. A small branch had broken off one of the trees, its flesh showing pale against the bark.

Rising, she held the twig against the break. It fit.

Less than a foot from the tree, she discovered another print, more ambiguous than the first. This one resembled an oval except for the slight imprint of the ball at the front of the print.

Rick grunted.

She turned toward him. "What now?"

He was ten feet away, staring at the footprint, hands on hips. He chewed the corner of his lip as he tilted his head to squint at the print.

The grunt had sounded closer. Much closer.

Freezing the rest of her body, she surveyed the trees by moving only her eyes. A shadow shifted.

She concentrated on the spot. Two pinpoints of red glared back at her.

The thing growled.

Out the corner of her mouth, she whispered, "Rick!"

He didn't respond.

"Rick!"

He stepped toward her. "What?"

"It's watching us. Don't move."

"I'm coming."

"No." Foliage rustled. She glanced at the shadow. "We don't want to alarm it."

"It! What about me?"

The creature strode out of the brush in front of her. It halted a dozen feet away.

"Where is it?" Rick asked.

"Right *there*," she said, rolling her eyes in the direction of the creature.

Shadows cloaked the creature. It looked seven or eight feet tall, bulky, hairy. She could make out no details on its face or body. Its eyes glowed red.

The smell washed over her. Rotten eggs served with decaying flesh.

She breathed through her mouth.

"I don't see it," Rick said. After a pause, he added, "What stinks?"

The creature looked behind, rotating its head and shoulders together. When the creature turned back to Katy, it snorted. "Oogah-oogah."

She looked past the creature into the woods through which she'd come, the woods through which Warner now came, somewhere back there. The creature might sense his approach before she could—smell him or hear him or both.

"Oogah." The creature jerked its head. "Oogah-oo."

The creature bolted past her. It smacked into her shoulder. She spun, tripped, hit the ground shoulder first. Branches snapped. Bits of foliage rained on her.

She twisted her head around to see where the creature had gone.

The beast bounded through the trees, grunting with each footfall.

She leaped onto her feet and ran after it.

"Katy!"

Rick's voice sounded distant. Everything faded into the background as she tore through the forest after the creature, following in its wake, jumping over its tracks. Ahead, the huge figure bobbed in and out of sight. Branches snapped and tumbled. Leaves showered behind the creature. The cracks and crunches merged into a chorus of destroyed foliage.

The woods rushed past in a blur.

The creature veered left. She sprinted after it. Her pack jounced on her shoulders and back, its forty pounds pummeling her. She kept running.

"Katy! Wait!"

Footsteps behind her.

The creature sped up. Its grunts ran together like the chugging of a train racing at full speed. Her own breaths shortened into gasps.

The woods opened. A stream cut through the clearing.

The creature sprang across the stream.

Katy leaped into the water. The mud sucked her boots down. She floundered, yanked her feet free, scrambled onto the shore. Her boots slipped on the sand.

Cursing, she pushed through the sand and rushed into the trees.

The creature had surged ahead. She could no longer see it.

Careening through the trees, she followed the creature's track. Then she spotted the creature. It ran toward a shaft of sunlight that broke through a thin spot in the canopy.

She raced after the creature.

It disappeared.

She stopped. Breathing hard, she tiptoed into the sunlight. The creature's footprints ended in the midst of the sunlight. Where the prints stopped, the feet were side by side, as if the creature stood there and simply vanished.

Impossible.

Wheezing, she collapsed onto her knees. She shrugged the backpack off her shoulders. Sweat glazed her face and neck, soaked her shirt. From the knees down, she was wet and muddy.

Leaves crackled. She reached into her fanny pack for the Taurus.

Rick sprinted into the light. He halted beside her.

She zipped the pack. Not Warner. This time.

Panting, Rick scowled at her. "Don't ever do that again."

"Do what?"

"Take off like that. You could've gotten killed, by the bad guys or whatever you were chasing."

"It was a hairy hominid." She laid down on her back, arms and legs splayed. "It sensed something coming, probably Warner. I think it was trying to warn me."

Rick sat down. He let his pack slide off his shoulders and onto the ground behind him.

"That was no bear," she said. "You didn't see it, so you have the luxury of denying it. I don't. It was real, it was huge, and it warned me."

"Where did it go? Nothing that big could just disappear. Or maybe you didn't want to catch it because then you'd see it was a bear." He rubbed his eyes. "Sorry, I didn't mean that. Truth is, I don't know what the thing was."

"It did disappear." She gestured at the parallel prints. "Right there. Look around, there aren't any more prints and, unless I missed something, hairy hominids don't fly."

Rick, raising onto his knees, leaned over the prints.

After a moment, he sat back on his heels and shut his eyes. "Shit."

Yeah, that was the word all right.

THEY DIDN'T MOVE FOR FIVE MINUTES. WHEN KATY FINALLY SAT UP, SHE DRAGGED her pack in front of her. Unzipping a pocket, she brought out a freezer bag full of beef jerky strips. She tossed a few strips to Rick.

They landed on his lap. When he picked up a strip, he curled his lips. "I hate beef jerky."

"Get over it." She bit off a chunk. "This is lunch."

"I thought we were catching lunch."

"No, we're catching dinner. We don't have time for catching lunch." She finished off one strip and grabbed another. "You can have granola bars if you'd rather."

He shoved a jerky strip into his mouth. As he chewed, he twisted his face in disgust. After his third strip, he said, "I think my taste buds are numb."

She suppressed a smile. "If you hate this, wait until dinner."

"I'm afraid to ask."

She closed the bag of jerky, stuffing it back inside her pack. She wiped her hands on her jeans. "You have your choice of Thumper or Rocky."

"I'd rather not eat Sylvester Stallone for dinner."

"Didn't you ever watch the Rocky and Bullwinkle show?"

He curled his lip again. "The squirrel."

"You can always starve, if you prefer."

After his last bite of jerky, he grabbed the round canteen tied onto his pack. He unscrewed the cap and swigged water.

The canteens, one tied to her pack and one to his, came from an army surplus store. Forged from metal, they were more durable than the plastic ones in fashion these days. Besides, inside the canvas cover the canteen sat in a metal cup shaped around its bottom. The cup could be removed for use as a bowl, a drinking cup, or whatever you needed.

She swallowed a few mouthfuls of her own water.

The sweat had dried, leaving behind a chill. Her calves and feet were wet, cold. Her boots were waterproof, but nothing could protect her when she fell into a stream. She ought to change her socks. They would never dry inside her boots, and wet feet would mean trouble when the temperature dropped at dusk.

While she changed socks, Rick paced with his head down.

"What's wrong?" she asked, tying her boot laces.

"That thing could not vanish into thin air. There must be more tracks."

"There aren't, I looked."

She knew of sightings where witnesses claimed hairy hominids vanished in flashes of light or clouds of smoke. While her hairy hominid hadn't gone in a blur of light, an interesting tradition existed concerning the creatures and lights. Down in Texas, residents of a town near Houston told stories about hairy creatures appearing from and disappearing into strange lights on a stretch of road called the Ghost Road. Stories from other locations told of the creatures vanishing in flashes of light. Often those tales came packaged with UFO sightings from the same area on the same night.

UFOs connected to hairy hominids? Perhaps. If the hairy hominids had a connection to UFOs, she had no clue what the connection was. In the course of investigating the true origins of humanity, she and Charlie investigated some UFO sightings. Though the sightings intrigued them, neither she nor Charlie could explain how the sightings pertained to human origins or hairy hominids. A connection existed, but one beyond their comprehension.

People had been seeing UFOs since the age of cavemen. Paintings on cave walls in France depicted disc-like objects flying through the air. A medieval painting showed, in the sky behind the Virgin Mary, a metallic UFO soaring while a man and his dog observed its flight.

The UFOs went way back. Hairy hominid sightings went back just as far.

Most historians, especially the ones with doctorates or other pieces of parchment hanging on their walls, discounted ancient sightings as folk tales. Native Americans believed hairy wild men had always existed and included the creatures in their pantheon of magical beasts. Europeans had long told myths about wild men. They even depicted the creatures in the literature of the Middle Ages. Most cultures throughout history took for granted that hairy hominids existed.

Until they forgot. As societies became more industrial, more "civilized," they abandoned the old ways and the old knowledge. Myths, they said, silly tales told around campfires.

Hairy hominids had many names now—Bigfoot, Sasquatch, almas, Yeti—but few believers within scientific circles. They had been demoted to folklore.

What she chased today, that was no myth.

Rick hefted his pack over his shoulders. "Let's go."

He helped Katy lift her pack on, and she took a step. He rushed past her out of the sunlight into the twilight of the canopy. The breeze had died. In the stillness, sounds echoed far. They must be mindful of signaling their location by sound. A conversation raised above a whisper might alert Warner from hundreds of yards away. A snapped twig could catch his attention from even farther.

Rick stomped across dead leaves. Crunch, crackle, crunch.

She grabbed his arm. Pausing, he looked back at her. Eyebrows scrunched. Lips flattened. Jaw tight.

"Quietly," she said.

Without a word, he headed off again, this time quietly.

Her encounter with the hairy hominid had gotten to him. Why should the incident upset him more than her? She saw the monster. Got knocked over by it. Jeez, she wasn't freaking out over the incident.

Men. Count on them reacting irrationally.

Rick stopped.

Her face smacked into his backpack. When he said nothing, she leaned sideways to peek around him. A few feet further, the land sloped upward. The trees continued up the hillside, shrouding the base of the hill. Scanning the slope, she saw what had stopped Rick. A backpack. Its shoulder straps were tangled in the lowest branches of a sapling. The pack dangled a few feet above the base of the hill.

Charlie's backpack.

It was identical to the ones both she and Rick carried. Charlie bought five backpacks, one for each of them—her, Jim, and Charlie—plus two extras in case one broke or got lost. Jim's was found in his truck near where his body ended up. Now they had found Charlie's. He would never leave his pack behind. It carried all his supplies, for the hunt and for emergencies. If his pack was here...

Oh Jesus.

She ran up the hillside.

8

ER FEET SLIPPED. KATY GRABBED THE SAPLING, FLOPPING ONTO HER BUTT
beside the backpack. She freed the straps from the sapling and set the pack
on her lap. The main compartment was unzipped, the contents spilled onto the
hillside. A freezer bag filled with trash had landed at the base of the hill. Leaves
had fallen on top of it. From this angle she could see the bag underneath.

Juice boxes lay scattered over the hillside. A fleece pullover ended up against
a pine several feet down the slope. She picked up the pullover, holding it close
to her face and sniffing. It smelled of dirt and pine needles.

She flipped over the pack. Along the back, a rip was torn from the left shoulder
halfway down the pack. Padding bulged out of the tear. Crumbs of tree bark
adhered to the padding. A branch most likely caught on the pack as it tumbled
down the slope. But why did it fall?

Setting the pack aside, she ascended the hill. Halfway up the slope, she found
a dent in the hillside, a sort of ledge with a sloping back wall and rounded rim.
The ledge stood a yard high and nearly as deep, twice that in width. Nestled
against the back of the ledge, beneath an awning someone constructed using
pine branches, she found the remains of a campfire. Bits of wood burned into
charcoal. Ash. Tinder stacked beside the remains. She touched the charcoal. Cold.

A scrap of fabric lay on the ground near the rim of the ledge. She grabbed
the scrap. Gray flannel. From Charlie's shirt. A stain darkened the fabric. She
held the scrap near her face, squinting at the stain. It looked dark red, almost
brown. Blood.

No, it wasn't blood, it couldn't be blood.

Rick strode up the hill toward her. "Find something?"

She stuffed the fabric in her pocket. "Just an old campfire."

"Dad was here," he said, reaching the ledge, "wasn't he?"

"Yes."

"He left his backpack."

"I know." *Don't tell him about the fabric.* "He's been gone awhile, the fire's cold. We should look around for more sign."

Rick arched an eyebrow at her. As she bit the inside of her lip, she turned around and examined the hillside. Surveying the area in widening circles starting from the campsite, she watched for any clue about where Charlie went or why. He must've left in a hurry. Either he forgot his backpack or, when it got stuck on a tree, he abandoned it because he felt he had no time for retrieving it. Something either excited or frightened him a lot.

A reflection caught her eye at the base of the hill, about thirty feet north of the campsite. The sun glinted off a shiny surface. She trotted down the slope to the object. She found, embedded in the dirt, Charlie's GPS radio. Though smeared with soil, the LCD screen still reflected the light. She backed away from the GPS radio. It had become embedded inside a depression. Branches, their leaves or needles attached, littered the area and concealed most of the depression.

She bent down, lifting away the foliage. The shape surfacing from under the litter was one she knew too well. A hairy hominid footprint.

A creature stomped Charlie's GPS radio into the earth. The print looked older than the ones she saw earlier, the ones made by the creature she chased.

She picked up one of the branches. The flesh along the break had darkened and hardened. Checking the other branches that masked the print, she realized all had broken at least several hours ago. The creature she chased snapped off branches as it bolted away from her. If the creature who made this print had been frightened, it might've bolted as well, inflicting similar damage.

The creatures normally preferred stealth. Most people who encountered them neither saw the creatures coming nor heard them departing.

The creature had been scared. Or angry.

A chill raised hairs all over her body. If the creature pursued Charlie…

Find more tracks.

Back on the hillside, Rick was squatting beside the backpack. He fingered the rip on its backside.

"I found his GPS radio," she said. "And tracks."

He pushed his finger through the rip. "What kind of tracks?"

"Hairy hominid. One of them stepped on the GPS radio. It looks like the creature was really moving when it came through here."

"Probably the one you chased."

"No, the tracks are a couple hours old."

She didn't mention the tracks might've been older. No way to tell, really, so why depress him with more bad news. He needed action, something to distract him from thinking about his father's fate. She needed a distraction too.

"Got to look for more tracks," she said, snatching the backpack from his hands and dropping it on the ground. "Help me look."

He stood. "Show me where."

As they descended the slope, Katy steered him toward the footprint she had found. He plucked the GPS radio out of the ground, wiping the dirt off the screen. When he flicked the power switch, nothing happened. The battery was dead.

She could've told him as much. He needed good news, though, so instead she instructed him in how to search the area for more sign.

"You sweep behind, I'll sweep ahead," she said. "Stop every few feet to scan the area visually in an arc. Look through the vegetation—and take your time."

Tucking Charlie's GPS radio in his jacket pocket, he began searching.

The odds of finding sign backward from the print were low. He had little experience in searching for sign, which lowered the odds further. But it gave him hope, and she realized he needed that more than sign. Any evidence would await her ahead of the print. What she would find, she didn't know.

And that scared bejesus out of her.

FIFTEEN MINUTES LATER, SHE LOCATED ANOTHER PIECE OF CHARLIE'S EQUIP-ment, his Game-Vu camera. Designed for hunters, the camera detected motion within twenty-five feet and snapped a digital image of the perpetrator. The camera, a black box with a motion sensor and lens on the front and an awning shielding the lens from sun and weather, was secured on a tree by a chain and bicycle lock. At eye level, the camera had a view of the surrounding trees. Anything wandering by posed for a photo.

The camera came with a handheld monitor for viewing the images. If she located the monitor, she could examine the photos. Maybe, just maybe, she'd see something useful. Since the camera stamped the date and time on the images, she would have some idea of when Charlie last checked the camera.

She jogged back to the hillside. Rick returned a moment later as she was digging through Charlie's backpack.

"Mission aborted," he said, stooping beside her. "There's nothing between here and the stream. No point in going back across the stream."

"I found Charlie's camera." She pulled a handful of granola bars out of the pack, dumped them on the ground. "It takes pictures of anything that moves. He locked it on a tree further ahead. If I can find the monitor, we can see what it captured lately."

In a side pocket, she located the monitor. The silver monitor, the size of her hand, included a cable for hooking it into the camera.

They trekked back to the camera. Katy plugged the monitor into the device.

The screen displayed black-and-white snapshots. The first showed trees. A squirrel or wind-blown branch could've set off the camera. She clicked through the images. One sequence caught a pair of does meandering past the camera. Another captured a rabbit in mid-jump, its legs stretched out behind it. Others, like the first image, showed nothing. The twentieth image made her heart skip.

Charlie. Walking toward the camera. Reaching for it. Behind his head, the top of his backpack and its metal frame were visible. He had his mouth open, tongue on his lower lip. The look he always got when he concentrated.

Rick leaned over her shoulder, his arm bumping her backpack, gaze fixed on the monitor. The date stamp said October 15, 9:54:20 AM. Two days ago Charlie had stood in this spot. Alive.

She advanced to the next image, taken thirty seconds later. Charlie—no longer reaching for the camera—stared back over his shoulder, squinting. He had slung his Remington .30-06 rifle over his left shoulder. Next. He had stepped back from the camera and now faced camera right. Next. Eyes and mouth wide open, he supported the rifle's barrel in his left hand while his right grasped the grip. His left cheek rested on the stock as he aimed through the sight mounted atop the rifle.

Her heart hammered as she advanced to the next image.

The picture was blurry. She squinted at the image. Black, like a shadow. A paler shape hovered near the top of the screen. A brown line extended down from the pale blur.

She stared at the image until her eyesight swam out of focus. Like sorting out one of those "magic eye" paintings where it looked like nonsense until your eyes lost focus, she suddenly saw what the image depicted.

A black figure hoisting Charlie over its head as his rifle tumbled downward.

A hairy hominid had attacked him.

The next twenty images showed wildlife or nothing at all. Since the camera could store as many as sixty images, she skimmed the rest. As she flipped past a series of deer photos, she noticed something strange. They were galloping past the camera.

She backtracked a few images. The deer rushed past the camera in a throng, wild-eyed, ears flattened back. Several of the deer twisted their heads around, gawking at a sight behind them. In the last photo of the deer, their hindquarters showed on the left of the screen as they galloped away. At the right, a shadow loomed on the ground. A long, wide shadow with no neck.

She skipped ahead a few images. The shadow disappeared. The next image was black. The one after that, the same. And the one after that. Five images of blackness. Had the camera malfunctioned?

The sixth image of blackness looked different. A bit of light peeked through a crack in the dark. The light illuminated hairs. Black ones. On a hand. The fingers had parted slightly, admitting the light. Three more images of blackness followed.

The hairy hominids knew about the camera.

She clicked ahead to the next image. A shadow darkened the ground. In the following image, it was gone. More images of trees followed before the camera had run out of memory.

"Dad was here two days ago," Rick said. "He looked scared. A bear must have attacked him before he had time to shoot."

A bear. She had no energy for arguing. She needed all of it to puzzle out what happened here two days earlier. Rick could hug his denial awhile longer.

She turned around and examined the ground. From the photos, she surmised Charlie struggled for his life in this spot. The struggle should've left sign—footprints, shell casings, broken branches, indentations where Charlie hit the ground after the creature threw him, tracks from the deer that galloped through. Even after two days, the place should've been a mess. It was clean.

The footprints belonged to her and Rick. Otherwise, the ground looked undisturbed, as did the vegetation. Leaves had fallen, nothing else. Unbelievable.

The images. A hairy hand blocking the camera.

She flipped back through the images, stopping at the last image before the hairy hand appeared. A large branch lay on the ground, its broken end jutting into the air, the fronds of needles splayed across the earth. Charlie's backpack sat a few feet away on its side.

Someone took his pack back to the campsite. Someone? Some *thing*.

Though the smallness of the image made identification impossible, she could tell the picture revealed marks and tracks in the soil.

A hairy hand. Blocking the camera.

Holy heaven, the creatures had recognized the camera and blocked its view while they brushed the track. They cleaned up after themselves.

They brushed the track.

Afterward they carried the pack to Charlie's campsite, rifled the contents, and threw the pack down on the ground. Thrown it so hard the pack bounced down the hillside and landed in a tree. Then they stomped the GPS radio into the ground. Or perhaps they looted the campsite before brushing the track.

Did it really matter?

Rick tapped her shoulder.

She jumped.

"You found something," he said.

"Yes." She looked straight at him. "You won't like it."

"Tell me anyway."

"No bear attacked Charlie, it was a hairy hominid." She clicked back until the monitor displayed the blurred image of Charlie's attack. She handed Rick the monitor. "Look at that picture and tell me what you see."

He looked at the image. "Nothing."

"Let your eyes go out of focus."

He gazed at the monitor for a minute. He made a face. "Looks like a furry thing throwing another thing in the air. Don't know what that line is."

"The line is Charlie's rifle."

Rick stared at the picture. His face paled. "You don't mean—"

"That hairy thing is tossing your father around like a Nerf ball."

He looked at her with such despair that she wanted to hug him and kiss him and tell him everything would be all right. She had no idea whether anything would be all right. Ever. A hairy hominid might leap out of the trees any second, intent on disemboweling both of them. If Charlie's .30-06 couldn't stop the creatures, she wondered if anything could.

Rick's expression hardened. He hurled the monitor into a tree.

She clasped his hand. "He could be alive. We have to keep looking."

"If that thing attacked Dad..." His nostrils flared. "You could've been next. When you chased that thing like you were running after a dog."

"I'm fine."

"These are animals," he said. "I may not have hunted in awhile, but I know how to kill an animal. If we see one, I say we shoot first and figure out what they are later."

She shook her head. "They're smart. They knew to block the camera so we couldn't see what they were doing. They brushed the track, Rick. Who knows what else they can do. If they want us dead, we may never see them coming."

"Are you saying these things killed my father and covered up the evidence?"

"They covered up, yes, but we can't know for sure that Charlie is dead."

"He's dead, Katy."

"No."

Rick gave her that look again, the one she couldn't decipher.

"Believe what you want." She glanced at the cleansed area. "But we must keep looking. We must be careful."

"We have to stick together." He clasped her hand. "Promise me you won't run off again."

Lacing her fingers through his, she pulled him after her. "Come on, we better stash our packs at the campsite and do another search before it gets dark."

"We can't camp at Dad's site."

"It's the best place around. Up on the side of a hill but still sheltered by the trees. If we start a fire, the smoke will dissipate before it gets out of the treetops. It won't give away our position."

"We should pick a different spot."

Halting, she wrapped her other hand over the top of his. "I know it's weird because Charlie was there and now he isn't. But it really is the best place to camp. Okay?"

"Fine."

She led him toward the campsite.

THEY SPENT TWO HOURS SCOURING THE WOODS AROUND THE CAMPSITE. RICK spotted deer tracks not far from the spot where Charlie had left his camera. When Katy examined the tracks, she noted how they dug into the soil. When fresh, they had probably shown kickback of dirt. Old, they illustrated that the animals had fled in a hurry. But the kickback had worn away.

She and Rick spent another three hours hunting for food.

Katy knew about tracking and hunting animals. She was rusty, though, and getting back into the groove of it took her awhile. After an hour, she finally felt comfortable stalking the woods. An hour and half after that, she found the sign of a squirrel—tiny, amorphous pellets in a pile on the ground beside oblong prints, two larger on the outside and two smaller on the inside, leading away from the scat. In her mind, she drew long toes and claws on the prints. A tree squirrel made the track.

The prints stopped at the base of a nearby pine.

Rick approached from behind, where he'd been gathering wood for the fire.

"What are you staring at?" he asked as he kneeled beside her. He cupped small sticks and pine needles in his hands.

"Squirrel scat." When he gave her a blank look, she said, "Scat is animal feces."

"Squirrel poop fascinates you. I'll remember that at Christmas."

"It leads me to our dinner."

"How should we kill it?"

"Hit it with a big stick."

"Nice."

"This is survival, not home ec." She took the wood and tinder from him, stuffing them into a plastic bag she had shoved in her pocket, and looked up into the pine tree. "I have a slingshot in my pack, but I might lose the squirrel if I go back for it. A stick works about as well anyway."

Rick snatched an inch-thick, foot-long stick from the ground. He thwapped the stick on his palm. "Ready."

He wanted to kill their dinner, she realized, and it surprised her. Maybe she underestimated his wilderness skills. Maybe following her lead all day made him feel unmanly. A confidence had infected his demeanor in the last hours, and she liked how it looked on him.

Gazing up into the tree, he thwapped the stick again.

She hated the idea of killing a cute squirrel, but they needed food. Carrying food with them would've taken up space they needed for sleeping bags, water, spare clothing. She could hardly call herself a hunter if she shied from catching her dinner. Survival required killing. That was that.

About twenty minutes later, they brought the carcass of a black squirrel back to the campsite. The sun had sunk nearer the horizon, halfway behind the treetops. The chill of dusk settled over the woods.

Katy got the skinning knife, a small blade with a curve in it, from her pack. She gave Rick the knife.

"Clean the squirrel," she said. "I'll start the fire."

While he skinned and gutted the animal, she gathered the rocks, sticks, and tinder they had collected. She cleaned out the area where Charlie had burned his fire. Digging a small pit, she lined it with the rocks. The pine needles, dead grass, and leaves she piled on top of the rocks. Atop that she stacked small sticks in a circle, their ends joining over the center of the pile.

Instinctively, she reached into her pocket for the magnesium block. She stopped. Why struggle with magnesium chips and flint when she had matches in her pack? Her father had left her the magnesium block—a four-inch rectangle, black on the outside and silver inside, with a rod of flint embedded in one side—and the service issue .45. The magnesium block was a fire-starter. Flake off the magnesium, let the flakes fall onto the tinder, and strike the flint for a spark. The method gave her a headache, along with hand cramps. Her instinct made her reach for the block because she'd been practicing with it for months now. Practicing.

And practicing.

Forget the magnesium. From her bag, she retrieved matches, which she stored in a Zip-Loc bag. After striking a match, she let it burn down a little and shoved it underneath the sticks. The tinder smoked. Little flames erupted.

The flames grew until the sticks caught fire. As the fire expanded, she added larger sticks. She kept the fire small, about eight inches in diameter, adjusting the placement of sticks as the fire expanded in one direction. After a few minutes, she had a good fire going.

Rick brought the skinned squirrel. He had cut off the legs and head and removed the entrails.

She pulled a scrap of aluminum foil from her pack. After wrapping the meat in the foil, she buried the packet in the fire, on top of the rocks. She placed more sticks on the fire. The awning of pine fronds sheltered the fire. The smoke that sneaked around the awning dissipated as it snaked through the trees overhead.

Warner would not see the smoke of their fire. Unless he got close, he wouldn't see the glow of it either. He might smell it, but there was no way around that.

"So now we twiddle our thumbs," Rick said.

"Hardly." She dug in her backpack. "We have more hunting to do."

"What, you want sautéed rabbit for dessert?"

"Hunting for hairy hominids." From her pack, she retrieved the binoculars and a night vision scope. "And some non-hairy ones."

"Warner. You think he's close?"

"Not too close, but we should look for them. In the dark, we have a better chance of sneaking up on them."

"Oh great, let's do that."

"You can stay here."

"Hell no." He settled a hand on the .45 holstered on his belt. "Just don't get why we have to look for trouble when it comes right at us regularly."

Rick grabbed the night vision scope, a box-like unit with a lens protruding from one end. A button on the top activated the unit. A second button turned on the infrared illuminator, which provided extra light when needed, as on a moonless evening like tonight. The scope was more expensive than regular binoculars, but cheaper than most night vision products. Charlie bought three, of course, one for each of them.

The scope looked small in Rick's hand. He shifted his hand as if testing its one-pound weight. "Where did he get the money for all this?"

"All what?"

"Night vision, digital cameras, GPS radios, a new truck. Didn't think he made that much as a professor."

"Not after they cut his salary as punishment for the spring semester fiasco."

"What fiasco?"

Katy told him about Charlie missing final exams and cutting out for two days in the middle of the week.

Rick whistled. "Spiegel put up with that?"

"Charlie's popular with the students. Spiegel wanted to fire him, but the kids signed a petition demanding Charlie stay. So Spiegel gave him a second chance, though he made sure Charlie understood there was no way he'd ever get tenure."

"The money," Rick said. He leaned toward her, head down, eyes upturned to gaze at her. "Tell me where he got it."

"By pimping me on the streets of Anameka. It's a rough town, you know."

He leaned close. His breath tickled her face. "Where, Katy."

"I can't tell you."

He shrugged his eyebrows. "Can't or won't?"

Charlie made her swear she wouldn't divulge the truth. She didn't know the whole truth anyway, only the fragment Charlie shared before she left for Texas. When he handed her the airline ticket—first class—and an envelope stuffed with hundred-dollar bills. You're going to Texas, he'd said, to investigate those human footprints we keep hearing about. Jim found a map on the web, take it and have a good time. Bring back some photos, Katy, I know you can find those prints.

He told her he made reservations for her at the Worthington Hotel in Fort Worth. Another extravagance. Once he convinced her she should go, he laid the truth fragment on her.

Now Rick wanted that fragment. But she promised Charlie, and she despised breaking promises.

Charlie could be dead. Rick was alive, here, and he wanted the truth about his father. He deserved that, after traipsing through the woods after her, entrusting his life to her, a woman he barely knew.

He was so close she could feel his body heat.

"He told me the money came from a sponsor," she said.

"What sponsor?"

"I don't know. A rich guy who made anonymity a condition of the donation. Charlie knew but he never told me. He didn't even tell me about the money until last week. Tuesday he gave me an airline ticket, hotel reservations, and some traveling money to go to Texas. I left Thursday."

"How much traveling money?"

"Six thousand dollars."

His eyes widened. "And you didn't wonder where he got it?"

"Of course I did." She looked at the fire. "I demanded he tell me the sponsor's name and how much money the guy had given him. Charlie clammed up. The sponsor is rich, local, and well-connected, that's all I know."

"I believe you." Rick backed away. "Now explain to me why we should go after Warner."

"Not go after him, look for him. To make sure he hasn't found our sign and, if he has, to mislead him again. While we're out, might as well look for hairy hominids too. A lot of sightings happen at night."

She got up.

He pulled her back down. "I will go. You will stay here."

"No."

"Yes." He leaned close again, his nose brushing hers. "Or neither of us goes."

They stared at each other.

Rick held her upper arm in his hand. His grip felt strong and warm.

She could not let him shut her out of the hunt. This was her expedition. She brought him along as backup, a bodyguard perhaps but not a commando. Did he have any clue what night stalking entailed? And could he do it without getting himself caught? They had worse problems than Warner, they had hairy creatures who might kill to defend their territory.

Rick denied their existence. No man could defend himself from an enemy he denied existed.

Her shoulders ached. She rolled them forward and back.

Leading was tiring, and she had led all day. All her life. Everybody expected her to be strong and in command, the daughter of a soldier couldn't show weakness. Suck it up, move on.

Rick didn't expect that. He wanted to take the lead.

So let him. She could get some rest. And maybe he'd see enough that his dam of denial would crack. Then the truth could flood in at last.

"Fine," she said. "Go alone."

"I can do this, Katy."

"I know." When he moved away, she grabbed his shirt and pulled him back until their eyes were inches apart. "Don't you dare get yourself killed."

He kissed her forehead.

In less than a minute, he vanished into the night.

DARKNESS. TREES. AS RICK SNEAKED THROUGH THE WOODS, HIS VISION ADJUSTED to the dark. Every minute or two, he looked through the night vision scope. The woods in shades of green. Despite the distortion around the periphery of the field of vision, he could see the leaves on the ground, the branches on the trees.

Crickets screeched. An owl hooted. He looked up, through the scope, at the trees. The owl perched fifteen feet above in a maple.

Behind the hoot of the owl, voices murmured.

Knees bent, back stooped forward, he crept toward the sound.

Look *through* the vegetation, he reminded himself. Katy knew about tracking, he should pay attention to her advice. He'd worried she might argue about staying behind at the campsite. He hated leaving her alone. She looked tired, though, and he didn't want her getting sick out here because she pushed too hard.

Dad was dead. Their goal had changed from rescuing his father into finding out what killed him and why. Katy could never accept that he had been killed. Her desperation told him everything he needed to know.

She loved his father.

Sure, she liked him. But she loved Dad. Why else would she deny that he was dead despite all the evidence? Why else would she hide things from him? She found more than a campfire on the ledge. He saw her stuff something in her pocket before he got up the hill. Back at the parking lot, she had said she knew Dad's shoes. Sounded awfully intimate.

He understood why Dad got involved with her. She was smart, beautiful, independent. She let no one push her around, and she radiated the kind of energy that infected everyone around her. She had will too, which—though irritating as hell—made him like her even more. Katy Gallagher was strong, yes. She also had a softness that balanced the willfulness. That made him want to protect her. Take care of her.

When she ran off after that hairy beast, he felt like strangling her. When he caught up with her, he had almost hugged her. But she had been fixated on the creature, so he yelled at her instead.

He frowned at his own ineptitude. He'd had girlfriends, of course, but none of them stalked hairy monsters in the wilderness or ate squirrel for dinner. If he had served those women whole milk they would have screamed at him. *All that fat, are you insane?* No wonder he hadn't dated in two years.

It didn't matter if Katy saw him as temperamental. She was in love with Dad.

A glow up ahead caught his eye. He lowered onto hands and knees, crawling toward the light. The voices, though still soft, grew louder.

He hid behind a pine sapling. As he peeked through the branches, he saw the source of the glow and the voices.

Warner and his friends huddled around a small fire drinking from plastic mugs. The woman sidled up to Warner. Grimacing, he pushed away from her.

Ivan grunted. "Lukewarm soup. This is the life."

"This is the wilderness," Warner said. "Not the Hyatt resort."

"No kidding." Ivan sipped his soup, winced. "How long we gonna sit here? Oughta go after her while she's sleeping."

"And do what?"

"Beat it out of her."

"She knows nothing—yet," Warner said. "We must wait until she finds him before we confront her."

Ivan rolled his eyes.

"Sleep," Warner said, "and at dawn we will find her again."

"And follow her around like lost puppies some more."

Warner glared at him. Ivan pulled out his sleeping bag and unrolled it. While Ivan flattened out his bag, Warner stared into the trees. He cocked his head, opening his mouth.

Diane unrolled her sleeping bag.

Warner scanned the woods.

The crickets ceased singing. The owl hooted twice.

Warner looked straight at the pine sapling.

Rick froze. He held his breath. Warner's gaze seemed locked on his, yet the sapling hid him. Didn't it?

His father's lessons came back to him now, the words he had heard over and over throughout his childhood and memorized because it made Dad happy. If they see you, freeze. Do not move until you're sure they lost you. Movement gives you away, stillness disguises you.

"They" had meant deer back then. Now it meant humans.

Warner closed his mouth. He turned his attention on Diane as he grabbed her sleeping bag and showed her the proper way of laying it out on the ground.

They would do nothing until dawn. He should tell Katy.

Rick eased backward.

Movement flashed on the opposite side of Warner's camp.

Motion behind the trees.

Rick stopped. He raised the binoculars.

Warner stopped as well. He zeroed in on the trees over Diane's shoulder.

Rick focused on the trees. As he studied the outlines of branches and needles, working at looking beyond them, a silhouette emerged from the chaos. A humanlike silhouette.

A large, thick-necked man.

No, wait. He had no neck. The shoulders tapered into the head. The massive shoulders. No wrestler or Marine had anything on this guy.

Guy. What if that wasn't a—

Of course it was. What else would it be? Somebody besides Warner trailed them out here. Somebody besides Warner wanted to find his father.

The figure retreated and disappeared.

Katy. He should get back to her.

He lowered the binoculars so they hung around his neck on their strap. The scope, which he had set on the ground, he took in his hand.

Warner looked away from the woods. Rick headed back toward the campsite and Katy. She would think he had seen a Bigfoot. He hadn't, of course.

He *hadn't*.

Tasted like chicken." Rick wiped his hands on his pants. Having consumed the last of the squirrel, he reclined against the rear of the ledge.

Katy folded the aluminum foil in which she had cooked the meat and tucked it in her pack. To her, the squirrel tasted greasy like the dark meat of a chicken. But, hey, if Rick liked it…

Since returning from his reconnaissance, he'd said nothing about what he saw or heard except that Warner would stay put until dawn. When she asked for details, he lapsed into silence.

She tried again. "What's bothering you?"

He got out his sleeping bag. As he unrolled it, he faced away from her.

"Not enough room up here," he said. "I'll sleep at the bottom of the hill. Better view of the woods there anyway. I can keep watch."

"Rick."

He clomped down the hill.

Some event had unsettled him, she could tell that much. If he'd seen a hairy hominid—or, as he called them, Bigfoot—he would keep it a secret, especially if he believed it was a hairy hominid. The truth frightened him. It frightened most people. They had a narrow definition of reality and anything that didn't fit into their definition got thrown out altogether.

For anything it couldn't throw out, the mind dreamed up nonsensical explanations. UFO? No, just the planet Venus. Never mind the sky was cloudy. Bigfoot? A bear, of course. Don't mention the creature had humanlike feet, no snout, and was bipedal. Prehistoric human footprints? Just erosional depressions, my dear. So what if the depressions showed clear toe impressions and dermal ridges.

Laymen needed no help coming up with ludicrous explanations. Scientists and the government did it for them.

Katy rolled out her sleeping bag. The mummy bag hugged the body, curling around the head as protection against the elements. Because of its compactness, the bag was also lighter and easier to carry in her pack. Rick's was identical, although longer.

She could see him below, a shadow at the base of the hill.

Let him sleep down there. In the morning, after a cold night alone with his denial, he might feel more inclined to share his experience and accept the truth. She wouldn't wait up for his epiphany.

The rip-stop nylon of the sleeping bag shooshed as she crawled inside it. Cushioned inside the bag, she drifted into sleep.

When she awoke awhile later, the moon peeped through the trees at her. The air was still. The owl she had heard earlier must've fallen asleep too. She closed her eyes. The sleeping bag felt warm, soft.

Katy bolted upright, eyes wide. The moon set an hour after the sun.

That light was not the moon.

She heard no thwopping of helicopter rotors. No sound whatsoever.

The light hovered behind the trees that lined the hillside. Fumbling out of the sleeping bag, she ran up the hill. At the summit, she halted.

The light floated above the lower trees surrounding the hill. Round and bright as a full moon, the light cast a false daylight on the woods. A hush had come over the wilderness, a hush so profound she wondered if she had died in her sleep and the light was guiding her into heaven.

A shiver shook her body. She turned around to wake Rick. Someone else must see the light. Someone else must verify that she had not lost her mind or died.

Static electricity surged over her. She whirled around.

The light was gone.

K ATY AWOKE MUMMIFIED IN HER SLEEPING BAG BESIDE RICK, WHO SLEPT
half out of his bag a few inches away. For a second, she couldn't remember
how she got there.

The light hovering. The hair on her head prickled by static electricity. The
light gone.

After the sighting, she had stumbled down the hillside, grabbing her sleeping
bag as she sprinted past it, and curled up beside Rick. She felt safe there next to
him. When she first saw the light she thought of waking him so someone else
could witness the event. After the light disappeared, she decided a midnight round
of skepticism and argument sounded less appealing than keeping the secret of
what she had seen. The memory lingered as a pit of ice in her gut.

She crawled out of her sleeping bag. Rick stayed asleep, his body slack, his lips
curved in a slight smile. Wonder what he was dreaming about. Had to be better
than her dreams. Strange lights burning her body into cinders. Hairy beasts
using her as a basketball. Amazing she got any rest at all. The fuzz on her brain
would clear after breakfast.

Despite the crazies chasing them, despite the mysteries that popped up at
every bend in the landscape, she felt at home in the woods. A lifetime of moving
here and there had ended when she drove through Anameka eight years ago, saw
the lake with its crystalline blue waters, smelled the trees and the rain-soaked

earth, felt the roots sprouting from her feet, planting themselves in the ground here. She belonged.

It was more than the town and the people, both of which she loved in spite of the townsfolk's assumptions about her lifestyle. The woods seduced her. The first time she walked under the pines and white birches and maples, she knew she never wanted to leave. Maybe her love of the woods explained her commitment to uncovering the truth about hairy hominids.

The creatures *were* the woods. They seemed connected with it in a manner she couldn't comprehend. Maybe she envied them a little.

Maybe she felt really stupid for thinking such a thing.

She prodded Rick. When he opened his eyes, she said, "Better get breakfast and get moving."

Sunrise snaked across the sky like rainbow-colored serpents as the daystar nudged its head above the horizon.

Katy strode down the hill, carrying the canteens by their straps, to where Rick stood at the base. Rick had already dragged their backpacks down the hill. During breakfast, she had checked the GPS and discovered they'd penetrated ten miles into the triangle of sightings. Their investigation of and searches for sign, stops for misleading Warner, and timeout for catching dinner slowed their progress. Looking at the map she compiled from the sightings data, she estimated another few miles would take them as far as they need go. Three days had passed since Charlie's attack. The longer the search took, the lower the chances of finding him plummeted.

The attack had looked vicious. Could anyone have survived it?

She handed Rick his canteen. "We need to fill them. The stream is the natural choice. Where was Warner camped?"

"This side of the stream."

"We'll make a wide arc around them. Gotta be vigilant, though, they might be going for water too."

"Yes, ma'am." He saluted and took the canteen. "Any other orders, captain?"

"I prefer general."

"Aye-aye, General Katy."

She smiled. "Better be careful with your sarcasm. I am a soldier's daughter, you know. We learn how to kick butt early."

"Good to know." He turned. "Follow me, general."

Katy stayed behind him as he guided her toward the stream. She had kept the incident with the light to herself and he had kept whatever he saw last night to himself. They should've talked, but she sensed time dripping out of her cupped hands. When her hands were empty, Charlie was dead.

Rick thought his father was already dead. He was wrong, he must be. If someone she loved died, she would feel the black hole wrenching the light from her soul. She would know.

They passed under a maple tree. Its leaves, having turned a bright red, spattered on the ground like blood.

Rick marched onward, oblivious of the imagery. She had death on her mind now, there was no escaping the pictures that flashed in her mind's eye.

Jim floating face-down in Lake Anameka.

The blood-red leaves splattering the ground.

A creature hurling Charlie.

Bloody leaves.

A branch smacked her in the face. She ducked under it and kept going. Her cheek stung where the branch nailed her. Rubbing the spot, walking right behind Rick, she studied his footprints. Though the marks on the soles of his boots matched Charlie's, he left different tracks. Larger, yes, but also more precise. Charlie staggered a little as he walked because his left leg was shorter than his right, so his track often S-curved like a snake's. Rick's track moved on a straight line of travel. When he turned, his track angled sharply into the turn. When he stopped, he halted both feet, no meandering or foot tapping while he decided which route he should take.

Like most people's footprints, his prints angled out from the line of travel. Hardly anyone walked with their toes pointing straight ahead.

Next she observed how he moved. He held his head high, his shoulders back, spine straight. Charlie slouched and hung his head forward.

Rick dropped into a crouch. She hunkered down as well, crab-walking up behind him.

He whispered, "Heard something."

She listened. Ahead, water gurgled. The stream. She couldn't see the stream through the trees, yet it must lay nearby. The gurgling sounded close.

A ticking issued from near the stream.

She touched Rick's shoulder. When he looked at her, she mouthed, "Stay low."

Rising into a half crouch, he tiptoed ahead. She proceeded behind him. A minute later they reached the border of the stream where the woods ended along the narrow, sandy shore. The ticking was louder. Rick stopped at the edge of the tree line. She came up alongside him. The ticking originated from the right, further downstream.

A tall oak, its branches expanding over the stream, shaded a portion of the shoreline. The shadow could've covered a porcupine or a man. So long as the perpetrator held still, he was hidden.

The ticking stopped.

Katy squinted at the shadows. A tiny form hopped out of the darkness into the golden light produced by the sunrise. The green frog bounded past them. Its yellow throat, visible from a dozen feet away, sexed it as a male. The frog hopped upstream out of sight. The frog could've made the ticking sound. Somehow.

No, the source stayed in hiding.

The ticking began anew. Faster now. The ticking faltered. A scrape ensued. "Ahhh!"

A man stomped out of the shadows, kicking at the sand, grasping a rock in one fist and a small knife in the other. Ivan repeated his curse.

Wood debris, fallen or blown off the trees, lay scattered along the shore. He kicked some of it into a pile. He kneeled beside the pile and, stacking several twigs atop it, held the rock over the debris. As he struck the knife on the rock, he flattened his lips against his teeth.

"Gah!"

He pitched the rock into the stream. It splashed and sank.

Katy stifled a chuckle. The idiot was trying to start a fire with a lump of conglomerate. He couldn't tell the difference between flint and other rocks but, like most people, he'd heard flint would spark when struck.

Ivan stalked into the shadows. He emerged with a plastic water bottle, the kind with a filtration system built into the top. He kneeled at the stream. As he dipped the bottle into the stream, water seeped through the filtration system. Katy had tested one of those bottles a few months back because she wondered if they really worked. While the bottle did work, it was so bulky she opted against using it. The iodine tablets she used took half an hour, but they weighed little and took up even less space. With space in her pack limited, she needed compact equipment.

While Ivan waited for the water to filter, he sat down and lit a cigarette.

Katy and Rick huddled behind a pine.

A breeze whispered in the trees. A few hairs that escaped her elastic band tickled Katy's face. She dared not move to resituate them.

Ivan suckled his cigarette. He closed his eyes.

The stench of his smoke wafted over her. She breathed through her mouth.

Across the stream, the treetops deeper into the woods waggled. The movement traveled from tree to tree, nearing the stream. Two trees at the edge of the shore shimmied.

A figure traipsed out of the woods.

The hairy hominid strolled along the shore as a tourist might. Though the auburn-haired creature glanced at Ivan, her pace did not change. Her breasts dangled as pendulums while her arms swung in rhythm with her footsteps. She looked a bit over six feet. Because she hunched her torso forward as she walked, her standing height could've topped seven feet. The creature had no discernible neck, broad shoulders, and distinct buttocks. Hair covered her entire body save for areas under her eyes, over her nose, and around her lips. Her mouth was wide, the lips flat. The nose was flat and wide as well. The crown of her head tapered into a what looked like a cut-off cone. No, wait. The cone flapped as she walked. A crest of hair standing erect created the illusion of a cone shape.

As she sashayed down the shoreline, the muscles worked beneath the skin, shifting and tightening as needed. If Katy had harbored any doubts about the creature so far, seeing the movement of the muscles would've erased them. No one, not even an Oscar-winning Hollywood effects artist, could manufacture a suit or a robot whose skin and sinew moved over the musculature so naturally.

Katy's throat went dry.

The humanness of the creature's face stunned her. If the creature shaved her face and body and wore a hat to disguise her brow ridge, she could blend into any street in America. She would never win the Miss America Pageant, but she wouldn't frighten children either. Witnesses often spoke of how human the creatures' faces appeared, yet their descriptions failed at conveying the image. Katy needed to see one to understand, a fact she had missed until now. In essence, you had to see one to understand that you had to see one to understand.

The creature walked no more than thirty feet from where Rick and Katy hid. As the creature raised her hand and swatted a fly, Katy saw the palm was hairless. The soles of her feet should've been hairless too, according to the sightings.

Katy couldn't take her gaze off the creature. She was beautiful.

Ivan yelped.

The creature halted. She turned her head and torso to study Ivan. She grunted.

Ivan dropped his cigarette.

Katy looked back at the creature.

The female furrowed her brow, crinkling her nose.

"Hey girl," Ivan called, his voice trembling, "whatcha doing over there? Want a cigarette?"

Ivan plucked his cigarette from the ground. He waved it at the creature.

"See it, girl?" he said. "Polly want a cigarette?"

The creature bared her teeth, growled.

"Dumb ape."

Ivan threw the cigarette at the creature. It landed, smoldering, near her feet.

She bent down to pat the cigarette. As her finger touched the burning end, she yanked it away and leaped upright. She concentrated on Ivan.

Grunting, Ivan scratched his underarms in a schoolboy imitation of a monkey.

The creature bounded across the stream.

Ivan shouted.

The creature grabbed at him. He rolled away. She swooped toward him, her features contorted, low grunts issuing from her throat. He bolted into the trees.

She thundered after him.

Ivan's voice shrieked through the wilderness. "Warner! Help me!"

Rick moved forward in the direction Ivan and the creature had gone. Katy seized his arm.

"No," she said. "Get the water first."

"But—"

"No."

When he looked at her, his expression dismayed her. His face was pale, eyes wide, forehead and mouth marked by lines. He had seen the creature he refused to believe existed, the animal he considered a figment of imagination, a communal hallucination spread through the air or the water like a disease. His denial had been ripped from him. She could practically see him bleeding.

"Oh honey." She took his face in her hands. "It's not the end of the world. Your world has changed, that's all, and the worst thing you can do is keep denying it. Accept the truth. There are beings and events you cannot explain. What you must do now is accept that and move on."

"I can't—it was—I mean—"

"I know." She brushed away the hairs that had fallen over his forehead. "The unknown is frightening. Believe it or not, I had never seen a hairy hominid until yesterday."

"What?" The pallor vacated his face. "I thought you saw them all the time."

"No, honey, I look for them. Never said I saw one. Unlike you, I can believe in something I have no firsthand knowledge of."

She lowered her hands.

He tilted his head down, gazing up at her. "But you knew I thought you'd seen them. You let me believe it."

"You believe whatever you want. Don't need my help lying to yourself."

He surveyed the area where the creature had first appeared. "Doesn't really matter I guess."

She headed for the water. Survival above all else, she must adopt that as her motto on this expedition. Living by it meant quelling the urge to pursue the creature that took off after Ivan. She had another reason for staying put. Ivan had screamed for Warner. She wasn't ready for a confrontation with him.

The way the creature went after Ivan...

She could hear the fading cacophony as the creature charged after Ivan.

If he lived, he'd have a heck of a story.

WARNER! SHOOT IT! *SHOOT IT!*"

Ivan's cries resounded in the distance. He couldn't be far from the camp.

Warner, snuffing out the coals of the fire by kicking dirt on them, paused to listen. Footfalls crashed. Ivan wailed above a background of grunts.

Diane, still dozing inside her sleeping bag, roused. "What's that?"

"Sh."

The treetops wobbled.

Curse the fool, he warned Ivan about flag waving. If you leaned on a tree as support or bashed into one as you moved, the trunk telegraphed the motion into the treetop like the waving of a flag. Everyone could pinpoint your location.

Ivan burst through the vegetation into the camp. His eyes bulged. His hair was mussed, his face pale and sweaty. He dropped onto his knees at Warner's feet.

The treetops flapped. Leaves rained down from the branches.

A screech deafened Warner. He glared at Ivan.

"It's her," Ivan said, jabbing his finger at the woods in the direction from which he had come. "She is going to kill me, Warner, you have to shoot her!"

Warner stared at the trees. "Gallagher?"

"No, you Teutonic freak, *her.*"

As Warner opened his mouth to ask who, the creature barreled into the camp.

One of her pendulous breasts whapped him in the face as she shoved him aside and clenched Ivan's arms. Diane shrieked. Stunned, Warner thrust a hand against a tree to halt his tumble. The creature hoisted Ivan over her head.

Ivan screamed.

Warner snatched the Glock from its holster.

The creature held Ivan suspended above her head, shaking him. His arms and legs flailed. He screamed again, louder, shriller.

Warner aimed at the creature's head.

She twisted sideways as he fired. The bullet hit her shoulder. She dumped Ivan onto the ground. In slow motion, she turned on Warner.

Diane collapsed.

Warner fired. The creature's torso jerked. She whirled and fled.

He kept pulling the trigger until the clip emptied. The treetops shimmied. As the creature fled, the crashes of her footfalls and the waving of the trees subsided.

Lying on his side, clutching his arm, Ivan whimpered.

Warner exchanged the empty clip for the spare he kept in his pocket. When he approached Ivan, he pointed the Glock at the man's head.

"Your screams have alerted Gallagher to our presence and our location." He chambered a round. "Give me one reason why I should not kill you now."

"That monster was chasing me." Ivan's voice grew shrill. "So excuse me if I screamed a little."

"What did you do?"

"Nothing."

"That *monster* was angry. You provoked her."

"Did not." Ivan scrambled onto his feet. "I want my rifle."

"*Nein!* We can't go back for it."

Warner went to Diane. When he checked her pulse, it throbbed against his fingers. She had simply fainted. He reached for the water bottle clipped onto the side of her backpack. He drizzled cold water on her face. Her eyelids fluttered and opened.

Ivan stomped his foot. "I want my rifle!"

Warner, cradling Diane's head in his hand, glanced over his shoulder at Ivan.

The man's face had reddened. His nostrils flared.

"By all means," Warner said, "go and get your rifle. If you can find your way."

"Bet your concrete britches I will."

Warner said nothing. He squirted some water onto Diane's lips. She licked it away. Her face still looked pale, her lips colorless. He slipped the mouth of the water bottle between her lips. She drank.

Ivan hefted his backpack over his shoulders. As the weight settled onto him, he stumbled backward. He snatched up his Desert Eagle from the spot where he'd left it, on the ground by the pack. The sun glinted off the pistol' s gold finish. He turned toward the path the creature had torn out of the vegetation.

A distant shriek echoed through the woods.

Ivan turned around. "Don't need the rifle when I got my Desert Eagle."

Warner sighed.

K ATY AND RICK HAD NO TROUBLE LOCATING WARNER'S CAMPSITE. THE FEMALE creature left a trail of severed branches, crushed leaves, and scarred trees aside from the inch-deep footprints her feet carved into the earth.

Warner and his companions had departed the campsite. They left no trash, no footprints. They cleansed the area thoroughly of any sign, including the creature's. By now they must've reached the spot where she and Rick had camped, but she and Rick also left no sign. Don't show me yours and I won't show you mine.

Katy crossed the campsite. Despite Warner's efforts, some sign remained. He could not eradicate the damage the creature had inflicted on the vegetation. When she reached the other side of the camp, she found where the creature exited. She also found blood.

It was smeared on a juniper about five feet off the ground. Some blood also drizzled onto the ground.

The blood trail stopped after a dozen feet. There, the hominid's tracks got sloppy. She had tripped—her footprints showed the slide-in of the heel as it contacted the ground and slipped forward before the full weight of the body came down, creating a panhandle effect behind the heel. The track staggered sideways, straightened for a few steps, staggered. The stride length shortened as she stumbled over a dip.

The yards passed and the creature's tracks continued in the same fashion. Trip. Stumble. Stagger. Get it together for awhile, then lose balance again.

Katy wished she could've helped the creature. Ivan tormented the poor thing into a response. Certainly, she reacted with an anger far beyond what Ivan's actions merited. Still, she couldn't help sensing the creature's pain. Would the female survive, or would they discover the body a few hundred yards ahead?

What if the creature made it home? How would her fellow hominids react? If her anger gave any clue, they might charge at anything human. Following the tracks might prove dangerous.

But she must follow. She must know.

The quest for knowledge got Charlie attacked, perhaps killed. If she ended up like him, no one would search for her. If she got Rick killed on her quest, because of her inattention to dangers—

Never mind.

"Is this such a good idea?" Rick asked. "This thing is probably ticked off at humans right now."

"I know."

"I notice you're still moving."

She concentrated on the track.

"Nice to know my opinion counts."

Halting, she angled her body to face him while keeping watch on the track ahead. "I know it's crazy and I have zero evidence to support this, but I have a gut feeling Charlie is wherever the hairy hominids are. This female might lead us there."

"A gut feeling."

"Out here, you have to trust your instincts. They could save your life."

He scrunched his face. "Instincts."

"Why do you repeat everything I say? It's slightly annoying."

"Sorry." He shifted the weight of his pack. "I have to trust your instincts too. I don't know what to think, which means I don't know what to do either."

"Right now we need to find this hominid."

"Whatever you say." As she turned away from him, he muttered, "You'll do it anyway."

Her *instincts* urged her to wallop him with a retort. She bit the inside of her lip and tromped ahead. The sighting earlier, whatever he'd seen last night, and her encounter yesterday had all sensitized his nerves. She understood that. Yet she sensed another emotion underneath the anxiety and fear, one her presence irritated, one he refused to discuss.

Later. They could yell at each other after they found the hairy hominids.

She tracked the female through several hundred yards of woods before the footprints crossed into a small field. The landscape rolled upward into the slope of a steep hill. Trees cloaked the hillside. Grass, dead now, speckled the field. In the middle of the area, the sun burning on its lumpy surface, sat a boulder.

It looked as out of place as a tiger swimming in the Atlantic Ocean.

The footprints drew a line toward the boulder. Katy followed it. The boulder was angular and irregular in shape, its gray surface flecked with blue. Sure, Michigan had rocks, big ones even. A boulder sitting alone in the middle of field, however, was unusual. Considering the hominid tracks leading up to it, the rock seemed downright freaky.

The female's track circled the boulder. After she walked around the rock a few times, she trod eight or ten feet north and stopped. Her prints, like the prints of the creature Katy chased, ended with a side-by-side pair. She stood in that spot. Motionless. Waiting.

For what?

Katy dropped onto hands and knees. Her left ear brushed the dead grass as she studied the prints from the side. The dirt had caved into them a bit. Behind the heel, earth had sprayed backward from the print. The creature's feet sunk deeper at this point than in any of the previous prints. Even when she stumbled, her feet made shallower impressions than here. Looked like she planted her feet firmly before leaping off a cliff. No cliff existed here.

To test her theory, Katy stood. She matched her stance to that of the hominid, feet parallel about shoulder's width apart, planted firmly. Bending her knees, she swung her arms and jumped forward, both feet airborne until they clapped down half a foot from her starting position. When she looked back at the prints she had made, she held back a smile.

They matched the hominid's. Her prints hadn't dug into the earth one-fifth as deep as the hominid's, yet they looked similar enough that she had no doubts.

"Either you've lost your mind," Rick said, "or you found something."

She pointed at the prints.

"Look at the prints I made when I jumped." She waved at the hominid's track. "Now compare them to the creature's prints."

"They look the same."

"Exactly." She kneeled in front of the hominid's prints, her gaze traveling from them back toward the track encircling the boulder. "She walked around that rock, looking or waiting for something, then she walked straight to this spot and jumped."

"Into thin air, I suppose." He bent down beside her. "If we could actually find what she jumped into, that would be too easy. Nothing with you is easy."

"Easy is boring."

"If there's one thing you're not, it's boring."

When she glanced up from the footprints, she caught him looking at her. He turned his head away.

"You know," she said, standing, "we're only a couple miles from where the other creature disappeared. They must have a nest or homestead—whatever you want to call it—nearby."

"Of course we're going to look for that."

"What else have you got to do?"

He traced the horizon with his gaze. "I can't get the picture out of my head. Of that thing throwing Dad around."

She had no response. What could she say that would make him feel better? Nothing. She couldn't vouch for his safety or guarantee Charlie was alive. If he was alive, she couldn't guarantee they'd find him. She could try. That was it.

"Let's go," she said, trudging out of the field. "We shouldn't stay in the open. Warner might think of tracking the creature and come here."

Once they penetrated the woods far enough that they could no longer see the field, she halted. An idea had occurred to her. If the hairy hominids maintained a nest nearby, the odds of seeing them increased dramatically. But if she and Rick wandered through the woods in search of tracks or other sign, they might miss the creatures. Like an asteroid streaking within a million miles of Earth, the creatures could slip past them.

Hairy hominids were a lot harder to see than asteroids.

The one she chased had stood mere feet from her and she had looked right past it until the creature moved. They had an uncanny talent for blending into the shadows. Perhaps their desire for stealth explained their affinity for the forests of the world. Plenty of shadows in which to hide.

Her idea had nothing to do with the creatures' talents for blending into the background. It involved *her* blending into the background. If she and Rick could become a part of the woods, they could wait for a hairy hominid to pass by then tail the creature back to its lair. The creatures seemed aware of their surroundings. If the creature yesterday had been warning her of Warner's approach, they must have keen hearing. Or smell. Either way, hunting them would take patience and vigilance. It was worth a shot.

She told Rick her plan.

He leaned against a tree. "So we sit here and wait for Bigfoot to waltz by us."

"Basically. For efficiency's sake, you should sit under your tree and I should sit under a different tree. The more distance between us, the better shot we have at seeing one of them."

"We are not separating."

"It's the best way."

"Meanwhile, Warner can shoot you in the head and I won't know about it."

"He won't shoot me. He needs to find Charlie first, otherwise he would've shot us before we left my cabin."

He folded his arms over his chest. His expression pinched, he glared at the treetops. "Those GPS radios have buddy tracking, right?"

"Yes."

"The *only* way I agree to this is if we have our GPS radios on so I can see where you are all the time. If you move *one inch*, I'm getting on the radio and you better answer. Otherwise, I'm coming to get you no matter how much noise I make or how many signs I leave."

The intensity of his stare shot a bolt of lightning through her body.

"Agreed," she said.

"Damn right agreed." He dug his GPS radio out his pocket. As he flicked the power switch, he said, "I'm not leaving until I see your little blip on this screen. Or whatever the heck it's supposed to show."

Retrieving her radio from the fanny pack, she switched it on. Satisfied, he cupped his radio in his hand, lowering his arm to his side.

"You take this tree," he said. He strode past her and, as his shoulder grazed hers, he said, "Don't go running after those monsters either."

"Yes, Dad."

He tramped past her. Turning partway, she watched his figure diminish until he became another shadow in the forest. Soon, even his shadow disappeared.

The tree he had leaned against looked as good as any for hiding. After grabbing her binoculars, she hid her pack under a low branch and climbed to a height that should have placed her above the heads of any hairy hominids who happened by the tree. The ground felt far away, although it couldn't have been more than eight feet below her.

She found a sturdy branch. Testing its six-inch width by bouncing it with her foot, she then settled her butt into the crook where the branch segued into the trunk. With her back against the trunk, she stretched her legs out onto the branch.

A sparrow chirped from a higher branch of the fifty-foot oak. Through the binoculars, she looked up at the bird. She glimpsed its wings as it flew away.

She took the GPS radio out her fanny pack. It showed Rick had progressed three hundred yards northeast and was still moving. Good. The farther he went, the better their chances of seeing a hairy hominid. After his demands for her to stay put and refrain from chasing the creatures, she thought he might walk to where she couldn't see him but he could see her and stop there. That was no good.

Thankfully, his faith in her instincts overcame his male nature.

How anyone could witness a hairy hominid, in daylight and in plain view, yet keep denying the creatures existed confounded her. If he needed time to absorb events, she'd give him until lunchtime. Then he was talking, whether he wanted to or not.

The GPS showed him a quarter mile north-northeast of her position. When she watched the screen for several minutes without seeing him move, she tucked the radio in her fanny pack. She leaned her head on the tree. Now came the waiting.

A breeze rattled the trees. Katy yawned. Scanning the woods, she saw nothing.

A big black squirrel skittered up the tree. It stopped inches from her face to eye her. She returned the gaze. The squirrel scampered up into the top of the tree.

The wind sighed. The hairs on her arms stiffened. She picked up the binoculars. Nothing. The sound repeated, and she knew it was not the wind. The sigh rumbled inside a massive chest as the creature expelled it. But she couldn't see the creature.

Squinting, she scrutinized the shadows, the spaces between branches of neighboring trees. Her gaze swept over a misshapen tree.

She looked again. The tree seemed more than misshapen. Its gray surface looked fuzzy. Its trunk widened upward before angling in about seven feet off the ground. A foot higher, two knots glistened as if filled with water. The bark around the knots was darker. Strange.

She swung the binoculars up to her eyes. As she focused on the knot-like blemishes, the creature blinked.

She jerked. The binoculars thwacked into her face. She gasped.

In one fluid motion, the creature stepped away from the tree and hopped over a fallen branch. It rushed toward her like an apparition soaring through the air.

Katy hopped onto her feet. The branch shimmied beneath her. She hugged the trunk, flattening against it.

The creature reached the tree. Silently, it stared up at her. Its eyes glowed with a faint redness.

Her heart beat faster than a hummingbird's.

The creature pounded its hands on the trunk. Its hair, longer than that of the other hominids she had seen, flapped as it thrust its fists into the tree. Wrinkles covered the hairless portions of its face. Its hair was the color of tree bark, flecked with white.

The creature leaned backward, inspecting the tree.

Katy glanced left and right. None of the nearest branches looked capable of holding her. Maybe the creature would get bored and give up. Maybe he just wanted to make friends.

The creature barked. Shoving his stubby fingers into knotholes, he pulled his body up the trunk. His first effort surged him four feet off the ground. He looked directly at her and growled. His lips peeled away from his teeth.

No friend-making today.

She lunged at the nearest branch. As her right foot contacted the wood, the branch cracked but held. She swung her left foot across to the limb. The branch split in two.

Her shoulder hit the ground first. Pains ricocheted through her torso.

The creature sprang off the trunk. He landed with his feet straddling her hips.

She slithered between his legs and bolted.

His footfalls thrashed behind her.

10

LEAVES CRACKLED, BOOTS POUNDED, BREATHS GASPED AS SHE TORE THROUGH the woods. A glance backward and she saw the creature a car's length behind her. Not a big luxury car's length either. Nothing larger than a VW Bug could have snuggled between them.

Her chest ached. Her legs burned. Blood trickled down her cheek from where a branch had snagged her. She pushed harder.

The creature kept coming.

The Taurus. She had a gun in her fanny pack, for God's sake, so why was she running? If the beast wanted a piece of her, it could have the lead from her .357.

Dropping onto her stomach, she rolled sideways out of the creature's path. On her side, flat on the ground, she unzipped her fanny pack and yanked the Taurus out of its holster.

The creature skidded, halting a few feet from her.

She aimed the gun at him.

He grunted. He resembled a gray variant of Yoda, the character from the *Star Wars* movies, if Yoda had stood eight feet tall and sneered. The creature could've had pointy ears. Under all that hair, who could tell?

Since he lacked a name tag, and a formal introduction seemed unlikely, she decided to call him Yoda. Better than "the nasty tangle of hair with eyes and a serious case of body odor."

Yoda, eyeing her, clenched and unclenched his fists as if contemplating squashing her skull between them. The glow in his eyes flared into twin stars. The eyes of the creature who chased Ivan had not glowed. The eye glow could be a male trait, though what purpose it served eluded her. She could mull it over after she got rid of Yoda.

Despite his hostility, she couldn't shoot him. His face looked so human behind the hair. And he had stopped attacking. He wielded no weapon. She couldn't shoot a human in those circumstances.

She lifted her finger off the trigger but kept the Taurus trained on him.

A breeze gusted, rustling the treetops. His odor surrounded her. Rotten eggs and decayed flesh.

Yoda stiffened. His nostrils wiggled as he caught a scent. He canted his head. Two hairy hominids, one black and one cinnamon-colored, both male, tramped out of the shadows behind Yoda. He whirled a half turn toward them.

The black creature gazed at Katy with…recognition? He could've been the one she pursued yesterday. The glimpses she'd gotten of him gave her little to use for identification. He had the yellow eyes of a cat. Garfield, she'd call him, after the cartoon cat.

The cinnamon one, taller and thinner than Garfield, nevertheless sported a more pronounced brow ridge, or maybe the hair thinned over his brow making the bone appear thicker. He looked like the classic depiction of a Neanderthal, save for the elongated cranium. Call him Neander.

She was naming them now. Rick would love that.

Well, she had to call them something.

Garfield grunted. "Ook."

Yoda jabbed a finger at Katy. "Oogah."

Though they exchanged grunts and mumbles, the utterances sounded eerily like a language. A few sightings mentioned sounds resembling speech, though witnesses couldn't understand the meaning. Those sightings comprised a small percentage of the total literature. The creatures might speak only to each other, or most humans might've misinterpreted their language as nonsense. After all, the Romans labeled the Celtic tribes barbarians because the Celtic languages sounded like the baaing of sheep to them.

Garfield stomped toward Yoda. "Oogah-oogah."

Yoda honked at him, waving both arms and bearing his teeth.

Neander sidled into the shade of a tree. He hunkered down as if trying to merge with the shadows. Yoda and Garfield glowered at each other. Their eyes burned red. Yoda, wrinkles deepening as he scrunched his face, glanced at Katy. His eyes were red dwarfs twinkling in the void of space.

Inside the fanny pack, her GPS radio crackled.

The creatures jerked in unison. Six eyeballs focused on her.

The radio crackled again. "Katy, what's going on?"

Rick. He said if she moved one inch he'd get on the radio. He'd come after her no matter how much noise he made. The creatures didn't seem fond of noise.

"Katy. Answer me!"

Yoda shrieked.

She winced. The scream sliced through her eardrums.

Garfield bellowed. Yoda scooted away through the trees. He made no sound, left no sign besides his footprints. Katy lay still, the Taurus clutched in her hand, ears ringing.

Footfalls clomped up the path she and Yoda had ripped out of the woods.

Garfield jogged past her. Neander followed, and they morphed into the woods. Katy stared after them.

The footfalls crunched closer. Seconds later, Rick burst out of the path in front of her.

Halting, he frowned at her. "What are you doing?"

"Sunbathing." She pushed up into a sitting position. "What do you think? A hairy hominid came after me so I ran. Should I have let him disembowel me instead?"

The angry lines on his face smoothed. Kneeling, he touched her cheek. His finger came away bloody.

His voice softened. "You're hurt."

"A scratch, nothing serious. But I think Yoda had bigger plans for me, possibly involving fire and skewers. If Garfield hadn't stepped in, I'd be shish ke-Katy."

"Garfield?" Rick flopped onto his butt. "Yoda? Did you hit your head on the way out of that tree?"

"How did you get here so fast?"

"I started running the second I saw you'd moved. Got on the radio en route. Figured you wouldn't answer and, what do you know, I was right."

"I was occupied."

"Who are Garfield and Yoda?"

She slid the Taurus into its holster. Head down, she pretended to concentrate on zipping the fanny pack shut. "Hairy hominids."

"You named them." He tightened his lips, the corners curving up a bit. "Sounds like something Dad would do."

He was right. Charlie would name the creatures. He named the nine deer in the herd that frequented his backyard. While she hadn't named the deer on her property, she did christen the squirrel living in the pine tree behind her cabin Sammy. Rick wouldn't understand. She couldn't imagine him naming wild animals.

"Guess you have to call them something," he said.

That he said exactly what she had thought moments earlier blocked her throat like a rock lodged inside it. She thought he was so different from her that they operated on separate levels of reality. Sometimes when she spoke he stared at her as if she jabbered in Linear A, the language of ancient Knossos which no one could decipher. Sharing one thought did not make them twins. Didn't even make them compatible.

Compatible? What did that matter? They could die in these woods, killed by hairy hands or Warner's gun. *Focus, Katy.*

The scritch of a zipper interrupted her musing. Rick was digging through the contents of his pack.

"Looking for something?" she asked.

"First aid kit."

"Left side pocket." While he pulled the kit out, stuffing the junk back in his pack, she said, "Cut yourself?"

He turned to her. Flipping the kit box open, he grabbed a piece of cotton gauze.

When he reached for her cheek, she ducked sideways. "I don't need that. It's a cut, not a mortal wound."

He met her gaze, hand suspended near her cheek, jaw tight. She rolled her eyes and shifted so he could reach her cheek better. Relaxing, he daubed the cut with the gauze to wipe off the blood.

As he concentrated on rendering first aid, he asked her, "What do you think those things are?"

"Pieces of the branch that scratched me. Or else I'm infected with alien spore."

"No." He dabbed antibiotic ointment onto the cut. "Those hairy monsters."

He ripped open a Band-Aid packet. She waved it away. He shot a glance at her meant to irritate her into acquiescing. She ignored it.

"There's a lot of debate about what they are," she said. "Of course, there's even more debate about whether they really exist, although a handful of scientists have accepted their existence. Some people say the creatures are *Gigantopithecus*. There are several problems with that theory. First, everything we know about *Gigantopithecus* is based on teeth and a jawbone. Second, if *Gigantopithecus* existed it was a huge ape. Not all hairy hominids are eight feet tall."

"I thought they were."

"That's what the media wants you to think. If they can convince everybody Bigfoot is a huge apelike creature that exists only in North America and is probably a bear or a prankster in a suit anyway, then no reputable scientist will look into it."

"They've got the Yeti in the Himalayas," Rick said, reclining on his side with his head propped up on one arm. "I've never heard about Bigfoot anywhere else."

She couldn't stop the smile from inching across her face. Chomping the myths Hollywood and the scientific establishment had created into bits the mind could digest and excrete as the crap they were gave her an all-over glow. Kind of like the feeling she got on a hunt last year when she and Charlie ran into a redneck bent on killing a deer for the sport of it. The creep had hunkered in his deer blind with a beer clutched between his fingers waiting for the Bambis, which he had been feeding corn all summer, to poke their heads into view. She asked him how tricking the deer into sitting on his lap made him feel manly. Glancing at the Taurus strapped on her hip, he made a crack about "little ladies who play with guns cuz they ain't getting any."

She had shot the beer bottle out of his hand. The shards lacerated his alcohol-bloated fingers. One fragment lodged in his cheek. She had patched up his wounds, despite his threats to call the cops. He never did call them.

Go figure.

Rick poked her knee. "Gonna laugh at me or explain it to me?"

Her smile broadened into a grin. "Hairy hominids live all over the globe, sweetie, all over it. From Nepal to Canada, Russia to Africa, and even down into Australia. From South America to Asia. Everywhere. Even the desert."

He arched an eyebrow. Disbelief. They always doubted her assertion until she blasted them with the facts. Some clung to their disbelief afterward, but many succumbed to her arguments. She felt a little like Darth Vader seducing a Jedi to the dark side. Except her side represented the light of truth.

Jeez, that sounded corny and self-important.

She inhaled and dived into the water. "Hairy hominid or wild man sightings date back at least as far the Etruscans, whose art contains depictions of hairy humanoids. But the sightings could go back as far as humanity itself. Could be as long we've been around, they've been around. In the Middle Ages, people of Europe called them *wodewose* and reenacted captures of them during festivals.

"In Guatemala the *sisimite* are giants, while pygmy-size wild men are called *dwendi* in Honduras and *shiru* in the mountains of Ecuador. The Himalayan yeti sounds something like our Bigfoot, but the *almas* of Mongolia are shorter and more humanlike. In China the wild men have various names, including *yeren*. In fact the Chinese have investigated their wild men extensively. The Beijing Museum of Natural History even got into the act.

She took a breath and let it out slowly. "Sumatra has the *orang pendek*, which has apelike feet but walks upright, and Africa boasts numerous varieties from the little *agogwe* to the giant *muhalu*. Australians call their version the yowie. Even here in America we have dozens of names for the creatures—Bigfoot, Momo, Skookum, Skunk Ape, Sister Lakes Monster. Truth is, humans have as many names for hairy hominids as we do cultures. The old sightings get brushed off as folklore because we're arrogant enough now to believe we're smarter than the people who lived a hundred or a thousand years ago."

She paused, planting a palm on each knee and rolling her shoulders back. The crick in her neck ironed out a bit.

Rick's face had slackened. His eyes had glazed over too and, although his gaze stayed trained on her, he looked past her rather than at her, as if trying to see through a dense fog. She had pummeled him with facts. Regaining his composure might take a minute.

She developed her tactic of shattering the wall of myth from a person's mind after countless attempts at reasoning with people. Most humans had a powerful ability to block facts that disturbed them from entering their psyches. They ignored the truth, laughed at it, concocted far-fetched explanations meant to discredit it, and—at the extreme—destroyed those who defended it. In the arena of cryptozoology, especially as it pertained to hairy hominids, careers were ruined, reputations shredded.

Did Jim die for that reason?

She had discovered one tactic worked for convincing people. She must treat the truth as a battlefield and attack. Her weapons of choice were facts. The tactic garnered her some enemies. It also cemented friendships. Jim started out believing hairy hominids were apes, until she barraged him with her missiles. The wall erected by society and science vaporized. He listened to her arguments and, even when he disagreed, he acknowledged she made a good point. Her method didn't include brainwashing. She penetrated the wall, inserted the facts, and backed off. Everybody needed to make the decision alone.

Now she awaited Rick's judgment. Wacko theory or rational argument?

The life came back to his face. He nodded slowly, humor sparkling in his eyes.

"Okay," he said. "You got me."

She exhaled, suddenly aware she had been holding her breath.

"I get it, they come in every shape and size in every country." The smile he suppressed drew lines around his eyes. "And they're not giganto-whatevers. So what are they, professor?"

"I didn't say they're not *Gigantopithecus*, I said there are problems with that theory. Most of the researchers who subscribe to the Giganto theory also believe the hairy hominids of Northwest America either exist nowhere else or are a separate species from the others."

"You don't think they're a different species."

"They are taller and have thicker coats of hair than some varieties, like the agogwe and the almas. But humans can be tall or short, more or less hairy, muscular or skinny. We don't say Michael Jordan is of a different species than Danny DeVito."

She scooted backward to lean against a tree. "They could be Neanderthals or *Homo erectus*. They could even be *Homo habilis* or *Australopithecus*. The problem is, nobody can agree on what those hominids looked like or in what order they arose. If hairy hominids turn out to be an already-known member of the hominid family then evolution goes out the window. How could *Homo erectus* have evolved into *Homo sapiens* if *erectus* still exists?

"The Neanderthal theory wouldn't be so devastating to evolution. Scientists can't agree on whether Neanderthal man was an ancestor of modern humans or not. DNA evidence has suggested they're a distant cousin at best. So saying hairy hominids are Neanderthals would be okay because that could still make them a separate branch of the hominid tree, *Homo neanderthalensis*. Most scientists would rather make them apes. It keeps them at arm's length from us."

A fluttering erupted nearby. Rick jerked the .45 out of its holster on his hip.

Katy laid a hand on the gun. "It was a leaf falling. Happens a lot out here."

He set the .45 on the ground. His hand rested on its grip.

The hairs on her neck bristled as a shiver winnowed down her spine. She felt a gaze on her. Rick was squinting at the trees. The shiver strengthened, like worms of ice burrowing through her body.

"What is it?" Rick asked.

"We're being followed."

"Yeah, by Warner. That didn't give you the creeps until now?"

"Not him." She looked into the leafage and glimpsed a shape that could've been a head, but it melded with the shadows before she could identify it. "Them."

She rubbed her arms. The chill remained. She knew his next question before his mouth opened.

"They're keeping tabs on us," she said. "The hairy hominids."

Katy crunched a strip of beef jerky. The chewing provided an outlet for the nervous energy that buzzed through her body. Rick chewed his jerky while watching the woods. His nose crinkled and his lips crimped after each bite.

Finishing off a strip, he said, "I don't see why it would throw evolution out the window if these creatures turned out to be *Homo erectus*. Some of them could've evolved into us while the rest didn't."

"Sure, but we live in the same environments as the creatures. Why would *Homo erectus* split into two separate species in the same environment? Evolution supposedly arises as an adaptation to the surroundings, so if we shared the same surroundings we should be hairy like them."

Her butt ached. She shifted to relieve the pressure. "Current evolutionary theories say three forms of humans existed simultaneously. *Homo erectus*, *Homo neanderthalensis*, and *Homo sapiens*. According to the theory, we gradually replaced all the older forms of hominid."

"What is a hominid anyway?"

"Any member of the human family, from the most ancient types, such as *Ardipithecus*, to modern people. A hominoid, on the other hand, is any member of the primate family including us and the apes. The definition presumes humans evolved from the ancient hominids."

Rick, grabbing his canteen, gulped down some water. "Tastes like pool water."

The sanitizing tablets she used on the stream water worked in two steps. First iodine tablets cleansed the water, leaving it yellow and sour. Step two comprised neutralizing tablets to eliminate the iodine color and taste, replacing it with a mild chlorine smell. It tasted fine to her. Of course, she'd drunk it on dozens of hunts.

Swallowing another mouthful, he said, "If these things are an older form of human, evolution needs a little tweaking. But it doesn't throw it out altogether. What about the DNA evidence? I heard they could trace humans back through their DNA."

"Despite what the proponents of that theory claim, there is nothing close to unanimous agreement on the validity of those tests."

Biologists used mitochondrial DNA, or mtDNA, as a kind of time machine to trace human origins backward through genetic markers. Everyone inherited mtDNA from his or her mother. Since men contributed no mtDNA to their offspring, this method could track only the maternal lineage.

But like a computer file copied onto a floppy disk a hundred times, with each iteration overwriting the older copy, mtDNA could become corrupted over time. Biologists called these corruptions mutations. The mutations, passed from mother to daughter to granddaughter and so on, formed the basis for the modern theory of human evolution. We know we evolved from the ancient hominids, scientists said, because we can trace our mtDNA back in time for 200,000 years. Since modern humans had recently evolved at that point, according to the dogma, we must be tracking our lineage back to the African hominids. Also, since people of African descent had a higher rate of mutations and therefore a higher genetic diversity we must have all come from Africa, because higher genetic diversity must equal an older population. The older population must've evolved from the ancient hominids and later given birth to the rest of us.

Biologists ignored one pertinent fact about genetic diversity. A population bottleneck could squeeze the diversity right out of human genes.

As recently as the Middle Ages, the bubonic plague killed at least a third of the European population. An ancient bottleneck occurred between 27,000 and 53,000 years ago. Though the bottleneck could've reduced the population in northern Europe to as few as fifty individuals, most geneticists estimated the numbers crash to more like 15,000 individuals. Either way, the bottleneck must have caused a matching contraction in the genes of northern Europeans. No one could say whether current genetic differences stemmed from a recent African origin of humanity or the bottlenecks that afflicted European populations.

Then you had to consider that scientists based their studies of mtDNA on the rate of mutation. For their studies, they assumed mutations occurred regularly and that nothing aside from time mutated the mtDNA. Yet they admitted to discovering mutations that occurred for other reasons, irrespective of time.

Even the fossils failed to support the Out of Africa theory. Including Mungo Man in the family tree introduced a serious dilemma for the anthropologists. Mungo Man was the nickname for the skeleton of an ancient human unearthed in New South Wales, Australia, back in 1974. The skeleton—dated at 60,000 years old—appeared modern, no argument there. The Australian scientists, however, claimed to have sequenced the mtDNA of Mungo Man and discovered it contained genes both older than and different from the African *sapiens*. If true, their claim disproved Out of Africa. If 60,000-year-old Mungo Man's genes dated back earlier than the African migration, and were distinct from that genetic lineage, then all humans did not come from Africa.

Against the evidence, scientists talked as if they had proved beyond any doubt humans originated in Africa between 100,000 and 200,000 years ago. The opposing theory, multiregionalism, purported *sapiens* evolved separately but concurrently around the world, arising from local populations of *erectus*. Katy saw problems with this notion too.

If humans had evolved separately in each area, why were we not separate species? Why did we share so much DNA in common?

Greater genetic distance existed between two mountain gorillas living in a tightly-knit locale than between an Inuit and an Australian aborigine.

All the evidence, and the quandaries inherent in it, gave Katy a headache.

After she explained all this to Rick, he said nothing for several minutes. Eventually he squirmed in place, his facial muscles taut.

"Maybe we don't understand how evolution works," he said, "but that doesn't mean the theory is wrong. And these hairy things existing still doesn't make evolution wrong."

He had a point. And she had more facts.

"Yes," she said, "if the existence of hairy hominids were the sole evidence against evolution."

"What else is there?"

"Plenty." She took a swig of her own water. "Evolution is an unproven idea. Darwin has become God to the anthropologists, so they defend his theory like the Ark of the Covenant. Alfred Wallace, the man who shared the credit with Darwin for discovering evolution by natural selection, later realized there was too much evidence of man's antiquity for us to ignore it. Darwin considered him a heretic for even thinking such a thing."

"He went senile. That's hardly evidence."

A retort popped into her mind. She clamped her jaw shut and waited for the urge to subside. She said, "Scientists distort the facts to support evolution. Consider the case of *Sinanthropus*."

Starting in the 1920s, a team of paleoanthropologists excavating in a cave near Zhoukoudian in China uncovered the fossilized remains of hominids. The first find consisted solely of three teeth. Based on that evidence alone, team leader Davidson Black declared a new species dubbed *Sinanthropus*, or Beijing Man. But science didn't leap for joy at the discovery. Basing a new species on such scant evidence seemed hasty. So Black found more.

The next year Black's team uncovered half a jawbone with three molars intact. The discovery of a nearly complete, fragmented skull followed. Black immediately embarked on a publicity tour to convince the establishment his finds confirmed evolutionary theory. Soon everyone hopped aboard the Beijing Man train.

Black could've faked what evidence he had found, but Katy doubted it. He did exploit his meager finds for the publicity. The bones, fragments really, he'd uncovered could've come from several individuals of different species. No one could prove they belonged to one individual.

Beijing Man, an archaic hominid, became celebrated as the missing link in evolution. Anthropologists deemed him incapable of hunting or tool-making. However, finds of stone tools and ash from fires in Zhoukoudian Cave hinted at the presence of modern humans, *sapiens* or Neanderthals. Since the remains at the cave were dated at between 460,000 and 230,000 years ago, and scientists assumed *sapiens* departed Africa no more than 120,000 years ago, the cave could not have housed *sapiens* concurrently with Beijing Man.

The finds of fire and tools soon became irrelevant. Once the paleoanthropologists realized the implications of tools and fire, they revised their opinions about *Sinanthropus*. No more did they depict him as an apelike cretin. Now he had been transformed into a cunning hunter who built fires in his cave and chipped stones into tools. Despite his apelike bones, *Sinanthropus* became a human.

Meanwhile the bones of the original Beijing Man, placed on a train in 1941 on the first leg of their journey to America, vanished en route.

Sinanthropus himself didn't disappear, although his fossils did. In the decades after Black's discovery, Chinese scientists claimed additional skulls found at Zhoukoudian exhibited an evolution in cranial capacity, a measure of brain size. Archaic humans, including *erectus*, sported smaller brains than *sapiens*. Only the Neanderthals, our extinct cousins, boasted brains larger than ours.

While the Chinese scientists claimed the skulls increased in cranial capacity from the oldest to the youngest, they ignored the fact that the oldest skull—dated at 460,000 years—was a child and that another skull found amongst the oldest layers had the largest cranial capacity. Only by ignoring some evidence could they create an evolutionary progression.

Even the dating of the Beijing Man finds was fudged in the name of evolution. Paleoanthropologists often relied on dating by morphology to settle incongruities in the physical evidence. Morphology, or the form and structure of a specimen, required every modern human skull be dated to the Late Pleistocene because *sapiens* could not have existed until that period. What if the faunal evidence, consisting of fossilized animal bones found alongside the skull in the same layer, suggested the skull must date to an earlier period? No problem. The skull would be dated by morphology to nudge it into a later period.

At Tongzi in South China, faunal evidence suggested an earlier date for the *sapiens* bones found there. Remains of giant tapirs, hyena, and an extinct species of elephant indicated the finds were older than the accepted Late Pleistocene date, possibly the Middle Pleistocene. Since the Pleistocene period extended from 2 million years ago until 10,000 years ago, a Late Pleistocene date fit into the evolutionary framework. A Middle Pleistocene date would shake its foundation. So the scientists nudged the date forward.

When in doubt, morphology won out.

Katy explained the Beijing Man story to Rick. When she finished, he lay silent again for several minutes.

"I'm confused," he said. "How did the animal fossils date the site earlier?"

Picking up a twig, she scrawled in the dirt EP, MP, and LP. She etched vertical lines between them creating a chart. Pointing the twig at each abbreviation in turn, she said, "Early Pleistocene. Middle Pleistocene. Late Pleistocene."

In a column down the side she wrote Hyena, Tapir, Elephant, and Site. Then, stretching rightward from the species names, she drew a thick line representing their accepted dates of existence for each animal, leaving the Site column empty.

"If we mark where the dates for animals overlap, we get a date for the site." She drew a line next to Site. "As you can see, it ends at the late Middle Pleistocene."

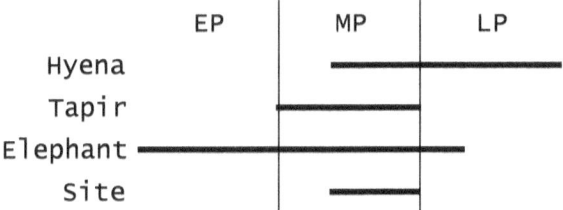

"Because dating by morphology says this can't be, we ignore it." She stamped her foot on the chart, swiping her sole across it, wiping the ground clean. "We draw a new chart that looks how we want. Voila! Evolution."

Rick grabbed a handful of dirt from the spot where she had drawn the chart. He let it drizzle out between his fingers.

"At Liujiang," she said, "they completely ignored the faunal evidence to place the human fossils tens of thousands of years later than the latest faunal fossils indicated."

"Why would they do that?"

"Evolution tells us modern humans have existed for about 250,000 years and came out of Africa about 120,000 years ago. Humans couldn't have been in China 230,000 years ago."

"If the evidence shows they were, I don't get why scientists would fudge anything. They can rewrite their theories and get rich discovering the new dates."

"Remember," she said, "paleoanthropologists are academics, not scientists. They have to worry about prestige and career advancement, tenure and crap. Careers are made based on these kinds of discoveries. Davidson Black convinced the Rockefeller Foundation to fund his research. Can you imagine what a coup that was? When money and truth bid for a scientist's loyalty, truth has a hard time competing. It's one of those slippery-slope issues."

She stared at the dirt as she said, "Besides, academia rewards conformists. Look what's happened to Charlie since he went against the flow."

Rick scribbled in the dirt with his finger.

She had battled his denial enough today. Let it sink in, let the water weaken the mortar, and soon the wall would crumble. Besides, she wanted to discuss other subjects with him.

"What did you see last night?" she asked.

"One of those things spying on Warner and his gang. Seems like nothing after what we saw today." He locked his gaze on hers like a laser sight. "What did you see last night?"

She hesitated. "A light. At first I thought it was the moon but last night was the new moon. I went up the hill for a better look. When I turned around for a second, it disappeared. I felt static electricity right before it disappeared. I don't know what the light was."

"What does a light have to do with hairy hominids?"

She grinned. "You called them hairy hominids, not Bigfoot."

Blushing, he looked away. His change in phrasing signaled a major shift in his attitude. He finally accepted the existence of hairy hominids and no longer considered them silly. In a few hours she might have him convinced of their intelligence. Once he gave up the notion society ingrained in people's heads, the idea that anything outside the bounds of normality was nonsense, he could accept the truth about the world. She already knew.

Everything they taught in school was a lie.

Well, maybe not *everything*. Nearly everything. The hard sciences—math and physics, for instance—were taught honestly because they must be. The history of humankind could be manipulated as easily as clay to suit the agendas of anthropologists and archaeologists.

"Why do you call them hairy hominids?" Rick asked. "Instead of Bigfoot, or even Sasquatch."

"Bigfoot is a pop culture term with negative connotations. People think of Bigfoot as a cartoonish oaf. Anthropologists who believe the creatures exist like the term Sasquatch because it sounds more scholarly, when in fact it's another pop culture term with the same problems as Bigfoot." She stretched her legs, easing out the kinks. "I call them hairy hominids because it describes them the most accurately. They are hominids. And they are definitely hairy."

"Did my dad get you calling them hairy hominids?"

"No, he was calling them mystery primates when I met him. I was calling them Bigfoot at the time because I'd grown up with the term. The more I thought about it, the less appropriate it seemed. I got hairy hominid from a book and I adopted it. After awhile, I got Charlie saying mystery hominid." She feigned an evil smirk and switched into her wicked witch voice. "Eventually I lured him over to the dark side where we call such things hairy hominids."

She cackled.

Rick shook his head. "I think your nose is turning green. I see a couple warts cropping up too."

The treetops swayed. They turned their heads simultaneously in the direction of the movement. Katy saw nothing move apart from the trees. If a hairy hominid concealed itself in the shadows of those trees, it deserved the Nobel prize for stealth.

The creatures were watching. Following. For what reason, she couldn't say. She could guess they thought she or Rick had shot the female who chased Ivan or maybe they disliked humans intruding on their territory. Her ideas were all guesses at best. Guesses without facts.

The treetops shimmied further away. Whatever was observing them had backed off.

For now.

THE PROTEIN DRINK MIX TASTED LIKE CHOCOLATE DIRT AND HAD THE CONSISTENCY of gritty mud. Warner gulped down the last of the drink.

He mixed the ingredients himself from a breakfast shake mix, a protein powder made for athletes, and ground ginkgo biloba. Cocoa, sugar, and a touch of cinnamon rounded out the flavor. The gingko provided increased blood flow to the brain and body, which he sorely needed on this trip.

Chasing after Katy Gallagher was monotonous. He couldn't close in on her until she found Charles Bergren, yet he must sneak closer to ascertain whether she had found the professor. Her knowledge of tracking and experience in the wilderness, coupled with her intelligence and drive, complicated his efforts.

His attempts to force Ivan to stay behind while he edged closer complicated the situation further. The idiot felt he had a right to tag along everywhere Warner went. After the fiasco with the angry creature, Warner had enjoyed a respite while Ivan cowered in fear behind him, trailing in his shadow, obeying his commands.

The shock had worn off now. Ivan squatted on a rock in the center of the clearing, tracing with his gaze the path of the beast's footprints as the tracks circled the rock and headed in a straight line for the edge of the clearing. The prints stopped short of the edge, however, and Warner hadn't decided what that meant. Alongside the last pair of prints the beast had made, he found two boot prints. Gallagher's boots. She had matched the beast's stance and hopped forward. While he could see where she landed, if the creature had jumped as well its prints had vanished. Perhaps Gallagher he erased them.

Seated on the rock, Ivan guzzled his drink. He coughed. "Jesus, Warner, this stuff tastes like elephant dung."

"Have you ever seen an elephant?"

"Course." Ivan retrieved a sketch pad from the pack at his feet. "I've been to Africa too. Seen things you never saw."

"The inside of an elephant's rectum does not interest me."

"I'm talking about Border Cave. Sterkfontein. Laetoli."

Ivan flipped the sketch pad to a blank sheet. From the pack he pulled out a plastic bag filled with charcoal pencils. While he talked, he sketched.

"Your problem, Warner," he said, "is you think everybody should be like you. Well, not everybody likes fighting. Some of us enjoy peace and quiet."

Warner snorted. "You enjoy money. My money, to be precise. And I fight only when it is necessary to maintain order."

"Yeah-yeah, I've heard all about your grand and noble motives. You're a saint. With blood on his hands."

Warner walked behind Ivan where he could peer over the idiot's shoulder at the sketch pad. Ivan had drawn the outline of the female beast's head and facial features. He was filling in the silhouette. Within a few minutes, he finished the general look of the face and started sketching in the hair that shrouded most of the features.

"A waste of time," Warner said.

"You got no scientific curiosity. Besides, this'll make a great image for my slide show at the monthly meeting."

"You cannot say what happens here."

"Course not." Ivan snapped the pad shut. "But I can use the drawing. Our agreement said nothing about drawings."

Warner simmered for a moment. Ivan was right. Their agreement took no account of drawings of the creatures. An oversight on his part, perhaps. Nevertheless he always abided by his agreements.

"Fine," Warner said.

He strode across the clearing toward the tracks.

"Use the drawing. But say nothing of this expedition." As he stopped at the footprints, he turned his torso to look straight at Ivan. "And remember the punishment for violating our agreement."

The smugness faded from Ivan's face, replaced by lines and shadows. He stuffed the sketch pad and pencils back inside his pack. Diane hurried out of the trees nearby. She rubbed her buttocks. Warner and Ivan stared at her.

Rubbing her arms, she focused on the ground. "Sat on a pinecone."

"Ain't the bathroom at the Ritz, is it?" Ivan said.

Warner helped them heft their packs onto their shoulders then hoisted his own onto his back. He led them toward the edge of the clearing, straight ahead of the parallel tracks. Gallagher went this way. He was certain of it.

Once they entered the woods, he found proof of his hunch. Boot prints. The prints looked recent. He kneeled beside them, scooped dirt from inside the print into his palm, and sniffed it. An hour at most passed since she trod through here.

Ten minutes later, he saw the tree. Scrape marks, made by boots, marred the trunk. Scratch marks looked like those made by claws or fingernails. A large branch had snapped in half. The flesh of the branch, pale and soft, indicated the break occurred recently. Boot prints and the deep tracks of a creature led away from the tree. A second set of boot prints, larger than the first, overran the first prints. The track would lead him to her.

He glanced back at Ivan and Diane. He held two fingers against his lips. They nodded. Gallagher was getting sloppy. Finding her would become simple.

When she found Bergren, he would be there.

11

A BREEZE HAD AWAKENED. IT SNATCHED UP LEAVES, WHIRLING THEM BETWEEN the trees before releasing them. The leaves fluttered onto the ground. They danced as the breeze flared up once more.

Rick looked at the spot where Katy had drawn her chart. Yes, her evidence sounded convincing. A part of him, probably the part that followed the rules no matter what, questioned her facts. She must've exaggerated or bent the truth a little.

He couldn't believe that either. Katy just wasn't the type to distort the facts for her own agenda. He knew some people would, people in positions of power and influence, like politicians and CEOs. And the head of the accounting department at Waterman & Associates, the conglomerate law firm he worked for in Boston.

Just crunch those numbers a little looser, kid. Nobody'll know the difference.

Kid. The word made his skin itch. When it rolled off the forked tongue of Mitch Atkins, the word made him want to deck the dirtbag. But no, he followed the rules about not decking people in the workplace. He should've done it. Mitch couldn't have screwed him any worse than he already had.

The world was home to plenty of dishonest people. Men and women who cared more about money than ethics or pride in their work. Why should anthropology be different?

Still, chucking evolution out the window…the idea hit him like a red-hot spike shoved up his spine into his brain. He grew up believing what teachers told him in school. Humans evolved from apelike creatures in a progression spanning millions of years. *Australopithecus. Homo habilis. Homo erectus. Homo sapiens.* He knew the names of human ancestors better than he knew the Declaration of Independence. His father had seen to that. Dad insisted everybody should know where they came from, and he didn't mean finding out whether your grandfather immigrated from Ireland or Wales. He meant where humankind came from.

Dad believed in evolution too, back then. When did belief transition into doubt? When did the doubt push him into a quest rivaling the Crusades? When did he decide evolution was garbage? Why had he decided it?

And why hadn't he talked to his own son about it?

His father had tried, Rick realized, but he'd been too busy or too jealous to hear. Jealous of Dad's relationship with Katy. Jealous his father found a mission, a purpose in life, while he worked for a crook who respected money and nothing else.

The jealousy seemed stupid now. He could live out here if he wanted. Shoot, he could probably live with Dad.

Dad was dead. He could live in Dad's house, when he inherited it. What a jerk. Thinking about inheritances when his father's body hadn't been found yet.

His inner eye returned to the present and he looked at Katy. "I'm having a little trouble getting my brain around this. Even if the anthropologists fudge some of the facts, there still isn't any evidence modern humans existed for a lot longer than they say. And how did we get here if we didn't evolve?"

"Good question. I don't have the answer. I hoped finding out about hairy hominids would answer it for me, or at least point me in the right direction." She shrugged her eyebrows. "As for the other thing, loads of evidence has turned up that shows a human presence millions of years ago."

"Never heard about it on the news."

"Of course not, but the evidence exists. You name it—from femurs, skulls, and other skeletal evidence to stone tools, metal artifacts, and coins."

She jerked her head toward the path he had come down when she ran away from the hairy hominid. Unblinking, she held her gaze on the area. Then she turned her eyes downward. He traced her gaze and his jaw tensed. Footprints. The two of them had left clear tracks, not to mention vegetation so disturbed it looked ready to strangle the next passerby.

Warner could follow the track. He could find them.

Katy leaped up without a sound. Rick rose too and helped her get the pack over her shoulders. She headed away from the tracks. Swinging his pack on, gripping the .45, he hurried after her. He had learned by watching her how to move quietly without shaking trees, breaking twigs, or leaving noticeable imprints in the soil.

Instead of planting the heel first and then rolling the foot forward, she stepped down on her toes and lightly rolled the foot backward. The technique gave her gait the bobbing of a hop when she moved fast, the glide of a ghost when she slowed down. Although the gait got tiring after a few minutes, they used it for short periods when Warner closed in on them rather than for the duration of the journey.

Katy halted. His chest bumped into her pack.

She ducked behind a tree. He followed her a dozen yards until they crossed into a lineup of dense pines. There she paused for a second, two at the most, before rushing back the way they had come.

What the blazes was she doing?

He hopped after her. His arches ached from the tension of supporting his weight. He prayed she had a plan.

Katy slowed. As they crept forward, he tapped her shoulder. She kept moving. He jabbed his finger into the soft flesh of her arm. She ignored it. Up ahead, he recognized the tree Katy had leaned against while they ate lunch.

They stopped and Katy kneeled. Reaching behind her back, she grabbed his shirt, pulling him down too. Off and on the sound of crinkling paper originated overhead, tumbling down around him. Sometimes he spied the leaves falling, other times he hoped it was leaves because the sound of hairy monsters swinging down from the treetops might sound the same.

Crunching issued from the other side of their picnic spot. He bent his head down to peek through the branches.

Warner strode out of the path.

KATY EXHALED AN OUNCE AT A TIME. SINCE THE BREEZE HAD DIED, THE WHISPER of her breathing might alert Warner to her location. On a still day the human ear could almost detect a pine needle hitting the ground from a mile away.

The falling leaves provided some cover. Their crackling, while intermittent, could confuse the ear.

She should've kept walking in the opposite direction. Gotten as far from Warner as she could. Knowing the enemy gave her an advantage. If she understood what he wanted, why he wanted it, she could estimate just how far he would go to capture his quarry. To capture her. And Rick. She was the baby rabbit hopping across an open field while a hawk circled overhead.

Screw the hawk. She was no baby. She could outsmart a bird, despite the years of experience he had on his side and his innate skill for sniffing out blood. She had intelligence, initiative, and a Taurus .357 on her team.

And she had Rick. She sensed him behind her, although she dared not look back. Knowing he was there quieted the prickling of her nerves.

Warner approached the tree where she reclined during lunch. From her vantage fifteen feet away, she saw the marks as well as he did. The smooth spot where her butt rested. The indentations from her heels. The dead grass provided a medium in which her pack had painted a picture of her presence in displaced and squashed blades.

The earth illustrated Rick's presence too. His body had mashed a long, narrow swath of grass, leaves, and dirt. When he had stood, his heels dug chunks out of the soil. Warner turned in a circle, scrutinizing their sign.

Dammit. She should've known better, should've been more careful. She let herself relax, the worst thing to do on a hunt. Especially with Warner sniffing out her trail like a beagle on the scent of heroin in an airline passenger's suitcase. Rick entrusted her with his life. She could've gotten them both killed.

Ivan and Diane moseyed out of the path. Diane stopped an arm's length from Warner. Her smile melted into a slight upturn of the lips coupled with a pallor that lent her the look of a mannequin.

Ivan tromped past Warner straight to the clump of saplings she and Rick hid behind. Katy froze. *Don't even blink.*

Lips twisted in a half frown, Ivan hunched a foot from her nose. He stared over her head into the woods. If he had seen a hairy hominid, he gave no clue.

A leaf crackled as it tumbled down through the treetops. Ivan peeled back his jacket and caressed the huge pistol holstered on his hip. The gun's ten-inch barrel stuck out the bottom of the holster, parallel with his thigh. Its gold finish glistened in the sunlight filtering down through the treetops. If he drew his *Pistolus giganticus*, the glare would blind every hairy hominid within a half mile. Good thing for him, since he probably never fired a gun of such power before. Had probably never touched one until he saw it in a catalog and just had to have it. He'd miss the hairy hominid and shoot his own butt.

She envisioned him squatting in a deer blind, beer in hand. Yeah, he'd look at home there.

The gun gave a clue. He had money. Did he earn it, or extort it?

Ivan removed his Stetson hat. His black hair was receding at the crown. Huddled a foot from him, swaddled by trees, Katy got her first good look at the man's face.

He looked about thirty-five, though the jaundice of smoking infused his skin. When he smirked, lines stretched outward from the corners of his lips and eyes. His eyes were dark, almost black. His nose hooked downward from a bump midway up the bridge.

Recognition teased her brain. She might have seen him before, or she might've gotten confused after stalking hairy hominids for two days. The nose. She remembered seeing the nose before.

Yeah, like yesterday when she watched Ivan goad a hairy hominid into running after him.

Warner marched past Ivan along the route she and Rick had taken moments earlier. Ivan and Diane fell in behind him. Warner's little army. If they had goose-stepped while chanting "left, right, left right," it would have seemed perfectly natural. For now, Warner had control of his troops. Fear was the factor controlling their behavior, rather than loyalty. Once Ivan's nerves settled, he'd return to the cretin she observed on the stream's shore.

Good. Warner's problems were her solutions.

She trailed after the threesome. When she glanced behind, she spotted Rick following, his expression the model of focus and determination. She hoped she looked as confident but suspected her face displayed a mixture of anxiety and uncertainty. Some fearless leader.

Upon reaching the point where she and Rick had angled right before turning back, Warner paused. He bent down to run his fingers over the soil. Eyelids half shut, he surveyed the wilderness around him. He froze.

He knows. She held her body as still as a mountain. Warner frowned, straightened, and started off again.

Katy sneaked after him.

❧

TEN MINUTES LATER, WARNER STOPPED HIS GANG ON THE SLOPE OF A HILL. KATY stopped where she could see and hear them clearly without getting so close they might see or hear her. Rick sidled up beside her. He tightened his lips in a half smile. She looked away toward Warner.

He and his gang sat down on the slope. Diane was sipping water from a bottle while Warner unfolded a map. Ivan, seated facing Warner, leaned over the map. He traced a line with his finger. Warner scowled. Ivan shrugged.

She could not shake the feeling she had seen Ivan before.

She leaned close to Rick. Her lips touched his ear. "Had you seen Ivan before Charlie disappeared?"

He shook his head.

Warner pointed out spots on the map. Diane thrust her finger onto the map. She stabbed it down three times, scrunching her face.

Katy pressed her mouth to Rick's ear. "I have to get closer. Gotta see what they're fighting about."

She stepped sideways. He grabbed her arm.

Pulling her close, he whispered, "They'll see you."

"Gotta take the risk."

He held onto her arm. She glared at him.

"Aw hell!"

Rick's grip loosened as his focus shifted to the source of the expletive. Katy looked at Ivan as well.

Warner's face had gone red. If he clamped his teeth together any tighter they might shatter. Diane's pallor had deepened until her red hair glowed like a halo of fire.

Ivan snatched the map from Warner. The paper snapped.

"No," Warner growled.

"Yes," Ivan said. "You are not the boss anymore, Warner. You lost them."

Though his face remained red, Warner spoke calmly. "You cannot find them again. But if you want to try, go ahead. On your own, of course."

"Course."

Ivan hopped up, whirled around. The map fluttered in his fisted hand. He stumbled over a hole and, shoving a hand against a sapling, righted himself as he stomped away. Warner moved neither his body nor his eyes to observe Ivan's departure. Diane watched Ivan until he disappeared in the trees.

She turned to Warner. "You can't let him go."

"Let him try. Failure might make him wiser."

"He could die, with those monsters out there nobody's safe." She hugged herself. "And what if he finds it."

"He will not."

"Not on purpose." She settled a hand on his thigh and squeezed. "He's not smart like you, Errie. But he could stumble on something. We can't stop him if we let him go off on his own. He has no respect for life."

"He has respect for my money."

"There's more money in finding it than losing it."

Warner met Diane's gaze. Her cheeks flushed. She averted her eyes. Warner studied the spot where Ivan had disappeared from view. With a loud sigh, he jumped to his feet, stalking after the wayward fool. Diane lagged a few steps behind him.

Katy lifted her foot to follow them then stopped. They were looking for something. Charlie, she had thought, except they called their quarry "it." Even when you hated someone you called them he or she. Whatever "it" was, they could make money if they found it yet Warner wanted it unfound. Diane hinted they could make money by not finding it too, though not as much as if they found it. So money did not drive Warner, not solely. He had another agenda, one that required finding Charlie but not finding "it," while preventing Ivan from finding "it" because he cared more about money than life. Whose life? What did it all mean?

A woman could get brain cramps from pondering those questions.

Rick tugged her sleeve. "Aren't we following?"

"No." She stood. "They'll be distracted with Ivan for awhile. We need to find the hairy hominid nest."

He rose beside her like a fire-truck ladder stretching its rungs toward the fortieth floor. "Don't suppose we have any idea how to do that."

She tilted her head back to see his face. "Same as before. Only this time we share a tree."

"It's a little soon to move in together."

"You can have your own branch."

Five minutes later, they found a pine tree with two branches at the same height capable of supporting them. After stowing their packs behind the tree, under a pine frond she snapped off a branch, they climbed into position. Rick took the thicker, shorter branch while Katy crouched on the other. She sat as before, her butt crammed into the intersection between the branch and trunk. Rick balanced a few inches out, long legs dangling, one arm slung over a higher branch. The needles of the tree shrouded them. And tickled them. And poked them in the eye, the butt, the cheek, anywhere the buggers could reach.

She suppressed an urge to scratch her neck where a needle grazed her.

Rick sat motionless, suspended like a huge pinecone.

Sure, she had known him for two years. Their dozen meetings during that span, however, consisted of eating dinner at Charlie's house while chatting about the weather, the economy, anything except the Human Origins Project and hairy hominids. If Charlie broached the subject, Rick excused himself for an alleged visit to bathroom. He would return when the subject had changed. If she dared mention the project or the creatures in Rick's presence, he aimed a twisted-mouth, wrinkled-eyebrows, squinty-eyed look at her while leaning backward as if afraid the spores of her insanity might float into his nostrils.

If she avoided the subject of hairy hominids, Rick was amiable. She had even let herself imagine he liked her in a way unrelated to friendship. Several times, when Charlie had left the room, Rick leaned across the dinner table, lips parted, blue eyes locked on her face, muscles tense. She thought he was about to ask her out for a date, but he'd shut his mouth, flopped back against his chair, and looked away.

She'd gotten used to living alone and had convinced herself she enjoyed the solitude. She did, to a point. Some nights, though, she lay in her bed staring out the window at the snow-covered hill, sleep thwarted by worries about the project and Charlie, thinking she might be asleep if she had someone there to comfort her. Someone like Rick.

Heat flushed her cheeks. Get real, if he wanted her he would've acted by now.

Goose bumps prickled her arms. That old feeling had returned, the sensation of someone or something watching. Waiting. This time she knew it was not Warner.

The knowledge failed to settle the goose bumps.

Leaves fell. birds chirped. an hour elapsed.

The noise of the woods still surprised her every time she ventured beyond the boundary of her own property. The leaves crackling, the trees creaking, the distant sounds of animals moving. People usually talked of the woods as silent, like in the old saying if a tree fell in the woods and no one was there to hear it, would it make a sound.

The sounds of the woods gave it character. Made it interesting. A person could sit in a tree and listen for hours. If they could relax.

She could not. Yoda's face flashed in her mind at each crunch of leaves or snap of a twig. Yoda climbing the tree. Yoda pursuing her.

She swallowed. Hard.

This time Yoda would not chase her and neither would his friends. She would pursue them. She would find their nest or lair or whatever it was and learn the truth of what happened to Charlie and Jim. What was happening to her now. What could happen to Rick.

Keeping her vow of stillness, she moved her eyes to glance at Rick. He sat motionless, an arm over one branch, body poised on another. He darted his eyes back and forth. Checking the woods. Like she should be doing.

Leaves crunched below. Breaking through a veil of vegetation, a doe pranced past the tree. Another trotted after her. The pair stopped a few feet beyond the tree, lowering their heads to sniff the ground.

Their heads snapped up. Eyes wide, ears twitching, they listened.

Katy heard nothing unusual. The deer might've smelled a bear.

The does sprinted away.

A breeze wafted the stench over her. A hairy hominid was nearby. She scanned the trees but saw nothing. *Do it slowly*, she reminded herself, and recommenced the search. This time, she scanned in widening arcs of 180 degrees starting at the base of the tree. Each arc took longer as she studied every leaf and shadow before moving on to the next. Still nothing. Maybe she should turn to scan the area behind the tree.

The creature strolled out from behind a wall of branches. He ducked under a low branch, approaching the pine. Katy held her breath, didn't blink.

The dark brown male walked within a yard of the tree. His head passed less than a foot beneath her branch. The muscles in his buttocks flexed and shifted under the skin as he moved. The hair on his head, a bit longer than the rest, ruffled in the breeze created by his movement. The tuft of hair sticking up on top of his head, which reminded her of a mohawk haircut, gave the impression his skull had the shape of a cut-off cone. The crest of hair flopped as he walked.

He continued through the forest. Gently, Katy lowered herself out of the tree. Rick did the same. He held her pack while she snuggled into it, then hefted his own pack onto his shoulders. They headed out after the creature.

THE CREATURE LEFT DEEP, CLEAR TRACKS EVEN WHERE HE CROSSED EXPANSES of leaves. Katy had experimented months ago with creating tracks as deep as hairy hominid tracks. She discovered her feet impressed deeper when walking purposefully as opposed to jogging or walking briskly. Yet she couldn't impress her feet as deeply as the creatures' feet pressed into the soil.

From her experiment she knew the creature impressed deep prints because he walked in a slow, purposeful gait. He hadn't detected them. Except for the track, the creature left no sign. The breeze, intermittent as it was, blew toward them. Any scent they gave off would travel away from the creature. Unfortunately, his odor blew right into her face. When she glanced at Rick, he crinkled his nose.

The track turned left. Katy swung left after it. Rick seized her pack, jerking her backward. She stumbled, twisted around, and fell face-first into his chest. She grabbed a handful of his sleeve, along with some of his flesh. As the kinetic energy of her fall pushed him backward too, he threw one arm around her while with the other he grasped a branch. With her face jammed against his chest, she inhaled the pine scent that had infiltrated his shirt during their sojourn in the tree. And the distinct, though not unpleasant, smell of him.

She shuffled backward. "What did you do that for?"

He gestured at the hominid's footprints.

She glanced at him sideways. "Those are footprints."

"Not those." He slapped a hand on each of her shoulders and angled her toward a maple tree alongside the track. Bending near her face, he whispered, "There was something behind that tree. I saw its eyes."

"I don't see anything."

"It's gone now."

"I see."

"Somebody's following us."

Hands on hips, she said, "I already told you the creatures are following us."

"Doesn't it bother you? They could be leading us into a trap."

"Guess we'll find out."

He gaped at her, waving his hands at his sides as if the motion could stir up a retort in his brain. She resumed tracking the creature. The thwapping of Rick's footsteps behind her assured her she had his company. After a minute, his footfalls shushed. When she checked, he was still there.

Rick had a point. The creature could be leading them into a trap. She hadn't considered that angle, probably because deep down where hope bubbled like champagne she wanted to believe the hairy hominids meant no harm. Her presence might have frightened Yoda into responding as any animal would. He might've thought she shot his girlfriend. He could've had any number of harmless reasons for his actions.

The red in his eyes, the sneer on his lips, she couldn't erase the image from her memory. Some pictures, once painted, lasted forever.

The trees opened around a stream. Whether the same stream as before or a different one didn't matter. The creature's track veered left to skirt the shoreline. Katy walked alongside the footprints. The shore here consisted of rocks and dirt with an outcropping of trees jutting into it occasionally. The branches from the forest on either side stretched toward each other, lovers reaching out but never quite making contact, their fingers trembling. The branches trembled from a breeze, rather than the strain of holding themselves up.

The track traveled so near the water's edge, where fewer rocks littered the earth, that stream water had run into some of the prints.

Tick-tick.

The sound stopped her. It came from the other side of an outcrop of trees blocking her view upstream. She canted her head, mouth ajar, in that direction. The ticking came again, this time intermingled with splashing and shuffling. After half a minute, silence ensued.

Rick slipped around her and tiptoed nearer the outcropping. She trailed him as fast as she could, but her soles kept sliding on the rocks. To maintain silence she crept forward, making certain each foot found traction before settling her weight onto it.

As she neared the outcropping where Rick crouched at the base of a short slope, she spotted another track near the creature's. The second track emerged from the water then crisscrossed underneath the creature's prints. For a space of three feet the creature had paralleled the animal's track instead of tromping right over it. Webbing splayed between the digits of the hand-sized tracks. A wide ribbon of smoothed earth cut across the prints and nearly obliterated some of them. The hairy hominid was hunting a beaver.

Katy sneaked up beside Rick. He was staring, eyes narrowed, at an area beyond the outcropping. The slope on which the trees hunkered came up to her forehead, so she rose onto tiptoes. Her eyes cleared the summit.

The creature was stooping at the water's edge. He picked up a stone from the streambed and dropped it onto a pile a few feet away. Tick. When he adjusted his footing, turning slightly, she saw the object of his attention. A beaver dam. He was digging under the dam, removing rocks in an attempt at either scaring the beaver out or uncovering the animal in its lair.

The creature grabbed a thick branch that fortified the dam. He pulled. The branch shifted but held. When he released the branch, he stumbled backward. His feet splashed in the water. He scrambled back to the dam. Grunting, he seized a handful of pebbles and mud from the streambed, thrust it onto the bank, shoved his hand down into the water. His arm submersed up to the elbow.

A growl gurgled from his throat. He dove his arm deeper. Half his forearm sank into the stream. With a cry, he yanked his arm out of the water. In his dripping hand he grasped the beaver.

He wiggled the animal and bared his teeth like a virgin hunter grinning at his first catch. Then he trudged away from the stream. The slope blocked her view.

She planted her hands on the slope, pulling herself up. Despite the risk of the creature spotting her, she must see.

The creature kneeled on the shore. The beaver squiggled and cried. The hominid took the animal's neck in one hand, its body in the other.

Rick settled his hand atop her head. *Get down*, he was urging her. She could not move.

The creature jerked its hand. The beaver's neck snapped with a sharp crack.

Rick shoved her head down.

Her gorge rose in her throat. She gulped it back. She had seen animals killed before, had killed a few herself for food or in self-defense. The creature's ease as it snapped the beaver's neck, she'd seen nothing like it. Ever. Her throat constricted. She felt hairy fingers around her neck, squeezing her bronchial tube until it ruptured. Fracturing her spine. Separating her skull from her neck.

Rick's hand on her cheek shattered the sensation. She let out a long breath.

He whispered, "You okay?"

"Yeah."

The creature. She spun around and popped her head above the slope.

The hairy hominid was gone.

"Oh no." She jumped to her feet. "We lost him."

She jogged around the outcrop to the spot where the creature slaughtered his meal. The footprints led upstream. She marched after the creature.

The track drew her forward as surely as a rope tied around her waist and pulled by oxen. She was aware, subconsciously, of Rick's footfalls behind her. She stayed zeroed in on the track. The creature. It was taking dinner home. She would find its nest. She would find Charlie.

The track veered into the woods.

She swerved left into the trees.

Wait. This wasn't right. She whirled around, trotted back to the stream. A cloud of mud was dissipating in the water, spiraling away from the epicenter. Halfway across the stream a second cloud curled into the current. She glanced back at the where the track had turned. A line of three large rocks zigzagged from the tree line toward the stream. She bent beside the nearest rock. Dirt smeared across one corner. The creature walked into the trees far enough to make it seem, superficially, like he went that way. He then doubled back—using the rocks as stepping-stones to avoid leaving footprints—hopped into the stream, and sauntered across it.

He laid a false trail.

A shiver rattled her teeth.

Rick hunched a few feet away studying the track. He said, "The thing went back into the woods I guess."

"No."

She crooked a finger at him, and he trotted up beside her.

"He did that for our benefit," she said. "He knows we're following him so he's trying to shake us off his tail."

Kneeling, she dipped her finger into the water where the mud was clearing. "He stepped here. Couldn't keep the mud from rising. Over there too."

"You're saying this thing knows how to lay a false track like we did? That implies analytical thinking."

She smiled inwardly. He sounded like her. Pretty soon he'd spout words like stratigraphy and dermatoglyphics too, when referring to the layers of artifacts at an archaeological site and the science of fingerprints respectively.

"We can debate their intelligence later," she said as she hopscotched across the stream using small rocks as her stepping-stones. "Right now our goal is him."

"The hairy hominid."

She hopped onto the bank. "Of course."

Rick strode across the stream. The water sloshed up to his knees, soaking his jeans. Once he reached the bank where she stood, he shook his boots. Water spritzed her calves. She frowned.

"I'll dry my socks later," he said.

"If you get pneumonia, don't blame me."

She located the creature's tracks and started after them. Behind her, the squishing of Rick's socks inside his boots betrayed his every footstep. No good.

Katy stopped. "Change your socks. Unless you want the hominids to hear you coming and organize a surprise party. Trust me, they wouldn't be singing happy birthday."

So he wouldn't need to remove his pack, she rooted around inside it until she found his socks. He changed into them and squeezed the water out of his boot insoles as best he could. They headed down the track in silence.

The creature tried a few more tricks. He led them in one direction by impressing prints in soft soil before doubling back through a leaf patch or an area of firmer ground. Twice his track ended as abruptly as the female's had in the field. He hadn't vanished, however. Both times she located his tracks several yards ahead. From the depth of the first footprints in the new track and the bent branches overhead, she surmised he climbed a tree, swung or climbed forward, and jumped down again. He was smart.

Paleoanthropologists claimed the early hominids were incapable of such thinking. They were not self-aware, couldn't plan ahead, knew nothing about deductive reasoning. If, as some people claimed, hairy hominids represented relict Neanderthals or *erectus*, an isolated population who survived into the present, they should possess the same mental capabilities as their ancestors. The human brain had not changed since *sapiens* came into existence. Yet these creatures knew just as much as she did about tracking—maybe more. And they understood deception and strategy.

The fist in her gut turned to ice. *Analytical thinking.*

She tramped after the track. The trees rose over a low rise, a hill that slumped like a turtle shell to a height of ten or twelve feet. The tracks disappeared into a clump of fallen branches at the base of the hill. A clump similar to the one Pete Kryszka found, the one stuffed full of deer kills. Katy leaned closer. These branches, rather than being arranged in a dome, looked as if someone wove them into a sheet a little taller than her. A wall.

No. She jiggled it. A door. Scrapes on the ground demonstrated where the creature dragged it out of the way. Perhaps he swung it open and shut similar to a hinged door.

Rick tugged on a branch. "Looks like a door almost."

"I think it is." She straightened. "Help me move it."

Before she could grasp a piece of the contraption, Rick grabbed either edge and lifted it aside. He set the thingamajig down beside the opening the door had concealed. "There you go."

A different kind of shiver rippled through her. "Thanks."

She dug the flashlight out of her pack, removed the red filter, and walked toward the opening. Rick, thrusting an arm between her and the doorway, snatched the flashlight from her hand. He ducked inside the opening. She went in after him.

The flashlight's beam revealed a cave cut out of the dirt. The passage was a hair under six feet tall, forcing Rick to stoop as he walked, and twice as wide. Natural or hominid made, the cave had the feel of a burial mound. Whether it was the tang of earth in her nostrils or the moisture clinging to her skin, the sensation of being buried alive made her tense her hands into fists.

After a few yards, the earthen walls gave way to rock as the passageway descended and leveled out. It ended at a craggy wall. A rectangular slab of rock protruded from the wall. Rick shined the flashlight on the slab. Shadows delineated the seam between the slab and the wall of the cave. She explored the seam with her fingers. A draft tickled her skin.

"Shine the light on the floor," she said.

Rick complied. A gouge etched a semicircle from the right side of the slab out and around to the wall. She bent down. The gouge was fresh, but underneath the scars from older gouges marked the rock. The slab was another door.

Rising, she inserted her fingers as far as possible into the seam and pulled. Her fingers hurt, but the rock stayed put. She braced her back and buttocks against the wall, kicking at the side of the slab. The concussion sent pangs up her shin bones into her kneecaps. The slab did not budge.

"Let me try," Rick said.

He set the flashlight on the ground. As he pushed from the side his heels dug in and his face contorted, yet the slab remained in place. He pushed until sweat beaded on his face, until the tendons in his hands and wrists bulged. The slab groaned but held.

Rick collapsed against the wall. Between gasps he said, "If that monster moved this thing it must be stronger than Superman."

She contemplated the gouges.

"Wasted effort, I guess." He pushed away from the wall. "We lost him again."

"But we found the nest. It's the other side of this door. All we have to do is wait here for one of them to open it."

"And what? We say hi there friends and waltz past them?"

He grabbed the flashlight. Rays bounced off the walls, the floor, glinted off a patch of white further back in the passage.

Her heart thudded. She jabbed a finger at the area. "Shine the light over there."

Rick turned around. The light preceded him. When it struck the object lying on the ground along the wall, he halted. The light glowed on the white skull.

She shuffled closer. The skull was larger than a man's with a pronounced brow ridge and a heavy jaw. The eye sockets gaped as if they had startled the creature's spirit, waking it from a century's repose. The skull sat on the floor of the passage against the wall. Someone put it there.

Rick swung the light along the length of the wall. Another skull seemed to pop out of the darkness further ahead. And then another. And another. He probed the opposite wall. More skulls, each spaced to line up with the skulls along the other wall. They bordered the walls at even intervals. The hairy hominid's version of mile markers, she supposed.

Rick faced her. The flashlight's beam lanced across the floor. His face paled to match the glow from the flashlight.

She looked at the ground. Buried in the earthen floor was a skeleton, its ribs and legs and arms flush with the floor, its skull recessed so that the jaw stuck out just a sliver. The toes pointed at the doorway slab. She jerked her head up. Rick met her gaze, his eyes looking as haunted as she felt.

"Tell me what I'm thinking is wrong," he said.

"I can't." She lowered her gaze to the bones. "That skeleton is human."

THE YELLOW-BROWN TINT OF THE BONES SHOWED THROUGH THE ENCRUSTED dirt. Dozens, perhaps hundreds, of hairy hominid feet had trampled the skeleton. Desecrating a grave by their every step. Did they realize the import a human's resting place had for the other members of the species?

The creatures laid false trails. They deceived. They plotted.

They understood so much.

She had no reference point for determining where to draw the line between human and hairy hominid. When she started her quest for truth she believed the most shocking thing she might discover was that evolution didn't exist, at least not in the way most scientists believed. Here in this cave she was discovering a more frightening truth. She just didn't know what it was yet.

"Let's get out of here," Rick said.

"No." She scuffled backward toward the slab door. "I am not moving until this door opens."

"I'm starting to think you want to die."

"Got a better plan?"

"Yes."

He lunged at her, locking his arms around her waist, and hoisted her over his right shoulder, all without dropping the flashlight. Her head hung upside-down, her arms too, while he held her legs clamped under his arm. Her pack slumped against the nape of her neck.

Rick stamped out of the cave into the sunlight. He deposited her on the ground a short distance from the hill. She couldn't speak. No man had thrown her over his shoulder and carted her away before. He had been so presumptuous, so pushy, so…sexy.

She was still mad at him.

"Don't even think about going back in there," he said.

"Would you like to bind my feet together too?"

"Maybe later." His expression softened. "I'll make you a deal. Stay out of the cave and we'll find another tree to sit in. Wait for the things to come home."

"One already came home. And if I can't go in the cave, what good will it do to watch them come and go?"

She could practically see the thoughts bumping around behind his eyes. He had no answer. They both knew it. Her way might be dangerous but it would get them inside the nest. He wanted to protect her, an inclination she appreciated even if she disliked his method of hog-tying her curiosity. Which was impossible. Although she could've told him as much, he would've ignored her.

"Let's talk about this after dinner," she said. "I'm starving."

"Everybody craves roasted squirrel this time of day."

"If you're turning vegetarian, I see some moss on a tree over there. Looks yummy."

"I'll take the squirrel."

"Then let's find one."

They stashed their packs in a hollow on the far side of the hill, where the hairy hominids had no doors. Katy sent Rick on a scrounging mission for tinder and firewood while she searched for the tracks of their dinner. After about fifteen minutes, she spotted the delicate prints of a rabbit. The egg-shaped hind prints registered ahead of the smaller front prints because of the rabbit's hopping gait. Occasionally rabbits walked. Mostly they stuck with their diagonal hop, the gait most people associated with the species.

Rick caught up with her a few minutes later.

"Well?" he asked.

"Looks like rabbit tonight."

He lifted his hand. He held her slingshot, plus the pouch of steel pellets she had tied onto the slingshot with a rubber band to keep them together.

"Dug this out of your pack," he said.

"Now you're going through my stuff?"

"You weren't there to ask so I made a command decision."

She noticed how the rabbit prints ducked between a pair of saplings, where they disappeared into the shade of a shrub.

"Mad at me?" he asked.

Shaking her head, she bent down close to the ground. Beneath the shrub, a shadow twitched. Light glinted off eyes.

She raised onto her knees. "Let's get dinner."

H E WASN'T LOST. SCREW WHAT WARNER SAID, HE COULD FIND HIS WAY AS WELL as anybody. He had the map and his GPS unit. He didn't need Warner.

Ivan massaged the cramp in his calf. Squatting behind a tree put cricks in every part of his body. He needed to hide, though. He learned that much from Warner before he got sick of the Nazi ranting at him about every little thing. Don't scream when a monster chases you. Don't take your gun out, it's too big and gaudy. Don't smoke, don't talk, blah-blah-blah. Like he was the commander of the universe. Ivan could claim as much right to boss everybody around as Warner. He had degrees, three of them. Warner had none.

But Warner had bucks, and not the kind with antlers. Money gave him more power. At least Warner thought it did.

Ivan scratched his cheek. The pine needles tickled something awful. Sure, he liked the money Warner gave him. Taking a few bucks didn't make him Slave Number One to Errando Warner. So he took the payoffs. He performed a top-notch service for the bucks. For Warner. Who else could do what he did with as much eloquence and elegance? Warner didn't appreciate him. The hell with Warner.

The mission had changed. Ivan changed it. Forget finding the old fart and getting rid of the problem Warner's way. He would find the goldmine. He lost it once before because he listened to Warner. Never again. This time he'd hold onto it with all his strength no matter how many Sasquatches got in the way.

He patted the Desert Eagle through his jacket. Let the hairy freaks try. He would decapitate them with a lead projectile hurtling at them faster than the speed of sound. Okay, maybe not decapitate them. He'd sure enjoy watching them die anyway.

A memory replayed in his mind like an old home movie, the images jerky and blurred. The creature storming after him. Her breasts flailing. The sound she made as she moved, a cross between a grunt and a shout. Her hands around him. In the air. Screaming.

He shivered. Next time the hairy freak would die. Gallagher too. Both of them got in his way, which irritated him worse than the fungus he'd gotten under his toenails last year. He had to get rid of them. His way.

When he told Warner some people liked peace and quiet he implied he was one of those people. He was. Sort of. Long as nobody messed with his peace and quiet, he liked it fine. Charles Bergren messed with it. Gallagher messed with it. If they bugged him again, he'd strike back.

He pulled the crumpled map out of his pocket. Finding the red X he had scrawled on the paper, he brought out his GPS and checked his position. Not far. He could make it before sundown.

The goldmine would be his.

AFTER DINNER, THEY RELAXED ON THE HILLSIDE. THE LITTLE HOLLOW FORMED a natural sofa of sorts, the way it curved into the hill.

Katy leaned her head back. The earth felt cool and damp. The sun had sunk low in the sky, although the orb stayed visible above the horizon.

Rick, seated beside her, rolled onto his side to face her. "I have an idea. We can watch for the things to come home, see how they open the door. Then we can wait until they're gone and open it ourselves."

"What if they lift it aside like a cardboard box? We can't do that."

The hopeful upturn of his lips curved down into a frown. Lines knit across his forehead.

"I have an idea too," she said. "After dark, we sneak over there with my night scope and watch for them. We see what they do, maybe get an idea how to get inside the nest. Or we follow them in. They might not see us in the dark."

"They could have night vision like cats and other animals."

Now she felt her hopeful expression fading. He rejected her idea and she rejected his, both for good reasons. They had reached the point in a discussion where compromise becomes unfeasible. They needed to think of a new idea.

Rick fidgeted beside her. Light glanced off his wrist. She grabbed his arm, yanked up his sleeve. A gold watch hung around his wrist. Polished gold. Glittering in the sunset glow. Shine, a deadly problem when you were being stalked.

She tapped the watch. "Didn't I tell you about shine?"

"What's shine?"

"This." She tipped his wrist. Sunlight coruscated off the gold. "Might as well jump up and down screaming. Shine telegraphs your position like a flare. Take off the watch. Put it in your pocket."

He unhooked the watch's clasp.

She pulled her hand away. "Does it tick?"

"Yes."

"If you can take the battery out, do it. Otherwise bury it in your pack. Wrap it in your spare clothes and stuff it in the middle of the pack."

"Sounds a little paranoid."

"We're being hunted by the man who murdered Jim Van Owen. Want him to hear your watch ticking?"

Rick pulled the watch off his wrist. It slipped from his fingers, plunking onto the dirt at her feet. She picked up the watch. Lines on the underside of the watch captured her attention. She tilted the watch into the light. On the underside someone had engraved little pictographs. A shape like a cross with a noose at the top. A bird resembling a falcon. A crook. And a man kneeling with one arm bent before him, the other bent at his side.

"What's this?" she asked, handing him his watch. "Those look like Egyptian hieroglyphs."

"They are."

"What do they mean?"

"Nothing." He pulled out a pocket knife. As he threaded the tiny screws out of the watch's back, he said, "My mom gave it to me for my high school graduation. She didn't know what hieroglyphs meant so she picked ones that looked good."

"Why would she have hieroglyphs engraved on your watch when she didn't know what they meant?"

He muttered.

She leaned toward him. "Sorry, I didn't catch that."

The last screw fell onto his palm. He popped out the battery and replaced the screws. The shadows, nipping at the sunset's heels, darkened his face.

She poked his arm. "I said why would—"

"Because I was learning to read them." After he inserted the last screw, he tucked the watch in his hip pocket. Turning his head away, he said, "For awhile I wanted to be an Egyptologist. Stupid, I know."

"That's not stupid. Why didn't you?"

He shrugged. Shutting her eyes, she rested her head against the hill. He didn't want to tell her. She was too tired for prodding him into a confession. Besides, if he felt uncomfortable sharing his secrets with her she wouldn't force the intimacy. She had other things on her mind anyway. Like why hairy hominids would display a human skeleton as the welcome mat at their front door.

Why they hid in caves, she understood. Caves provided shelter with a steady temperature year-round. A cave also acted as a fortress, especially with a slab blocking the inner entrance. She knew of no natural caves in this area. On the eastern side of northern Michigan there were sinkholes. None over here. The hairy hominids could've found a cave humans had yet to discover. But the topography of the land consisted of rolling hills and forest dotted with lakes.

The hairy hominids might have dug out a cave.

Imagine the effort involved in such a task. Certainly the hairy hominids had the strength and, if their numbers tallied as high as she suspected, they had the manpower. Their intelligence was evident. If they lived in this area for tens or hundreds of thousands of years then they would've had the time for excavating a cave. They could've dug out a subterranean metropolis.

But a thousand generations of hairy hominids all working toward a goal implied more than analytical thinking. The idea implied loyalty, forethought, direction.

She pulled her coat tighter around her. More than the chill of nightfall seeped into her body. The hominid skulls troubled her. The human skeleton terrified her. Yes, she admitted feeling terrified, though she felt idiotic for letting a little thing like a skeleton doormat get to her. The hairy hominids could've killed the person.

People had disappeared in the woods before. The police likely maintained a chest-high file of people who wandered into the woods without bothering to buy a map or hire a guide and subsequently got lost. Usually they were rescued, at taxpayer expense. Occasionally their bodies were found within walking distance of safety. Rarely, they stayed missing. Forever.

Did the hairy hominids account for the missing? Was the skeleton a hobby hunter or an urban hiker who stumbled into the cave?

The skulls and skeleton could act as a security system. Scare off the humans. Make sure they never come back. It might work on most people. It failed with her. She must know the truth and she'd step over as many skulls and skeletons as necessary to find it. Bones wielded no power. Sure, they scared her.

Fear hadn't stopped her yet.

"We are not going back in there," Rick said.

"I didn't say we should."

"You were thinking it."

"What, are you suddenly psychic?"

"Don't need to be psychic," he said, "to know what you're thinking."

Arms folded over her chest, she tilted her head up to squint at him. "Well, if I'm that transparent it must be horribly boring for you to be stuck out here with me twenty-four hours a day."

"Like I said before, you're not boring."

He propped his head up with his arm. The sun had ducked under the horizon, leaving a wake of fire amidst the darkness. Because the sunset raged behind him while the night darkened in front, she couldn't make out his expression.

She picked at the dead grass. "I've never spent this much time alone with one person. It's weird."

"You go out with Dad all the time."

"Day hikes. We don't camp out here." She imagined that look took over his face again, the one whose source emotion she had yet to pin. "Think it's time I cleared up something. About me and your father. What our relationship is."

"None of my business."

His tone was gruff. He flipped onto his back, scooting away from her. She grabbed his arm but only succeeded in grasping a handful of his jacket.

She hissed, "Now listen to me and listen good."

Someone coughed from the other side of the hill. Footfalls shuffled through leaves, scraped across earth.

She let go of Rick's jacket. The footfalls ceased. Scraping and rattling ensued.

Katy rose onto hands and knees. She scuttled up the hill toward the sounds. Rick rushed up behind her, grasped her ankles, and pulled. She kicked his hands away. As she crested the slope, he tackled her. The weight of his body flattened her against the ground and she turned her head sideways to avoid smashing her face into the dirt. He draped his arm across her shoulder with his hand planted on the ground behind her head. She couldn't move.

But she could see the cave entrance—and Ivan fumbling with the woven-twig door.

Ivan clutched a flashlight in his left hand. He struggled to lift the door with his free hand, the flashlight's rays twirling around him, knifing through the shadows. He wedged the flashlight under his arm to grip the door with both hands. His features contorted. He heaved the door aside. It clattered against a tree.

Rick pressed his mouth to Katy's ear. "Stay here. I'll see what he's up to."

He clambered onto his knees. Below them, Ivan ducked inside the cave. The flashlight's glare faded.

Stay here? Fat chance.

She bolted down the hillside. At the entrance, she paused to look back over her shoulder. Rick was sliding down the hill toward her. She hurried into the cave.

The darkness struck her blind. She careened into the wall, stumbled sideways, hesitated for a moment until her senses oriented themselves. Although she was still blind, she could at least distinguish up from down. She hadn't realized how disconcerting total darkness was. When she half turned toward the entrance, the night outside seemed bright.

Until Rick stepped into the opening. His body blocked the view.

A chuckle bubbled up from the recesses of the cave, echoing off the rock walls further inside. Ivan.

With a hand on the wall, she trotted into the blackness. Her fingertips traced the wall and bumped over the transition between earth and rock. Ahead, a light cleaved the dark. She stopped. Ivan squatted beside the skeleton. A grin revealed his white teeth. The light glittered in his eyes.

He shoved his finger into the dirt filling the skeleton's mouth. A giggle made his gut tremble. Katy clenched her teeth, fisted her hands.

The giggle mutated into a cackle. Tears welled in his eyes. He yanked his hand back, rubbing the dirt off on his pants as he collapsed onto his butt. His lips tensed though they held the curve of the grin. His skin was pale, she saw now, his lips too.

He wasn't gleeful. He was terrified. Good.

"Holy crap." He wiped his nose on his sleeve. "Nobody'll believe this."

He unzipped his backpack, which lay on the floor beside him, and dug out a camera. He stood to snap photos of the skeleton. The flash pulsed.

Katy flinched at the brightness. She pulled the Taurus out of her fanny pack. With it gripped in her hand, she surged forward out of the darkness.

At the instant she passed in front of the flashlight's beam, Ivan glanced up at her. Before he could react, she snatched the camera from him, slapped her hand onto his chest, and thrust him backward into the wall. She tossed the camera onto the ground. With the Taurus jammed under Ivan's chin, and her hand flat against his chest, she glared at him.

Rick moseyed up beside her. He shook his head.

Ivan swallowed. His Adam's apple bulged against the muzzle of the Taurus. He winced.

She rammed the gun deeper into his throat. "Who do you work for?"

He croaked, "Warner."

She let off the pressure enough for Ivan to speak. "Who does Warner work for?"

"Nobody."

"Why are the three of you following me?"

Ivan chuckled. "To find out where you're going, obviously."

She flashed back to her conversation with Pete Kryszka. She had no time for verbal tap dancing. If Ivan refused to volunteer information, she'd surgically remove it from his brain.

She looked over Ivan's pack, his camera, the flashlight, the skeleton.

"It's fossilized, you know," Ivan said. "Looks male too."

She glanced sideways at him. "How do you know?"

He sucked his lips between his teeth. The smirk glimmered in his eyes.

"Have we met before?" she asked.

"Not formally."

"Explain."

He smirked. She punched him in the gut.

Rick shook his head.

Gasping, Ivan clutched his abdomen. Between breaths, he said, "You've probably seen me around. I've seen you but we never actually spoke."

"Who are you?"

"Ivan Thaw." He straightened. "You may know my professional name."

"Which is?"

A groan, which seemed to come from all around, stopped the conversation. Sounded as if the hill had moaned.

The rock groaned again. Katy glanced at the slab door. As another groan quaked the ground, the slab inched outward.

She released Ivan. He grabbed his pack and sprinted out of the cave. His flashlight, still on the floor, rocked with each groan of the slab. The grinding of stone against stone rattled inside her bones. She looked at Rick. Although his lips moved, she heard nothing he said.

He grabbed her hand and pulled her away from the slab. She ran out of the cave after him without looking back. She was afraid of what she might see. Ridiculous. She would see hairy hominids, something she had seen before, so why the thought of seeing them now frightened her made no sense either.

Outside, they ducked behind a pine tree.

Seconds later the first creature emerged from the cave. He paused to study the twig door Ivan had moved aside. As a second creature appeared in the entrance, the first one held up a hand and grunted. Both creatures stared into the woods.

They dashed back inside the cave. The slab door groaned. They had retreated into their nest.

Katy headed back over the hill to their campsite.

SOMEHOW SHE FELL ASLEEP. THE CREATURES HAUNTED HER DREAMS, PHANTASMS of fur with red glowing eyes. They pursued her through a woods where trees had arms and faces, teeth sharp as razors. The creatures dragged her into their nest and hoisted her over a fire. They grunted, danced, splashed blood over her.

A stick poked her in the arm. She rose from the dream like a deep-sea diver surfacing. Her eyelids refused to open. The stick jabbed her. She opened her eyes, rolled onto her back. She felt his presence before she saw the figure looming over her. The man prodded her shoulder with a long stick.

She snatched the stick away and pitched it aside. The man crouched beside her. In the ambient light, she could make out a beard and white hair.

"Come with me," he whispered.

That voice. She knew it.

He clasped her wrist in his hand, urging her onto her feet. Her mind fuzzy, she stumbled after him as he rounded the base of the hill. Near the cave's entrance, he stopped. He pulled a pen-sized flashlight out of his pocket.

The man directed the beam at his face. "It's me, Katy."

She blinked. "Charlie."

He shut off the light.

"Wait…" She spun around. "Rick…"

He seized her arm. "No."

"He thinks you're dead, you have to let him know."

"Tell him later. Right now I need you to listen to me."

Her mouth was cottony, her eyes gritty. Her brain felt stuck in the twilight world between sleeping and waking. Her thoughts blossomed in slow-motion. Charlie stood before her as an apparition, his white hair and beard glowing in the half-light, his dark clothing melding with the night. When he spoke, his voice sounded distant.

"Go home, Katy, they won't let you alone until you leave. They would kill to protect their secret. I understand why but I don't expect you to." He grasped her shoulders. "I couldn't stand it if you or Rick got hurt because of me."

"I will not leave you out here."

"They can protect me. I can't convince them to take in anyone else. When I've finished my work here, I'll come home."

She studied the blur that was his face. His words got tangled in the fuzz blanketing her mind. They. Kill. Protect.

"Who's protecting you?" she asked. "Warner? I thought he wanted to kill you. And I seriously doubt he'll let us leave without finding you."

Syllable by syllable, as if the word derived from a long-dead language, he said, "Warner?"

She rubbed her temples. The sleepiness lingered.

"Have you seen him?" he asked. "He's out here?"

"Yeah, he killed Jim and now he wants the three of us. You, me, and Rick."

"Jim's dead?"

Oh God. She'd forgotten. He couldn't know about Jim's death because he came out here before the body floated to shore.

His shoulders slumped. His voice sounded weak. "How did it happen?"

"He drowned. I don't know how, Warner must've killed him."

"No."

"What do you mean no? He's a killer. He's stalking me and he had his goons break into both our houses."

"Yes, but he wouldn't—after what he said—" Charlie hesitated, his expression unreadable in the dark. When he spoke again his voice betrayed nothing. "Stay away from Warner. Go home."

He walked past her.

She twisted her neck to peer over her shoulder at him. "Wait, what about the Human Origins Project? You said we couldn't stop until we figured out what the hairy hominids are. I'm so close to the truth I can almost touch it. I *will not* leave until I have it. The truth is my life."

"It shouldn't be. You're young, you should be hanging around with people your own age instead of keeping an old fart company." He sighed. "The truth is dangerous, Katy. You won't like the way it feels on your conscience."

Her protestation came out as a squeak. She clamped her hands into fists.

He said, "The project is terminated."

The footfalls shooshed to her left. She panned her head in that direction. A figure was tromping around the slope toward her.

When she glanced back, Charlie was gone.

Rick stomped up alongside her. Though she couldn't see his expression, she felt the anxiety radiating from him.

He stood close. His shadow blocked what little light penetrated the dark. "What are you doing? I thought those things had kidnapped you."

"I—" Her throat constricted, choking off the words. *I saw your father and then he vanished.* Sure, Rick would understand that. He'd tell her it was a dream, and he might be right. Until the second she saw Rick coming down the hillside she had felt stuck in a dream, uncertain what was real. Yet the conversation had seemed real.

"What were you doing out here?" Rick asked.

"Thought I heard something."

As if in support of her lie, a groan resonated from inside the cave. The door was opening.

Rick dodged behind a tree, pulling her with him. The maple, split at the base, looked like two trees. The dual trunks and the branches intermingling between them provided good cover for two human bodies. His hands squeezing her shoulders, he held her close against him.

The groan escalated into grinding. The noise ended. The night plunged into a hush deep as the earth's core. Two creatures emerged from the cave. While they angled into the woods, another pair exited the cave. And another. She watched, her jaw tight, as two more pairs succeeded the first two into the woods.

She started to go after them. Rick's hands restrained her.

Katy asked, "Don't you want to know where they're going?"

Rick freed her shoulders, pushed past her, and strode in the direction the creatures had gone. She jogged after him. A box-like object dangled from his belt. Not a flashlight. The night scope.

The creatures led them through an area of thicker vegetation, over a hill, into a clearing. Rick halted at the edge of the clearing, where he crouched behind foliage. Katy dropped onto her knees beside him. The creatures walked into the center of the clearing. Their grunting carried on the breeze.

Rick unhooked the night scope from his belt. He lifted it to his right eye. When he clicked the power button, a tiny green light popped on. From the front, no one could see the light. He handed her the scope.

She raised it to her eye, adjusting the focus. The creatures came into view awash in green. They huddled in a throng bobbing their heads at each other as they grunted. Discussing strategy, no doubt. She scanned the clearing. Eight or ten feet behind the creatures she spied a rock like the one in the clearing where the female had vanished.

The creatures congregated in a circle around the rock. They stood motionless, arms at their sides, faces tilted toward the sky.

She handed Rick the scope.

Even without the scope, she could see the creatures' silhouettes in a ring around the rock. They were waiting. The hairs on her neck stiffened. Static electricity tingled over her body.

A light appeared above the treetops. Since its daylight glow lit the slope of a hill in the distance, she judged the light to be no more than a half mile away. The light was a perfect orb, pure white in color, brighter and larger than the full moon. The orb swelled. Her body tingled as if she had jammed her finger in an electrical socket. It was coming.

Rick dropped the night scope. It thunked onto the ground.

The creatures held so still she wondered if they'd turned into wax figures.

The light drew nearer. The air seemed to crackle on the verge of erupting into lightning. The orb, its diameter now as wide as the clearing, hovered above the creatures and their rock.

A flash of light blinded her. A crack split the air like thunder.

Ghosts of the flash danced in her vision.

The creatures—and the light—had vanished.

13

RICK GRABBED THE NIGHT SCOPE. WHILE HE SURVEYED THE CLEARING, KATY let out the breath trapped in her lungs. A cloud roiled away from her mouth. She zipped her jacket, hugging it closer.

The creatures. The light. All gone.

If they fled during the flash, that answer left her with questions about the light but at least gave her a real-world explanation for the disappearance of the creatures. The flash scared them and they fled. Yes. It made sense.

Hopping up, she burst out of the trees into the clearing and sprinted toward the rock.

"Katy!"

Get to the rock. Find their tracks leading away from it into the woods.

Rick's footfalls clomped behind her. She skidded to a stop a yard from the rock. A flashlight, she needed a flashlight. She whirled around. Rick stopped with a huff in front of her.

She said, "I need a flashlight."

"Don't have one."

"Give me the scope then."

He tossed it at her. She caught it, spun on her heels, and peeked through the scope. The night came alive around her in shades of green. Aiming the scope at the ground, she could see little. She hit the button for the infrared illuminator. It spotlighted the clearing, the rock, the trees. She discovered the footprints immediately. As she circled the rock, the little voice in her head whispered, *this can't be real.* Eight pairs of footprints encircled the rock, the feet in each set parallel, no sign of movement, no tracks leading away from the rock.

The creatures simply…evaporated.

She lowered the scope. Her fingers trembled as she clicked the buttons that shut off the illuminator and the scope itself.

The creatures vacated the cave, hiked here, waited for the light, and disappeared into it. Into a UFO. It was insane. Sure, she believed in UFOs. If hairy hominids shared a connection with them, however, what did that mean for humanity? What truth lay behind the facade?

You won't like the way it feels on your conscience.

An inkling of what Charlie meant tickled her mind. Since she probably imagined Charlie, the thought came from her own mind. A warning to herself because she sensed a discovery coming, one so cataclysmic she wanted to hide from it. She couldn't. She ventured out here for one reason.

For the truth.

Saving Charlie and finding Jim's killer would flow out of the truth. She had believed that. But was it true? Or had she come out here to satisfy her curiosity? No, she couldn't be so cold.

Maybe she could.

The creatures left their cave to join a UFO. Left their cave.

She exhaled with a gasp. Steam jetted out of her mouth. They opened the slab door. She'd heard the eardrum-thrumming groan—just once. They left the front door open. A way in.

She dashed past Rick. He grasped her arm and yanked her backward.

"Where are you going?" he demanded.

"The cave, the door's open."

He freed her arm.

She raced into the trees.

KATY RESTRAINED HER CURIOSITY LONG ENOUGH TO RETRIEVE THE FLASHLIGHT from their campsite before she charged into the cave, past the skulls, halting at the head of the skeleton.

The door stood ajar.

The creatures had pushed the slab out halfway, enough for them to exit. Darkness awaited beyond the opening. She stepped around the skeleton and through the doorway.

Rick, panting as he caught up with her, trailed her through the door.

The flashlight lit a tall, narrow passage cut out of the rock. Beyond the light's beam, blackness pooled in the passageway. She slunk forward. Half a minute later, the passage widened into a cavern about twenty feet across and ten feet long. Another passageway forked off the short side.

Katy stopped. She swept the light over the walls. Images scrolled in and out of sight as the beam swept past them, lines and dots comprising the bodies of animals, spears, hominid figures. Cave paintings. She was standing inside a gallery of hairy hominid art rivaling the Lascaux cave art in France. The art looked so much like the Lascaux paintings that the notion rippled through her mind she had stepped through a space warp into the cave at Lascaux.

When darkness splotched her vision she at last remembered to breathe. The hairy hominids painted.

While some of the images seemed abstract, most were familiar to her. A deer. A black bear. Hominid figures with no necks and red eyes. One image depicted a bird with a long, thin beak curving downward at its end.

Rick moved closer to the drawing of the bird. He touched the black line delineating its body. "Looks like an ibis."

"Wasn't the ibis a sacred bird in ancient Egypt?"

He gave her a look she would've expected if she just discovered the secret of cold fusion. "That's right."

With most guys, she needed to evince a thorough knowledge of pro football statistics or the workings of internal combustion engines to impress them. She impressed Rick by recognizing the name of a bird worshipped by a long-dead culture. Go figure.

She stared at the bird painting. "Ibises are common worldwide."

"What about this one?" Rick snatched the flashlight from her hand, pointing it at a figure sketched on the far wall. "Looks like a hippo to me."

She tromped across the cavern. The closer she got to the figure, the more it resembled a hippopotamus. The ears. The muzzle. Stocky legs. A little tail.

Definitely no hippos in Michigan.

In the painting, a hominid running behind the hippo raised a spear over his head. Hunting. If the hairy hominids depicted themselves hunting hippos they must've hunted, or at least seen, hippos at some point in their history. Hippos lived in Africa. Unless the hairy hominids visited the Detroit Zoo, they hadn't seen a hippo in Michigan.

Rick swung the light up toward the ceiling. Katy gasped. Painted across the ceiling in shades of black and red, in a near life-size portrait, was a giraffe.

"My God." She faced Rick. "Hippos. Giraffes. You know what this means."

He traced the hippo's silhouette with his finger. "They've been to Africa."

"Or they came from Africa."

Neither option soothed her nerves. Whoever or whatever picked up the hominids in the clearing could've taken them to Africa. For what, a vacation? Their species could've arisen in Africa and migrated here thousands of years ago, painting these images back then as a sort of keepsake from their homeland. Yet for all she knew they had painted these pictures yesterday.

She took the flashlight from Rick. "I'm going further into the caves."

The passage leading off the gallery had rough walls. She passed a recess that delved three feet into the walls, a natural fissure in the rock some eighteen inches wide. A matching fissure cleaved the opposite wall a few feet further along the passage.

Rick's breathing echoed behind her. Her own breaths ricocheted off the walls. No helping that. The rock took the slightest sound and magnified it.

Rick grunted.

She glanced back at him. "Sh."

"Wasn't me."

A second grunt reverberated down the passageway. The echo gave the illusion the grunt originated close by when it must've come from up ahead. A hairy hominid was advancing on them.

She pointed at the larger fissure. Rick sidled into it. After she squeezed into the second fissure, he quelled the light. The rock swaddled her in its chill embrace.

Bare feet slapped nearer. The creature grunted. The susurrations of its breathing echoed and multiplied into a burbling, as of water.

Her teeth chattered. She squished her tongue between them.

Yellow light flickered on the rocks. The creature strolled past her carrying a torch fashioned from a tree branch split at one end to form a slot. Into the slot the creature had jammed a length of birch bark, folded several times. The bark, burning at its tip, bathed the passage in amber light. In his other hand the creature grasped a pair of rocks. The rocks were gray in color, shaped like rounded triangles, and rough in texture.

The creature ambled down the passage.

Katy poked her head out of the fissure far enough to see down the passage into the gallery, where the creature had paused. He turned his head side to side, his nostrils wiggling. He shook his head as if satisfied and rotated in a semicircle toward the passage from which he had come. Kneeling, he shoved the torch into the dirt until it stood erect on its own. The creature straightened.

He clapped the rocks together.

From deeper inside the caves, rocks clacked.

The creature trotted down the connecting passageway toward the entrance to the caves. His torch splashed flickering tides of light on the gallery walls.

Hairy hominid voices murmured deeper inside the caves.

Rick stepped out of his fissure. He motioned for her to follow. For once, she shared his concern. If more hairy hominids came through here they might spot her and Rick hiding in the fissures. One creature missed them, but dozens of hairy hominids meant dozens of chances for discovery. She had no desire to find out how hairy hominids punished trespassers.

She and Rick hurried out of the cave. As she hopped around the skeleton outside the door, her throat constricted. A trespasser?

If so, he trespassed long ago. Although Ivan might've lied about the skeleton, hoping to frighten her, she doubted it. He should've known by now fear wouldn't stop her. Besides, he and Warner expected her to lead them to Charlie. He had no reason for wanting her scared off. She believed him about the skeleton.

Believing engendered more questions about the bones. Who, what, why. Fossilization took thousands of years, at least. Answers must wait.

At the mouth of the cave, Rick hesitated. With the night scope, he checked the area outside. Standing on her toes, Katy peeked over his shoulder out the entrance. Shadows on shadows, that was all she beheld.

Rick sneaked out of the cave. He moved by stepping down on his toes the way she did. She hadn't demonstrated the technique for him. He must've picked it up by watching her. Closely.

She grinned, then clamped her lips together. Teeth had shine too.

When they reached the campsite and sat down on the earthen sofa once more, she relaxed. A bit. The creatures were roving the woods, probably hunting. The creature she saw had carried no weapon, only rocks. Based on what she witnessed the other creature do to a beaver, they needed no weapons. Their hands, their enormous strength, were their weapons. Any creature capable of wheeling a rock slab the size of a door in and out of position could surely break a deer's neck. Or a human's. The man whose skeleton now adorned their doorway could've died that way.

The creatures used rocks to communicate or perhaps to frighten their prey. After what she saw and heard the night Pete Kryszka showed her the deer kill stash she'd assumed they used the sounds to communicate, to triangulate their prey's position and telegraph it to each other. If the sound also frightened the prey, the effect was a bonus.

Clack!

Katy froze. Clack-clack! Pulling the Taurus out of her fanny pack, she glanced at Rick. He gripped the .45 in his hand. The clacks hammered in machine-gun bursts now, the beats from two or three sets of rocks overlapping.

The racket stopped. The night sank into a silence deep as the vacuum of space. Katy snatched the night scope off Rick's lap. In the green brilliance she searched for the creatures but found none. Wherever they went, they hid themselves well. The rock clapping had sounded close.

Clack. Even closer. She scanned the base of the hill.

Clack. Clack. Clack!

She surveyed the woods, switching on the illuminator to spotlight the areas between trees. The clacks resounded like drumbeats. A deer scurried out of the trees on the other side of the hill. It galloped past the hill, crashing through saplings and crunching over leaves. A creature bounded after the deer, his footfalls hushed.

The deer and the creature ran into the trees. Foliage veiled them. The deer's crashing silenced. Katy trained the night scope on the spot where the two beasts had gone into the trees.

The creature lumbered into view. He had slung the deer over one shoulder, grasping the animal's rear hooves in one hand. A trio of creatures disunited with the shadows. The foursome trudged around the hill and, momentarily, she heard the woven-twig door scrape shut. The earth groaned as the creatures shut the slab door.

They had carted the deer into their cave. Not a stash pile.

Rick slid the .45 into its holster. "Better get some sleep."

She looked through the woods, between the trees, in the trees, over the top of the hill. Seeing nothing, she turned off the scope and set it on the ground beside her. She felt one of those creepy-crawly sensations in her gut, the kind that made her think someone was watching. Of course someone was—Warner. How close had he gotten? He must've either found Ivan by now or given up on the idiot. A man like Warner wouldn't waste all day searching for Ivan. He would save time for sniffing out her and Rick. While they played in the cave, he could've located their campsite and staked out the location. He might be watching her through his own night scope right now.

She pulled her rolled-up sleeping bag out of her pack. "I have this feeling Warner is close. We better sleep in shifts."

"You sleep. I'll watch."

She wriggled into her sleeping bag. Instead of lying down, she zipped the bag up to her waist and reclined against the hill. Rick sat a few feet away, the .45 in its holster on his lap.

Katy shivered inside her sleeping bag. The temperature was dropping lower than the previous night, possibly near freezing. She pulled the sleeping bag over her arms but left it unzipped. The bag warmed her outside. Inside she had turned into a snowman. Strange lights. Disappearing hominids. Skulls in a cave. Paintings depicting animals found nowhere except Africa.

She wriggled toward Rick. He said nothing when she snuggled against him, her head tucked into the hollow of his shoulder. After a moment he slid his arm around her shoulders.

"I saw Charlie," she said.

He leaned his head back on the hillside.

"He told me the project is over," she said, "and I should go home. Maybe I dreamed it. I really don't know anymore. Could be my subconscious desire to give up or fear about what I'm going to find out here."

"Shut up." He slipped his other arm across her, linking his hands to cradle her against him. "Think about it in the morning."

She closed her eyes. Her mind had slipped partway into sleep. She felt like a feather floating on the ocean. Think about it tomorrow. She liked that idea.

Saturday, October 19

Katy woke an instant later. The sun already peeked over the horizon, spinning pastel streamers of light out across the landscape, winding them between the trees. Not an instant. She had slept for hours.

Rick's arm was still draped around her shoulders. He lay with his head on the hill, eyes shut, mouth open slightly. His free hand rested on the .45, which balanced on his thigh. So much for sleeping in shifts.

She sidled out from under his arm and shimmied out of her sleeping bag. By the time she retrieved the granola bars from her bag, Rick was awake. Sort of. He gazed at her with bleary eyes.

Tossing him a granola bar, she said, "You fell asleep."

"I was resting my eyes."

"Resting." She fought against smiling. "You were practically comatose."

He bit into the granola. While he chewed the bar he watched her eat, sip water, and yawn. She stretched her arms to iron out the kinks. He stared at her. She got a bottle of eyedrops out of her pack. He watched. She dropped the moisturizing liquid into her eyes. He studied her.

She dropped the bottle into her pack. "What is it with you? The staring is giving me the creeps."

He finished the last bite of granola. "You know what happened last night."

"Lots of creepy things."

"No." He looked at her without expression. "We slept together."

She rolled her eyes. "If you want to take it literally. I suppose you'll brag to the hairy hominids about your conquest."

"I think the black one has a thing for you. Might have to fight him for you."

"You'd do that for me?"

"Absolutely."

Sitting back on her heels, she picked up the night scope, which she had left on the ground last night. She tucked it inside her pack.

"About last night," she said. "What we saw in the cave bothers me. But what we saw outside it bothers me more. First there's the light gobbling up those creatures. Then there's the deer they killed and took inside the cave."

"They got hungry. So what, we killed a rabbit."

"Remember what Pete Kryszka showed us, the deer kill stash?"

"I remember you sticking your head in it."

"Do you remember how angry the creatures got when we invaded their stash?"

Rick fidgeted, the cloud of a bad memory settling over his features. "Yeah."

"Those hominids used the same hunting technique—the rocks banged together—but they hid their kill in a stash. These hominids took their kill home."

"They were right outside their cave. Why bother with a stash when you catch dinner right outside your front door?"

"Exactly," she said. "I suspect these creatures have a network of caves under this entire area. They could catch a deer anywhere in their home range and bring it into the nest. I don't think they made the stash."

"Since bears don't make stashes, and I really can't see Pete faking one, I don't get who else could've made it."

"Hairy hominids."

"You just said they *didn't* make it."

"I said *these* creatures didn't make it. I think I know what Charlie saw, why he got excited about the sightings. We have two tribes of hairy hominids out here. One tribe seems relatively benign, the other prone to violence. The violent ones have been encroaching on human territory, making stashes of deer kills and attacking people. For some reason, they aren't satisfied with staying in their own territory."

Rick jumped up. He paced the length of the earthen sofa.

"Maybe," she said, "they're having a war. The one tribe might be pushing the others out because of their violence. The ones encroaching on human areas could be like criminals, cast out for the good of the tribe. The creatures don't realize their fugitives pose a danger to us."

"Or they don't care."

"Possibly."

The idea had quickly sprouted in her mind. Call it a flash of insight or even a revelation. Whatever it was, she felt certain she'd latched onto the reason for Charlie's disappearance. He embarked on a hunt because he realized the creatures had separated into two bands, and he realized what it could mean for humans. A tribe of violent hairy hominids invading human territory. Creatures with enormous strength. Who hated humans. She shivered.

"Still doesn't tell us what they are," Rick said.

"I think the cave paintings are a clue about their origins."

The light she could not explain.

How did a UFO fit into the equation? Accounting for the light was like trying to divide thirteen evenly by two. She had trouble reconciling the cave paintings with the creatures too. If they came from Africa, if they painted the images on the cave walls shortly after migrating, they must've migrated here eons ago. The caves seemed unnatural, more like tunnels carved out of the bedrock than natural hollows. The creatures had thousands of generations to carve out the tunnels. How did they do it? They had no shovels, no tunnel boring machines, nothing more than rocks and possibly spears.

The wind gusted. Leaves rattled down from the treetops. Someone was watching.

Yeah, hairy monsters bent on using her as a doormat.

No, someone else...

Rick paced past her and stopped. With his back to her, he said, "Last night you told me you saw Dad."

"I did." Her mind traveled back in time to the moment she saw Charlie hovering over her. "I thought I did. I don't know."

"He told you to go home."

"I'm not going home."

"Didn't say you should." He turned to her. "Too late for running and hiding. We have to find my father, dead or alive. And we have to figure out what happened, what is happening. I need to know."

"Ivan knows more than he let on. If we can find him, maybe we could drag the truth out of him. Somehow."

Rick stooped beside her. He said with a quiet fierceness, "Let me alone with Ivan and I'll get the truth out of the little toad."

Contemplating the hillside, in her mind she relived the confrontation with Ivan back in the cave. He spoke about the skeleton as if he knew a great deal about bones, especially fossilized ones, and human anatomy. She could think of a dozen explanations for his knowledge. He was lying. He was a doctor. His parents were doctors. The list would fill ten pages. She must find Ivan. Question him.

Let Rick question him. Even better.

Warner was close. She sensed his approach as she might perceive a storm front inching closer by the increase in air pressure, the tang of ozone in the air, and the cloying humidity. He would find them soon, if he hadn't already. He could be watching them now. Waiting. Scheming. Looking for a lake to drown them in.

She clenched her teeth.

"Okay," she said, "we find Ivan. Make him talk."

"Good."

"Then we go back in the caves."

"Don't make me throw you over my shoulder again."

"Don't try it again."

He frowned at her. She stared at him. He looked away first.

She grabbed her pack. "Better hide these. Since Ivan's close by we won't need to carry them with us."

"How do you know he's close?"

"Because he wants what I want." She hopped up. "To get inside those caves."

"You're both suicidal."

"If you want to find your father, if you want to know what happened, the answers are in those caves. Charlie may be in those caves."

Rick picked up his pack. He fumbled with the zipper.

From his demeanor she figured he wanted reassurance she wouldn't risk her life for the truth. She could no more promise him that than she could verify she actually saw Charlie last night. She wanted the truth more than money, more than respect, more than life. It *was* her life.

Charlie said it shouldn't be. He had a point. But she couldn't stop now.

Ivan couldn't stop either. For different reasons, with different intents, they worked toward the same goal. He was close. She could find him.

She must find him.

Ivan crawled out of his sleeping bag, elbowing the pine fronds off himself. He piled them over his sleeping bag and head as protection, should Warner decide night was a good time to search for him.

Or should the Sasquatches decide to hunt him down for trespassing.

No one had found him. Either they didn't care or his trick worked. He decided to think his cleverness paid off. This trip may have been his maiden voyage into the wilderness, but he knew a few things about survival. Staying alive at work had a lot in common with staying alive outdoors. You couldn't let anyone see where you really stood.

So he lied. To most everybody. Big deal. He lied to Warner and the Nazi believed him. Mr. Brilliant Entrepreneur fell for fibs told by his stooge. The guy he paid to spread lies everywhere else. Somehow Warner thought his money made Ivan tell him the truth.

Instead it encouraged him to lie even more. Couldn't let on where he really stood, now could he? The intravenous money drip would shut off.

The caves caught him off guard. Those skulls, that skeleton, holy crap. He'd never seen anything like it, never dreamed of anything like it. Whatever these monsters were, they hated people. Used them as doormats, literally. The bones had fossilized, which meant they either laid there a long, long time or the Sasquatches dug them up elsewhere and reburied them in the cave.

He rolled up his sleeping bag and crammed it inside his backpack. He had a mission now. Get back inside the caves. Get through that monolithic door. Imagine what he'd find beyond it.

The goldmine.

A face materialized in his mind. A voice intoned in his ears. He felt the revolver jammed into his chin. He cleared his throat. Slipping a hand inside his jacket, he caressed the Desert Eagle. From his backpack he got the silencer he had ordered special-made to match the gun. Its polished gold finish glistened in the fire of the rising sun. He screwed the silencer onto the Desert Eagle. He had another mission before he entered the caves. Get rid of Katy Gallagher.

If her boyfriend got in the way, take him out too.

WIND RIPPED THROUGH THE TREETOPS. BELOW, AT GROUND LEVEL, THE GUSTS twirled leaves into mini-whirlwinds then faded into a whisper.

Katy zipped her jacket. Before leaving the cabin, she had checked the weather forecast online. The forecasters called for a front to slide through Saturday afternoon, dropping the temperature a few degrees and generating some showers. Two days had gone by since then. Knowing how weather predictions went, the forecast had likely switched to hurricane-force winds leading into a blizzard.

Though a blizzard concerned her, its hazards dwelled in the future. The wind troubled her now. Its noise masked sounds. A hairy hominid could steal up behind her, knock her skull between two rocks, and drag her back into his cave before she detected his presence. More frightening creatures could sneak up on her too. Like Warner.

She unzipped her fanny pack partway. If anybody attacked, she could reach her gun.

Rick walked ahead of her. They both searched for any signs of Ivan. Though she had wanted to lead, because she knew what to look for, Rick had insisted. Because arguing took time, something she lacked, she let it go. Two days of searching. Eight days since Charlie took off on his hunt. Four days since the hairy hominids attacked him. Too long.

Less than twelve hours since she saw him. Or dreamed him. The incident had felt so real, yet she had felt groggy at the same time. While she trusted her instincts, they could mislead her.

Logic could too. The world didn't always operate on logic, because people ran the world and people often acted in direct opposition to both logic and instinct. She must trust her own instincts. She had nothing else.

She had seen Charlie. He was alive. They were protecting him.

Great. They. She needed more ambiguity in her life.

The wind blustered in her face. She squinted at the trees around her, stripping the vegetation away in her mind, revealing what lay behind it. Trunks. Roots. She looked at the ground. Sign, she must locate Ivan's sign.

She passed a sapling. As her head cleared its trunk, a thin branch cracked and separated from the sapling, tumbling to the ground at her feet. She picked up the branch. It had split. The limb, tipped with green leaves, looked healthy. She bent the limb. The flesh flexed. She dropped the branch.

"Ouch!"

Rick jerked to a halt. He massaged his left forearm.

Katy jogged to him. "What happened?"

"Branch scraped me I guess. Felt like a sandblaster." He lifted his hand. His shirt was ripped. His fingers and shirt were daubed with blood.

No branch scraped him. The sapling branch. Rick's arm. Realization teased her brain. She turned in a circle, slowly, scanning the woods as she turned. Her eyes caught the shimmer of movement. She froze. The sun glanced off a shiny surface no more than twenty yards away. Then it was gone. Someone was shooting at them.

Katy dropped flat on the ground. She yanked Rick down with her. He flattened as she did, his face angled toward hers. The wind masked sounds. She could risk a whisper.

"A gun with a silencer," she said.

"Warner."

"If Warner shot at us, we'd be dead. It's Ivan. It has to be."

Ivan lugged a huge, shiny handgun that she doubted he ever fired before. The weight of it alone could throw his shots off course. The kickback would intensify his mistakes. When he hit Rick's arm, he must've aimed for the head. Luck helped him graze Rick. She could rely on luck to aid the enemy. For herself, she must force luck and opportunity. Ivan had no clue what he was doing. She had some clue. She held an advantage, however slight.

She slid her hand under her belly into the fanny pack. The instant she felt the Taurus' grip in her hand, she slid out the gun.

"Look for the shine," she said. "He's got that absurd gun, look for the flash."

Rick withdrew the .45 from its holster. He rose onto hands and knees.

She tugged his pants leg. "Don't shoot unless you have to. Try to catch him." He nodded.

She gestured past his shoulders. "You go that way. I'll take the other side."

He stared at her briefly. Then he dropped onto his belly and slithered away. The crackling of leaves under him couldn't overcome the whistling of the wind. Katy started in the opposite direction. She would circle around Ivan. Sneak up on the little creep.

She glimpsed a flash and angled toward it. As she neared the spot she crept forward, slinking a hand out ahead, feeling for twigs, lifting them out of the way, pushing her body forward with her toes. The wind calmed for a moment and she stopped to listen. Breathing. Panting. Straight ahead. She inched closer.

Around the trunk of a maple, she spied the toes of boots.

She slithered closer. The boots were attached to legs. Closer. Ivan's head came into view. With the pistol clutched in front of him in his right hand, he supported the weapon with his left. He squinted down the barrel. Sweat rolled over his temples.

She pushed up onto hands and knees. Ivan was fixated on the area where she and Rick had ducked below the vegetation.

She raised the Taurus.

A figure arose from the shadows beside her. She noticed the gun too late. It was already aimed at her head.

She glanced at the Taurus in her hand. Warner shook his head. In her mind, she cursed herself. Beyond Ivan, she caught a wink of movement. Rick.

She lowered her arm but kept the Taurus in her fist. "Hey Ivan."

Warner grabbed her hair, yanking her head backward. She gasped. Her scalp burned. Pains shot over the crown of her head, down her face.

Ivan spun toward the sound. His arms wavered, the gun jittered. Noticing Warner, he dropped his arms to his sides.

"Dang, Warner," he said, "I wanted to waste her."

"I am not killing her." He aimed his steel-cold gaze at her. "Yet."

She said, "You mean ever."

"Drop the pistol."

"Shoot me. I'd rather die than be your prisoner."

She avoided looking in Rick's direction. Though she had seen movement, which must've been him, she couldn't let Warner know about it. One twitch of her eyes and he would know. He was that kind of man.

The most dangerous kind.

Charlie acted surprised that Warner had come after him, that he would use her to do it. That he would kill her. That he had killed Jim. She had no idea

Charlie knew Warner. If he did, she had no idea how he could believe Warner innocent. Looking in the man's eyes gave all the proof she needed that he had killed before and would kill again.

Ivan sauntered closer. "Your Glock can't blow her brains out as good as my Desert Eagle. Let me do it."

"*Sit down.*"

Katy studied Warner peripherally. She could shoot him now, while he and Ivan bickered. Her instincts warned her his reactions were faster than hers. He exuded the calmness of a panther stalking its prey.

Ivan aimed his gun at her.

Two guns on her. One idiot who would miss but might still hurt her. One killer who would never miss.

Come on, Rick, hurry up.

R ICK EASED THE .45'S BARREL BETWEEN TWO BRANCHES. THE PINE NEEDLES obscured his view. He had no choice. He needed the cover.

Katy looked mad. Furious, actually.

He leveled the .45 at Warner's head. He had one shot. If he missed, Warner would kill Katy. He hadn't shot a gun in months. If he missed...

Katy would know to duck as soon as he fired. He had *no choice.* Hooking his finger over the trigger, he closed one eye and sighted down the barrel.

The instant he squeezed the trigger, a mass of black hair descended out of the maple tree beside Katy and Warner. The .45 jerked. His shot veered right of Warner.

The creature shrieked. It smacked Warner across the face. The gun flew out of Warner's hand. The creature slugged him in the chest. Warner's mouth dropped open. He wheezed, stumbled backward. Ivan screamed.

Katy rolled away.

Rick bolted through the pine branches toward her.

Warner collapsed onto his back, gasping.

Ivan screamed and fled.

The creature lunged at Warner. It seized his jacket, hoisted him overhead.

As Rick raced past the creature, Katy leaped up. She took off after Ivan.

"Katy no!" Rick shouted.

She kept going. He rushed after her.

Warner howled behind him. He glanced back. Warner lay sprawled on the ground, dazed and panting. The creature had dropped him.

It was hurtling after Rick.

14

HIS LEGS PUMPING AS FAST AS HIS HEART, RICK CHARGED AFTER KATY. HER head bobbed in and out of the foliage. He no longer saw Ivan ahead of her. The creature grunted behind him in time with its thundering footfalls.

The wind cast flurries of leaves everywhere. The treetops swayed. Each gust shoved him sideways. He stumbled, lurched forward several feet, leaped upright, and hurtled after Katy. Her hair, flying around her head, guided him. If he lost sight of her—

He wouldn't.

The creature snorted. Closer.

Katy's head dipped out of sight. A hairy hand clutched at his arm. He pushed harder, his leg muscles burning, his chest aching. Katy, where was Katy.

The creature clawed at him. Its fingers snagged the collar of his jacket, pulled, slipped. The motion threw him off balance and he plunged into a pine sapling. Needles scratched at his face. He stumbled through the branches into a clearing and slumped onto the ground. The creature stomped past him.

He rolled onto his side. This was the same clearing he and Katy found last night. The clearing where the creatures disappeared into the light. He lay at the end farthest from the rock.

His pursuer stopped in the center of the clearing. Sighting Rick, the creature strode toward him. The hominid had set his mouth in a firm line and fisted his hands at his sides. The longer hair on his shoulders flapped with each step. Eyes narrowed and glowing red, he glared at Rick.

The creature growled.

He looked like the creature Katy chased their first day in the woods. The one she named Garfield or Yoda. Like Katy said, you had to call them something, so he'd pick Garfield. Katy said Yoda was dangerous, but she thought the creature she chased was harmless. This must be Garfield. He sure didn't look harmless now.

Rick swung the .45 toward the creature's head.

Garfield halted at Rick's feet. He canted his head, nostrils flaring, eyes widening.

Rick tensed his trigger finger.

Garfield bared his teeth. A growl germinated deep in his chest.

Shoot. Don't shoot. Damned if he knew which was the right thing to do. Garfield chased him, tried to grab him, but didn't hurt him.

Garfield darted his gaze around the clearing. He let out soft grunts reminiscent of "oomph-oomph." His nostrils wriggled as if he had caught a scent or was trying to catch a scent.

Rick breathed through his mouth. He caught a scent all right. The fumes wafting off Garfield could melt silver.

A gale tore through the clearing. Garfield sprinted across the clearing into the trees, moving in silence.

Rick collapsed onto his back. His chest heaved. Despite the chill borne on the wind, sweat beaded on his forehead and dribbled down the bridge of his nose. He swiped it away with the back of his hand.

Katy. He jumped to his feet. Where was Katy?

He lost sight of her when she entered the clearing. Her head dipped below the vegetation. If she had fallen, he should've noticed her lying on the ground inside the clearing. She could've gotten up and taken off after Ivan again.

Sign, Katy would look for sign. He should do that now.

A search of the clearing netted him nothing. His own footprints and those of the creature obliterated anything else. He found no prints leaving the clearing other than Garfield's. He should've seen Ivan's prints exiting the clearing. Ivan must not have come this way.

But Katy came this way. She was following Ivan.

Rick circled the perimeter of the clearing one more time. As he walked past a large pine, a patch of leaves drew his attention. He backed up to analyze the leaves. Some were tamped down. In his mind he traced a line around the tamped-down area. It was the shape of a boot print. The toe pointed at the pine's trunk.

He tiptoed closer to the tree. Another print had squished pine needles into the earth at the base of the trunk. The other foot came down behind it to leave a partial imprint. Rick scrutinized the tree. He found, stuck to the bark partway up the trunk and smeared with dirt, a leaf. Yes.

The pine creaked in the wind. Rick tilted his head back, squinting up the trunk into the mesh of branches above. At first he saw nothing, until he remembered what Katy said about looking through the vegetation. He let his eyes lose focus. A shape emerged from the chaos, a form huddled on a branch ten feet off the ground. Boots jutted out underneath. Ivan was hiding in the tree.

The pine stood fifty feet tall, its branches fanning out six feet on either side. The tree, a foot wide at the base, narrowed higher up the trunk.

Rick found a foothold and hoisted himself up the trunk. He planted his right foot on a branch. From here he could use the branches as a ladder. They were close together, thick enough to support most of his weight. He pushed up a few feet.

Ivan stirred. Rick paused, glancing up at him. The Desert Eagle glimmered.

"Don't move," Ivan said, his voice quavering. "I'll shoot you. I will."

"I've seen your shooting. Gotta say, not impressive." Rick grabbed a higher branch, pulled his foot up. "I'm betting I can get up there and wring your neck before you get off a shot that even grazes me. Fear makes a person unsteady. Now which one of us looks scared?"

The gun trembled, shooting off rays of sunlight. Ivan holstered the weapon. He pushed onto his feet. The branch undulated. Ivan grabbed another branch for support.

Rick surged upward.

Ivan leaped out of the tree. He thudded onto the ground below.

Rick jumped down. He landed alongside Ivan, who had ended up on his belly. Eyes shut, face pinched, Ivan rolled onto his back and clutched the left side of his abdomen. Rick thrust a hand inside Ivan's jacket. He yanked out the Desert Eagle.

Ivan whimpered. "Think I cracked a rib on that pistol."

"This is no pistol." Rick tucked the gold gun inside his waistband. "It's a pocket cannon. You don't have the muscle for it."

He seized Ivan's jacket, hauling him onto his feet. Ivan grimaced. While he held Ivan with one fist, Rick rammed the .45 into the man's temple.

"Where's Katy?" Rick asked.

"If you lost your girlfriend, it ain't my problem."

Rick hoisted him off his feet. "It is now."

"I don't know," Ivan whined. "The earth swallowed her."

"Wrong answer." Rick lunged forward, pinning Ivan's back against a tree. "Talk sense. I'm out of patience."

"That's what it looked like, I swear! She was there and then she wasn't. Looked like she fell through the ground."

Rick studied Ivan's face, the lines engraving valleys across his forehead and around his mouth, the color leaching out of his skin more each second. He wanted to believe the man was lying because, if Katy had "fallen through the ground," he'd lost her. The hairy hominids must've taken her into their caves. How could get to her there?

In Ivan's face, he recognized the signs of a man telling the truth for the first time in years, maybe in his entire life. Rick swallowed hard despite the grit in his throat. They had Katy.

He smashed his elbow into Ivan's gut. "Tell me *exactly* what happened. Starting with the second Garfield came out of that tree."

"Garfield?"

Rick hesitated. "The creature."

"You naming them now? How domestic."

"The creature came out of the tree. Then what?"

"I ran of course! No idea where I was going, I just had to get away. Your girlfriend started after me and she looked so ticked I thought—anyway, I was running. About then a second monster came out of nowhere ahead of me and I went after it, don't know why. Seemed like the thing to do. It led me into this clearing. When I got here the monster was gone but your girlfriend was still coming, so I hid in the tree. That's when she ran into the clearing and fell through the ground. Hell if I know what happened."

Rick glared at him.

"If you don't believe me," Ivan said, "go see for yourself. Her gun's on the ground where she fell. Must be footprints or something."

Rick glanced sideways into the clearing. "Where?"

Ivan flapped his arm toward the rock. "Over there."

Katy vanished near the rock where a light had swallowed eight creatures. He saw no light, which at least gave him hope she went into the caves instead of the heavens. Katy was right, Ivan knew more than he let on. Rick knew he should question Ivan. But he had to find Katy. She might be injured, lost, trapped under tons of rubble, tied onto a rotisserie while hairy hominids lit a fire beneath her. He must find her.

He couldn't let Ivan go.

He must find her.

Ivan squirmed. Rick shoved him aside. Ivan stumbled, hit the ground hip-first.

Rick strode into the clearing toward the rock. Behind him, leaves crackled and twigs crunched as Ivan scurried away. Rick stopped ten feet from the rock. In the brown grass, flat on its side, lay Katy's Taurus revolver. When he bent down to grab it, he scanned the area beside it and the boot prints mashed into the earth there. Katy's boot prints. After following her for three days he knew her boot prints as well as he knew the layout of his apartment in Boston.

Backing up, he traced the prints into the melee of markings he and the creature engraved nearer the trees. Katy had run across the clearing toward the rock. Back where he found the gun, he noticed how her right boot had impressed a clear outline of the sole, including its pattern of ridges and grooves reproduced in the negative. The left print, ahead of the right, had impressed only the heel, which slipped forward obliterating the pattern. The heel print was cut off at the back.

Cut off. He dropped onto hands and knees until his cheek rested flush with the ground. The ridge around the print plunged downward as if the print continued under the ground. As if someone raised a section of earth and flopped it back down after Katy passed through the area. But Katy's prints ended here.

The earth swallowed her. He had taken Ivan's statement for an exaggeration. Maybe he shouldn't have.

An animal growled nearby. He held his breath, turned his head toward the sound. The wind gusted. The trees swayed and creaked. He must've heard a tree groaning.

Lying on his stomach, he scanned the ground for any hint of what happened. The ground looked like ground. What did he expect? A door knob?

A door. Since the hairy hominids used a rock slab as a door, why not the earth itself? If they cut trap doors into the ground that would explain how the creatures could disappear. Although it didn't explain the ones who disappeared into the light, he'd take whatever explanations he could get.

The unknown is frightening. Katy was right again.

He felt along the ground for a seam. When he found none, he dug his fingers into the earth at the point where Katy's boot print ended. His fingers slipped down into the dirt. Too easy. He pulled his fingers out and shoved them back into the gap. He'd found a seam.

Retracting his fingers, he rose onto his knees and plunged both hands into the seam. At first no more than his fingertips would fit, but the more he pushed the more of his hands he got into the seam. He pulled. Nothing moved.

At the third knuckle his hands would go no deeper. He pulled up until his shoulders throbbed. Nothing happened. The door was meant to open from the inside.

He yanked his hands free. Dirt speckled his fingers, crusted under his nails. He wiped his hands on his jeans. Katy was under there. He felt it.

He must find a way in. Planting a hand on either side of the trap door, he stared down at it as if he could will the contraption to open.

Hang on, Katy.

DARKER THAN NIGHT. NO MOON. NO STARS. COLD EARTH PRESSED AGAINST HER backside. Katy turned her head, but the blackness surrounded her. Falling, she remembered falling.

She was not alone.

The sensation struck her a second before the creature moved, its feet swooshing on the earthen floor. It grunted. Hairy hands slipped under her body, lifted her into hairy arms that carried her through the blackness. As they traveled, the ground descended. She felt the forward motion of a downhill grade.

A glow seeped into the darkness up ahead. As they neared it, the light strengthened, flickered. The creature carrying her rounded a bend into a chamber carved out of the bedrock. In the middle of the chamber stood a torch, its end shoved into the dirt. Another torch was posted near a passageway at the other end of the chamber. An auburn-haired creature slept near the passageway on its side, facing the wall.

The creature plopped her down at the corner farthest from the sleeping hominid. Her benefactor, a tawny-haired female, watched her for a moment before walking into the far passageway. Katy leaned against the wall. The rock chilled her through her jacket.

The creature returned a few minutes later with a pile of twigs under one arm and a clump of dried moss in one hand. In her other hand she cupped two rocks. Because of the golden hues highlighting her tawny hair, Katy named the female Goldie. The creature kneeled before Katy, the longer hairs on her head falling over her face.

Katy's teeth chattered. She pulled the jacket tighter around her.

Goldie set the larger sticks aside. She stacked the twigs into a teepee shape around the moss. She picked up the rocks. Spotting the flecks of gold within them, Katy recognized the rocks as iron pyrite, fool's gold. Goldie struck the rocks against each other. Sparks flitted off the stones onto the stack. Within five minutes smoke spiraled up from inside the stack.

In less than ten minutes Goldie had a small fire burning. Snapping a larger stick into quarters, she set the pieces onto the fire.

Katy stayed against the wall. The fire looked nice and warm, but for all she knew Goldie made it for roasting the filet of Katy she intended to slice off her body.

Little flames licked the air. Goldie gestured at the fire.

Katy held still. Goldie waved at the fire, Katy, the fire.

Katy slid closer. Goldie held her hands over the fire and nodded, grunting. Katy stretched out her hands. The warmth penetrated the chill that had overtaken her.

Goldie exited via the passageway.

Once the chill dissipated from her bones, Katy sat back. The chamber was oblong in shape with a passageway leading off one end, where Goldie had exited. At the opposite end a tunnel formed a T intersection—the tunnel through which Goldie carried her into the chamber. The tunnel was bored out of the earth, descending toward the chamber and the system of caves connected to it. The passageway was hewn from solid rock like the chamber and the caves she and Rick explored last night. The hairy hominids had quite a subterranean world.

The creature reclining against the far wall moaned.

Katy slipped a hand inside her fanny pack. The Taurus was gone. Uh-oh. She must've dropped it when she fell through the earth. She hadn't even noticed. She had no explanation for how she ended up in the tunnel. Falling. Darkness. Hitting the earth. The world disappeared like the sun dipping below the horizon, except the horizon rose instead of the sun setting.

The creature rolled over. Her breasts flopped onto the dirt. She glared at Katy with eyes so dark the pupils blended into the irises. From deep in her chest rumbled a growl.

It was the creature that chased Ivan. The creature he or Warner shot.

Katy grabbed a stick. At six inches long and a quarter-inch wide it hardly qualified as weaponry. She'd take what she could get. At least she felt armed.

The creature edged closer to the nearest torch. The light dispersed the shadows from her body, revealing three wounds across her chest and shoulders and one in her arm. Blood caked around the holes, matted her hair. Her lips vibrated as she uttered a growl.

Katy dropped the stick. The creature was injured, possibly dying. She posed no threat. For the moment.

Goldie marched out of the passageway holding a wooden bowl. She approached the wounded creature, kneeling beside the female. With her fingers Goldie applied a gooey substance from the bowl to the injured creature's wounds. The substance glistened golden in the torchlight. Honey.

She remembered reading honey had antibacterial properties. If applied to a wound it would prevent infection. The hairy hominids must know.

The injured creature howled. She knocked the bowl out of Goldie's hand. The injured female focused on Katy. She screamed and slammed her fists into the dirt.

Goldie grunted. The creatures exchanged a series of grunts, growls, and hacking sounds. Finally, the injured female flopped over to face the wall. Goldie left again.

Katy relaxed against the wall. Great. They left her alone with a homicidal hominid.

She had thought of a name for the injured female. Bonnie, as in Bonnie and Clyde. How long would the creatures leave her here? What would they do with her later?

She hugged herself, drawing her knees up to her chest. Maybe she didn't want to know. So she'd sit here awaiting her fate?

No way. She stood. The smoke from the little fire drifted into the tunnel. Bending over the torch nearest her, she clasped both hands around it and pulled. The torch popped out of the ground. She careened backward, caught herself. From the corner Bonnie snored softly. Katy marched into the tunnel.

The smoke guided her left. The ground ascended. The earthen walls narrowed. She reached a dead end. From the boot prints impressed in the floor she surmised she'd fallen into the tunnel here.

She raised the torch toward the ceiling three feet above her head. The creatures had affixed a wood peg to the ceiling. Around the peg, a line incised a rectangle in the earth.

A portal.

At three feet by two feet the opening would admit one hairy hominid. The system must require one creature to shove the portal open for the other who waited above. They must have a signal to let the doorman know when his brethren needed the portal opened.

They knocked rocks together as a signal when hunting. The creatures had proven their ability to plan ahead. They might simply agree ahead of time where the ones who ventured outside would reenter the caves. The doorman could wait here and, when he heard the thundering of hominid feet overhead, shove the portal open. The other creature jumped in, the portal was shut.

She craned her neck back, gazing at the portal. Rick was up there. Undoubtedly mad at her for chasing Ivan but more concerned for her safety. She had no way of letting him know she was okay. No way of letting him know where she was.

Of course she had a way. She had a GPS radio in her fanny pack. The buddy tracker would lead him straight to her, if he thought of checking it.

He would think of it.

Withdrawing the GPS from her fanny pack, she flipped the power switch. Now it emitted a signal Rick could trace.

She looked up at the portal. *Please remember the GPS.*

Rick CROUCHED AT THE TRAP DOOR. MAYBE THE HATCH NEEDED A MAGIC SPELL to open it.

He'd tried prying at it with his fingers. That accomplish nothing except making his fingers ache. He located a small branch and tried levering the door out of its slot. The branch got stuck. It snapped in half when he yanked on it. He had used up every idea in his brain.

He sat back on his heels. The door refused to open for him.

Although the idea sounded ridiculous, he swore he felt Katy underneath the door, gazing up at him. If he uncovered another way in, if he figured out where the creatures took her, he had a chance of finding her. Alive.

The GPS radio. He had watched Katy check hers in case Dad's radio still gave off a signal. It didn't, but watching her had familiarized him with the GPS's tracking feature. If she had hers with her, if she turned it on, he could track her.

She had it with her. She kept the radio in her fanny pack, which she wore even while sleeping. The question was, had she turned on the unit.

One way to find out. Unfortunately, he forgot his GPS radio in his pack. They hid their packs under a tree and piled leaves over them. He needed to find his way back to the hill where they had camped before he could locate Katy.

He laid a hand on the trap door. He hated leaving, especially when he sensed Katy so close. What did he think, he was psychic now?

A gale ripped through the clearing. He shut his eyes until the gust subsided. Clouds had moved in, blotting out the sun intermittently, painting shades of gray and purple across the sky. A storm was coming. Before they left Katy's cabin, she had said no rain until Saturday at the earliest. Today was Saturday, wasn't it?

Each time the wind blustered it felt chillier. Might snow instead of rain.

He had to find Katy.

Three people and two hairy hominids careening through the woods left a trail a nearsighted person could track from outer space. He let the mess of prints lead him back to the tree where Garfield attacked Warner. If a herd of cattle stampeded over the tract, they could not have disturbed the ground more. He backtracked along the route he took in sneaking behind Ivan. Though he had crawled on his belly most of the way, his toes and knees had imprinted the ground. Here he thought he did such a good job of hiding his presence.

Half an hour later, after three wrong turns and five minutes during which he etched a circle in the woods with his footprints, he found the hill. At the base, on the side opposite the cave entrance, he located their packs. After he dragged his out from under the leaves, he stuffed Ivan's Desert Eagle inside it. He got out his GPS radio, flipping the power switch. The buddy tracker latched onto Katy's signal.

Thank goodness, she had her unit on.

He turned to leave, hesitated. If she was hurt, he would need the first aid kit. Water too. The hairy hominids might prevent them from coming back to this spot. The creatures didn't like humans poking around their territory.

He couldn't carry both packs, they were too big. He consolidated their equipment as much as possible and hefted one pack onto his back. The weight pulled on his shoulders. Leaning forward as a counterbalance, he followed the route prescribed by the GPS.

After fifteen minutes he realized it was taking him back to the trap door.

KATY HUDDLED NEAR THE FIRE. GOLDIE HAD COME BACK TEN MINUTES EARLIER with more tinder, refueling the shrinking blaze. Bonnie was still asleep. Or unconscious.

Katy wrung her brain for at least half an hour for a way to access the portal, yet squeezed not one drop of an idea from her cerebrum. The portal was too high to reach. She needed a stool or a ladder. Goldie supplied her with no ladders, and the chamber held nothing she might fashion into one. Unless she could levitate, she was stuck.

The passageway must lead somewhere.

She got up. Goldie left minutes ago. She must've gone out of earshot, and eyesight, by now. The creature's demeanor gave Katy the impression she better stay here, despite Goldie's generosity in providing a fire.

Katy tiptoed over the threshold of the passageway. Dark. She retrieved the torch. No creatures guarded the passage. She skulked down the rock-hewn corridor, feeling the chill close in around her. The torch lit the passage for fifteen feet ahead of her, where the darkness devoured its light.

The passageway widened. She crossed a threshold into a chamber whose walls spread further apart than the torch's light stretched. The dirt floor was lumpy. She stiffened, a gasp trapped in her throat. The floor wasn't lumpy. The bumps were bodies. The slumbering forms of hairy hominids.

Some reclined on their backs, their chests rising and falling, their breaths echoing off the walls, a dozen sighs coalescing into the susurration of waves lapping against the shore. Others dozed on their sides with arms draped over their hips and down their thighs or bent with hands under their cheeks. The creatures slept in two groups. A three-foot-wide space, a walkway, separated the groups.

If not for the hair, she might've mistaken them for humans napping.

A creature near her stirred. He mumbled, his lips twitching.

She backed into the passageway. She kept backing up until the torch no longer penetrated the sleep chamber.

Tawny-haired arms grabbed her around the waist. Goldie plucked her off her feet. The torch slipped from her grasp, rolled across the floor. Goldie swung around and stomped down the passageway, through the opening, and into the chamber where Bonnie rested.

Goldie threw Katy down on the floor. Her shoulder landed on a rock. Her hip smacked into the compacted earth. Pangs ricocheted through her body. She turned over onto her back. Goldie yelled at her, the sound a cross between a lion's roar and a shriek.

Goldie stamped out of the chamber. She returned a moment later carrying the torch. As she jammed the torch into the dirt, she snarled at Katy.

When Goldie was gone, Katy scrambled to her feet. Time to get out. Now.

Wrenching the torch out of the floor, she hurried down the earthen tunnel. Once she reached the portal, she stopped to glance around the area. Nothing but dirt. If she piled the dirt high enough, she might reach the portal by standing atop the mound. Shouldn't take too much dirt.

She planted the torch in the floor. With her hands she clawed at the walls. Chunks of earth broke away, toppled onto the floor. She swept the chunks into a pile and tamped them down under her feet. She pawed more chunks out of the wall. The pile enlarged. After she dug a hole in the wall large enough to accommodate a coffin, she tested the height of the pile by stepping onto the summit and hefting her weight onto it. The dirt shifted. A mini landslide slumped onto the floor. She steadied herself and stretched her hands toward the portal. Her fingers grazed the ceiling. She grabbed at the wood peg. Her hand closed around it.

"No, Katy."

She swiveled her head toward the voice. At the periphery of the torch's light, hands grasping the Remington .30-06 rifle, aiming the muzzle at her, hunched Charlie.

"Come down from there," he said.

The peg clutched in her hand, perched on tiptoes, she stared at him. He was real. She had seen him. He had told her to go home. She did not dream the conversation.

He shuffled into the torchlight. She noticed his finger cupped around the trigger. He was threatening to shoot her.

She opened her mouth. The words lodged in her throat.

"If you try escaping," he said, "they'll kill you."

"If they wanted me dead they'd have done it already."

He scrunched his forehead. "No, not them. The others."

She let go of the peg. "What others? Stop talking all mysterioso like we're in a horror movie and you're the gypsy fortune teller. Tell me what on earth is going on."

The Remington's muzzle pointed straight at her head. If he pulled the trigger, the bullet would splice her skull.

She hopped off the mound. "You really going to shoot me?"

"No." He slung the rifle's strap over his shoulder. "Safety's on."

"Why threaten me at all?"

"To get your attention. Takes a lot to break through that steel-reinforced will of yours. Thought a rifle might do the trick."

"First you threaten to shoot me, now you insult me. Don't think I like you anymore, Charlie."

"Sorry."

She rushed forward and hugged him quickly, backing away before he could reciprocate. Didn't want him thinking she forgave him. Since she last saw him a week ago, discounting last night, a hug seemed appropriate. Especially since she had thought he might be dead.

He plucked the torch from its roost. "Let's get you back to the holding cell before the warden comes back."

"Holding cell. Am I a prisoner?"

"In a way." He proceeded down the tunnel with her in tow. "They want to protect you but they can't risk letting another human into the fold. That's why you wound up in the holding cell with the condemned female."

"They're executing her?"

"Not precisely."

They entered the holding cell. Charlie shoved the torch into the floor and sat cross-legged against the wall near the fire. He gestured for Katy to join him. She sat down beside him, knees drawn up to her chest, arms wrapped around them.

"They only execute for murders," Charlie said. "This one caused a ruckus but didn't kill anyone. She will be transferred."

"Where?"

"They had been banishing the delinquents to the perimeter of the forest. They've been getting in trouble with humans, though, which puts the entire population at risk. When the outcasts attack humans, they bring attention to the species, attention which could bring hunters and scientists into the area. The creatures want no attention. They can't banish anymore."

Slipping the rifle's strap off his shoulder, he dropped the weapon on the floor.

Katy glanced at Bonnie. The creatures had begun attacking humans. People wouldn't accept hairy monsters attacking their loved ones, threatening their lives, invading their territory. Just as the creatures disliked humans entering their territory, humans disliked the hairy hominids infringing on theirs. The two species could never live together.

The hairy hominids did more than endanger human lives, they endangered a mindset ingrained in the human psyche—namely, the belief *Homo sapiens* evolved from apelike hominids over millions of years. The belief humans represented the pinnacle of evolution. The need to believe humans alone possessed the capacity for self-awareness, forethought, culture.

These hominids had a culture. They had morals, laws, and paradigms to follow. Perhaps humans couldn't understand the hairy hominid culture, but an inability to comprehend did not nullify its existence. Humans no longer reigned on the throne of evolution.

"What *do* they do with the outcasts?" she asked.

"Send them away." He rolled his eyes heavenward. "Far away."

"The ones who disappeared into the light last night. They were outcasts?"

"No, that must've been a tribunal going to commune with the gods."

"How do you know all this?"

Charlie shrugged. "Context. Assumption. Logic. In other words, pure guesswork."

"Why would they care about protecting me?"

"They sensed I care about protecting you. They're very intuitive creatures. Blackie saw a picture of you in my wallet and, when he saw you in the woods, he followed you."

"Blackie? Guess you mean Garfield."

"Afraid I'm not terribly imaginative with names." He grabbed a twig and stoked the fire. "Yes, Garfield. He was watching over you. For me."

She looked at him sideways. "You have a picture of me in your wallet?"

"Of course. Right next to Rick's picture." He winked at her. "Seemed fitting."

Her cheeks flushed. She fussed with her hair as an excuse to shield her face.

"Apparently they decided you should be here," Charlie said. "For protection. They probably chased or led you to the trap door and—floop!—in you went."

She recounted the chase in her mind. She had pursued Ivan, Rick pursued her, and Garfield trailed after all of them. Though Ivan led her into the clearing, she'd spied a brown shape ahead of him. The memory of it had slipped to the back of her mind. It could've been another creature. They lured her into the clearing, using the tools at hand, namely Ivan. They captured her.

"What will they do with me?" she asked.

"Keep you."

RICK STOOPED BEHIND A VEIL OF PINE BRANCHES AT THE EDGE OF THE CLEARING. He watched the trap door.

No way in. He had tried everything. Now he could think of nothing else besides waiting for a creature to happen by and use the door. Once the creature jumped in, he would follow. He could hear Katy's voice in his head saying, *what if they slam the door shut before you get there?*

The plan stank. He was waiting at the wrong door. When the creatures abandoned their cave last night, they left the slab door open. They might do it again.

He could wait hours for them to come out of the cave. Unless he gave them a reason for showing themselves.

What would inspire a hairy hominid to step outside?

An idea came to him. He trekked back to the hill. The creatures had replaced the woven-twig door. He hefted it aside and marched into the cave, pulling out the flashlight as he descended into the darkness. The beam cut a swath through the false night. Rays bounced off the skulls. In a couple minutes he arrived at the skeleton. The slab door hulked before him. He clipped the flashlight onto his belt.

Scenes of the worst-case responses flashed through his mind.

Zipping his jacket to hide the .45 holstered on his hip he collected Ivan's gun from the pack, along with cotton gauze from the first aid kit. The gauze he stuffed in his ears. Shuffling backward a few steps, he raised the gun at the door and fired. The shot exploded, earsplitting despite the cotton. Shards of rock sprayed from the door. He fired another round.

The explosion sucked the silence into it like a black hole consuming light. When the echoes died, he pulled the cotton out of his ears.

Minutes ticked past.

He leveled the Desert Eagle at the door. Looked like he needed another shot to wake up the sleeping giants.

The cave groaned. The ground trembled.

The door crept outward in an arc, a millimeter per second. As the door parted from the wall, a creature came into view behind it, his hand flat against the door, biceps bulging, teeth bared and clenched. With the door open halfway, he stopped. He glowered at Rick, the backs of his eyes aglow with red fire.

The creature shrieked.

Rick tossed the Desert Eagle at him and threw up his hands.

Nose twitching, the creature nabbed the gun. He flipped it over in his hand, caressed the gold finish.

He hurled the gun at Rick. The pistol bounced off the wall and landed near Rick's feet.

The creature lunged at him.

Footfalls echoed down the passageway into the holding cell. Charlie rushed to the threshold. He peered into the shadows beyond, mouth ajar, tongue on his lower lip.

The photo from the Game-Vu camera flashed in her mind. Charlie making that face. A few images later, the creature attacking him.

The footfalls pounded closer. More than one set of feet. Katy leaped up from the floor. Charlie had left his rifle on the ground. She grabbed it, disengaged the safety, braced the butt against her shoulder, and slapped her right hand over the grip. Her left hand supported the barrel. With her finger hovering over the trigger, she aimed at the doorway.

Charlie scuttled away from the threshold. His heels bumped Bonnie, who snorted in response. He trotted toward Katy.

Footfalls shook the floor. A creature bellowed. A second voice shouted "ook-ook" under the first creature's cries. Bonnie raised her head, grunting.

A creature with silver-streaked brown hair surged through the doorway. A black creature hauling a man over his shoulder trotted in behind him.

Katy recognized the boots and clothes. Rick.

The creature hurled Rick across the room. He hit the floor, rolled twice, and wound up on his side facing the tunnel junction. He lay motionless, arms askew, torso twisted.

Katy turned the rifle on the creature who had thrown Rick.

Charlie yanked the gun out of her hands. He locked the safety, then dropped the gun.

Katy ran toward Rick. Charlie thrust an arm in front of her. She felt the anger rising in her chest, distorting her expression, scorching her cheeks. She slapped his arm down. He clamped his arms around her chest to pin her arms at her sides.

His mouth near her ear, he whispered, "Stop fighting or we all die."

Katy slackened her arms and legs. She tried to erase the anger from her features. Didn't feel like it worked.

The creatures retreated. Charlie released her.

She hurried to Rick. His eyes were closed but his breathing seemed normal. When she checked his pulse, it throbbed against her fingers. He had no obvious wounds. Her heartbeat slowed. She took a deep breath and sat down beside Rick. She lifted his head onto her lap, stroking his forehead.

Charlie squatted alongside her. "How is he?"

"Ready for the Olympics, how does he look?" She scowled at him. "How could you do that? They throw your son around and you stand there like it doesn't matter. Should've let me blast them to oblivion."

"They would've killed us all. When they feel threatened, they get very angry. Rick must've upset them."

"It's not his fault."

"I meant inadvertently. You have to understand the way these creatures think. Where humans are concerned, they don't distinguish between accident and intention. They mistrust us, for good reason."

"Evil humans, misunderstood creatures." She shook her head. "You've been living with them too long, Charlie. You are a human, remember? Humans first, creatures second."

"You don't understand."

As she looped an arm around Rick's neck, she flattened her free hand across his forehead. "I understand you'd let them kill Rick rather than throw a stick at one of them."

"Rick was never in danger."

"You said they'd kill us all."

"If we turned against them." He settled a hand on her shoulder. She shrugged it off. "As long as we obey them, they won't hurt us. If they perceive a threat, they react. Sometimes violently."

Rick moaned. His eyelids fluttered. Katy brushed the hair from his forehead. He opened his eyes. "What happened?"

"You almost got yourself killed," Charlie said.

"Dad?" Rick, eyes half shut, gaped at his father. "How…"

"Later."

While Charlie paced the length of the cell, Rick sat up to brace his body with one arm, his palm flat on the floor. Despite the confusion clouding his features and the redness in his eyes, he had returned to normal. When he rubbed his neck, his fingers pushed his shirt collar aside. Bruises had materialized on his neck.

"What did they do to you?" Katy asked.

"Not much." He glanced at his father, who now paced back and forth past the doorway, and then at Katy. "The GPS said you were down here. I needed a way in so I improvised. They weren't happy with me."

Charlie paused. "What did you do?"

"I went back to the cave, the rock door. I shot at it until one of them opened the door. I gave him the gun but he jumped me anyway. Last thing I remember is huge hands around my neck."

She imagined the scene. Her hand ached. She looked down to find her fist clutching a twig. She dropped it. Another snapshot projected on the screen in her mind. Rick tossing his gun at the creature. Her father's gun. Rick's life meant more to her than the gun, but the .45 represented one of the few items of value that belonged to her father. The gun might've saved his life once or twice, and when she looked at it or held it she felt him with her. When she thought of the creatures owning it, her throat constricted.

Trying to sound nonchalant, she asked, "They have the forty-five?"

"I used Ivan's gun. The creature threw it back at me. Probably still in the cave."

"Then you have the forty-five?"

He unzipped his jacket, flipping one side out to show the .45 snug in its holster. She let out her breath.

Rick touched her knee. "You okay?"

She nodded.

Voices murmured in the corridor. Charlie trotted away from the doorway. The murmur silenced, replaced by the rapping of bare feet on the dirt.

"The creatures are coming back," Charlie said. "Do exactly as I say and we might survive."

"I will not kowtow to hairy hominids," Katy said.

"You have to. They don't trust you or Rick, you saw to that."

Her gaze locked on the doorway, her heart beating hummingbird fast, she searched her brain for a plan. None came to her. Obeying Charlie meant ignoring the inner voice warning her of danger ahead, trusting creatures who strangled Rick and attacked Charlie. How Charlie maintained good will toward a species that unleashed its derelicts on humanity baffled her. Why he harbored such an affinity, and perhaps preference, for the hairy hominids she couldn't guess.

If the creatures jumped her, Rick would defend her. If they jumped Rick, she would defend him. What would Charlie do? A week ago, she would've said he would defend her. Now...

The footfalls slapped across the threshold.

"Oh!" Rick pulled her Taurus out of his pocket. He offered it to her, butt first. "I found this."

She accepted the gun. A grunt echoed right outside the doorway. Charlie looked at her, then the gun. Despite the inner voice, despite the tightening in her gut, she tucked the Taurus in her fanny pack and zipped the pack shut.

Two creatures waltzed through the doorway, Goldie and the silver-streaked male. Goldie clutched a torch in one hand. They stopped, one on each side of the doorway. Goldie jerked her head at the passageway.

Charlie walked out of the cell.

Katy followed him. Goldie bared her teeth at her. The creature seized her wrists. The male rushed at Rick, grasping his wrists, and hauled him through the doorway. Goldie dragged Katy after them.

Katy made no struggle. She prayed Charlie knew what he was talking about, prayed he actually had gained an insight into the creatures' mindset during his furlough with them. She prayed he hadn't gone senile.

The creatures dragged them through a series of tunnels. After they rounded a corner into a large chamber, Goldie propelled Katy into the middle of the room. The male dumped Rick nearby. Charlie hunched against the wall.

Goldie drove her torch into the dirt. Its light flickered on the walls. Ghosts of darkness flitted across the rock. Goldie and the male left.

Among the shadows playing over the walls Katy discerned shapes and lines, images of creatures long gone from the planet, scenes of life and death drawn in red, black, and brown. On one wall a hairy hominid, spear in hand, pursued a woolly mammoth while three of his comrades observed. To the left of that scene, a mother hominid carried a baby on her back. She had slung one breast over her shoulder for the baby to suckle. In her hand she carried a small animal akin to a beaver, which sported six-inch teeth lancing down from its upper jaw.

Further left, a herd of creatures similar to horses—except for their long necks and snouts that curved down like mini trunks—grazed while hairy hominids observed.

As she turned a quarter-circle, the images grew stranger. An eel-like creature with a whip tail and a maw that gaped three times the width of its body swam across the wall. A saber-toothed cat snarled at a figure clad in a jumpsuit. A globe-shaped helmet concealed the figure's head. At the front of the helmet, two black eyeholes shaped like enormous almonds gaped back at the cat.

She returned her attention to the hunting scene. An element of the scene she missed before leaped out at her as if someone shined a spotlight on it. Above the heads of the hominids, emitting a beam of what must've been light, hovered an ovoid craft.

And in the beam, rising toward the craft, a hairy hominid.

15

KATY STARED AT EACH IMAGE IN TURN, HOPING TO BURN THEM ONTO THE disk of her memory. She must remember them. She must find out what they were. The images meant something. If she identified the animals in them she might have a clue what the paintings meant.

The saber-toothed cats and mammoths she recognized. First-graders knew about those animals. The animal the mother hominid toted, the fish, and the horse-like animal eluded her. She read books about prehistory and ancient history, and knew she saw these creatures in books, yet the memory lingered beyond her grasp. Her neurons couldn't bridge the gap.

Later. She must remember the images, to look them up at home. If she ever got home.

What will they do with me?

Keep you.

A chill shimmied up her spine. Keep me for what, she had almost asked. Now she was about to learn the answer. This room had the feel of a meeting hall. Humans decorated their courthouses and meeting halls with images of their past—George Washington, Abraham Lincoln—and mythical figures with meaning for them, such as Justice and her scales. Perhaps the hairy hominids observed a similar tradition.

Against the far wall, animal hides lay spread out as blankets over piles of grass and leaves. A rock identical to the ones in the clearings outside sat before the hide seats. A bone rested atop the rock. The arm or leg bone of an animal, a deer perhaps.

She turned to Charlie and Rick. Both men craned their necks to gaze up at the images on the walls. Charlie raised his hands as if to touch the images, a slight smile on his lips. Rick shoved both hands in his pockets, frowning.

To Charlie, she said, "Explain to me what's going on."

"Judgment Day," he said.

"I meant with you."

He jerked his head to look at her, eyes wide. The smile had slipped open.

She crossed her arms over her chest. "Don't give me that innocent look. You know what I mean. What were you doing down here for a week?"

"What we talked about. Studying their behavior, charting their social structure, integrating myself into the group to facilitate further study."

"We talked about watching them from afar in the woods, not living with them. Let me guess, you've taken a mate too. A young blonde?"

"Don't be vulgar."

"Now you're offended." She stalked toward him, jabbing a finger into his chest so hard he winced. "I'm offended! While you were playing Jane Goodall down here, Rick and I were up there risking our lives to find you. Worried you were dead or maimed or worse. Being stalked by murderers and crazy hominids. *You don't even care.*"

His face paled. An emotion flickered in his eyes she had never seen in him. It snuffed out before she could identify it.

Rick took hold of her hand. He pulled her finger away from Charlie's chest as he enfolded his hand around hers, though she tried twisting her hand free. His hand felt hot against hers. She was cold. She hadn't noticed. Her hands were shaking. She'd missed that too.

The shaking spread up her arms into her shoulders, through her neck, chopping her breaths into bite-size bits that stuttered from her mouth. The tremors infected her head, chattered her teeth. They leached down through her abdomen into her legs where her knees quaked, threatening to give out altogether. Her eyes stung. She sniffled.

Rick pulled her closer. Hugging her, he cradled her head against his chest, pillowed her face in his jacket, defeated the chill in her with his own warmth.

The quakes broke the levy and tears flooded down her cheeks. She buried her face in his shirt. If only she could slip through another hole in the ground into darkness where no one would see the tears, where no one could hear her crying. She despised crying, especially like this. A total weep-out. What kind of a weakling had she become?

Rick stroked her hair. He murmured sounds meant to soothe her, which only made her cry harder because she didn't deserve his sympathy. She screwed up. She believed Charlie needed saving, she underestimated the threat posed by Warner and Ivan, she misread the entire situation. She put them all in danger by thinking she was an expert tracker. Some expert. Warner had caught her sneaking up on Ivan.

After the tears stopped, Rick kept his arms around her. And she let him.

Charlie scuffled up beside them. He bent over to peek at her through the strands of hair that fell over her face. His face was pale. His wrinkles had deepened but the corners of his mouth turned down, the start of a frown.

"I am sorry, Katy," he said. "I didn't know you were out here until yesterday."

She pushed the hairs away from her face.

"Last night I was trying to say I'm okay and you shouldn't worry. Guess I mucked that up."

"You said the project is terminated. That means I'm terminated."

"What? No. I meant the hairy hominid project is over, Katy, not the Human Origins Project." As he glanced at Rick, a Santa-like humor glimmered in his eyes. "But if my son would get a move on, I wouldn't need the project to keep you in the family anyway."

Rick tensed. Katy stepped back from him. He pulled a handkerchief from his pocket, handing it to her. She wiped the remnants of tears from her face. Her eyes felt gritty and hot, her throat parched. The aftermath of a freak-out.

"You know," Charlie said, "October is a good month for a wedding."

Katy bit back a chuckle.

Rick pinched his lips. His jaw looked tight enough to grind diamonds into dust. He locked his gaze on the walls and jammed both hands in his pockets.

Charlie continued, "Of course if you wait until December there might be snow."

Katy advanced toward the animal-hide seats and rock table. She picked up the bone, turning it over in her hand.

"Though in my opinion," Charlie said, leaning toward Rick, "you've waited far too long already."

"Give it a rest, Dad."

"How long do you usually wait before you ask a girl out? Two years isn't long enough?"

"Can we talk about this later?"

"Are you afraid of her?"

Rick said nothing. His jaw muscle twitched.

Charlie pressed on anyway. "A lot of young men fear a strong-willed, independent woman. Thought I raised you better—"

"Dad!"

Katy bit her lip to ward off a grin. Over her shoulder, she said, "If you boys can't get along, I may have to separate you."

Rick stomped toward her.

Charlie muttered, "Two years..."

Spying the redness on Rick's face, she said, "Charlie, what do you make of these paintings?"

"They're animals. Extinct ones, I'd say."

"Duh."

"You're the bone freak, you tell me."

"That sounds like an insult. I merely have an interest in paleontology and archaeology."

She set down the bone. As she contemplated the images, she flipped through her memory for information. It was right there, inside her head, if she could just access it.

A horse-like animal with a long snout. She folded her arms across her chest. Horse-like. She tipped her head left.

She clapped her hands. "*Macrauchenia!*"

Rick and Charlie gave her identical looks. Eyebrows scrunched, lips puckered. She bobbed on her toes as she pointed at the horse-like creature.

"This animal," she said, "is called *Macrauchenia*. It's a mammal that lived in South America up until 20,000 years ago. Nobody knows much about it, whether it's related to modern-day mammals or what."

She raised onto her toes, feeling a grin tug at her mouth. "*Macrauchenia.*"

Charlie exchanged glances with Rick. "Knew she'd figure it out."

"What I really want to know," Rick said, "is if the creatures will give me my backpack."

"They took it?" Katy asked.

"I had it when the thing jumped me. Woke up without it."

"They wouldn't take it," Charlie said. "They have no use for it."

Katy gazed at *Macrauchenia*, her moment of discovery gone, the starburst of energy from knowing something no one else did fizzling.

"If they don't have my pack," Rick said, "who does?"

WARNER STUMBLED INTO THE CAMP.

Diane gasped. "What happened?"

He shook off the hand she clasped around his arm. He must appear as beaten as he felt, although the creature had not injured him. His journey back to the camp took longer than expected. The creatures were following him. He saw their eyes in the shadows, heard their breathing beneath the wind, sensed their eyes focused on him like telescopes. He knew what they wanted. His corpse.

They could not have him. His mission was uncompleted. Gallagher and the Bergrens were still out there. Still searching. They came so close to it, to Ivan's "goldmine," that they might have uncovered it by now. He must locate them. Stop them. By whatever means the task required. He had hoped to find Ivan as well, keep the dolt from interfering, but Gallagher and those creatures thwarted his attempts. Gallagher thought he tracked her to the tree.

Good, the knowledge would eat away at her confidence. She need never know his real target had been Ivan.

Warner flopped onto the ground. He rested his head on his backpack, which he left in Diane's care. She crouched beside him. His body ached in places he never imagined possible. A weariness infiltrated him so profoundly he wanted nothing more than to sleep. He must stay awake.

"You should rest, Errie." Diane hugged herself. "I can watch out for the monsters."

"No." He propped himself up on his elbows. "Take my pack. Find the metal box inside and take it out."

She obeyed, retrieving the square box from the bottom of his pack. He had buried it there to conceal it from Ivan. The turncoat might rifle through his pack, however he would give up before reaching the bottom. Ivan lacked patience. It was his greatest weakness and the quality that made him dangerous now.

"Open it," he said.

She flipped up the lid. When she saw the syringes, her jaw dropped.

He laid down. "Fill the syringe to the red line."

"What is this?"

"Vitamin solution."

She grabbed the bottle tucked into the compartment beside the syringes. In her other hand she grasped a syringe.

The bottle did contain a vitamin solution. She might think he lied and was asking her to inject him with amphetamines or opiates. He despised drugs. He dealt with pain and infection in the manner of his ancestors—the Germanic tribes of Europe—by self-medicating with herbal concoctions and poultices, willpower and time.

Nature's remedies had worked for millennia. Modern men believed they knew better than nature, that they could manipulate genes and bombard the body with poisons to eradicate disease. Only now were the ramifications becoming apparent.

Modern men believed they had mastered their world. In reality, they did not even understand their own history. To be precise, their own *prehistory*.

Ivan understood it least of all. Yes, he aided Warner in his mission. Ivan's brain, shriveled from years of disuse, failed to comprehend the truth. Warner had beheld the truth. He had held it in his hand.

The UK and Canadian expeditions changed him. He knew the truth before but seeing it, touching it, made the concept material. The leathery texture of the UK artifact lingered on his skin even now, while a vision of it manifested before his eyes. He slipped a hand into his hip pocket. His fingers grazed the Canadian artifact. He kept it near him always. Its smoothness surprised him each time he touched it. An artifact of such antiquity should feel rough, not glassy.

Unfortunately, the Canadian expedition ended early. The professional he hired contacted the media. Warner spent weeks repairing the damage.

He must return to Canada.

His concern now was Katy Gallagher. What awaited her, and all searchers, out here could destroy his world. Unlike the artifacts he unearthed in Canada and the UK, this truth lacked the power to shatter the whole world. It did however possess the strength to crush *his* world. If Gallagher found it she would use it. She would play a round of show-and-tell certain to destroy him and ravage his family.

He could not allow that.

Meine Kinder, I will defend you. To the death.

Diane tapped the bubbles out of the syringe. She squirted out a jet of the solution. Warner took the syringe from her. He jabbed the needle through his pants leg into his flesh, depressing the plunger.

In a few minutes he would feel better. The vitamins would restore his energy. His resolve needed no restoring. Katy Gallagher could not hide forever.

But he could wait forever to find her.

Diane took the syringe, stuffed it into the box, and snapped the lid shut. After she stuffed the box deep into his pack, she asked, "What will we do now?"

"Wait. The patient hunter finds his prey."

"She won't wait. If she finds it, she could ruin us all."

"You learn your impatience from Ivan."

"No, I learned it from reality. I can't afford the consequences, Errie, my whole life depends on these woods."

A figure shambled out of the shade of a tree. The sun behind him shadowed his features. His voice betrayed his identity.

"As a hunter," Ivan said, "you stink."

Warner stood. He rolled the tightness out of his shoulders. "You went off to be the great woodsman. Now you crawl back to me. Which of us is weak?"

"Ain't crawling back, Warner. I wanna make a deal."

"You have nothing I desire."

"Wrong." Ivan whisked his arm out from behind his back. He clasped a backpack by its metal frame. "Belongs to Gallagher's boyfriend. Found it in the cave. But this isn't the most desirable part."

"You ransacked the contents."

"No, I made a little shrine where I worship it." Ivan thrust his hand into a pocket of the pack and withdrew an electronic device the size of his hand. "This is the deal-making find, my friend. Guess what it is."

Warner scowled at him.

"Two guesses." When Warner said nothing, Ivan huffed. "Jeez, Warner, you're less fun than a tooth extraction. It's a GPS radio."

Ivan held up the device with its LCD screen toward Warner. It was a GPS unit. Warner carried his own GPS. What could he want with Rick Bergren's?

"You're wasting my time," Warner said.

"This GPS has a buddy tracker." Ivan punched keys on the unit. "Right now I'm looking at the exact position of Katy Gallagher. Of course if that doesn't interest you…"

"Give it to me."

"Huh-uh. I want a raise. Triple my current salary."

Warner ripped the Glock from its holster. He trained the muzzle on Ivan's forehead. "I have a counteroffer. Give me the GPS or die."

"Even you aren't that cold-blooded."

Warner tilted his head, letting a hint of a smile grace his lips. "You made a career out of groundless theories. Care to test this one?"

Ivan slouched his shoulders.

"You have five seconds to decide," Warner said. "Four, three, two—"

"Fine!" Ivan lobbed the GPS radio at him. "Take the bloody thing."

The Glock in his right hand, Warner plucked the GPS radio off the ground with his left. Ivan had left the tracking feature on. The screen displayed Gallagher's position along with the best route for getting there.

Warner clapped a hand on Ivan's shoulder and squeezed. Ivan grimaced.

He smacked the Glock into the back of Ivan's head. Ivan crumpled.

To Diane, Warner said, "Tie him up. We are going after Katy Gallagher."

THE THUMPING OF THE CREATURES' FOOTSTEPS PRECEDED THEM. KATY RE-treated to where Charlie stood near the wall, farthest from the rock table. Rick loped after her.

Two brown creatures swaggered into the room armed with rocks. They selected positions on either side of the animal-hide seats, backs against the wall. A white-haired, wrinkle-faced male sauntered through the doorway next. He crossed to the table where he settled himself onto the middle seat. He grasped the bone. He concentrated his hazel eyes on Katy.

A female entered next, accompanied by a short creature Katy assumed was a youngster. The duo seated themselves on the animal-skins at either side of the white male.

Next came Goldie and Garfield. They posted themselves along the wall adjacent to the doorway, right of the white male and his family. The last creature through the door snarled when he spotted Katy. His gray hair flapped as he jerked his head toward her.

Yoda positioned himself left of the doorway, opposite Goldie and Garfield.

Witness for the prosecution. Had Goldie and Garfield come to defend her?

Rick inched closer on Katy's left. He placed a hand in the small of her back. Charlie joined them on Katy's right, hands coupled behind his back. He glanced at her sideways, flashed a smile, and turned his attention to the hairy hominids.

The white-haired male, the chief she supposed, grunted. He tapped the bone on the rock. The others bowed their heads.

Half a minute later, the chief vocalized a string of grunts and noises, "oogah" and "umph" mixed with huffing. Once he finished, Yoda approached the rock. He pointed a finger at her.

The chief shrugged. Yoda uttered chimp-like cries that echoed off the walls. The chief bared his teeth. He slammed the bone down on the table. Yoda backed away.

The chief looked at Charlie. The creature grunted.

Charlie stepped forward. He waved at Katy. Stabbing his fisted hand down as if holding a knife, he shook his head.

The chief mumbled a syllable she swore was "huh?"

Charlie told Katy, "Bow your head."

"Are you kidding me?"

"Now." She complied, and he spoke to the chief. "Oogah."

She clamped both lips between her teeth to suppress the laugh threatening to explode from her. Charlie talked like them too. What next, running through the woods naked and shrieking?

"Oogah," Charlie repeated, gesturing at her.

Garfield echoed, "Oogah."

Goldie nodded.

The chief grunted. He waved at the sentries on either side of him.

They rushed at Yoda, who shrieked and whirled around, heading for the doorway. The sentries pummeled him with the rocks. He fell to his knees, moaned, slumped forward onto his belly. His eyelids drooped shut. His body slackened. His breaths puffed fast and shallow.

The sentries scooped up his body. They ferried Yoda out of the room.

Charlie waved at the doorway.

The chief pointed at the painting of a helmeted figure, then the ceiling. The creatures exited in the order they had entered.

"They're sending him away," Charlie said.

"What does oogah mean?" she asked.

"Safe, I think. Or else danger."

"Great, either you told them I'm safe or I'm dangerous. They could've decided to send *me* away."

"It worked, that's what matters."

"Quite a chance to take without warning me."

He gave her the same look Rick had given her when she chased the creatures. The look Rick gave her quite often. A lot of people gave her that look. Go figure.

"What, are we supposed to sit in here twiddling our thumbs?" she asked.

Charlie shrugged. Rick kicked his heel into the floor.

Perfect. They could stand here until the sentries returned to drag them back into the holding cell or someplace worse, like the landing pad for the "gods" or the hairy hominid tannery where they skinned humans for leather. If the creatures got mad, they got deadly. She'd ticked them off enough for a decade's worth of animosity. Charlie saved her butt once. He couldn't keep intervening. They might decide he was trouble too. But she must keep searching.

Searching? For what? Her life's mission had consisted of finding the hairy hominids and proving they existed. She found them all right. Proving they existed she could accomplish by killing one and hauling its body back with her. She had vowed not to kill them. After witnessing their culture, their intelligence, she could no more kill a hairy hominid than she could kill Charlie or Rick.

She might convince one of the creatures to go back with her. Sure, and she might get elected Queen of the World too.

She'd found the hairy hominids. Now what?

Her mission consisted of more than hairy hominids. It included a task more important than hairy hominids, a task she believed in enough to join Charlie's project, a task that drew her to Texas and the footprints fossilized in 100-million-year-old rock.

Tracing the true origins of humanity.

The hairy hominids were a piece of the puzzle. So what if she couldn't see the other pieces and had no clue what the puzzle should look like when finished. So what if she had no clue where to continue the search. Ignorance never stopped her before.

The truth was like footprints on water. You saw the ripples circling outward from where the truth had been yet the truth itself stayed invisible. She must find a way of seeing it.

The hairy hominids were one of those ripples. She felt it. She must trace the ripple back to its source. At least then she would know where the truth last impacted the water. A clue could lead her…somewhere.

She marched to the doorway.

Charlie grabbed her arm. "No, Katy."

"I'm really sick of you two telling me no." She wrenched her arm away. "I have to investigate these caves. I have to know what the creatures are protecting."

"You've seen what they can do when humans anger them."

She thought back to the photos on the Game-Vu camera, the clean-up of the scene, the destruction of Charlie's campsite. A creature stomped his GPS radio into the ground. Yes, she knew what they could do when angered.

She must know.

"This time I have a choice," she said. "I'll take the risk. You stay here."

"I'm no safer if they think I let you escape."

She stepped into the doorway. Pounding erupted down the corridor, feet impacting earth. She squinted into the darkness. Torchlight shimmered in the distance like memories of daylight. The footfalls ceased.

Rick, behind her now, poked his head around her shoulder into the corridor.

The footfalls pounded again, louder. The light glimmered nearer, while the silhouettes of hairy hominids bobbled within it.

They were coming. Fast.

Rick pulled her backward out of the doorway.

The creatures raced past the opening. The lead creature grasped a torch in his hand. The others ran after him in the light's wake. None made any sound except for the thumping of their feet. She gave up trying to count how many passed. The light receded. The figures blurred into one long shadow the torch inside the meeting room could not penetrate. The pounding diminished into distant thunder, and then silence.

"What was that?" Katy said.

Brushing past her through the door, Charlie stared after the procession. "I have no idea."

Rick plucked the torch out of the floor. He strode past her into the corridor, pushed around his father, and halted.

"Let's find out," he said.

He started in the direction the procession had taken. Katy tagged along behind him. Charlie lingered at the doorway chewing his lip. With the torchlight dwindling around him, he jogged after them.

He woke up with a bad headache. The spot where Warner clouted him throbbed. He lifted his head. Pain pulsated through his skull. The cord binding his hands behind his back chafed his wrists each time he shifted his weight. More cord shackled his ankles. Ivan kicked his feet. His wrists jerked downward, tearing the muscles across his chest and shoulders. He wailed. The Nazi connected the cord around his wrists to the one around his ankles.

He'd kill Warner for this.

Warner and Diane had abandoned their backpacks, a sign they'd come back. After they caught Katy Gallagher using the GPS radio *he had found* and made her tell where *his goldmine* was and destroyed it. Warner forced him into signing an agreement wherein he promised to destroy the goldmine if he found it. He had no intention of honoring the agreement. What could Warner do, sue him?

Ivan chuckled. His chest muscles twanged. He whimpered. Damn Warner.

Spotting his backpack ten feet away beside Warner's, he wriggled toward it. Pain seared his chest, pulsed through his skull. His vision blurred. The world gyrated. He squeezed his eyes shut. In a moment his vision stabilized and the pain subsided. He flopped onto his belly. Slithering snake-like he reached his backpack in a few minutes.

Maneuvering into a sitting position in front of the backpack, facing away from it, took several minutes longer. At last he reached behind him into the side pocket of his pack. His fingers touched the handle of his knife. He pulled it out and flicked the sheath off the four-inch blade. A minute later he severed the cord around his wrist. Seconds after that he liberated his ankles.

Warner's backpack slumped beside him. The flap was unzipped.

He folded back the flap. Warner had crumpled his clothes into the pack. How uncouth of him. His great German ancestors would flay him for his carelessness. Ivan tossed the clothes out, along with a plastic bag filled with packets of Warner's protein drink, the liquid elephant dung he called food. Ivan closed the pack.

From deep in his pack he dug out the Desert Eagle. He'd thought Warner would want the GPS so bad he'd do whatever to get it, hence no need for the gun. Besides, he learned dragging Rick Bergren's pack took both his hands. How in tarnation that cowboy lugged the thing on his shoulders Ivan couldn't figure. Since the gun seemed unnecessary anyway, he had put it in his backpack.

All right, he miscalculated his advantage. One penalty didn't forfeit the game.

He slipped the Desert Eagle into its holster. Back to the cave.

THE CREATURES CONGREGATED AT THE END OF THE CORRIDOR WHERE IT widened into a sort of cul-de-sac. Rocks, in all shapes and sizes, were stacked nearby. The lead creature had embedded his torch in the dirt. The others, a dozen or more, clustered around it.

Katy huddled behind Rick, who positioned himself far enough back the congregation either failed to see them or dismissed them as no threat. Charlie was several yards behind her still chewing his lip. She leaned sideways to peek around Rick's arm.

The creatures muttered to each other for a few minutes. The leader detached from the group, strolling into the corner amid the shadows. His head nearly bumped the ceiling. It rose two feet over Rick's head. The creature reached up, pushed something.

Sunlight burst into the cave. The glow surrounded the creature in a block of brilliance.

He reached into the sunlight and heaved his body upward, through the portal into the world above. The others emulated his ascent, some seizing rocks before departing. Soon the creatures were gone. The portal slammed shut. The sunlight winked out.

"Danger," Charlie said.

Katy whirled on him. "What?"

"Oogah means danger."

"Great, you told them I'm dangerous."

"No no." He walked into the cul-de-sac. "I heard one of them say oogah just now. Since they were obviously on alert, it must mean danger. They've left to investigate and, if necessary, eliminate the danger."

"You told them I'm oogah."

"They must've assumed I meant you were *in* danger, not that you *were* danger." Head tilted back, he looked at the portal. "Question is, what oogah are they after now?"

"Warner."

He jerked as if she'd hurled a rock at his head.

He still believed Warner posed no danger. The creatures must've beaten him good and the concussion made him loopy. Maybe he ate hallucinogenic mushrooms with the hairy hominids. No one who met Warner could think him harmless. He aimed a gun at her temple. He murdered Jim.

"Warner won't hurt us," Charlie said.

Rick stalked toward his father. Scowling, he said, "He tried to kill Katy and he probably killed your friend Jim. He'll shoot us too if he gets the chance."

"You must be mistaken."

"Open your eyes, Dad! He's a murderer."

"He may have killed before, but he is not a cold-blooded murderer. He won't hurt us, he can't. We have an agreement."

Rick threw his hands up and kicked the wall. She felt like kicking something. Not the wall though. She wanted to kick Charlie's butt. A throttling might jostle his brain free of the muck Warner had slathered over it.

We have an agreement. Charlie said those words as if Warner would keep whatever agreement they had made. She would trust Warner's word when the hairy hominids sang a round of "Row, Row, Row Your Boat." What kind of agreement did they make anyhow? You can kill my friends and I won't say anything so long as you don't kill me too. What a deal.

The money.

The truth smacked her in the face. She should've seen it before. Warner tracked them into the wilderness but let them live. He must've ignored chances to kill them. He held back. There was one explanation.

"The money," she said. "For the new truck, the fancy equipment. You got it from him."

Charlie averted his gaze. He hunched his shoulders forward, crammed his hands in the pockets of his jacket.

"Warner paid you off." She slammed her palm against the wall. "Dammit, Charlie, how could you do that?"

"When you've lived a little longer, you may understand why I did it. Money isn't everything, but it makes everything possible." Charlie's gaze was sharp, his posture erect. "To study human origins you need financing, Katy. Anthropologists accept corporate sponsorship."

"Let Coca-Cola pay you. Not a murderer like Warner."

"I understand why you dislike him. He is a corporate sponsor, Katy, he owns one of the largest conglomerates in the world. His umbrella covers logging, mining, paper production, real estate, museums. He both founded and finances seventy-five percent of the Museum of Prehistory in Chicago. He paid for the construction of the new wing himself."

"To bury his enemies in the concrete for the foundation."

He refused to look away until she admitted he had a point. Because she refused to admit it, he bored his gaze into her brain. Sure, he might have a point. Admitting it meant admitting Warner might have a decent side. Then again, funding a museum wing hardly proved his magnanimity.

The Human Origins Project needed financing. Charlie disregarded his instincts to accept Warner's cash, because no one else proffered a grant. Desperation, rather than curiosity, killed the cat.

"Why does Warner care about hairy hominids?" she asked. "And if he paid you to look for them, why is he trying to stop us now?"

"I suspected from the start he wanted me to find them so he could get rid of them. I thought I could change his mind. Thought by the time I brought one back and proved they existed, he'd have no choice. I overlooked the possibility he was having us watched."

"Why does he want them gone?"

"He hates them. Not sure why." Charlie raised onto tiptoes, stretching his arm toward the portal in the ceiling, and stumbled. "When I realized he'd been watching us, I decided to find the creatures before he did. He could've gone through our records, read all the sightings, figured out what I'd recently realized. The creatures are concentrated in this area but are spreading outward. He, of course, doesn't realize the spread is because of the outcasts. Not all hairy hominids are a menace."

Katy leaned against the wall. "They send their outcasts straight into human territory. Not exactly a sign of friendship."

"They want to rectify the problem. They seem to be organizing a bounty hunt to capture the outcasts and send them away."

"Another guess based on context?"

"I developed a rudimentary means of communicating with them."

"Which is?"

"Charades."

She shook her head. "As a history professor, Charlie, you are brilliant. As an anthropologist, you're useless."

"It works better than you think."

She spun on her heels and headed straight into the corridor. "I'm checking out the caves."

Rick fell into step alongside her, torch in hand. He kept quiet as she angled left into an offshoot corridor. Boots clomped behind them, Charlie jogging to catch up. She'd heard enough of his rationalizations. She'd heard enough from him period. The fact his arguments might have validity set her stomach churning. She tightened her fists until they ached. She wanted no part in a world where killers funded research, her friends preferred the company of hairy beasts, and lunatics pursued her for reasons she had given up understanding. The world should make sense. Though she investigated the true origins of humanity, believing generations of scientists deluded themselves and the public, at the end of each day the world made sense. She understood the motivations.

Charlie's motivations vexed her. Warner's confounded her.

She wanted to break something, anything. Instead she stomped through a doorway into an oblong cavern.

And tripped over a rectangular pit in the floor.

Her feet slipped out from under her. Rick shoved his hands under her arms. She hung suspended over the pit for a heartbeat before he pulled her backward. Her feet touched the floor. He retracted his arms.

The pit was six feet long, two feet wide, and at least three feet deep. In the bottom, carved out of the earth, was the outline of a skeleton.

Stones shaped into chisels lay in the pit alongside round stones perhaps used as hammers. A tuft of fur rested near the tools. She hopped down into the pit, straddling the outline. She picked up the tuft, a hand-size clump of rabbit fur. She shook the tuft. Dust plumed out from the fur.

She grabbed a chisel. If she had used these tools, she might've chiseled at the compacted soil to excavate a skeleton, brushing away debris with the rabbit fur. The hairy hominids freed a skeleton from the rock. The skeleton at the cave entrance.

"Good lord," Rick said.

He had moved into the center of the cavern. His torch illuminated paintings on the walls. When she saw the painting that attracted Rick's attention and incited his exclamation, she leaped out of the pit.

The painting covered the full expanse of the twelve-foot wall. The artwork depicted hairy hominids massacring an enemy. They tore the enemies' heads from their bodies, lifting the trophies high. They crushed the enemies under their feet, pummeled them with rocks, drowned them in a river. The enemies had no weapons, no strength comparable to what the creatures possessed, nothing aside from the spears the creatures had torn from their hands and snapped in two.

The hairy hominids had annihilated the humans.

16

THE TORCH HAD BURNED DOWN TO A SLIVER OF BIRCH BARK AT THE HANDLE'S apex. Its light no longer saturated the cavern. Now the torch lit half of one wall, most of the twelve-foot painting depicting the hairy-hominids-versus-humans battle.

"The torch is going out," she said. "We need more birch bark."

Charlie hustled out of the cavern.

"Where are you going?"

He had either gone out of earshot or ignored her. She checked the cavern for bark but found none. Though the rabbit fur might ignite, it would burn down too quickly.

Rick had not moved. He stood three feet from the painting, turning his head left and right, bending his neck side to side, squinting and widening his eyes.

"Maybe these aren't people," he said.

"They are."

He shuffled backward. "Yeah. They are."

Like the Paleolithic art of Europe, these paintings evinced sophistication in their accuracy. The hairy hominids looked like hairy hominids. The humans looked like humans. No one could mistake either for bears.

Charlie stumbled through the doorway. In his hand he clasped a section of birch bark three feet long and a foot wide.

"We'll have to douse the torch," he said. "Add the new bark and relight it."

"Relight it?" she said. "With what?"

"I have a lighter."

"How do we add new bark in the pitch dark?"

He jammed a hand into his pocket, brought out a pen light. "For getting around in these caves, it's worthless. It ought to give us enough light for the task though."

Rick kneeled. As he smothered the torch in the dirt, darkness drew its shroud around them all. Her chest tightened. She felt the walls closing in. An illusion. The walls could not move, the darkness could not strangle her, the cold could not freeze her bones. Yet she felt the cold infiltrate her body, felt the hardening as her molecules transformed into ice.

Charlie clicked on his pen light. A blade of light perforated the dark. He folded the bark three times, forming a yard-long strip. As he lodged the strip into the eight-inch slot in the handle, he stuffed a hand into his pocket to retrieve his lighter. He flicked the starter. Nothing. He flicked it again. A tiny spark dissipated before lighting on the torch. He flicked once more and nothing happened.

Flick, flick, flick. Not even a spark.

He shook the lighter. "Out of juice. Got any matches?"

"Why didn't you check before we killed the torch?" Rick asked.

"Sorry."

The chill radiating from the rocks frosted through her body. She shoved her hands deep in the pockets of her jeans. Her fingers bumped a hard object.

She yanked out the magnesium block, jingling it by its metal chain.

Charlie and Rick scrunched their eyebrows at her.

"It's a fire starter," she said. "A magnesium block with a flint core embedded in one side. Magnesium is flammable. Flint sparks."

"Nice," Charlie said. "How do we get the magnesium onto the bark?"

She left her knife in her pack. Aboveground.

"You're men," she said, "one of you must have a pocket knife."

Rick slid a folding pocket knife out of his hip pocket. He handed it to her.

Oh great. They expected her to start the fire. Her father had shown her how, but she had little luck with the technique. She could do it. She must.

"Hold the torch lower," she said.

Rick balanced the end on the ground. The tip of the bark was at hand level for her. Unfolding the knife, she held the blade and the magnesium block over the torch. She scraped off flakes of magnesium until it tinged the bark silver. Rick and Charlie awaited the amazing fire she had promised to light. She swallowed. As she flipped the block over to the flint side, she lowered it closer to the bark. She struck the knife against the flint. A spark danced off it. No ignition.

She struck the knife five times. Sparks rained onto the bark. Smoke drifted out from inside the folds of bark and died. She struck again, again, again, faster, showering sparks onto the bark. Smoke curled upward. The spark snuffed out. She struck the knife so fast her fingers hurt. Smoke trickled up from the torch. She kept striking sparks onto the bark. She puffed at the smoke and was rewarded with a glow inside the folds of bark.

More sparks. The glow intensified.

She puffed at the fire. The glow erupted into little flames. She hopped backward. The flames escalated into a torch. Light beat back the gloom.

Holy cow, she'd done it.

The torch ignited blue flames in Rick's eyes. He said, "That was incredible."

Charlie murmured agreement. Of course. *Now* they were impressed. When she recognized a prehistoric beast from a cave painting and remembered its name, they shrugged. When she made fire, they thought she was a goddess.

Rick helped her onto her feet. The torch lit the entire cavern. The light revealed, on the wall opposite the massacre painting, more artwork. This time the artist portrayed daily life among the hairy hominids—as seen by their cavemates, the humans.

In the images creatures and humans shared a campfire, hunted mammoths, prepared meals. A mother hominid cradled both a baby hominid and a human baby in her arms. A human mother watched over a nursery of human and hairy hominid children.

To the right, the paintings showed the humans cowering while the creatures brandished spears at them. No more children in the paintings, only adults. The creatures pointed accusing fingers at the humans. The humans kneeled before them, heads bowed. Ovoid crafts hovered overhead. In the next image, beams transported the creatures into the crafts. The humans shielded their eyes.

She turned. On the far wall, across from the doorway, a series of paintings depicted humans hunting mammoths, saber-toothed cats, and the horse-like *Macrauchenia*. In the last scene, ovoid crafts soared overhead casting beams downward. Inside the beams, hairy hominids floated upward.

The next painting was the massacre scene.

She whirled toward the first paintings beside the doorway. In the images of humans and hairy hominids hunting she noticed the gestures the humans made. Some pointed at the quarry animals while others lifted their spears or locked arrows in their bows. The hairy hominids watched, lifting their own spears in imitation of the humans. The humans were teaching the creatures to hunt with spears and bows and arrows.

When she had seen the creatures hunt, they used rocks or bare hands. She hadn't witnessed a hairy hominid hunting with a spear or bow and arrow. Yet in every image in this cavern they hunted with those weapons.

It meant something. Darned if she knew what.

She turned around twice to scan the paintings. All the images seemed to show the human point of view. When the hairy hominids vanished into the crafts, the paintings portrayed the humans' activities but left out what happened to the creatures, until they returned from the crafts.

And massacred the humans.

Sometime in the past, humans lived with hairy hominids. They painted a history of that time in these caves. Then the peace ended. The paintings offered

THE HUNT FOR BIGFOOT

no clues about what pushed the hairy hominids to mass murder. Unless the clue was the ovoid UFO.

The crafts. The lights. Someone guided the hairy hominids. Someone didn't want them mingling with humans. Someone convinced the creatures to exterminate a population of humans to protect the secret of their existence.

She had no proof. Just a theory. And a gut feeling. A very bad gut feeling.

Rick waved the torch in front of her. "You okay?"

"Depends what you mean by okay."

"Are you sick?"

She forced a smile. "I'm fine."

She was fine in the sense she had no injuries or illnesses. Instead of a virus, knowledge infected her. Knowledge of a past no one remembered and a danger lurking on the limen of reality. If whoever flew those crafts decided the three of them had violated the creatures' privacy, they might star in the revival of *Hairy Hominids Vs. Humans.*

Peripherally, she glanced at the massacre scene. Crushed ribs. Decapitation.

She rubbed her neck. A hairy hominid throttled Rick. The creature let him live, though, when it could easily have killed him. Rick shot at the door. The creatures had tempers more flammable than propane.

She clomped to the doorway and the pit in front of it. A painting she missed before embellished the rock above the doorway. An outline of black filled in with red formed a triangle.

Walking closer to the pit, she bent down beside it. Depressions, varying in shape and size, surrounded the pit. Stones, piled near the doorway, bore smears of dirt. She grabbed one of the stones and dropped it inside each depression in turn. One hole matched the stone's dimensions. When she tried more stones, she discovered each fit inside one of the holes. Somebody removed the stones from the holes, where they had encircled the grave of a human.

She dug through the pile. Near the bottom, she found one stone larger and more rectangular in shape, its surface encrusted with dirt that obscured its color. No holes matched the stone. She waddled toward the head of the pit where the skull's removal had left a depression. There, several inches outside the perimeter of stones, was a faint rectangular impression. She dropped the stone into it. The two fit together.

She picked up the stone. With her fingernails she pecked at the dirt. Bits flaked off in her hand. She spit on the rock. The moisture loosened fragments which dropped away. In a minute she'd removed most of the encrustation. She rubbed at the stone with her jacket, then held the cleaned stone at eye level.

On the stone an artisan had inscribed, over the background of a red triangle, a tiny figure. The figure wore a loose-fitting jumpsuit and a spherical helmet with dark, almond-shaped eyeholes. On either side of the figure hovered ovoid crafts.

She set the stone inside its depression.

The grave had reclaimed its headstone.

THE WIND GUSTED. BENEATH THE STIRRING RESONATED A GROWL. WARNER stopped in the center of the clearing. He had heard the growl. The creatures tried hiding their sounds in the gusts. He listened through the wind, down to the level of their voices. Twisting left, he watched between the branches and through the leaves swirling up from the ground. He turned in a circle. The wind might have displaced the sound. There. He discerned the shape as he circled past it. He swung back to the right, squinting at the woods. Masked by branches, hunched to minimize its profile, hid a creature.

A red fire ignited in its eyes.

He brought out the Glock.

Beside him, Diane hugged herself. Half-moon shadows darkened the skin beneath her eyes. She clamped her teeth over both lips.

"You should have brought a gun," he said.

"I hate guns."

"Then I hope you enjoy dying."

The wind scattered leaves across the clearing. Within its roar, multiple voices grunted and snarled around them. Pinpoints of red flashed from all directions.

He checked the GPS. It still showed Gallagher two hundred yards due west, beyond the boulder. Dead center in the herd of creatures. Herd, flock, gaggle, what term applied to a tribe of shaggy titans?

A figure disengaged from the shadows. The creature, a red-haired male, strolled to within ten feet of them. Diane sucked in a breath.

Warner aimed the Glock at the ground.

The creature curled his upper lip back, revealing teeth stained beige. The hair covering the dome of his head ruffled in the wind. His shoulders seemed to undulate as a gust rippled the hair. His arms hung at his sides, the hands stubby yet massive.

The creature grunted.

Warner curled his finger around the Glock's trigger. He should have brought a Tommy gun.

The creature raised his left hand over his head, palm open.

More creatures materialized from the shadows. They surrounded Warner and Diane, fists clenched, exuding an anger that permeated the air—along with their stench.

Diane slapped a hand over her nose and mouth. Eyes bulging, she looked from one creature to the next.

"Do not move," Warner whispered.

Her hand muffled her voice. "I *can't* move."

Diane's eyes had gone bloodshot, her skin white. She pinched her nostrils shut with trembling fingers.

Taking her free hand, he transferred the Glock into her palm. He curled her fingers around it.

He said, "It's simple. Aim and pull the trigger."

"What will you do?"

He eased his knife out of its sheath, which he had clipped onto his belt. He snapped the knife open. The six-inch blade glistened. "I will survive."

The red-haired titan screeched.

The creatures stormed the clearing.

Diane screamed.

A creature cinched its arms around Warner's waist. He thrust the knife behind his head, felt it sink into flesh, twisted. The creature gurgled. Its hold slipped. He kicked its shin, yanked the knife out, spun around. Blood matted the fur on the creature's chest. With a shout, Warner leaped at the beast. He jammed the knife into the creature's throat. The creature dropped onto its knees. The glow faded from its eyes.

Warner pulled the knife free. The creature collapsed.

Two more beasts rushed him. One seized his ankles, flipping his legs out from under him, while the second clamped its hands around his throat.

A shot exploded.

The blast paralyzed the creatures. A voice wailed.

The two holding him relaxed their grips and he rolled away. Diane huddled near the rock, the Glock gripped in both hands, a creature dead at her feet. Another creature flung itself at her. She fired. The ground hit the creature's chest. The animal whumped onto the ground face-first.

The pair who had escaped lunged at Warner. He kicked one in the teeth. The creature howled, stumbled backward. The second creature snatched a branch off the ground and swung it at Warner. He ducked. The branch connected with a tree. The creature swung it back for another try.

Warner stabbed the knife into the creature's ankle. He sliced through sinew. The creature dropped the branch. It seized a handful of Warner's shirt, hoisting him four feet off the ground.

Another gunshot exploded. Over the creature's head, Warner saw one of its brethren topple backward into a sapling.

The creature holding him roared. It shook him hard. The knife flew from his hand as pangs erupted behind his eyes. His arms and legs flailed.

Boom!

The creature's fist slackened. Warner hit the ground tailbone-first. Pain spread through his hips into his back and legs. His head smacked into the ground. Lights flashed before his eyes.

The creature crumpled onto the corpses of his brethren.

Diane, the Glock in her hands, stood behind where the creature had fallen. She chewed her lower lip. A pink flush chased the pallor from her face. Her eyes were narrowed. Her stance was solid.

She lowered the gun.

A creature bolted out of the trees. Blood dribbled from its mouth.

The one he kicked in the teeth. The creature grabbed Diane's arm and jerked her sideways. The Glock slipped out of her hand.

Warner rolled toward the gun. The creature wrapped its arms around Diane's waist. He squeezed the trigger. The shot punched into the creature's shoulder. The beast shrieked and ran. Warner fired another round. The creature disappeared through the trees.

Warner pushed into a sitting position. "You said you hated guns."

"I do," Diane panted. "But I know how to use one. My dad was a cop."

She wrapped her arms around herself.

Warner, on his feet now, slid the Glock into its holster. The creature who lived had fled. Five corpses lay strewn around the clearing.

He checked the GPS. Gallagher had not moved. He led Diane through the woods to the spot where the tracker showed Gallagher's position. He found solid ground.

Ivan mentioned a cave. She could be underground.

Ahead, a shadow shifted.

Warner took off after the creature. Its pace quickened into a gallop when it saw him coming. He matched its speed, his chest aching. Behind him, Diane's footfalls crunched.

The creature absconded to a hill. The beast ducked through an opening in the hillside. Warner slowed to a fast walk. Ivan's cave.

He strode into the cave. Despite the darkness, he followed the slapping of the creature's footsteps. With the wall as a guide, he inched forward like a blind man feeling his way through a new house.

The footsteps silenced. He halted.

A hand clutched his jacket sleeve. He touched the fingers, feeling the smoothness of nail polish at the ends. Diane had joined him. Her fingers were cold.

A light washed over them from behind. He squinted. Diane cupped a hand above her eyes. The light slanted down toward the floor. His eyes adjusting, Warner spun toward the light.

Ivan, camouflaged by the shadows behind his flashlight, waggled the Desert Eagle. The gun's gold finish cast off swords of brilliance.

"I know," Ivan said, "you didn't open that door."

Warner looked at the rock slab and the opening half revealed behind it. A doorway. The creature neglected to shut the door.

Ivan said, "You're not taking my goldmine this time."

"What will you do with it? Sell it?" Warner took a step toward Ivan. "I cannot allow that."

"Give me the GPS."

"No."

"I'll shoot your bowling-ball head off!"

"No."

Ivan pulled the trigger.

Click.

His face reddened. Ivan jerked the trigger three more times.

Click, click, click.

He whimpered.

"You did not think," Warner said, "I would leave you with a loaded gun."

Ivan popped out the clip. When he saw it was empty, he hurled the clip and gun at the wall. The gun smacked into the rock, bounced backward, hit the floor. The clip pinged off the wall.

Warner seized Ivan's shirt and flung him through the doorway. The flashlight twirled across the floor.

Ivan cowered on the dirt inside the doorway.

Warner sneered at him. "You may go first, *doctor*."

Ivan scrambled to his feet. Slouching, eyes wide, he stared into the darkness behind him.

Warner crossed the threshold.

In the doorway, Katy tilted her head and cupped her hand around her ear. The shuffling got louder. Voices murmured.

Rick laid a hand on her shoulder. "Hear something?"

"They're coming back."

Torchlight glistened further down the corridor. Dark ghosts writhed behind the light. The shuffling intensified as the murmurs silenced.

The torch holder trudged past Katy. He glanced at her sideways, his expression stoic, his posture stiff. After him came two creatures carrying a litter fashioned from pine fronds and branches, each holding an end of the contraption. On the litter reclined another creature. In the dimming light, the blood matted on his chest and neck appeared black. His eyes were closed. His breathing was shallow.

His comrades plodded past the doorway. As the wounded creature's head passed by Katy, he opened his eyes. Their gazes connected. A faint redness glimmered inside his eyes.

He shrieked.

Katy slapped her hands over her ears.

The procession hurried away.

Rick squeezed her shoulders.

"Humans did that to him," she said. "He hates all of us now."

"Looked like he was dying."

"Imagine how his friends will feel when he does." She moved into the corridor. "Or his family."

"We have to get out of here."

"Not yet. I need to look around more."

"Sure, let's hang around until that creature dies and his family decides all humans should pay for it. Good idea."

"We have some time."

She went into the cavern. Charlie waited near the wall, the torch in his hands. She grabbed the torch and tromped into the corridor. When she glanced back, Rick and Charlie were behind her. Rick, shoulders squared, pinched his mouth into a scowl. He clenched the .45 in his fist, the muzzle pointed at the ground.

The creatures tolerated their presence, so far. If the wounded creature died, their tolerance might snap. She had already drawn it tight by prowling their caves without permission. They liked Charlie, yet even that relationship was strained by her actions and whatever happened outside. A human had shot the wounded creature. Whether the shooter was Ivan, Warner, or a hunter who wandered deep into the woods made no difference. The creatures were fed up with humanity.

Still, she must search. A truth awaited her down here, a truth hinted at in the paintings. Humans and hairy hominids once cohabited. Until the hairy hominids went away. When they returned, they massacred the humans. At least one human survived to record the tale on the cave walls.

Katy, Rick, and Charlie traversed chambers full of rocks and wood, empty caverns, and the sleeping chamber she stumbled into earlier. This time, however, the chamber was empty. Though pine-frond mats evidenced where the creatures had slept, all were gone from the room. She crossed through the chamber, across a threshold into another corridor. Several hundred feet later the corridor dead-ended at a rock slab identical to the one barring the entrance to the caves.

She laid a hand on the slab. Cold. Immovable. A hairy hominid had the strength for opening such a door, not a human. Near the top of the slab, a tiny figure was drawn on the door. The figure stood before a red triangle, flanked by ovoid crafts. The same symbols had marked the grave from which the creatures excavated the human skeleton.

Rick shouted.

She spun around. Charlie was backed up against the wall. Rick sat on the floor a few feet away, hair tousled, his scowl directed at a creature who loomed over him.

Garfield wriggled his nostrils. He muttered, "Oogah."

"Oogah to you too," Katy said.

He furrowed his forehead.

She needed a way of communicating with him.

Charlie claimed charades worked. He relied on the method to communicate with the creatures during his weeklong stopover in the caves. The idea seemed ridiculous. A child's game used as a language. But gestures might provide a platform for communication, a shared concept. She knew oogah meant danger. The rest of their language remained as cryptic to her as the barking of dogs.

Worth a shot.

Emphasizing each word with representative gestures, she said, "Can you open the door?"

Garfield grumbled.

She repeated the gestures.

He shook his head. "Oogah."

Danger behind the door. She was danger for the door. The door was dangerous.

Garfield voiced apelike ululations. Clenching her wrist in his hand, he towed her away from the door. Rick leaped to his feet. He punched Garfield in the shoulder. Garfield held her wrist tight.

Rick slugged him in the side, beat his fists into the creature's neck.

Garfield groaned.

Rick swung his arm back for another blow.

Katy said, "Stop it! He's trying to tell me something. You're not hurting him anyway."

Rick lowered his arm. "He was dragging you off."

"Because he thinks I'm in danger."

Garfield pointed down the corridor. "Oogah."

He hauled her away from the door. Rick tensed as if to punch the creature. Katy shot him a glance coupled with a shake of her head. He relaxed his fist and trail after them with Charlie close behind.

Garfield guided them left, then right, through a chamber littered with tiny pine-frond mats. The mats looked dusty. They were the size of babies and children, yet she had seen no infants in the caves. The youngest creature was the chief's son, who seemed like a teenager, if she could judge a hairy hominid's age by human standards.

The floor ascended as they continued into another corridor. One more turn and they entered a passage that dead-ended at an earthen wall. Two wood pegs stuck out of the wall at human eye level, three feet apart. A portal.

Releasing her wrist, Garfield clasped the pegs. He pulled. His muscles bulged and the portal popped out of the wall. As he hefted the plug aside, her torch's light trickled into the space beyond. It was a hole dug out of the earth, six feet wide and perhaps ten feet long, four feet in height. Garfield motioned for her to enter.

She didn't move.

Garfield honked. He nabbed the torch from her hand. Looking past her head, he said, "Oogah."

She bent over and walked into the hole.

"Are you nuts?" Rick said. "This could be a trap."

"He wants to help us." She dropped onto her knees. "If you can't trust him, then trust me. Trust my instincts."

Grumbling, he stooped over and clomped into the hole. Charlie crawled in after him.

As Garfield shut the door, Rick said, "I hope there's ventilation in here."

Darkness. Except for the stars overhead.

She bent her head back. Stars. No. Bigger than stars. Rising into a crouch, she stretched her hand toward the ceiling. Her fingers blocked one of the lights.

She felt around the area. Her index finger dipped into a hole. The lights shined through holes drilled in the ceiling.

Barely wide enough for her finger, the holes nonetheless provided ventilation for the room. Since her finger had not exited the other end, the holes must've extend upward for more than a few inches. A foot, possibly two.

Rick yelped. "What the—aw, yuck."

Her stomach flip-flopped.

Charlie clicked on his pen light. He swooped the beam in Rick's direction.

Rick was sitting on a pile of deer parts.

Charlie shined the light around the room. Bones cluttered the floor. She recognized a deer's bones, a bear's skull, assorted small mammal bones. They were in the hairy hominid butcher shop.

Charlie's pen light flickered. He shut it off.

She sat down. "Charlie, you said in your itinerary they are watching. Who did you mean?"

"The hairy hominids. I'd seen them loitering in the woods near my house. They knew I was coming."

"How could they know?"

A long pause, then: "I'd been writing about my plans in my journal."

"How would they get a hold of your journal? And even if they did, how could they read it? You can't be saying they understand English. If they do, you wouldn't need charades to communicate with them."

The chirping of birds filtered down through the ventilation holes.

"Well?" she said.

"I saw…"

She hugged her knees to her chest. The dirt was cold. Her butt had gone numb.

When Charlie said nothing more, she asked, "You saw what?"

He coughed. "A light. I woke up one night because there was a spotlight shining on my face, through the window of my loft. It got brighter, almost blinding. I felt static electricity all around me. Then I blacked out. When I woke up in the morning, my journal was on the bedside table."

"So?"

"I left it in the drawer."

"Jeez, Charlie, do you know what you're saying?"

"Yes. We are dealing with a foe of unimaginable power. Not aliens or paranormal beings, but people with technology and resources far beyond our comprehension."

"How do you know they're people? Have you seen them? What are you hiding? And why? I thought we were friends."

"Leave it alone, Katy. The truth is dangerous. You won't like the way it feels on your conscience."

"You said that last night."

He lapsed into silence. She hugged her knees harder. A familiar hand grasped hers. Rick sidled up to her, slipping an arm around her shoulders.

A foe of unimaginable power.

She had seen the lights. She watched the hairy hominids go into them. She saw the skeleton, the grave, the paintings. She trod so near the truth she couldn't possibly turn back now. If she faced an enemy with unimaginable power, she must understand that foe. She must know how to fight them.

She must get inside the secret room marked with the triangle logo.

Outside the door, creatures shrieked. Footfalls thundered.

A gunshot exploded.

17

THE GUNFIRE BOOMED IN BURSTS OF TWO OR THREE SHOTS, THE SOUND muffled by the door. Feet thudded throughout the caves, shaking the walls, vibrating the floor. Within the clamor of hairy hominid wails and roars, human voices hollered.

Rick crawled to the door. With both hands flat on the portal he pushed against it. Charlie shined his pen light on the door, more as emotional support than actual illumination. Despite pushing until sweat trickled down his forehead and his face turned red, Rick could not budge the door.

Katy took the Taurus out of her fanny pack. Screw what the hairy hominids thought. If anybody came through the door, she wanted protection.

Panting, Rick sat down beside her. Charlie shut off his pen light.

The gunshots boomed closer. The walls trembled.

A hairy hominid screeched. A human shouted.

A mass thumped into the door.

Her heart skipped. She clutched the Taurus.

The gunfire ended. The footfalls dwindled until a silence pervaded the caves. Even the birds aboveground stopped chirping. Or else she'd gone deaf.

No, she could hear her own breaths gasping from her, Rick's breathing whispering beside her. She reached for his hand and found the .45 instead, which actually comforted her far more than his hand. She scrambled into a crouch.

The silence lasted forever. Seconds, minutes, she lost all concept of time trapped inside the hole. The sunlight percolating through the ventilation holes had dimmed. Late afternoon. Soon the sun would dunk below the horizon. Night would flood the landscape. Last night she witnessed bizarre events. What would tonight bring?

A lump lodged in her throat. She gulped it down.

The door popped out of its niche. Torchlight assaulted her eyes. When her vision had acclimated, she noticed two figures outside. Garfield held the torch. The other hominid lagged behind Garfield, his face hidden by Garfield's massive shoulders.

Garfield turned around and motioned for them to follow him. The other creature waited by the door, his brown hair glistening in the torchlight. She recognized the brown creature from the meeting hall. He was one of the sentries who guarded the chief, if she grasped their social customs correctly. Either way, he stood beside his leader during her trial.

She had a feeling her trial wasn't over yet.

Charlie left first. He walked bent over for a few steps, with his hands on his lower back, then leaned Backward. With a little cry he straightened. Rick enclosed her hand in his and departed next, tugging her along behind him. Once out of the hole, Katy released the breath she'd held for...she didn't remember how long. Though claustrophobia had never affected her before, getting locked inside a dirt dungeon had stabbed cold spikes through her gut.

She and Rick walked hand-in-hand down the corridor behind the creatures.

The sentry sealed the door and trudged after them.

The hairy hominids could handle the confined spaces because they knew nothing else. The creatures alive now spent their entire lives down here. They ventured above to hunt, guard their subterranean fortress, and meet with the gods. Their lives they spent underground. While a few sightings mentioned finding hairy hominid beds in the woods, places where creatures piled leaves and grass to make a sleeping mat, most people saw the creatures on the move—or on the hunt. Now she understood why. They lived underground. It was the one place they could rest undisturbed.

The procession rounded a corner into a narrower passage. The sentry jammed his fist into her back. She moved faster. Rick, matching her pace, tightened his hand around hers. They angled around another corner.

Garfield and Charlie ducked through the doorway into the holding cell.

Bonnie was gone. Yoda squatted near the doorway.

Katy halted on the threshold. Rick stopped a foot ahead of her.

Crude ropes bound Yoda's wrists and ankles. Nothing, however, bound him to the floor or the wall. Seeing Katy, he hopped onto his knees and growled, lips peeled back over brown teeth. One tooth was missing, another blackened. His gums gleamed pale and blotchy. Warts dotted his face, lips, and palms. He glowered at her with glowing, bloodshot eyes.

The sentry shoved her across the threshold. She tripped, floundered three steps, smacked into the floor hip-first.

Rick slugged the sentry.

Katy rolled onto her back and sprang upright. She aimed the Taurus at Yoda. The sentry grabbed Rick's shirt, lifted him off his feet, and hurled him into the cell.

Katy swung the Taurus toward the sentry. He barked. She jumped up. He scampered off down the corridor.

Garfield hulked against the wall beside the doorway.

Rick hit the ground flat on his back. He sat up. "I'm sick of these things tossing me around."

"Quit irritating them," Charlie said.

"He pushed Katy."

"Chivalry will get you killed down here. To them, it's another human trait they can't understand, so they fear it."

Garfield stepped away from the wall. As he trudged into the doorway, he signaled to Charlie in a come-with-me gesture. Garfield sidestepped through the door into the corridor. Charlie started after him.

Katy nabbed his arm. "You can't go with him. They might be expecting you to answer for all our crimes."

"Then I shall."

"Don't martyr yourself on my account."

Rick stood. "No, she can do that on her own."

Charlie brushed off her hand. He strolled into the corridor after Garfield.

Yoda snarled.

She leveled the Taurus at his forehead. In a vicious tone she hoped conveyed the meaning of her words, she said, "Shut up or I'll blow your head off."

Yoda closed his mouth. The glow petered out in his eyes. The glower, however, remained.

Her watch told her an hour elapsed before footsteps clapped in the corridor.

It was a quarter past six. The sun had set.

Charlie shambled across the threshold. He had his hands in his jacket pockets, gaze cast downward, shoulders slouched. His face was pale. A frown infected his features, accentuating the wrinkles. His white hair seemed whiter somehow. The torch in the center of the cell bathed everything in a golden hue, but did nothing for Charlie's appearance.

He stopped on the threshold, leaning against the doorway. When he looked at her, a chill penetrated her bones. When he spoke, the hairs on the back of her neck stiffened.

"They made some decisions. I have to leave in the morning. You..." He sagged his shoulders further. "Both of you are to be sent away."

"Sent away?" She pointed at the ceiling. "You mean up there? Into one of those craft?"

He nodded.

Rick stomped toward his father. "We won't go."

"You have no choice, I—I tried to convince them to let you go. They wouldn't listen. At midnight tonight, when they send this gray fellow away, you will go with him. The gods will decide your fate."

"You told us they aren't gods," Katy said, "but people."

"The words make no difference. The people in those ships care about the creatures, not us." He walked halfway to Katy, between her and Rick. "You were right, I have seen them. I sneaked out one night and followed the creatures to their rendezvous. The craft landed that night. People as human as you or I came out of it, but they wore strange clothes and spoke a language I couldn't understand. I watched them converse with the creatures, then get into their craft and leave. They treated the hairy hominids like their children. I have no evidence to support this, but I had the most disconcerting feeling during the whole event. I felt that if those people saw me, they would kill me. I would simply disappear from the planet."

He closed his eyes. "Do you know how many hunters and hikers have disappeared in these woods? They probably ran afoul of the creatures and were sent away. The gods already know about me. Now they know about you. The creatures who left in the craft last night went to tell them."

"And you're going to hand us over," Katy said.

"No." He opened his eyes, squared his shoulders. "I have a plan. It's risky, we could all die, but at least you can't be sent away if you're dead."

"We escape."

"Yes. It's more dangerous than it sounds. They have guards watching all the entrances twenty-four hours a day, even the trap doors. I'm sure they alerted the guards we might attempt an escape. If they see us, they will stop us. By whatever means necessary."

Charlie's rifle still rested on the floor where he set it earlier. Rick picked up the rifle and tossed it to his father.

"Let's make sure they don't see us then," Rick said.

If the creatures attacked, they might have to kill some of them. She and Charlie—and Jim—had vowed not to kill the creatures. She didn't want to do it. She understood their fear. If the choice came down to her life or theirs, though, she chose hers. She thought back to the butcher shop and whoever shot at the creatures. Was it Warner? Had they killed him?

She felt for the speed loaders in her fanny pack. *Please don't let me need them.*

Rick strode toward the doorway. Footsteps down the corridor sent him scuffling backward.

Charlie cleared his throat. "That reminds me, there was one more decision."

The footsteps echoed through the caves. The creatures' feet slapping on the earth. And boots clomping.

"*Nein!*" a voice shouted.

Charlie stepped aside. "They're being sent away too."

The sentry stopped outside the doorway. He shoved a man, then a woman, into the holding cell. The woman bumped into Yoda. He snarled. Diane yelped and dodged sideways, away from him.

The man stumbled, righting himself in front of Katy. Inches separated them. As he recognized her, a sneer parted his lips.

Warner chuckled. The sound, more of a growl than laughter, rumbled from deep in his throat.

She raised the Taurus in front of his face. Its muzzle grazed his nose.

He raised a 9mm Glock at her.

Warner retracted his arm. He kept the Glock at his side, the barrel pointed at the floor.

He settled his hand over hers, over the Taurus. A shiver snaked through her body. She jerked her hand away, bounding backward a few steps. He had presence, an aura of danger and sensuality that evoked a primal response in her.

The moment had ended. She wanted to kill him again. He was like a white tiger, attractive but deadly.

Warner took a step toward her.

Rick lunged at him. He socked Warner in the chin and swung his fist back for another blow. Warner stumbled backward.

Katy grabbed Rick's arm. She shook her head. He dropped his arm, keeping his fist tight.

Rick hissed between clenched teeth, "Don't ever touch her."

A droplet of blood poised on Warner's lip. Swiping it away with the back of his hand, he said, "We could help each other. If you do not kill me."

Though Warner deferred this time, a glint in his eyes warned he might not restrain himself next time. Rick would punch him again anyway, if he looked askance at her or twitched his finger in her direction.

She considered herself independent, capable of caring for herself, defending her own life. She could in most situations, though as a woman she had no prayer of fighting off a full-grown male without firepower. Sure, in the movies women beat up men bare-handed. In real life she had more chance of jumping to the moon than of pummeling a man into submission, no matter how much she worked out.

With her Taurus she could defend herself. Now, in a chivalrous manner she'd thought existed only in Arthurian legends, Rick wanted to defend her. She might let him.

She could still be independent.

To Warner she said, "I don't need your help."

He palpated his lip. "You haven't thought of escape?"

"We can escape without your help."

"Dozens of creatures wait for us out there. They protect the entrances. You need all the help you can get."

He murdered Jim, she knew it, in spite of Charlie's defense of him. He had the demeanor of a man who had killed. She could not trust him. And yet...

Rick arched an eyebrow at her.

Grasping his wrist and dragging him into the far corner where the others couldn't hear their conversation, she said, "What do you think?"

"Don't trust him. If the creatures attack, I'd much rather they kill him than us."

"So we take him. But we never turn our backs on him."

"Let me worry about him. You worry about you."

"Thought you were doing that for me."

"About time you helped in that department."

She ambled into the center of the room. Although she sensed him staring at her, she kept her head turned away. He sauntered up behind her, settling his hands on her shoulders.

His lips brushed her ear. He said, "I'll handle Warner. Just don't you go running off again."

"I'll try."

His fingernails dug into her shoulders for a second. Then he strode toward Warner.

Waving the .45 at Warner's chest while acting as if he had no idea the gun was pointed at Warner, he jerked his head toward the doorway. "You go first."

Warner's gun hand twitched. The flashlight clipped onto his belt wobbled.

Katy glanced over her shoulder at the tunnel through which she had first entered the caves. The memory of falling through the trap door flashed through her mind and she winced. The trap door.

Warner stalked toward the corridor.

"Wait!" Katy said. "I have an idea."

Four sets of eyes focused on her, five including Yoda, whose lip flapped as he exhaled. A growl grumbled in his chest.

She charged into the tunnel, toward the trap door. At the dirt pile she'd erected earlier, Rick trotted up beside her. He hopped onto the pile and grabbed the wooden peg in the trap door. He pulled.

The door held.

He strained against the portal. His features contorted. His tongue poked out between his teeth. He listed backward but the door remained sealed. Panting, he dropped his arms. His shoulders heaved with each breath.

"Stuck?" Katy said.

He sucked in a breath and pulled once more. The rest of the gang congregated behind her. Diane rubbed her arms while Warner observed without expression.

The portal sprang open. Rick tripped, skidded off the mound, and plunged into Katy, his face smacking into her chest. She shoved him away. Looking at the aperture the trap door had concealed, she bit her lip. Solid stone blocked it.

Charlie blinked slowly. "Of course."

"What do you mean of course?" Katy asked.

"They've locked us in." He gestured at the portal. "There are always rocks near the trap doors. Sometimes they're obvious, but mostly the creatures hide them in brush. I wondered what the rocks were for."

Katy rubbed her forehead. The beginnings of a headache twanged behind her eyes. She had seen the rocks too. She didn't notice they stood near trap doors. It made sense. The creatures needed a way of barricading the entrances in an emergency. Despite the doors opening from the inside, someone might figure out how to pry the doors up or push them down into the tunnels. Disaster for the creatures. Cover the door with a rock and, voila, the leak was sealed.

Except they had become the leak. The creatures sealed them inside.

Until midnight.

"Gotta be a way," Rick said. "Anybody remember where the front door is?"

"Yes," Warner said, slipping a device out of his pocket. "I marked it as a way-point on the GPS."

His GPS looked a lot like hers. Katy patted her fanny pack and felt the outline of her GPS radio.

Warner punched buttons on the GPS. "Follow me."

He headed down the tunnel. Rick fell in step a foot behind him. Katy hurried after them. Charlie, wrenching the torch out of the floor as they crossed the holding cell, hustled after her with Diane in tow.

Once they passed through the threshold into the corridor, Warner's flashlight blinked on ahead of her. Rick glanced back at her, his face half shadowed.

They traveled several hundred feet before Charlie sprinted past Katy and Rick to Warner. He said, "What about your friend?"

"He is not my friend," Warner said.

"They're going to kill him."

"He made a bad decision. Now he must pay for it."

"He's still a human being."

Warner snickered. "There is debate over that point."

Katy jogged to catch up with Rick, who lagged behind Charlie. She said, "You're talking about Ivan."

Neither man spoke. They were talking about Ivan all right. Although she disliked Ivan as well, they couldn't let the creatures kill him. He was an idiot, a completely irritating cretin who deserved much, nevertheless execution by hairy hominids was not one of the punishments he deserved. She saw how the creatures killed animals. She saw the massacre painting. No one deserved to have his neck snapped, his chest crushed, his head torn from his spine. Except maybe Warner.

"If they have Ivan," she said, "we have to go and get him."

Warner wheeled around to face her. His mouth was twisted in a cross between a frown and a sneer. "He is not worth the effort."

"Why?"

His lip twitched.

"He's a human being," Rick said. "No matter how obnoxious he is, we can't let him die."

Warner glared at Rick, who returned his glare twofold. Charlie watched with a blank expression. Diane loitered ten paces behind the group. Katy scrutinized the wall.

When trying to escape, the last thing anyone wanted was an impasse. While someone must compromise, she sure didn't want Warner getting his way. Because she despised him and because her conscience would wither if she let a man die knowing she could've saved him, she must make Warner compromise.

While she pondered a compromise, she studied Diane. The woman hugged herself as if she feared her arms would fall off if she let go. Her cheeks were colorless, her eyes wide. Though she bit her lip to quiet the tremors in them, the shaking leeched into her jaw, eliciting a faint chatter.

"Who are you?" Katy said. "What are you doing out here?"

Diane gnawed the inside of her cheek.

"She's Diane Frasier," Charlie said.

"As in Diane Frasier Realty?"

"Didn't you recognize her? Her picture is in the paper every Sunday, in those real estate ads."

"I never look at the ads."

Katy tromped closer to Diane. "Why does a real estate agent care about hairy hominids?"

Diane looked at Warner, who simply returned her gaze. If she hoped for her savior to step in, she had misjudged his compassion.

"To save my livelihood," Diane said. "The way Ivan explained it, these creatures could mean the end of real estate development in this area. In any area where those monsters are."

She met Katy's gaze, tears welling in her eyes. "I don't just sell real estate, I invest in it. Imagine what would happen if you prove these creatures are real."

A tear traced a rivulet down Diane's cheek. She sniffled and averted her gaze.

What would happen? Katy had thought about one consequence. The chance for vindicating herself and Charlie, proving the skeptics wrong, invalidating a host of ludicrous theories about the hairy hominids. From the *Gigantopithecus* theory to the psychic hippie nonsense, she could knock them all down like pins in a bowling alley. Where else the bowling ball might roll, she didn't consider. Over the past few days, she realized the creatures needed protecting from humans. If she exposed them to the world, hunters would swarm the woods in a competition to become the first to kill a creature. Anthropologists would stampede to reach the creatures first and capture one alive or observe them in their natural habitat. Environmentalists would argue the creatures merited protection as an endangered species.

Since the creatures either lived in small populations or hid their numbers, they would qualify for protection. The wrath of the EPA would be unleashed.

She imagined the headlines. *EPA Declares North Woods Bigfoot Sanctuary. Real Estate Values Plummet. Government Grabs Land for Bigfoot Sanctuary. Economy Flounders in North Woods.*

And it wouldn't stop there. The creatures inhabited other parts of the country. One by one communities would flatten under the heel of the United States government. The creatures needed protecting, but not at the expense of human lives.

She understood why Diane Frasier had come. The woman felt her livelihood—her life—teetering on the edge of a precipice. A breeze could knock her over the edge.

Katy knew she must protect the creatures from humans. Now she knew she must protect humans as well. She could never let the creatures' existence become known.

Rick and Warner resumed glaring at each other.

Katy rolled her eyes. "Come on, boys, we have work to do."

Warner stalked down the corridor. "I believe I can find the chamber where they are keeping Ivan."

Rick waited for Katy to follow Warner before he headed out too. If Warner led them to Ivan, good, they'd get the job done faster and get the hell out of this hole before the creatures realized they'd gone. If he lured them into a trap...

They would deal with it when it happened.

R ICK GRITTED HIS TEETH. THE SITUATION STANK WORSE THAN THE HAIRY hominids. Dad could handle himself fine. Diane Frasier was no concern. She was too anxious to do anything. He worried more about Katy. And Warner.

He wanted Katy in front of him, where he could keep tabs on her. Having Warner ahead of him, ahead of Katy, made his hand tighten around the .45 so much it ached. The joints in his trigger finger locked up too. Warner might swing around and shoot Katy, or grab her and shoot him.

Dad and Katy having an affair seemed stupid now. The way they interacted made it so clear he felt like a heel for ever thinking they were involved. No wonder Katy got irritated with him. She knew what he thought and was offended by it. He should apologize. Every time he tried the words paralyzed his vocal chords.

Now they were rescuing Ivan. He said, and he believed it, that they couldn't let Ivan die. The little rat annoyed everybody, with his head harder than steel and a brain he must've stopped using as a teenager. Ivan insisted on shooting a gun he couldn't handle, which meant he missed every shot. Ivan reminded Rick of the dentists who, on the weekends, dressed like Hell's Angels and mounted Harleys.

The corridor curved left. Warner halted in the bend. He held up a hand, tilting his head to listen.

Warner sprinted down the corridor.

Katy charged after him and Rick stayed right behind her. Warner had found a doorway. He stood in front of it, his flashlight directed at his feet, a hand over the flashlight's lens, fingers splayed to filter the beam.

"Through there," Warner said in a hushed voice. "We must be careful."

Katy screwed up her face the way she had when she noticed the skulls in the entrance cave. He squeezed between her and Warner.

The flashlight, hooded by Warner's fingers, lit the chamber in wedges of dull light. He and Katy passed through this chamber earlier. It had been empty then. Now eight hairy hominids slumbered on the mats.

Warner crept into the chamber.

Katy tiptoed in his wake. Rick followed. He glanced back to check that Dad and Diane hadn't gotten lost. Dad held the Remington in both hands, crosswise in front of him, close against his body. Diane shuffled along a foot behind him.

As they crossed the chamber the creatures stayed asleep, some snoring, others breathing heavily. Once they got through another doorway, turned into a corridor, and traveled a distance, Warner removed his hand from the flashlight. The beam brightened the corridor like a mini sun.

Warner stopped. Katy collided with him.

Rick hissed a breath. She shouldn't get so close to Warner.

Warner started walking. Rick sidled around Katy, putting himself between her and Warner. He glanced back every few seconds to check on her. Not much better, but at least Warner had to get through him to reach her.

She was still there.

He tailed Warner around a bend.

Although Katy lagged behind Dad, he could still see her. She was talking to Dad, who scrunched his mouth as if he disliked what she said.

The corridor descended. They advanced past a doorway.

She was there. Alongside Diane, urging the woman forward by cupping her elbow.

Ahead of him, Warner slowed. He swept the flashlight left and right. The hairs on Rick's neck prickled. Air gusted cold against his neck. He glanced back.

He trip-stopped. Katy was gone.

No, no, no…

"I have found him," Warner said.

Rick yanked the flashlight out of Warner's hand. He stampeded back down the corridor.

He paused beside Diane. "Where'd she go?"

"What?"

He shoved the flashlight under his arm and seized her shoulder. "Katy was right beside you. *Where did she go?*"

"I don't know."

Rick bolted down the corridor.

THE HAND, HAIRY ON TOP AND BARE ON THE PALM, SMOTHERED HER MOUTH and nose. She struggled for a breath, kicked her legs, but the creature had pinned her ankles between his calves. He clamped his free arm across her torso and arms as a restraining bar. Scratching her fingernails at the beast, she yelled. The thick pad of the creature's hand stifled her voice.

The hand slipped down a notch, freeing her nostrils. She snorted in air.

She stopped fighting. No point really, the creature had three feet and half a ton on her. Plus those muscles. They flexed and tautened around her. His hair tickled her face. When he dragged her into the crevice, he'd wrapped his body around her like a wetsuit. The two of them fit, though by a hair's breadth.

Rick ran past. The flashlight in his hand bobbled its beam across the walls.

She shouted and flailed. The creature's body muted the sound, thwarted her movement. The pounding of Rick's boots retreated down the corridor. The light dwindled.

Her heartbeat ticked out the minutes. Silence and darkness. The abysmal solitude of a tomb. Although she had never seen the tombs in Egypt's Valley of the Kings, carved out of a cliff face, she suddenly knew how it must feel inside those vaults. Sealed for millennia. Airless. Lightless. Populated by the dead.

She swallowed.

The creature pushed her out of the crevice. She shouted for Rick. The creature scooped her up in his arms. Footsteps clapped. A light flashed further ahead.

The creature trotted through a doorway.

"Rick!" she shouted.

The creature slapped a hand over her mouth. He tucked her in one arm and jogged through the darkness. The footfalls thumped closer, closer…

Rick passed the doorway. His footfalls retreated.

The creature carried her through the corridors. They ascended, turned, straightened, turned again. They went into a room lit by two torches. The meeting hall. She looked up at her captor. Garfield grunted.

Without setting her down, he kneeled and plucked a torch out of the earth with the hand he had held over her mouth. He gave her the torch. She took it in both hands. He left the room. Through the corridor they traveled, around bends and through doorways until they reached a dead-end. He plopped her onto her feet. They were at the slab door inscribed with the triangle logo.

Garfield planted his hands on the door's side and pulled. The muscles in his arms tensed and stretched. He gritted his teeth, his lips curling back over them. He pinched his face as he strained against the door. The rock groaned. He shifted position and pushed on the door's edge. Rock grated against rock. She winced.

He heaved the great door open.

Garfield moved aside, gaze averted, shoulders slouched, chin tucked. He faced the corridor wall. His shoulders rose and fell in time with his puffs of breath.

Jamming the torch into the dirt, she scuffled forward a few feet. The room was darker than dark. She had never seen a darkness so complete.

She neared the threshold. Inches from the room, she could smell the staleness within it. The sharp scent of a room that had seen no light, felt no circulation of air, in decades. Perhaps centuries.

Garfield pitched her into the room. She tripped, careened into the far wall.

She spun around just as he heaved the door shut. Rock screeched. The torch-light shrank into a wedge. She threw herself at the doorway and hit the floor flat on her belly an arm's length from the threshold. The impact knocked the breath out of her. The wedge of torchlight evaporated.

The door slammed shut.

18

W HERE KATY HAD BEEN, THERE WAS NOTHING. RICK SHUFFLED IN A CIRCLE. The flashlight's dove into a crevice and he froze. She might've ducked into the crevice. He sprinted toward it. No one there.

Why would she jump into a crevice? It was a stupid idea.

She had gone somewhere.

A minute earlier, as he ran down the corridor back to where Dad and the others waited, he'd heard Katy calling his name. Yet she was nowhere around. He must've imagined it. Wherever Katy went, he could neither see nor hear her.

A beeping interrupted his thoughts. Diane was squeezing her arms so tight her fingers had gone white. Dad thumped the stock of his Remington on the floor in a cadence. Warner waited further ahead, just outside the doorway he'd discovered, posture straight as a steel beam, pressing buttons on his GPS with his index finger.

"What are you doing?" Rick asked.

Warner said, "I can find her."

Rick sighted the .45 on Warner's forehead. "How?"

"This is your GPS. Ivan found it." He tilted the unit to show Rick the screen. "It has a tracking feature which is showing her current position."

Rick snatched the GPS from Warner. "Thanks, I can kill you now."

"If you fire that gun, the creatures will hear and come. Then you will never find her."

The sneer that had colored Warner's face earlier no longer warped his lips. Though he stood tall and kept his gaze trained on Rick, he had tucked the Glock inside his waistband. He hadn't reached for the gun in awhile. The confusion over Katy's disappearance gave him the perfect opportunity to seize control. Instead he lingered at the doorway, arms slack at his sides, watching.

The man was a murderer according to Katy. He sure didn't act like one.

Rick lowered the .45. Warner exuded tension, like a rubber band pulled taut until its fiber frayed. He seemed capable of killing. He'd had chances to kill them and done nothing. One more enigma. Rick came across so many lately he wondered if the sense of order he felt before had been an illusion. Maybe life was one mystery after another, always unsolved.

Dad cleared his throat. "She said something…"

Rick tipped his head toward his father. "What?"

"Katy said she thought we were being followed. By one of the creatures."

"They took her." Rick looked at the GPS. "I'm going after her."

Diane yelped.

Rick tracked her gaze to Warner, who had moved into the doorway. Warner aimed the Glock at the floor inside the doorway. Rick pushed in front of Diane. From there he could see past the doorway into the room, and spotted the boot-clad feet tied down by wooden stakes. Someone had driven stakes into the floor. He swept the flashlight across the room. The light revealed legs, followed by the torso, and finally the head. Ivan.

"Errie's going to kill him!" Diane said.

Ivan's wrists were also bound. He lay spread-eagled in the center of the room. Despite staring into the muzzle of Warner's Glock, he managed a smirk. The color, however, had bleached from his cheeks.

Warner exhaled in a growl.

Rick raised the .45 at Warner's head. "Kill him and I'll kill you."

"It would be worth the risk."

"You said he wasn't worth it."

"He isn't worth saving. He is worth killing."

Sand sifted out of the hourglass in Rick's head. He held the .45 level with Warner's forehead. The man really would give his own life to take Ivan's. With Katy he showed tolerance, even after she pointed her gun in his face. The guy even offered to help them escape. But with Ivan he wanted blood. Rick lowered his arm. He gave up understanding these people.

Rick said, "Fire and they'll hear, remember?"

Warner shot a sideways look at Rick. His jaw muscle twitched as he clamped his teeth together. His nostrils flared.

He stuffed the Glock inside his waistband.

"Knew you couldn't do it," Ivan said. "You got the attitude, Warner, but not the passion."

"Your only passion is for my money."

Warner retreated into the corridor.

"Somebody untie me," Ivan said.

The GPS showed Katy in the same spot she'd occupied five minutes before. She could be unconscious or injured or tied down like Ivan. What if the creatures hurt her?

If he let Ivan go and the little creep got in trouble, alerted the creatures somehow, they could all die. Katy would be alone.

Rick crouched beside Ivan.

"He will get us killed," Warner said. "He shot one of the creatures. He ran into a room where they sleep and shot one between the eyes before the others awakened and went after him."

"I suppose the other shots I heard were self-defense," Rick said.

"Ivan ran. The creatures didn't know which of us had done it so they came after all of us. I shot at them, yes, to no avail."

The ropes around Ivan's wrists and ankles were crude but strong. Rick freed Ivan without cutting the ropes, though untying some of the knots took longer than he wanted. Every minute he spent on Ivan meant less minutes for Katy. When he'd undone the final knot, Ivan ran for the door. Rick grabbed Ivan's jacket collar. He hauled the twerp backward.

Ivan sputtered objections. Rick twisted the man's hands behind his back, pulled them until he winced, wrapped a rope around the wrists, and tied a knot. Rick tied another length of rope to the binding as a leash.

"You freakin' cowboy," Ivan said. "Let me go!"

"There are two ways you can leave this room." Rick jabbed the .45 into Ivan's spine. "Your choice."

Grumbling, Ivan shuffled into the doorway. Rick trudged after him.

In the corridor, he checked the GPS.

Ivan swerved right. Rick tugged the leash. Ivan's hands jerked backward. He shouted, hopping in a half circle.

"This way," Rick said. "And you get to go first."

"Thanks, warden."

Rick snapped the leash taut.

Ivan stomped past him. "Get my backpack, will you."

The backpack rested against the wall in the far corner. Rick plucked it up, walked to Ivan, and slung the straps around Ivan's neck.

Rick tugged the leash. "At least you're carrying your own weight."

THE DIRT CHILLED HER BUTTOCKS AND LEGS. THE COLD SEARED HER LUNGS. Katy sat on the floor where she landed, in a room devoid of light, for many minutes before she dared move. Her pulse had calmed. She still felt the walls too close around her. She could stretch her arms out as far as possible without meeting the walls, yet she felt trapped in a tomb.

Get a grip, she told herself and raised onto her knees. Slowly, she stood. When she stretched an arm above her head, she could not touch the ceiling. The door was directly ahead, unless she was confused. In the dark, who could tell?

Holding a hand in front of her, she walked forward. Her fingertips bumped the door. Hands flat on the rock, she felt for the seam around the door. Her fingers found it a moment later. No draft leaked through the seam. Even her fingernail couldn't fit between the door and the wall. An airtight seam.

Seated on the floor, she'd tried reasoning out why Garfield locked her in here. He had stowed her, Rick, and Charlie in the butcher shop to hide them from the other creatures. They found out anyway. Maybe one of his buddies caught him stashing them there and told. Whatever the circumstances, Garfield came back with a sentry. The creatures left them in the holding cell believing they had no means of escape, because the doors were all sealed. Garfield, wanting to help, abducted her and brought her here. He took only her perhaps because his attempt at helping them all failed. He could sneak one human out, but three—not to mention five or six—created too many risks.

After opening the door, Garfield had turned away from her as if ashamed. She assumed he was ashamed of locking her in an airtight, lightless room. What if his shame stemmed from another source? The trouble he'd had opening the door, the airtight seal, both indicated no one had opened the door in ages. The door was engraved with the same markings as the grave of the human whose bones graced the creatures' front door. The triangle logo might signify a sacred object or place. Garfield might've felt ashamed at desecrating a sacred room.

A sacred room no creature had entered in years, if ever, was an excellent place to hide her. No one would look there. And no one saw Garfield spirit her there.

If he left her in here too long, she'd suffocate. Garfield might not understand humans needed air the same as hairy hominids, or he might not know the chamber was airtight. The creatures were smart, that she knew. She prayed he did understand.

She wanted to pound on the door and yell. Pointless. The sound might not penetrate the foot-thick door. If it did, no one waited on the other side to hear.

Running her hand along the wall, she passed over the seam. Her fingers bounced over indentations in the stone. She explored the indentations with her fingertips. Carvings. She slid her hand up the wall toward the ceiling, then down toward the floor. The carvings covered the height of the wall. They extended away from her as far as she could reach without stepping away from the door. She explored the wall on the other side of the door. More carvings filled that wall.

How far did the carvings go? She must abandon the door to find out, and she had no desire to do so. What if she couldn't find the door again? Blindness was new for her. She lacked the acuteness in her other senses that would let her navigate the darkness. But she must know.

What the heck. Things couldn't get much worse.

Hands flat on the wall, she felt her way toward the corner. There, she turned left and traced the carvings deeper into the room. The carvings covered the left wall too, floor to ceiling. The next corner steered her left. She felt more carvings.

They seemed to cover every wall of the room. If she could reach the ceiling she might've found carvings filled its expanse as well.

Her foot smacked into an obstruction. She bent down, keeping one hand on the wall. With her free hand she explored the obstruction. A slab of rock. The three-foot-high block sat a foot from the wall with its base buried in the floor. She felt along its backside. Smooth. On its front she detected more carvings. The slab, about three inches thick, was rectangular like a tombstone.

She jerked her hand away. A tombstone.

Find the door.

She tracked the wall to another joint that angled left. Her fingers skimmed over carvings. A moment later she met another corner, inched left, felt carvings, and a moment later crossed the seam onto the door.

Her breathing echoed off the walls. Yelling would waste oxygen. The oxygen would run out anyway. Why worry about losing a little now?

On the other side of the door, muffled by a foot of rock, someone screamed.

She pressed her ear to the door. Voices murmured like a distant brook. A voice shouted. She could neither make out the words nor discern the sex of the person. It was Rick, it had to be, the little jump in her heart rate told her. Wishful thinking?

It was him. She felt it. Right, she was psychic now.

Well, why not. If hairy hominids lived and humans had existed for 100 million years, she could certainly turn psychic.

Footsteps pounded outside, nearing the door.

She hopped back a step.

The rock groaned. The door popped out of its seam. A sliver of light sliced into the darkness. The rock shrieked, groaned, grated. The gap widened.

She felt like bolting into the corridor. Instead she waited, hands in pockets, as the door grated over the floor, out of its threshold into the room. When the slab cleared the doorway, she ambled into the corridor.

Rick pulled her into his arms. Relief surged through her. She flung her arms around him, squeezing until he gasped, then backed away one step.

He laid his palm on her cheek. "You okay?"

"Yes, yes. How did you get the door open?"

"Your boyfriend over there."

Katy glanced back. Garfield hunched between the open door and the wall.

"I think he was guarding the door," Rick said. "He came out of a hole in the wall and scared us half to death. He wanted to throttle me but Dad convinced him to open the door instead. Don't ask me how, he started waving his arms and grunting and for some reason it made sense to Garfield."

"Garfield?"

"Isn't that what you called him?"

"You never called him that before." She noticed Diane and Warner near the wall, close to Garfield. "You didn't get Ivan yet."

"Sure did," Rick said.

He looked at his hand, squinted, sighed. The sound reminded her of a water droplet splattering on a hot plate.

"I dropped the rope." He kicked the floor. "Where'd the little weasel go?"

No one spoke. Rick shined the flashlight down the corridor. Shadows flitted away from the beam. The light cascaded over dirt and rock, but no Ivan.

He jabbed a finger at Warner. "You kill him?"

"No," Warner said, "and I did not notice when he fled."

"Great. We better find him."

"Let the creatures have him. He will deserve whatever they do to him."

"You keep saying that."

Katy stamped toward Warner. Halting a few feet from him, glaring straight into his eyes, she said, "What aren't you telling us?"

"You will not believe. Your ideas about me will not allow it."

"Try me." She planted her hands on her hips. "Start with who he is. Ivan said he had a professional name."

Warner pursed his lips. "Fine. His professional name is Dr. Carl Ivan Thorson, founder of the Northern Michigan Sasquatch Society. Anthropologist for the Museum of Prehistory in Chicago."

"Your museum."

"I hired him. I created him."

No wonder Ivan looked so familiar. She had attended a half dozen meetings of the NMSS before she marked it as a sham. Carl Ivan Thorson espoused nonsense about the creatures having psychic powers as well as the ability to levitate, and claimed they evolved from *Gigantopithecus*. His Giganto theory, though she disagreed with it, seemed like his one concession to sense. She'd watched from the back row as he brought out casts of overlapping bear footprints which he identified as Sasquatch tracks. She listened to his lecture on human evolution in which he got half the facts wrong. He was an idiot.

He was Ivan Thaw. Of course.

She raised her eyebrows at Warner. "What do you mean you created him?"

"Ten years ago, he was blacklisted. He was fired from his job at Harvard when he faked evidence. No one else would touch him. Not only did he cling to the idea humans evolved from Neanderthals, he falsified DNA tests to prove it. The laboratory that performed the tests knew nothing of it. He gave them a Neanderthal bone which he had contaminated with modern DNA. They discovered his scheme, and Ivan Thaw's career died. I resurrected him as Carl Ivan Thorson."

"Why?"

"I needed a voice in cryptozoology. Someone who would say whatever I told him, destroy evidence if necessary, and keep me informed of new discoveries. I cannot let these creatures be proved real."

"I don't understand why you care."

"I own mines, lumber companies, sawmills, factories that create products from those raw materials. If these creatures are real, they are an endangered species."

"Diane will lose her real estate agency and you'll lose your companies. You're a billionaire, you could move on."

"My children could not."

She tilted her head. He clamped his jaw tight, narrowed his eyes. She glanced at his left hand. No wedding ring.

Diane scuttled toward him. Eyes bulging, she said, "You're married?"

She really zeroed in on the important information.

"No," Warner said, "I have never married. My children are my workers. The people in the factories, at the mills, in the mines. The ones who struggle to make their mortgage payments and save for their children's college education. I have a responsibility to them, to their families."

"If you lose your companies," Katy said, "they lose their jobs."

He nodded.

"With thousands of people unemployed, the competition for other jobs would be enormous."

"You understand."

"Yes, I do."

She looked up at the ceiling. Above her head, people struggled to survive on minimum wage. They fought to keep their families fed and sheltered. If they lost their jobs, if mining and lumbering and real estate were stopped to protect the hairy hominids, Warner's children would suffer along with thousands of others. She understood why he wanted the creatures to stay a mystery. They could become the biggest endangered species of all time, the gold medal winner in environmentalist circles.

Farmers in the Northwest had lost their water rights because of one fish. Californians lost their land to the kangaroo rat. Those cases were insignificant next to the hairy hominids.

She frowned at Warner. "That hardly justifies murder."

"I murdered no one."

"Jim Van Owen is someone."

"I was in Chicago when he was killed."

She let out a harsh laugh. "You expect me to believe you didn't kill Jim when you've been trying to kill us."

"Actually," Rick said, "he hasn't."

"Of course he has."

"Think about it. He never shot at us. Never attacked us."

"He held a gun to my head."

"But he *didn't shoot*."

He had a point and she hated it. Warner overlooked the chance to kill her. Sure, Garfield intervened. Warner had plenty of time before that. He could've pulled the trigger. If he really wanted her dead, why hesitate?

To find Charlie. He needed all of them dead. Killing her and Rick wouldn't erase the problem, because Charlie knew where the creatures lived. Warner needed her to find Charlie.

Which brought her back to the same problem. Why not kill them now? Plenty of opportunity, plenty of time, plenty of ammo. He might get shot in the ruckus, but a man like Warner would hardly consider that relevant. In this moment, after expending much time and money on the problem, he waffled. With victory so close.

"If you aren't going to kill us," she said, "why follow us out here? Why break into my house and rifle through my computer files? Why have me followed in town?"

"I believed you knew where Dr. Bergren was hiding. In your computer files my man found a map he thought would be useful. It gave an idea of where Dr. Bergren had gone into the woods. I needed more. My man broke into Dr. Bergren's house where he found nothing. He decided on his own to follow you, and he botched it. I realized I must follow you into the woods to find Dr. Bergren before either of you exposed the creatures."

In a fierce whisper, Warner said, "I will give you one million dollars to forget you saw this place."

"No," Katy said.

"Two million."

"I'm not for sale."

"Dr. Bergren was." He leaned toward her. "Name the price."

Charlie accepted Warner's money. Warner considered it a payoff, while Charlie believed he could take Warner's money and still do as he pleased. Warner thought more money would seal the leak in his ark. Paper was porous.

He had believed he controlled Ivan. No one controlled an arrogant moron for long. Ivan thought he knew better than everyone else, was cleverer, smarter, stronger. Despite Warner plastering more money over the leak, the water would burst through eventually. How desperate was Warner?

"Fifty million dollars," she said.

He clenched his hand in a loose fist. "All right."

For a moment her voice abandoned her. He would pay fifty million dollars to shut her up and keep the creatures secret, with no assurances she would stay quiet forever.

"No amount of money," she said, "will buy my conscience."

"Perhaps other enticements are necessary." He stepped closer, his face inches from hers. "An IRS audit might change your mind, or a visit from the DEA. Have you heard of asset forfeiture?"

His breath smelled of chocolate.

She knew about asset forfeiture. The government seized your house, your money, everything you owned without a shred of proof you'd broken the law. If they did want proof, Warner would fabricate some.

She exhaled in his face. He squinted. She said, "Either you make us rich or make us wish we were dead. But you won't actually kill us."

"There are fates worse than death."

She backed up beside Rick. He scowled at Warner as if he wanted to lock the man inside the airtight room until he suffocated. At the same time he believed Warner didn't kill Jim. Maybe he was as confused as she was.

Fates worse than death. Yes, she could envision plenty of them. False charges that forced them to spend years in court proving their innocence or got them sentenced to decades in prison. IRS audits that cost them their jobs, their savings, their futures. Suspicions that drove them out of town, rendered them unemployable, left them eating at soup kitchens and sleeping in alleys.

Maybe they ought to take the money.

She would hate herself if she did.

"Perhaps," Warner said, "you would like to know who did kill your friend."

She said nothing. The words she felt like spewing would only worsen the situation.

"I did not kill him," Warner said. "Ivan did."

Blood oozed from the abrasions on his wrists. It trickled down his hand, dripped off his fingertips onto the ground. Since the blood dropped intermittently, it left no real trail.

Ivan rubbed his back where an ache had cropped up a few minutes ago. The Desert Eagle had bashed a bruise into his spine when he got thrown into the rock wall by the creatures. He'd shoved it down the back of his pants before the creatures grabbed him. No one—not the creatures, not Warner, not Rick Bergren— thought to look for it there. One piece of luck after another. He must be blessed.

He lost his backpack, though. Because the pack weighed a ton, especially dangling around his neck, he bent his head forward to ease the pain. The pack slipped off onto the ground right behind the cowboy.

Oh well, he had the Desert Eagle.

He lunged onward, head bent. The crown of his head smacked into a wall.

Ivan bit back a curse. Screaming, no matter how good it felt, might give away his position. He didn't see the flashlight behind him anymore. This was far enough. His heel caught on something, he stumbled, fell, hit the ground butt-first. His tailbone smarted.

Blasted rope. Curse Katy Gallagher and curse her cowboy of a boyfriend.

There are two ways you can leave this room.

There was just one way Rick Bergren would leave these caves. Dragged by his heels while the blood settled in his backside because his heart stopped pumping.

Back on his feet, Ivan scuffled backward until his butt bumped the wall. Exploring the rock with his fingers, he located a point jutting out of the wall. Sharp enough to cut the rope. He positioned his wrists on either side of the point, hunching his shoulders and raising onto his toes to reach it. The rope was above the point. He jerked his hands down. The rope raked across the point. While the rope held, he felt a fray where the point had rubbed against it. He ground the rope over the point, up and down, over and over.

Nobody thought he had the brains to escape. Nobody thought he had the nerve either. *Dumb Ivan, poor slob, can't think unless Warner gives him ideas, can't shoot a bear at two feet.*

He showed them. He had the guts and the brains to get rid of Jim Van Owen in a way nobody would question his death. Of course the moron needed some cajoling before he'd swig the concoction Ivan brewed up special for the occasion—a mixture of plain beer and neutral spirits, alcohol so concentrated a person would get drunk on two beers, maybe one. Neutral spirits were tasteless, colorless, and odorless. The stuff burned going down but, with a bit of finessing, Ivan made sure Jim never noticed.

Ivan stole the neutral spirits from the distillery Diane's brother ran, during the tour last week. When her brother explained the liquid's properties, Ivan knew it would prove useful sometime. He hadn't realized how soon sometime would come.

At first, Jim refused the drink.

"One beer," Ivan had urged.

"No thanks," Jim had said, leaning on the tailgate of his truck, "gotta get home to the wife."

"Come," Ivan said in his imitation of Warner's accent. "One beer to celebrate your big break."

Why did he imitate Warner's accent? For the sheer fun of it, naturally.

Ivan called up the image of what he saw when he looked into the truck's bed. The parking lot lights tinted the body yellow. The body was small, a juvenile under six feet long, three hundred pounds in weight. Hair covered its body from head to toe, except around the eyes and mouth and over the nose. A genuine Sasquatch. The slimebucket found a type specimen, and he didn't even have to kill it. Just traipsed into the woods and found it.

After tailing Jim to Lake Anameka State Park, Ivan had waited until Jim moseyed into the woods before he parked his Mazda beside Jim's Ford truck. No other vehicles sat in the parking lot. No tourists this time of year.

Yet when Jim plodded out of the woods, huffing and dragging the specimen behind him, the ninny thought nothing of Ivan standing beside the Mazda like a tourist taking in the scenery. When Ivan offered to help carry the specimen, Jim thanked him. In his excitement, he'd blurted out how he found the body and what he intended to do with it. That's how Ivan figured out no one knew where Jim was. No one would miss him for awhile.

When Jim turned down another beer, Ivan waggled a bottle in Jim's face. Sucking in the outburst he felt rising in his throat, he had said calmly, "Just one."

A pause. The outburst, a curse itching to spew from Ivan's mouth, rose higher and higher in his gullet as the seconds ticked past.

"Okay," Jim said finally, "one won't kill me."

Then he took the bottle and gulped down some beer. Scrunching his face, he coughed. "What kinda beer is this?"

"German. You know us Nazis, we like stuff that burns your throat out."

"Maybe I shouldn't drink it. Don't want to get sloshed."

"Got the same alcohol content as regular beer."

Jim had studied the bottle, rotating it in his hand. With a shrug, he downed another mouthful.

Half an hour later they relocated to the cliff at the shore of Lake Anameka. Jim slouched at the edge talking to the moon. Ivan squatted near the fire they had built while Jim gulped down another bottle of pure alcohol.

Warner wanted the body destroyed. Screw Warner, Ivan decided. He deserved fortune and glory. He'd take the specimen for himself.

So he got rid of the one obstacle to his success. Jim Van Owen.

Ivan smiled as he recalled hurrying back to the parking lot while Jim sank into the lake. Ivan had left the fire burning to leave the impression Jim camped out there, got drunk, and stumbled over the cliff.

Ivan had hauled the body halfway out of the bed of Jim's truck when his cell phone rang.

"Have you obtained the specimen?" Warner said.

"No, he didn't have it."

"I tapped his home phone. He called his wife earlier to say he had found it. Do not lie to me, Ivan."

"It's mine, Warner, you can't have it."

"Norman is waiting at your house. Take it there. The two of you will burn it."

"Wait."

"*Do it.*"

Drifting back to the present, realizing he had stopped working at the rope, Ivan rubbed the fibers across the rock. Warner coerced him into destroying the goldmine once. Never again. This time he would get it and keep it. If Warner or Katy Gallagher interfered, he'd get rid of them the way he got rid of Jim Van Owen.

He might do it even if they stayed out of his way.

Snap!

The rope fell off his wrists. He yanked the Desert Eagle out of his pants. Nothing would keep him from his goldmine.

GARFIELD GRUNTED. HE DROOPED HIS HEAD DOWN TO HIS CHEST, EYES FIXED on the floor, hands fidgeting at his sides. He shook his head and laid a hand on the door. He was going to close it.

Katy raced toward the doorway. She stopped in front of the door but outside the threshold. Garfield would have to squash her if he wanted the door closed.

He grunted.

She didn't move.

He howled, waved his arms, stomped his feet.

A gunshot detonated in the corridor. She snatched the Taurus from her fanny pack. As she swung it up, another shot exploded. She dropped into a crouch.

Diane was flat on the ground, hands over her head. Warner stooped beside her, the Glock in both hands, gaze narrowed on the darkness further down the corridor.

Charlie had flattened himself against the wall. He grasped the Remington in both hands as he sighted down the barrel. Rick, across the corridor from him, aimed the .45 down the corridor. The flashlight rested at his feet, its beam pointed in the direction of the gunfire.

A chunk of ceiling lay on the ground.

She dodged inside the room and to the right, peeking around the doorway, her finger on the trigger. She sighted the Taurus around the corner. Her ears rang. Her nerves buzzed with electricity. The shot had been beyond deafening. Must be Ivan and his gold cannon.

Rick sidled down the corridor.

She whispered, "No!"

He dismissed her objection with a wave of his hand. If he lived, she'd kill him. She crept across the threshold.

Boom! Rock splintered off the door near her head.

Rick fired.

Garfield shrieked. Pounding his fists on his chest, he took off down the corridor past Warner and Diane, beyond Charlie to Rick. Garfield clenched a handful of Rick's jacket and hurled him at the others. Rick landed on his back ten feet in front of Katy. The .45 slipped out his grasp, clattered across the floor into the wall.

Garfield stormed down the corridor.

Three shots echoed off the walls in an earsplitting chorus.

Garfield jerked. He stumbled backward. With an apelike cry, he staggered into the darkness.

A man screamed.

No one moved. For five minutes or more, they trained their guns on the shadows, muscles rigid as the rock around them. When nothing happened, they relaxed.

Rick stepped into the middle of the corridor. Facing the doorway, he said, "Garfield must've gotten him."

Over his shoulder, a starburst exploded.

Katy lurched sideways and fired at the flash once, twice, three times.

Garfield limped out of the shadows. He stopped at the perimeter of the flashlight's beam, one hand shielding a wound in his arm. Another wound bled from his thigh. In his hand he clutched a lock of black hair.

He tossed the hair. It fluttered onto the floor. He pointed at the hair, grunted. When he saw the bewilderment on the humans' faces, he hooked a thumb over his shoulder, pointed at the hair, and stomped his foot. "Oogah."

Charlie clapped his hands. "Oogah."

Garfield hobbled away. Soon his figure merged with the shadows.

"He chased Ivan away," Charlie said, walking toward the doorway past Katy. "Or else he killed him. Not sure which."

Rick grabbed the flashlight. He marched down the corridor a ways. When he returned, he shrugged.

Behind her, Charlie said, "Forget Ivan. Better have a look at this."

She and Rick sneaked to where Charlie waited at the threshold of the sacred room. Charlie's pen light illuminated slices of the room. On the walls colorful symbols materialized then evanesced in the medium of the light.

Rick aimed his flashlight through the doorway.

Inside the room, the beam exposed the symbols as painted carvings rather than apparitions. The slab she took for a tombstone bore additional symbols, carved into the stone and then painted, like the walls. On the ceiling, a false sky glittered with stars. Embodiments of constellations, such as a lion and a crocodile, cavorted in the shelter of a goddess whose elongated body stretched over them. Beings, humanlike but sporting discs on their heads, lined up above the goddess. Around the pictures were more symbols. Not just symbols.

Egyptian hieroglyphs.

Rick whistled. "You know what that is."

"Yep."

"What does it mean?"

"Darned if I know." She squeezed past Charlie. "But something tells me we better find out."

19

KATY INCHED DEEPER INTO THE ROOM. CHARLIE, CLICKING OFF HIS PEN LIGHT, skulked into the corner behind her. He clasped his hands behind his back, head tilted up, clucking his tongue as he admired the ceiling.

Rick lingered in the doorway. His mouth dropped open. The flashlight beam reflected in his eyes.

"Come on in," she said. "We need your expert opinion."

"I don't see any account ledgers in here."

She made a face at him. "I meant the hieroglyphs. You know all about them, right?"

He shambled halfway into the room, five feet from Katy. She had stopped at the standing stone, a few feet from the wall. The room was about fifteen feet long, seven feet wide, and eight feet tall. The floor was compacted earth identical to the floors in the rest of the caves. The walls were carved out of the bedrock, smoothed until they appeared perfectly flat. Now that Rick had entered the room, the flashlight lit the ceiling better. She could tell the ceiling was concave with flat ends like the inside of a barrel.

"It looks ancient Egyptian," Rick said. "The curved ceiling. The hieroglyphic inscriptions. The stela."

"The what?"

"Stela." He gestured at the standing stone. "A standing slab with inscriptions on it."

"What about the hieroglyphs?"

He feigned an interest in the floor.

She cleared her throat so forcefully it segued into a cough.

Hunching his shoulders, head down, he looked at her. "I studied hieroglyphs years ago. If I mess this up…our lives could depend on understanding these inscriptions. I'm an *accountant*."

"Today you're an Egyptologist." She crossed the room to him and took his face in her hands. "You can do it, honey, I know you can."

For a moment he squinted at her, the blue of his eyes so intense, so alluring, that she waffled between wanting to kiss him and worrying that, should he still believe she was fooling around with his father, he might misinterpret such an overture.

He straightened. "I need some paper and a pen."

Her pack was outside somewhere. Charlie, regarding the hieroglyphic carvings, said, "Don't look at me. I keep notes in my head."

In the corridor, she asked Warner if he had paper.

"No," he said, "but Ivan would. I believe that is his backpack over there."

When he indicated a lump on the floor, she headed straight for it. Threads, frayed off the seams, frizzed on the outside of the pack. A rip spilled the contents of one pocket onto the floor. Inside another pocket she found a pad of paper and a pen. As she rose, she noticed the unzipped top flap.

She glanced at Warner, who turned his head away. Charlie had followed her into the corridor and now faced away from her with his hands hovering a hair's breadth above Diane's shoulders. Tears stained the woman's cheeks. Charlie, face crimped, murmured to her. His body blocked Diane's view. Katy flipped up the flap. Strangely, she felt like a criminal for peeking inside Ivan's pack.

A flannel shirt was crumpled into the pack. She pushed it out of the way, digging her hand deep inside. Grasping an object, she pulled it out. A digital camera.

She dropped it into her jacket pocket. Not stealing. Borrowing.

Besides, stealing from a murderer hardly counted.

Digging into another compartment, she discovered an extra ammo clip rubber-banded to a long metal tube. The tube's surface was burnished gold. A moment passed before the tube's purpose registered in her mind. It was a silencer for Ivan's gun. She stuffed it back inside the pocket.

After taking the pad and pen to Rick, she left him muttering to himself and scribbling on the pad. She strolled up beside Warner. She had moved the flashlight into the doorway and turned it on its end so the beam shined on the ceiling. It illuminated the hieroglyph room along with part of the corridor. Warner had positioned himself at the light's periphery, facing the darkened corridor. He held the Glock at his side, muzzle down, his arm dangling.

"Guarding us?" she said.

He didn't look at her. "Someone must watch for Ivan."

"But you hate us."

"No."

"You would've held me at gunpoint until I took you to Charlie." She folded her arms over her chest. "Forgive me if that doesn't breed trust."

"I do what I must. As do you."

She'd believed when she knew, for certain, who killed Jim that she'd want revenge immediately. Anger would take over her. She believed Warner, inexplicably. Ivan shot at her and Rick in the woods and at all of them here in the caves. He intended to kill them. Only his choice of weapons foiled his attempts. Warner offered bribes, threatened ruination, but he never threatened their lives.

He pointed his gun at them, more than once. If she accepted his money, he would expect her to follow his orders. He wanted control. He'd tighten the strait-jacket around her until she relinquished that control. Nonetheless, he stopped short of killing. He was a strange man.

"You don't like Ivan," she said.

"I would kill him for sheer pleasure."

"You said you don't murder."

"For Ivan, I would make an exception." He propped his shoulder against the wall. "I didn't want them to come. Ivan knew something of my past, and threatened exposure. Diane goes along with whatever Ivan does. She knew him before his resurrection."

"If they exposed you for paying off Ivan and inventing a new identity for him, they'd be exposing Ivan too."

"It has nothing to do with Ivan. They know of…another incident."

He would not tell her. Whatever secret Ivan and Diane knew, it must've been good to coerce Warner into taking the two of them on this trip. While he could've killed them instead, he was no murderer.

The realization hit her like a brick in the face. For days she convinced herself Warner killed Jim. The truth had spun 180 degrees, leaving her dizzy. She must concentrate on one thing at a time, leave Ivan for later, let Rick puzzle out the hieroglyphs. Another mystery, one she had shelved while searching for Charlie and trying to stay alive, tickled her brain.

What were the hairy hominids?

She read of the evidence humans had lived on the planet for tens, even hundreds, of millions of years. The footprint she found in Texas supported the idea. She had lost that evidence, to the fascist park rangers. Perhaps she struggled toward the wrong goal. Instead of seeking to prove her theories to the world, maybe she should concentrate on proving them to herself. For the moment, self-convincing would do. Once she connected the dots in her own mind, she could worry about convincing the world.

As if she could. The scientific establishment balked at any insinuation Darwin was wrong, any hint their theories were nothing more than fantasy. They quashed anyone who opposed them, sequestered the evidence, ridiculed what they couldn't bury. Most of them railed against the notion of man's antiquity because evolution had become ingrained in their psyches. For them, invalidating evolution equated with saying the earth was actually a basketball. Their minds refused to accept it.

A few scientists fought the truth out of fear for their prestige and salaries. They'd wagered their careers on this theory or that, all based on evolution. They must destroy the evidence.

The park rangers still bothered her. Why should they care if she found a footprint? No one would believe her anyway. Erosional depression, blurred dinosaur print, the skeptics had a litany of explanations. Why destroy the print? The rangers must've realized their actions would make her wonder and, possibly, investigate the issue. She could've called the Texas Parks & Wildlife Department, reported their actions, and demanded restitution or punishment for them. She could have made trouble. Yet they seemed unconcerned. While she could think of several reasons, one stuck in her mind. They knew she could never find them.

Because they didn't work for the parks department.

Did they have anything to do with the hairy hominids?

She believed evolution was crap—human evolution. What if evolution happened, just not with humans? The hairy hominids might represent the pinnacle of hominid evolution on Earth. Maybe evolution happened, but not with humans, and the hairy hominids represented the endpoint for hominid evolution. They evolved from *Homo erectus* and either *Homo heidelbergensis* or Neanderthals, according to the current ordering of the hominid family tree. Both *erectus* and heidelbergs were tall. The heidelbergs sported massive leg bones that must have supported massive muscles. The Neanderthals also had strong bodies, but were generally shorter. Both species shared with the hairy hominids their pronounced brow ridges.

The idea the ancient hominids were hairless sprang from the notion they must've sweated and therefore evolved out of their fur to aid in cooling. Their tall frames supposedly provided more surface area for heat loss. Anthropologists summoned, as proof of this theory, another hypothesis. They claimed modern humans who lived in tropical climates grew taller while those who lived in frigid climes became shorter and stockier, both as adaptations to their environments. A glance around the world disproved the notion. Not all Africans were tall, and not all northern people were short. Scandinavians lived in cold climates yet many had tall, slim frames.

In the animal kingdom, hair helped cool the body. Despite living in hot climates, out on the African savanna, lions and leopards had fur. Their coats insulated them from the heat. No one knew whether early hominids sweated. Even if they did, other animals sweated and still had hair—horses, for instance. The notion of the hairless *erectus* or heidelberg stemmed less from any hard evidence than from the assumption that, if they represent our ancestors, they must resemble us.

The hairy hominids could've evolved either from the heidelbergs or from Neanderthals.

She shut her eyes. The answer haunted the recesses of her mind. She needed to drag it into the light to understand it. Understand what? Who hairy hominids were, what they meant to humans, how humans fit into the world.

If humans fit at all.

A LIGHT GLIMMERED TWENTY FEET AHEAD THROUGH A DOORWAY. A SCRAPING issued from beyond the doorway while shadows of the room's occupant danced in the firelight.

Ivan paused at the bend in the corridor. His scalp and wrist abrasions had scabbed over, but still burned. The creature left him lying on the floor, assuming he was dead. Dumb animal. Must have the brain of a rat.

When he'd recovered from the attack, he checked the clip in his Desert Eagle. One bullet left. Couldn't waste it. He decided exploring the caves might give him an advantage. Navigating in the dark proved slow work. Still, if he knew the layout he might find a way to separate Rick Bergren from his gang. Alone, Bergren would be easier to kill. At first Ivan wanted Katy Gallagher dead the most. His priorities had changed.

He touched the abrasions on his wrists. He would kill the cowboy first.

Then he could take the cowboy's gun and slaughter the rest of them. Gallagher next, followed by Warner and the old fart. Diane he would save for last.

She betrayed him. And not for money, which he could understand, but for lust. She wanted Warner, and betrayed her oldest friend to get him. Ivan thumped his fist into the wall. He should've guessed. The way she acted around Warner, thrusting her bosom out until her breasts practically slapped her in the face, pouting like a supermodel, agreeing with everything Warner said, giggling when he made a stupid joke. He should never have introduced them.

How could he have guessed Diane would go for a Nazi? Since she knew about his deal with Warner, he figured they should meet. Besides, Diane kept bugging him about it. I want to meet the big man, I want to know what a mobster is like, let me come to your next meeting. When he said no, she got all doe-eyed and flapped her eyelashes at him. So he said yes.

For a long time he'd wanted Diane. Like Katy Gallagher, she preferred the cowboys. Both of them would be gone soon. It wasn't that he enjoyed killing. Sometimes he had to get rid of the competition. Sometimes he had to make them pay.

The best part about killing Jim Van Owen was outsmarting the jerk—and the police. When the cops "discovered" his evidence, like good little sheep they followed it home. No one could pin the murder on him. Nobody called it a murder. Accidental drowning. Dead-drunk jerk who fell into the lake, that was Jim's epitaph.

Ivan slunk around the corner. He tiptoed toward the doorway. When he reached the threshold, he peeked into the room.

A gray, wart-faced creature crouched on the other side of a torch, which the monster had driven into the floor. The flame danced, accentuating the jerks of the creature's movements as it scraped a stone across the ropes binding its wrists. The stone was as large as its palm and tapered into a blade on one side. On the left side of the room, a bed of coals evidenced where a fire burned earlier.

The creature sniffed. It crinkled its nose.

The beast set to work on the ropes. A second later the rope snapped. As the creature tossed the rope away, it untied the rope around its ankles.

If he had his GPS and the silencer for the Desert Eagle, he could really have fun with Bergren and Gallagher. The GPS and the silencer were in his pack. Which they had. To get it, he needed a diversion.

Wait, he had an awesome idea. Ivan sucked in a deep breath. He leaped into the doorway, leveling the Desert Eagle at the creature.

Lifting its chin, the creature sniffed. It bared its teeth at him.

Ivan held his breath. Slowly, he lowered the gun.

The creature growled. Its eyes glowed red.

Tucking the gun inside his waistband, he raised his hands, palms toward the creature. He ducked his head. Another growl. Softer. He peeked at the creature. It had closed its mouth. The red glow lessened.

"Hey buddy," Ivan said.

The creature snorted.

Emphasizing the words with gestures, he said, "You want the woman with long hair? The woman?"

The creature crinkled its brow. The skin folded into wrinkles across the monster's forehead, above its bulging brow ridge. Ivan grabbed a coal from the extinguished fire. With it he drew a quick sketch on the wall. The roughness of the surface made accuracy difficult, but he managed a portrait that looked enough like Katy Gallagher to do the trick. If the creature knew what she looked like. If it wanted her dead. The creatures seemed ticked at her. This one might be out of the loop, though.

He pointed at the sketch. "Want her? I can take you to her."

The creature grunted. It plucked the torch out of the floor and strode into the doorway. It kept its back to him.

Ivan started after the creature, hesitated. He swiped the tool the creature had used to cut its ropes. Ivan tapped the blade. It was an Acheulian handaxe, the type used by *Homo erectus*. The creatures must've found it and figured out how to use it. They couldn't have made the handaxe. Toolmaking would mean they were as smart as humans. As smart as him. Screw that idea.

They found it. By accident, they learned to use it. Much better.

He tossed the handaxe on the floor.

The creature stomped down the corridor. He sprinted after it, overtook the creature, and swerved in front of it. The creature lurched forward as if to grab his neck. Ivan raised his hands. The creature stopped. Ivan placed two fingers on his lips.

"Quiet, buddy," he said. "That's how you sneak up on people."

YOU KNOW WHAT THEY ARE."

Katy jumped at Warner's voice. "I've been thinking it over."

"Tell me your thoughts."

While he spoke, he maintained his vigil in the corridor. She had lost the fear of him, the ice ball in her gut when she saw him, the anger at his very presence. She had wanted to kill him. To find herself conversing with him about the nature of the hairy hominids was freaky.

What the heck.

She said, "I think they're descended from *Homo erectus* and, possibly, *Homo heidelbergensis.* Which would make them the endpoint of hominid evolution. Of course current theory says, in the past, several species of hominid coexisted, it's the natural order of things. Which means we could be related to them."

"You do not believe that."

"Until modern humans arrived about 200,000 years ago, hominids looked like a subspecies of ape. Then, sproing! Here comes *Homo sapiens.* No more brow ridges, no more small brains, suddenly we have noses and flat faces and language and art."

Archaeologists dated the oldest cave paintings in Europe at more than 30,000 years old. Yet they showed more sophistication than the later cave art in the same region. How did humans spring up and—in an evolutionary second— begin expressing themselves in sophisticated artwork? No one could explain the anomaly.

No one could explain why humans chose deep, hard-to-access caves as the galleries where they expressed themselves in art. Viewing most cave art required an arduous journey through narrow tunnels and holes a human must crawl through backward. In at least one cave, archaeologists discovered fossilized footprints indicating numerous people tramped through the cave in antiquity. The archaeologists, of course, attributed the activity to religious rituals. In archaeology, if the evidence is puzzling simply declare it a religious ritual. Problem solved.

"Besides," Katy said, "the evidence humans have lived on this planet much longer than 200,000 years is obvious. You just have to look at it with an open mind. Which scientists don't do. But the evidence is there."

Warner murmured, "I have seen."

"Seen what?"

After several minutes without a word or movement from him, she shrugged and walked into the room where Rick had sat down on the floor. He squinted at the hieroglyphs on the wall, lips squeezed together, forehead wrinkled. He tapped the pen on the pad.

"Problem?" she asked.

"Need my books. Can't remember all the symbols." He shut his eyes. "Feels like my head's about to explode."

"Time for a break. We need more light anyway."

"Don't see a lamp or an electrical socket around here."

Straddling the doorway, she glanced at Charlie and Diane. Charlie had quit pretending he knew how to comfort her. Instead, he sat back on his heels and nodded with his lips flattened into a grimace. Diane made no effort to wipe away the tears flowing down her cheeks. Her eyes were bloodshot.

Diane sniffled. "I c-can't believe Ivan would kill anybody, how could he do that? He promised."

Katy interlocked her arms over her belly. "Promises mean nothing to a man like Ivan. He's scum. Forget about him."

Diane looked at her. She paused in her sniffling.

To Charlie, Katy said, "When we needed more fuel for the torch before, where did you get it?"

"Supply room."

"Can you find the room from here?"

He stood. "Yes."

"Good, take her and bring back as many torches and extra fuel for them as you can carry." When Diane balked, Katy shot her a glance that silenced the woman. "I don't want Ivan sneaking up on us. We need to light this corridor for as far as possible. Plus our flashlight won't last forever."

Katy glanced at Rick. "Means sitting in the dark for awhile."

"No problem," he said.

She handed Charlie the flashlight. He grasped Diane's wrist, dragging her down the passageway beside him.

"Back soon," he said.

Katy watched the flashlight's beam fade.

Rick shuffled around beside her. He spoke her name, his voice near her ear. When he touched her shoulder, she relaxed, though the ball of tension in her gut remained.

He said, "I'll never get through all those inscriptions by midnight."

"Do the best you can."

His leg bumped hers and her jacket shifted. The weight inside her pocket thumped into her hip. Ivan's camera.

"I'll take pictures of the hieroglyphs," she said. "You can decipher them later."

"Take pictures?"

"Found a camera in Ivan's pack."

"Why bother? We might not live past midnight."

She turned her head toward him. Her lips grazed his. She thought of backing up but her head and body rested against the doorway…and she didn't want to anyway.

He pressed his mouth to hers. She felt his hands sliding across her shoulders, up her neck, searching for her face. When he found her cheeks, he slid his hands into her hair and drew her head closer. In the dark, they kissed again. And again.

A light flashed in her face. She opened her eyes. From behind the flashlight, Charlie smirked at her. Diane glared. In the backwash of the light, Warner stared down the corridor.

Heat flushed her cheeks. She pretended to consider the hieroglyphs. Rick jammed both hands in his pockets while inspecting a chip in the door frame, which he picked at with his fingers.

"You propose yet?" Charlie asked.

"Dad!"

Charlie dropped an armload of torch handles and birch bark strips. Diane dumped her pile. The sticks clattered. The bark crunched.

"Time for your magic block," Charlie said.

Katy reached into her pocket for the magnesium block.

A growl reverberated down the corridor.

A gray figure dashed out of the shadows. Yoda halted ten feet away, one step inside the perimeter of the flashlight. He thumped his chest. An apelike cry echoed out of his chest.

They gaped at him in unison.

Before they could react, he vaulted into the air, landed with a thump that rattled the cave, and roared at them. As the sound screeched in Katy's ears, Yoda rocketed back down the passageway until the shadows swallowed him.

"What was that about?" Rick asked.

Katy canted her head, as if a new angle would provide the insight she sought. What had it been about? Yoda inflicted no damage. He wanted her dead, she felt it in his gaze, saw it in his demeanor when he faced her. Why scream and run?

"There," Warner said, pointing at a spot on the floor. "Ivan's backpack is gone."

Yoda fled empty-handed. Which left one answer.

Ivan convinced Yoda to create a diversion so he could nab the backpack. She had seen his silencer and extra ammo in the pack. Now Ivan had those items. Worse, the incident meant he allied himself with a hairy hominid. Yoda was angry and violent, infected with a hatred of her more septic than a backed-up sewer. Ivan matched the same description.

She shivered. They were working together.

Rick aimed his .45 down the corridor.

"No," she said. "He's long gone now. He may be a lunatic, but he has enough sense to know he can't barge in here again. He needs a plan, and plans take time."

"How long have we got?"

She checked her watch. "Four and half hours."

A battery of whispered curses bounced off the walls.

Diane sobbed. Charlie cradled his head in his hands. Rick drummed his fingers on the doorway while Warner gave the dark corridor a look hot enough to ignite steel.

"Here's what we do," Katy said. "Warner will check the front door really is sealed. You've got it on your GPS, right?"

"Yes."

"Good. I'll start the first torch, then Charlie and Diane will light the others and set up a perimeter to stop Ivan from sneaking up on us. Rick will work on the hieroglyphs and I'll photograph them in case he can't get through them tonight. Got it?"

They all looked at her like she'd suggested they offer themselves to the hairy hominids as sex slaves.

Rick holstered the .45. "Let's get moving."

Charlie picked up a strip of bark. He folded it in thirds lengthwise.

Warner pulled out his GPS unit and clicked buttons.

"No," Diane said, hugging herself as she stumbled backward. "I will not do what she says. For all we know, she killed her friend. She likes those *things*."

The pitch of Diane's voice escalated. "We can't trust her, Ivan was right, she'll turn us over to them."

"Diane," Warner said.

"No, Errie, *she got us trapped in here*."

In one step Warner closed the distance between them and slapped her. A welt rose on her cheek. She widened her eyes. He ground his teeth. Her eyes bulged. A muscle in his temple danced.

Diane shuffled to Charlie, took a bark strip, folded it in thirds.

The first torch lay on the floor, the bark rammed into the split in the handle. Katy grabbed the torch. She corkscrewed the end into the dirt until it stood on its own. With the magnesium block in one hand and Rick's knife in the other, she worked on lighting the torch. Charlie and Diane assembled eight torches before she lit a spark on the bark. The spark fizzled. Four more torches joined the pile on the ground before a spark caught and the bark sizzled. The torch erupted into little flames that enlarged and spread. The torchlight licked at the walls.

She picked up another torch, lit it from the first. The second torch she carried into the hieroglyph room. There, she plunged it into the floor. She shut off the flashlight. The torchlight took over, its glow setting the hieroglyphs afire. The flicker of the flames animated the painted scenes, fostering the illusion the people depicted in them might shake free of the stone and jitterbug on the earthen floor.

Back in the corridor, she found Charlie and Diane lighting torches. A line of torches bordered the passageway on both sides.

Warner grabbed an unlit torch. He kindled it from the flame of another. When the torch had a solid flame going, he strode down the corridor.

"If you see any other doors," Katy said, "check them too."

She reentered the hieroglyph room. Rick kneeled in the corner, chewing on his pen. On the pad of paper he had scribbled letters and symbols as strange and unreadable as the hieroglyphs on the wall.

Katy flopped down beside him. "What is that stuff?"

"Transliteration. I'm not good enough to read hieroglyphs cold. I need to transliterate them before translating them into English. Transliteration is kind of like shorthand. The ancient Egyptians didn't write vowels, so you have to guess when you translate it into English."

"What do you have so far?"

"I got down to here." He tapped a line of hieroglyphs three-fourths of the way down the wall, between the doorway and the corner. "Haven't translated it yet."

"When you get to the floor, stop and translate. I'll be taking pictures."

"I need time."

"I can give you the time we've got," she said, "which isn't much."

Taking the camera out of her pocket, she studied the buttons. She used Charlie's digital camera when she investigated sightings. His camera was a Sony and Ivan's was an Olympus. It had different buttons. Might take a few minutes to get the hang of it. Great, she needed less time.

Tick-tock.

Katy snapped the last image. When she checked it on the lcd screen, the image looked good. She turned off the camera and dropped it in her pocket.

The light. The creatures disappearing into it. A massacre of humans.

They read Charlie's journal.

With the camera in her pocket, she popped out its memory card. Facing the wall, so no one could see, she tucked the card inside her bra. She trotted to Rick.

"Well?" she said.

"Doesn't make sense."

"Read it to me." She leaned close. "I'm crazy. It might make sense to me."

"Not crazy, stubborn." He flipped the pad back to the previous page. "Some of these hieroglyphs don't translate literally. I had to guess."

"Read it."

"Okay. It says the Planners seal this place in the name of Osiris, great god, lord of Abydos, et cetera, so he may give a voice offering...for the *ka* of the revered ones, the justified." He touched the hieroglyphs on the wall. "*Ka* is the life force, one of several souls the Egyptians believed everybody had. This inscription reads like a funerary offering, except there's no name for the deceased. References to the dead are in the plural. Plus the offerings are coming *from* Osiris instead of going to him and the offerings are, um, weird."

"Weird how?"

"Listen to this." He skimmed his fingertip down the page until he found his place. "Here's the part I left out before. So that he may give a voice offering of truth, of blood and *ka*, of everything good and pure which the something-or-others took."

"The who took it?"

"I told you I can't remember some of the symbols."

She kissed him. "You did great."

"Doesn't help us."

"Maybe it does." She thought back to the massacre painting. "You said references to the deceased are in the plural."

"Right."

"It could refer to the humans who died. The ones the hairy hominids massacred in that painting. If the massacre really happened, someone could've created this room as a memorial to tell the story."

"The painting tells the story. And I can't believe somebody capable of carving these hieroglyphs would also make cave paintings. It's quite a leap, either backward or forward."

"I know." She looked up at the ceiling and its celestial paintings. "Charlie said the beings in those crafts are human. It's possible there were two kinds of humans here. One less advanced yet sophisticated enough to create cave paintings, and the other far more advanced than even we are today."

Katy pushed onto her knees. "Keep working. I have a feeling this room holds the key."

She left the room. Charlie and Diane had extended the torch border for a hundred feet, curving it around a bend in the passageway as a buffer against Ivan. He must show himself if he wanted them.

Charlie was halfway down the torch-lit path, near the wall. He stared around the bend. Diane hunkered close by him.

Warner had not returned. Katy checked her watch. Three hours to go. If the creatures had abducted him, they had no time for a rescue.

Though she concentrated on other issues, in the background of her thoughts she carried on her quest to answer the question of what the hairy hominids were. She'd decided they must've evolved from *Homo heidelbergensis*. With its massive leg bones, heavy brow ridges, and tall physique, heidelbergensis both retained many features of its predecessor *Homo erectus* and added features found in the hairy hominids. She envisioned a line from *erectus* to heidelbergs to hairy hominids. While evolution was not a linear process, she needed to picture it in a fashion her mind could follow. The old question resurfaced. If she accepted evolution happened, except with humans, what did that make the hairy hominids? The true descendants of *erectus*, the children of the heidelbergs, the cousins of the Neanderthals. They fit into the family album far better than humans.

The culmination of millions of years of hominid evolution. It made them...

Homo sapiens.

20

THE HIEROGLYPHS ON THE WALL BLURRED. THOUGH SHE HEARD RICK CALL her name, his voice sounded muffled. She was aware of hands grasping her shoulders, shaking her, but her mind had sunk into the mud of her last thought.

"Katy?" Rick repeated.

They are us.

They could not be us, because we are us. Yet the creatures, if they descended from *erectus* and the heidelbergs as she suspected, were *Homo sapiens*. The term *sapiens* designated the species that evolved from the ancient *Homo* line, rather than specifically referring to humans. If we did not evolve from *erectus*, then we no longer deserved the title *Homo sapiens*. The creatures did.

Voices murmured like water in a stream, lying over a hill, beyond sight. She recognized them as voices. Knew she should understand the words. The more she concentrated on the voices, her mind switched back into reality and the murmurs transformed into the voices of Rick and Charlie. The haze cleared from her vision. They crouched in front of her, shoulders hunched, waving their hands in her face.

She blinked. "What's the matter?"

Rick frowned. "You go catatonic and you want to know what's the matter?"

"I was not catatonic." Of Charlie, she asked, "Warner back yet?"

"Afraid not. And we have less than three hours until blastoff."

She tipped sideways to peep around Charlie into the corridor. "Where's Diane?"

"Down the—" He glanced over his shoulder and stiffened. "She's gone."

"She might've wandered around the bend."

Charlie grumbled. "I'll get her."

He plodded down the corridor. At the bend, he poked his head around the corner.

Cricks harder than granite riddled Katy's legs and back. As she massaged her back, she wandered out of the room. The torches lit the passageway better than the flashlight. Some of the torches had burned down their bark strips. She roamed the length of the torch borders adjusting the flames by prying out the bark strips. When she reached the bend, she stopped. Charlie wasn't there.

The dirt was disturbed where he had stood. She dropped onto all fours and sniffed the disturbance. Fresh. A foot's length around the bend, indentations showed where Charlie's boots dug into the dirt. Skid marks connoted a slip. Or that someone dragged him. Her heart hammered. She searched the dirt for blood. She found none.

She sprinted back to the room.

"They're gone," she told Rick. "Charlie and Diane. I found signs of a struggle."

Rick leaped onto his feet. The pad and pen flew off his lap and scattered across the floor.

He hauled her into the room. Jostling her to the other side of the doorway, he drew the .45. She pulled out her Taurus. Together, they eased their heads into the doorway. In the corridor, nothing lurked.

The torch she'd planted in the center of the room flickered. Rick doused it in the dirt. She could hear his breathing, discern his silhouette in the glow from the torches outside. Anyone outside would have trouble seeing either of them—she hoped.

Tick.

This time the sound originated outside, past the lines of torches, instead of from the clock inside her head.

Tick-tick. Scraping ensued. Tick-tick. Scrape. Tick-tick.

It was Ivan, it had to be, Ivan and his new friend Yoda. Perfect. She should've named Yoda after Jeffrey Dahmer instead of a harmless, shriveled wise man.

"We have to go out there," she said.

"First you have to promise me no matter what happens, we're a team. You don't run off without me. Ever. No exceptions."

"I promise." She squinted into the shadows enshrouding him. "You have to promise the same thing."

"I do."

Why did it feel like they just got married?

Rick sidled through the doorway. She slunk out behind him. They tiptoed toward the ticking sounds, hugging the walls, ready to fire their weapons if Ivan revealed his position. Unless he got smart all of a sudden, he would reveal himself. They need only watch. And wait.

At the bend, Rick paused to reconnoiter. After a moment he tugged on her sleeve. They crept around the corner. The torches bordered the passageway for a further fifteen feet. Beyond that, the darkness devoured the light until none remained.

Her stomach muscles tightened. Felt like a fist clamped around her gut.

Rick grabbed a torch. Katy clasped his hand as they edged past the last of the torches. Rick's torch spilled a cone of light on the corridor around them. The ticking resounded nearby.

Clunk.

A stone landed within the cone of light. They froze. The stone came from the right. Rick swung the torch rightward and a doorway emerged from the darkness.

Katy picked up the stone. The hand-sized rock had been chipped away on both sides of one edge to form a blade. Bits of stone clung to the dimples the chipping created. The edges were sharp and rough rather than dulled by time or use. She grazed her hand across the edge and the dimples, wiping away the debris. She'd seen objects like this before. It was a handaxe, a tool used by ancient hominids. With the bifacial flaking, meaning the craftsman shaped it on both sides, the stone resembled a handaxe from the Acheulian kit used by *erectus*.

Through the doorway, breathing sibilated.

Rick hurled the torch through the doorway.

The room was empty. The axe in her hand, Katy walked into the room. Remains of a fire smoldered near the wall, while stone chips littered the floor. Boot heels had indented the earth among the chips and coals.

Rick shouted.

Katy dropped the handaxe. She spun toward the doorway. Rick slalomed into the far wall of the corridor clutching his abdomen. The .45 skittered halfway across the corridor. The torch rolled a few feet away from the gun, its flame faltering. She ran toward Rick.

A long shadow descended across the doorway.

She hopped to a halt, balanced on her toes.

Rick scuttled on all fours toward the gun. Yoda smacked him in the face. Rick fell onto his side, nabbed Yoda's ankle. The creature seized his shirt and hurled him into the wall. Rick crumpled.

Katy sprang into the corridor. She whirled left toward Yoda with the Taurus clenched in her hands.

Yoda kicked at her chest. His foot struck square over her sternum. The force threw her backward, her feet flipped up, the breath blasted from her. When she hit the ground the momentum wheeled her over and over. Her foot kicked torches out of their seats. Her head thwacked into the wall.

She sucked in air. Nothing happened, as if her lungs had ossified. She thumped the ground, pawed at the air. Her ears rang. Her vision shrank.

Down the corridor, Yoda growled.

Her lungs relented and she gulped in a chest-full of air. The ringing in her ears faded. Her vision normalized. Panting, she clambered onto her feet. She was at the bend. Yoda hunkered thirty feet away cloaked in shadows. Teeth bared, hands fisted, he glowered at her with red eyes.

She still clutched the Taurus in her hand.

Yoda shrieked. She fired once, twice. He roared and thumped his chest. She pulled the trigger. Click. Out of ammo.

Yoda stomped toward her.

She fumbled with the zipper on her fanny pack.

Yoda lumbered toward her—twenty-five feet away. His footfalls coursed tremors through the stone and earth.

She tore the zipper open. Her fingers closed around a speed loader and she yanked it out. Flipping out the cylinder, dumping the empty shells, she seated the bullets in the chambers while they remained locked in the speed loader. She pushed the knob on the speed loader to release the bullets. They stayed locked inside it.

Yoda snarled. Twenty feet.

She pounded on the knob, twisted it, cursed at it. The bullets stayed trapped. Fifteen feet.

Pull the knob *out!* She yanked it. The bullets, popping loose, tumbled into the chambers. She snapped the cylinder shut.

Yoda rushed at her.

She fired.

He stumbled backward. His lips parted in a snarl. He lunged for her.

She fired again, again, again, again.

Yoda hesitated.

She looked into his eyes. Reflected in the red glow she saw visions of her body sailing through the air, his hands tearing at her limbs.

He roared.

She fired straight at his head.

Blood oozed from his forehead, off-center. The glow in his eyes waned. His knees quivered.

Yoda collapsed.

Katy dumped out the shells and reloaded. She bolted down the corridor to where Rick had fallen.

He was gone.

The torch had died.

Katy snatched the torch off the ground. She dipped it into the flame of the nearest torch. The flame rekindled.

She kneeled where Rick had lain. Scuffs and gouges marred the floor. Feet, even those of a creature as heavy as Yoda, impressed no prints in the compacted-earth floor. To track Rick, she needed other sign.

In a crouch, she hop-stepped deeper into the passageway, feeling the dirt as she moved, scanning the floor and walls for sign. She found it, a minute later and four feet further, in the guise of a smudge on the wall. The smudge, as long as her hand and a fingernail's width above the floor, started as a clump of dirt. Where the smudge tapered away, she discovered dents in the dirt leading into parallel drag marks.

Ivan must've charged out of the shadows, hit Rick or shot him—with the silencer, how could she know—then dragged him away. Bleeding. Unconscious.

Her gut simmered. She stamped down the corridor along the path delineated by the drag marks. The trail veered left and she angled after it. Her hand ached. She kept her fingers tense around the Taurus, her index finger over the trigger. Behind her eye, a pang erupted. Her jaw ached from gritting her teeth.

Ahead, the trail terminated at the doorway to a room lit by flames, whether from a torch or fire she couldn't tell. She hesitated for a second. A shadow darkened the doorway. A voice moaned.

Bleeding. Unconscious.

She stalked into the room and raised the Taurus.

A fire, perhaps a foot in radius, burned in the center of the room. Rick sprawled on the floor against the back wall. His eyes were open partway. Ropes like the ones she'd seen on Yoda locked Rick's arms behind his back and shackled his ankles. Ivan stooped beside Rick's head. He held the Desert Eagle's muzzle, with the silencer attached, flush against the crown of Rick's head.

"I was going to kill him," Ivan said, "but then I thought no. You gotta see this."

He waggled the gun.

She scowled at him.

"Hey," he said, "you see my handaxe? Found it in another room. Apparently these moronic monsters dug it up and figured out how to use it."

"They made it."

He sniggered. "Yeah right."

She trained the Taurus on Ivan's head. "Don't make me kill you."

"The second you pull your trigger, I pull mine. How good is your aim? Can you hit me between the eyes at fifteen feet?"

Could she hit him? She practiced shooting once a month at most. Sharpshooting never seemed important for a website designer turned investigator of human origins. She would've practiced more if she realized she'd end up trapped in a cave with a psycho, if she'd realized the lives of everyone she cared about would depend on her.

Ivan had won. She let him implant doubt in her psyche.

Rick moaned. With his eyelids half closed, he glanced at her sideways with clear eyes. He winked.

A trick of the shadow?

He flung himself toward the fire, rolling away from Ivan.

She fired. The bullet hit Ivan's shoulder. He swooped the Desert Eagle toward her and pulled the trigger. The gun snapped back. The recoil drove him backward into the wall while the shot ricocheted off the ceiling into the fire, splintering a twig.

Ivan yelled. He fired again and the bullet fractured a chunk off the doorway.

Katy fired at his head. He jerked sideways. The bullet hit the wall.

Rick grabbed a stick from the fire. He jammed its smoldering end into Ivan's shin. Ivan screamed, stumbled closer to Katy. He swung his gun up toward her head. She fired into his chest. Blood soaked his shirt. His hand slackened. The gun tumbled to the floor. He slumped forward onto it.

His face smacked into the dirt.

She felt for a pulse in his neck. Nothing.

Stepping over the body, she kneeled beside Rick to untie his bindings.

"We have to find Dad," he said.

"And Diane, I know."

"Warner too I guess."

She tucked the Taurus in her fanny pack. As Rick stood, she glimpsed Ivan's body.

He said, "Least we don't have to worry about him now."

"But we are far from safe." She cast the ropes onto the fire. "Very, very far."

THEY SEARCHED THE CAVES FOR MUCH TOO LONG. THE BARK ON THE TORCH burned down until eight inches protruded from the slot. Katy slid the bark out a few inches. Side by side, she and Rick rounded a bend. Ahead a light glimmered through a doorway.

Rick mouthed, "Stay here."

She shook her head.

He laid two fingers on her lips. With his free hand he pointed at the ground. Though she wanted to say she'd understood the first time, his fingers prevented her from opening her mouth. Probably why he put them there. Sometimes she swore he read her mind.

She nodded.

The .45 drawn, he crept closer to the light.

At the doorway, he peeked into the room. He moved into the threshold and sighed, "Dad."

Rick walked into the room.

Charlie's voice echoed down the corridor. "No, Rick."

Then Rick's voice: "Give me the gun, lady."

Katy sprinted through the doorway. The room was half the size of the one where Ivan held Rick. A torch, propped up in the dirt, lit the interior. Charlie huddled near the torch, knees drawn up in front of him, an arm draped over each knee, frowning at the floor. Rick stood a few feet inside the doorway, to the left. The muzzle of Charlie's rifle poked Rick's nose. Katy traced the barrel back to the manicured hands wrapped around its grip, up the arms to a pale face fringed with red hair. The rifle trembled in Diane's grasp.

Diane swerved the rifle toward Katy.

"What are you doing?" Katy said.

Charlie answered. "She decided to help Ivan. She thinks you killed Jim and you're going to kill her and Ivan too."

"Half right."

Diane's face blanched. "What?"

"Ivan's dead. I killed him."

Rick ripped the rifle out of Diane's hands. He tossed it to Charlie.

Tears streaked down Diane's cheeks. Her chin quivered. Her teeth chattered. She choked off a sob.

"He was trying to kill me," Katy said. "He murdered Jim. He would've killed you too. He wanted the fortune and glory of discovering the hairy hominids for himself and he wouldn't have shared it with you."

Katy softened her voice. "I know you thought he was your friend, but you didn't really know him. He was evil."

Charlie offered Diane a handkerchief from his pocket, which she accepted. The sobbing subsided as she swiped her cheeks with the handkerchief.

She blew her nose. "Where's Errie?"

"Don't know," Katy said. "He never came back. We have no way of finding him."

Rick snapped his fingers. "The GPS."

"Won't work."

"Yes it will." Rick smiled. "He has my GPS. We can use yours to track him."

Katy dug her GPS radio out of her fanny pack. She had left it on. She switched the unit to buddy tracking mode, and it latched onto Warner's signal.

Stepping into the passageway, she said, "Follow me."

Rick took the torch from her. Charlie removed the torch stuck in the floor. When Charlie passed Diane the torch, she gripped it in both hands. The light reflected off the tear streaks on her face. Although her eyes had reddened, the color returned to her face.

Katy shepherded them through the corridor. The GPS gave her Warner's position yet it could not guide her through the caves because, well, Rand McNally never mapped them. Sometimes the GPS showed Warner twenty feet away—on the other side of solid rock. It was like navigating a maze on paper and in reality at the same time.

The corridor forked. She checked the GPS. Warner's signal blinked to the left on the screen, so she angled down the left fork. A minute later she spotted a glow ahead. The flashlight.

She stopped. Rick bumped into her.

The flashlight bobbled closer. Boots clomped.

Rick pushed in front of her. "Warner?"

"Yes."

Warner trudged into the torchlight. He clicked off the flashlight. Diane raced toward him. She touched his face, but he batted her hand away.

Behind him, the darkness bubbled.

Katy tiptoed sideways around Warner and Diane. She waved at Rick. He brought the torch closer. Her heart thudded.

The darkness did not bubble. Figures shifted amid the darkness, lurking nearer, their heads bobbing, shoulders undulating. The quartet of hairy hominids penetrated the torchlight.

A scuffling behind made her look back. Five more creatures closed in from the rear.

No doorways led off the passage. Their four guns against nine creatures equaled bad odds. She needed eight rounds to kill Yoda.

As if they had shared a realization, she and Rick and Warner holstered their guns. Charlie slung his rifle over his shoulder. Two creatures advanced on them, stealing the torches from Rick and Diane.

Hairy hands clinched their arms. The creatures propelled them down the corridor.

"THEY HEARD THE GUNFIRE."

"Gee, ya think?" Katy said.

Rick paced the length of the room. Since the room was twelve feet long, his circuit didn't take long. His heels dug into the dirt when he whirled around at the end of each circuit. He fisted and unfisted his hands in rhythm with his footsteps.

The creatures had brought them back to the room with the massacre painting and the grave. They'd stabbed the torches into the dirt in the middle of the room on their way out. Katy stooped between the torches while Charlie slouched near the wall, scratching his chin, his gaze on the paintings. Warner leaned against the wall furthest from the doorway with his arms crossed over his chest. Diane huddled beside Warner, her gaze on him, and chewed her lip. Through the doorway, Warner watched the two sentries posted outside.

From within the room, Katy could see one shoulder of each creature along with the corresponding arm, capped by a huge, stubby hand. Occasionally one of the creatures ducked his head in to check on them and growl. They had perfected the intimidation technique.

"We should've been more careful," Rick said.

"And let Ivan kill us?"

"Should've strangled him with my bare hands."

"As I recall," Katy said, "you were indisposed at the time."

"She saved your life," Charlie said with a Santa Claus smile. "You have to marry her."

A sentry snarled.

Rick curled his lip at the creature. Katy rose, stretching her legs. Although Diane had ceased glaring at her, the woman maintained a six-foot gap between them. Diane genuinely believed in Ivan. Katy couldn't change her mind. Didn't need to either. The opinion of a woman who'd aided Ivan and threatened their lives meant zilch.

Katy ambled past the torches to the grave's edge. The creatures must've dug it out by hand, or with nothing more sophisticated than rocks, perhaps the handaxes Ivan mentioned. If the creatures had shovels, they hid them. Like so-called cavemen, the creatures appeared intelligent yet primitive, incapable of creating the hieroglyph room or metal tools, yet savvy enough to navigate the tunnels in darkness. They used torches for light and rocks as communication tools. Despite their lack of speech, of the human kind, they had a social structure. They could easily have descended from *erectus*. Maybe they were *erectus*. Their identity depended on whether she accepted evolution happened to everyone except humans, or dismissed it as the daydream of anthropologists.

She didn't feel superior to the creatures. Since she killed a man, and felt no guilt over it, she might share more with the hairy hominids than she thought. Maybe she was worse than them. They at least shied from killing unless it became necessary.

Ivan shot at her, spurred Yoda to attack her, kidnapped Rick, murdered Jim…then he aimed his gun at her head with the intent of murdering her. How much more justified did self-defense get?

She had no reason for guilt. Besides, she had other concerns right now. Like how to escape before they got "sent away." She checked her watch.

Her stomach flip-flopped. 11:05.

Rick, done pacing, slid his finger up and down the wall. With a "hmm" he flattened both hands on the wall, gliding them up and down, side to side. As he explored the rock, he shuffled sideways along the wall's length. Halfway down the chamber, he stopped. With his index fingers he traced a line from the ceiling to the floor.

"Looking for hidden doors?" Katy asked.

"Not exactly." He gestured at the ground. "The floor is dirt."

"How hard did Ivan hit your head?"

He tilted his head down to gaze up at her. "I'm not finished. The floor is dirt but the ceiling and walls are rock. First, I don't think we're deep enough for bedrock and, second, if we are then why is the floor dirt?"

She surveyed the floor, the walls, the grave and, finally, Rick. "You're right. And the grave goes three feet into the dirt, not bedrock."

"Exactly."

"But the walls are rock."

He crooked a finger. She came as ordered. He settled a palm on her head, urging her closer to the wall, to the point where he had stopped feeling up the rock. He grasped her right hand, then skimmed her fingers over the rock.

"Feel that?" he asked.

"What?"

He brushed her hands over the area again. Her fingers skipped over bumps in the rock. Her fingernail caught on an edge. She tracked the edge up to the ceiling.

"I feel it," she said. "There's a seam in the wall."

"I bet there are more too."

She retraced the seam to the ceiling. On tiptoes, she grazed her finger over the curve where the ceiling adjoined the wall. The seam continued through the curve. As she traced the seam across the ceiling, her toes slipped. She toppled backward into Rick.

"Look," she said, "it goes up into the ceiling. Could be one U-shaped piece."

From the point where she stopped he followed the seam across the ceiling, down the opposite wall to the floor. "It is one piece."

"If these caves are man-made, whoever built them must've included ventilation shafts. The leakage from the doors can't be enough to ventilate these caves."

"And maybe we can get out through the ventilation shafts."

"That's what I'm thinking."

Rick meandered toward the door. The sentries barked at him. He swerved away from the door.

He hooked a thumb at the doorway. "First we have to get past them."

At the grave he picked up the marker stone. "This symbol, it's the same as the one on the door to the hieroglyph room."

"I noticed," Katy said. "I don't know what it means."

"The triangle could be a pyramid." He flipped the stone over and, wiping off the dirt, rubbed it on his jeans. "There are symbols on the back."

She crouched across the gulf of the grave from him.

He spat on his thumb, rubbed it across the stone. After a minute of spitting and rubbing, he held the stone so she could see it. Faint yet recognizable hieroglyphs decorated the stone.

"What's it say?" she asked.

"Gimme a minute." He tapped his finger on the stone. "It's a name and a title. Ranefer, priest of Amun, keeper of the Revered Ones. Looks like part of a funerary inscription but the hieroglyphs are…messy."

"Like they were in a hurry."

"No, whoever wrote this was careful to fit the inscription on the stone and arrange the hieroglyphs to fit the space, but it's bad handwriting. Like a kid who's learning to write." He squinted. "Mah-ah keh-roo."

"Excuse me?"

Rick indicated two hieroglyphs.

"Means true of voice or justified," he said. "It's what the ancient Egyptians called their dead, to make sure the gods knew they deserved a spot in the afterlife. *Maa kheru.*"

A gruff voice repeated, "*Maa kheru.*"

Katy looked up at the figure in the doorway who had uttered the phrase—one of the sentries, a black-haired male with a white streak down the middle of his head. His nostrils flared. He grunted, lifting his chin.

"Oogah," he said.

His voice, gruff and low, warped the words into near grunts. If she hadn't heard Rick speak the phrase first, she would've assumed the creature had grunted instead of spoken. Although their grunts resembled a language she had assumed, subconsciously, any speech should sound like human speech. The creatures grunted words exactly as they grunted grunts, hence their language seemed like gibberish. Unless you knew what they were saying.

Did she really hear it? Or did she imagine his grunts sounded like the phrase Rick read seconds earlier? The mind adapted sights and sounds to suit its expectations. Still…

"He spoke," she told Rick. "Say something else."

"I might not be pronouncing it right and, besides, we don't know if he understood the words or just repeated them. We might be sharing a hallucination too."

"Give it a try."

Rick said, "Ranefer."

The sentry nodded.

"Gee," Katy said, "I could've done that."

"Cut me some slack, I'm new at this."

"Show him the rock. Maybe he can read."

Rick proffered the rock to the sentry. When the creature took the rock and raised it near his face, his hand dwarfed the stone. He snorted. A growl rumbled in his chest, into his throat, resonating in his sinuses.

He hurled the stone at Rick, who dodged it. The motion lurched him backward into the grave. He plopped onto his butt at the grave's bottom.

"I don't think he liked it," Rick said.

The creature howled.

Rick leaped out of the grave. The creature thumped his foot. The second sentry clomped into the doorway.

Eyes bright and sharp as red lasers, the pair gnarled.

Charlie, fixated on the wall, said, "Bow your heads and get on your knees. Eventually they'll give up."

Katy bowed her head. Rick did the same and they kneeled beside the grave. The creatures watched for several minutes, alternating growling and snorting, before they stomped back into the corridor to resume their positions. Katy and Rick rose.

"This Ranefer," Rick said, "must be the one whose bones are outside the front door. Think he's a fossil like Ivan said?"

"No idea." She checked the time. "It's eleven-thirty. We have to get out of here."

Rick eyed the torches. "I have an idea."

"Yes?"

He glanced at the sentries. "Let's huddle."

At the wave of Rick's hand, Charlie and Warner joined them. Diane stared at the wall, hands jammed under her arms. Though Rick beckoned her, she only gnawed her lip. Katy whistled. The sentries grunted. Diane hustled into the circle. The sentries returned their attention to the corridor. Rick whispered instructions.

"Everybody squish against the wall beside the doorway. When I yell, run out the door. Got it?"

Katy raised her eyebrows. "And what are *you* going to do?"

"No time. Go."

She escorted the others to the wall, where they assembled in a line and squished themselves against the rock. Since Rick avoided explaining his plan, it must include some stupid action he knew she'd try to talk him out of doing. Oh well, if his plan could get them out of here she'd let him try. If he got killed, she'd never forgive him.

Seeing them huddled per his instructions, Rick grabbed one of the torches. He snuffed it out in the dirt. What on earth was he doing?

He snagged the remaining torch and pitched it out the doorway. The creatures grunted, snorted, huffed. Rick hopped into the grave. He wielded the doused torch like a baseball bat.

The black-haired sentry stormed through the doorway first. The torch outside had dimmed. The flame seemed in danger of extinguishing. It licked at the darkness inside the room, unable to penetrate further than the grave. Rick burrowed the toe of his boot into the soil. He kicked up a clod.

The creature growled. The second sentry loped through the doorway.

Their bodies left a few feet of clearance between them and the doorway.

Rick hollered.

Katy shoved Charlie out the door. Diane took off after him, dragging Warner by his coat sleeve. Katy ran into the doorway. She spun toward Rick, who shot her one of those looks she knew too well. She yanked out the Taurus.

Rick sprang out of the grave.

She jumped back one, two, three steps. Her butt bumped the wall. She leveled the Taurus at a creature's head.

Rick swung the torch stick at the nearest creature. The hominid caught the stick, tore it out of Rick's hands, clouted his neck with it. Rick doubled over, groaning. The black creature, pirouetting toward Katy, bellowed. His jaw gaped. Tonsils flapped behind mammoth molars.

She fired. The bullet grazed the creature's temple. A rivulet of blood trickled down his cheek. Just as she pulled the trigger again, the creature pounced at her. She flung herself sideways, landing on her side. Her hip whacked into the earth. Pain ricocheted through her legs.

The creature hit the wall. He turned on her.

The other sentry launched Rick into the air. He sailed into the corridor, crashing into the floor shoulder-first.

Katy fired at the creature. He clutched his gut. The second creature surged through the doorway into the corridor. As he stepped into her sight, she pulled the trigger. The bullet whizzed past the creature's head. She pulled the trigger again.

Click.

She plunged her hand into the fanny pack and pulled out the speed loaders. Empty. Oops.

The torch Rick had thrown rested a few feet away, its flame dwindling. She rolled toward it. The wounded creature slumped against the wall. His friend flailed an arm at her. She grasped the torch. The creature clawed at her neck. Bounding onto her feet, she thrust the torch in his face.

He bellowed. Hairs on his chin caught fire.

She lashed the torch at his chest. Hairs ignited. He shot past her. His arm thrashed into her, careening her into the wall. The other creature limped after his friend.

Footsteps clunked further down the corridor. Three figures detached from the shadows. Charlie, Diane, and Warner moseyed into the torchlight.

"I thought," Charlie said, "you were right behind us."

Rick scrambled onto his feet. "Got a little delayed. Katy wouldn't leave."

Katy smiled. "I promised never to run off without you, remember? No exceptions."

She considered reminding him he'd promised the same. The relief flooding through her overwhelmed that desire. He was okay. He could walk. He could annoy her. He was *alive*.

Her watch read 11:45.

"Let's look for those ventilation shafts," she said, heading down the corridor. "They should be near the ceiling or in it."

Rick jogged to catch up with her, then relit his torch in the flame of hers. While they traveled the corridor, they searched the ceiling and walls for a shaft or slot big enough to admit a person as well as air. Katy saw no shafts.

The flame of her torch wavered.

She raised a hand. "Everybody freeze and hold your breath."

Once they obeyed, she inspected the flame. It quivered. She licked her finger and held it in front of her. The left side cooled a fraction more than the rest.

She started for the left wall. Five minutes later, they found the shaft.

"Damn," Rick said.

Sighing, Katy sagged her shoulders. The shaft was cut into the rock where the wall curved into the ceiling. When she held a hand in front of the opening, a draft tickled her skin. The shaft must lead outside. It had one big problem, though.

The shaft was eighteen inches wide and four inches tall.

They located another shaft a few minutes later. It matched the first one—eighteen inches wide, four inches high.

Light quavered far down the corridor. Katy turned around but torchlight shimmered there too.

Within a minute, a dozen creatures surrounded them.

21

Sunday, October 20
12:01 AM

T HE CREATURES HERDED THEM INTO THE SAME CLEARING WHERE SHE AND
Rick had watched the hairy hominids disappear into the orb craft. Katy
felt the boiling in her gut that warned her she knew what would happen here.

The creatures abandoned their torches inside the caves. As her night vision
kicked in, she noticed some of the creatures clustering around the boulder. The
creatures who'd captured them now detained them at the edge of the clearing.
Ropes bound their hands behind their backs and restrained their feet. The
restraints permitted shuffling but prevented walking, running, or thrashing.
The creatures had confiscated her fanny pack with the Taurus inside, the .45
she'd given Rick, Charlie's rifle, and Warner's Glock. The items lay in a pile
along with Ivan's Desert Eagle, at the center of the clearing, an offering to
whatever god might appear.

Osiris? Rick said the hieroglyphs mentioned the Egyptian deity, so perhaps
the creatures worshiped him.

They certainly understood ancient Egyptian. Rick may believe the sentry
mimicked him when he said *maa kheru*. She had a feeling—one of those deep-
in-your-gut, makes-you-want-to-puke feelings— the creatures could read and
write. Since no one had entered the hieroglyph room in years, the creatures
must've kept up on the language some other way. Through speaking with the
people in the orb craft perhaps.

The thought seemed ridiculous. If the people in the craft were descended from ancient Egyptians and spoke the ancient language, the language shouldn't have remained stable for 3,000 years. English evolved from Old English to modern in less than 2,000 years. The evolution transformed Old English into a foreign language.

If the ancient Egyptians—what else could she call the UFO people—maintained the old language as a means of communicating with the creatures, and used a different language as their everyday speech, the old language might remain stable for millennia. It was possible. In spite of the Catholic church using Latin in its rituals, Latin was a dead language unchanged for at least 1,000 years. Language evolved when it stayed in everyday use, otherwise it lacked the means to change.

Charlie nudged her left shoulder. "When's the wedding?"

"Unless you have a plan, Charlie," she said, "shut up. We could all die in the next five minutes."

"Possibly."

"Possibly! We lost our weapons, we're tied up, surrounded by hairy giants who could kill us with their breath, and the mother ship is coming."

"Look on the bright side. We're out of the caves."

Rick's elbow jabbed her arm. He hunched beside her, wriggling his shoulders, pinching his features.

"What are you doing?" she asked.

"Trying to undo the ropes." He stilled. "Sick of getting tied up. I'm even more sick of getting thrown around."

"Then stop annoying the hairy giants."

He hrumphed. She wanted to get out of the ropes too. There must be a way.

"Got a knife?" she asked.

"Gave it to you."

She replayed the last time she used it, to strike the flint. "It's in my pocket."

"Get it out."

"My front pocket."

He looked at her jeans pocket. "Come around behind me. I can get it."

The creatures huddled around the rock tilted their heads toward the stars and moaned. Above the trees a moon-size light blinked on.

Katy shuffled backward a step. The creature posted behind her shoved her forward.

The light pulsed, enlarging with each wink. Coming closer.

The creature behind her was staring at the light. She inched backward and to the side, behind Rick. The creature ignored them. Daylight drenched the clearing. Static electricity raised the hairs all over her body. She leaned against Rick.

He dove his hand into her pocket. Finding the knife, he pulled it free.

The light hovered overhead, a little higher than the tallest trees, about eighty feet off the ground. The glowing craft filled the sky above the clearing. The creatures grew silent and still.

Rick flipped open the pocket knife and slipped the blade under his ropes. He worked it against the fibers.

The creature behind Katy snared her wrists. He propelled her into the clearing. Rick charged at the creature. "No!"

The creature punched him in the jaw, knocking him onto his knees.

Katy hit the ground on her side and rolled into the middle of the clearing, where she stopped on her back. The light overwhelmed her vision. She shut her eyes, rolling onto her side, pushing into a sitting position. The creature hooked his hands under her arms to hoist her onto her feet. Next he cinched one hand around her right arm while a second creature loped forward to clinch her left arm. They supported her on her tiptoes.

Lightning coruscated before her. Stars glinted in her vision.

A man stood before her.

He had the olive skin of a Mediterranean, dark eyes that shimmered like glass, and a clean-shaven head. A long tunic of linen, cut in the ancient Egyptian style, cloaked his body. Sandals shod his feet. A belt hung low around his waist, secured by a metal buckle inset with buttons.

And the triangle logo.

Rick had suggested the logo represented a pyramid. If she classified these people as ancient Egyptians, the triangle could be a pyramid. After all, the ancient Egyptians built over eighty pyramids. The shape symbolized the culture.

The man slithered his gaze up and down her body before settling on her face.

"Katherine Gallagher," he said.

A slight accent tinged his voice. Belgian? South African? Israeli?

"You know me," she said, "and you speak English."

"One of many tongues."

"Who are you?"

"If you require a name, call me Intef." He raised his hand near her face. "You seek answers you should not know."

"You don't know what I seek."

"I know." He lowered his hand. "We have watched you. We will always watch you and others like you, the ones who seek forbidden knowledge."

"You mean human history, the truth about where we came from."

"The truth does not belong to you."

"It belongs to everyone. Why don't you want us to know?"

"We protected you when we should not have. We will not repeat the mistake. You are too…inquisitive." He waved his hand past her face. "Now you must be silenced."

Her toes slipped. Her jacket swished, thumping the camera in her pocket against her hip.

Intef tapped her pocket and the camera within it. He plunged a hand into her pocket, extracting the camera. He caressed its casing.

"A cam-er-a," he said.

Intef handed it to one of the creatures as he decreed something in their shared language. The creature threw the camera to the ground and stomped his foot onto it. The casing cracked. He stomped until the camera shattered.

Intef pressed a button on his belt, then chattered at whoever listened on the other end. The creature grunted in a tone that sounded like "huh?" Intef must've spoken in a language the creatures didn't recognize.

Intef regarded the creatures gathered around the rock. She followed his gaze there. One creature turned his head toward them. Garfield.

Memories flashed in her mind. Lightning. The creatures. Gone.

Intef flicked a hand.

The creature posted behind Rick forced him into the clearing. With one hand, the creature impelled him forward until he was beside Katy. The creature waited behind Rick.

Intef held his hand, palm up, in Rick's face. "This one knows the language. He will translate as I speak your crimes."

Rick said, "I don't know it that well."

His sentry punched him in the small of his back. With a groan he dropped onto his knees, eyes wide. The rope, frayed and split in two, flopped out from between his fingers. He grasped at the ends, holding them together to maintain the illusion of being bound.

Silver shimmered in his hand. The knife. Rick slumped down onto his heels. He jabbed the knife down until it slid under the ropes around his ankles.

Intef snatched up Ivan's Desert Eagle. He cupped the gun in both hands.

When he spoke, he articulated as if speaking to a child and paused after each phrase. Rick translated during the pauses while working on his ankle bindings. She suspected the scrunching of his face, the wrinkles etched across his forehead, stemmed more from the strain of translating than the strain of severing his bindings.

"You have angered Amun-Ra," Rick said. "You have acted against the revered ones…wounded the justified…killed—no, blasphemed…the great god."

Rick hesitated. Intef repeated his last phrase. Rick squeezed his lips together. Intef flicked his hand. The sentry slugged Rick in the back.

Intef repeated the statement.

His voice strained, Rick said, "The…tribunal has judged you unworthy of life. We will offer your *ka* to Anubis, great god, lord of the sacred land…so he may judge it."

Charlie sprinted away from his sentry toward Katy and Rick. The sentry hurried after him.

Intef waved a hand. The sentry backed off.

Charlie squeezed between Rick and Katy. "I have a proposal."

"Dad!" Rick said. "Get back there."

Bending backward, Katy peeked around Charlie at Rick's feet. With one strand left to break, he poised the knife under the rope.

She told Charlie, "Get out of here."

"It's my fault they came out here," Charlie said to Intef. "If I hadn't gotten lost, Katy would be at home and Rick would still be in Boston. The creatures saved me, I owe them my life."

Charlie squared his shoulders. "Let me give my life in exchange for my son and his friends."

Intef looked from Charlie to Katy to Rick, and back to Charlie.

Katy's stomach did a backflip. She swallowed hard but the lump in her throat stayed put. He must be joking. Give his life for theirs? She couldn't let him. She *wouldn't* let him. She'd desert him in the caves first. Intef and his people cared about the creatures, not humans, Charlie said so himself. No way would she let him die or, worse, go into their craft.

"How do I know," Intef said, "they will not tell others of this place?"

"Long as you have me, they won't talk. What can I say, they love me." Charlie glanced back at Warner. "He doesn't love me, but he won't talk either. And he'll keep the woman silent."

Intef studied Katy. The reptilian sheen of his eyes rippled shivers through her.

"If you betray us," Intef said, "he will die."

"Forget it," Katy said. "No deal."

"The deal is not yours to forget."

Intef beckoned and Charlie took a position alongside him.

"It is decided," Intef said.

"Don't do this, Dad," Rick said. "You can't trust them."

Intef tapped a button on his belt. Light flashed where Charlie stood.

He vanished.

Intef, the Desert Eagle in his hand, looped a finger around the trigger. He aimed the muzzle at Katy's face.

"You will die as you lived," Intef said. "By the fire."

"We made a deal," Katy reminded him.

"He may prove useful. You, however, are not."

Rick whipped his hands out from behind his back and tackled Intef. They tumbled to the ground amid a flurry of flailing limbs. Intef's hand bumped the button on his belt. Light burst downward between Katy and the two men. Intef screamed. Where his feet had been, smoke curled up from blackened stumps.

Vaulting onto his feet, Rick slapped his arms around her. With the knife he snapped the ropes around her wrists and cut her ankle ropes.

Intef barked a command in his language. The creatures rushed at Katy and Rick. The sentries guarding Warner and Diane took hold of their charges. Though Diane tried to run, the ropes tripped her. She stumbled onto Intef just as he pressed the button on his buckle. He shouldered her off of him. Lightning split the air. Intef vanished.

Warner jostled out of his sentry's grasp. The creature grabbed at him. Warner dropped onto the ground and rolled.

Rick cut Warner free while Katy retrieved the .45 and Warner's Glock from the pile. Tossing the Glock at Warner, she located her fanny pack with the Taurus and her GPS radio inside it. Rick strode toward Diane. She floundered backward.

Warner reached for her. Diane jerked her head, stiffening. Warner pulled a knife from his back pocket and stooped beside her. She burbled nonsense as he slashed the ropes around her ankles.

Boom!

Behind Katy, Rick chambered another round in his father's rifle. The creature he had shot crumpled, bleeding from a chest wound. A creature looped its arms around her waist. She rammed the .45 into his chin and fired. His arms slackened. She fled toward Rick.

Diane shrieked. Hands still tied behind her, she bolted for the trees despite Warner yelling at her to stay put. A creature shot out of the trees in front of her. She smacked into his chest. The creature clamped his hands around her throat, lifted her off her feet, chucked her across the clearing. Her head whacked into the boulder.

Her body slumped like a sack of mud.

A creature snared Rick around his waist and hoisted him off his feet. He yanked the rifle's trigger. As the shot hurtled toward the heavens, the rifle tumbled out of his hand. Katy fired at the creature's head. The bullet nicked his ear. The creature squeezed Rick's chest. Eyes bulging, he clawed at the creature's face. Katy fired three times at the beast's legs before it released Rick. He landed on his buttocks, his leg twisted.

The creature turned on Katy.

She pulled the trigger. Click, click.

The creature launched himself at her. She staggered sideways, toppled onto her side, pushed up onto her knees. With the .45 stuffed inside her waistband, she crawled to Rick. He rose onto one knee, wincing when he bent the other leg.

The creature darted into the trees.

The howls of hairy hominids resonated through the clearing.

Warner ran toward them. "Diane is dead."

Overhead, the craft hummed.

"They're a little ticked off," Rick said. "We better get the hell out of here."

"What about Charlie?" she asked.

"He's gone."

The words slapped her psyche. She knew he was right, and that hurt the worst.

Katy draped Rick's arm over her shoulders. Leaning on her, he struggled onto his feet. A grimace contorted his face every time he put weight on his left leg. With Warner behind them, they hobbled toward the trees.

Lightning. Voices.

When she glanced back, four men dressed like Intef milled about in the clearing. They brandished objects the size of cell phones. One of the men shouted a phrase.

"Think it means kill them all," Rick said. "Or remove their vital organs."

"Big difference." Katy stopped at the clearing perimeter. "Can you run?"

All around, creatures growled and grunted. Red stars twinkled among the trees. Red eyes. To the left and right, ahead and behind.

"Hell yes," Rick said.

Warner leveled the Glock at her head and fired. The bullet zipped past her. Something grunted behind her. She whirled around to see a creature, its forehead bleeding, collapse onto a pile of leaves.

"Thanks," she said.

Warner nodded. "Run."

They ran.

As the distance between them and the craft's brilliance broadened, her eyes had trouble readjusting. She dodged a tree but ran into a low-hanging branch. Her forehead stung. She touched the skin. Her finger felt damp. Licking the tip, she tasted the tang of blood. Pairs of red eyes monitored their flight from all sides. She grasped Rick's hand to keep him close, which forced her to slow down. No way would she lose him out here. No way would she lose another person she loved.

Rick wrenched her backward. She collided with him. He mashed his mouth into her hair, near her ear.

He said, "Too many of them. We need a place to hide."

"Yeah, like a cave."

Gears clicked in her mind, thoughts coalescing into a plan. *A cave.* Well why not?

Growl. Boom. Fire sprayed from the muzzle of Warner's Glock. Brush crinkled and snapped. Silence.

Red eyes. Close.

Katy got out the GPS radio. The LCD screen lit up when she flipped the power switch. If she had marked the spot as a waypoint…nope. She shut off the unit.

She asked Warner, "Still got the front door marked on your GPS?"

"What front door?"

"The caves."

A pause. "Yes."

A square of green light glowed in the darkness. The GPS unit beeped as Warner called up the information. He slunk past Rick and Katy in the toe-down-first method she used to avoid crunching leaves. She hurried after him in the same manner, with Rick limping beside her, his arm over her shoulder.

The red eyes were gone.

Static electricity buzzed over her skin. She chanced a look at the clearing. The craft ascended until its radiance shrank into a spotlight above the forest, then it drifted over the forest. Its light broke through holes in the tree cover.

They're looking for us.

After an eternity of walking which probably took up fifteen minutes of real time, they arrived at the base of the hill. Warner guided them into the cave. The petrified muscles in Katy's gut softened.

Warner flicked on a lighter. Its flame wavered, burning away the fluid inside it, casting more shadows than it dispelled. Despite the lighting, Katy realized they'd stopped a few yards inside the cave's entrance. If she had a flashlight or a torch, she'd see the hominid skulls along the walls. Further down, deeper inside the hill, she would find Ranefer's skeleton safeguarding the slab door, which would be ajar in expectation of the creatures' return.

"Great idea," Rick said, "we hide in the main entrance to the hairy hominid caves. Where only every single one of them comes through."

"They won't be back for hours," Katy said. "They have to look for us."

"Kill us you mean."

"Whatever."

A flashlight lanced the darkness outside. Warner let go of the switch, snuffing out the lighter's flame.

Katy inched closer to the entrance. A foot from the opening, she was halted by Rick's hand on her shoulder.

Twin flashlight beams swept left to right through the trees. Two figures, their pale tunics aglow in the ambient light, trekked into view. The phone-size objects they carried emitted the beams of light. The men marched toward the entrance, from the left. A few feet from the opening they paused to chatter to each other.

Rick whispered in her ear so softly she almost missed the words. "They're not speaking ancient Egyptian."

One man moseyed straight out from the cave entrance, while the other strolled past it out of view. Soon the night swallowed their flashlight beams.

A shadow flitted past the cave. Katy covered her nose. Though his feet hit the earth soundlessly, the creature's stench betrayed his passing.

Katy and Rick felt their way along the wall back to Warner. She knew where to stop when she collided with Warner's shoulder. Rick positioned himself behind her with his hands on her shoulders, as if afraid she might float away. Or throw her arms around Warner and kiss him. No chance of either happening.

They spoke in half whispers.

"How long do we stay here?" Rick asked.

"Until it is safe," Warner said.

"Until they stop searching," Katy said. "It will never be safe."

"When the craft has gone," Warner said, "we go."

Rick squeezed her shoulders. She looked out the cave entrance, where she could make out ghosts of trees swaying in the breeze. Though she couldn't see it, she knew her breath condensed when she exhaled. She zipped up her jacket. The chill penetrated her jeans, numbed her nose. Her gloves were in her backpack, along with her knit hat. She buried her hands in her pockets. Her pack also held the extra box of ammo for the Taurus. Rick had stowed her pack on the other side of the hill.

She had forsaken Charlie to people who valued hairy hominids over humans. People who would kill to protect the creatures as well as a secret about human history. She must've gotten close. With the fossilized footprint in Texas? That was part of it. She must've gotten closer out here too, with the creatures. Their identity was the lasso she needed to capture the truth. Once she knew what they were, she would know what humans were.

Or were not.

Her teeth rattled. Rick circled his arms around her, enfolding her in his jacket. She rested her head on his shoulder.

Her skin tingled. A spotlight zoomed past the cave entrance. The craft.

Once it passed, the tingling subsided. The fluttering in her stomach persisted.

Intef and his friends were searching for them. Intef's gang wanted the truth hidden from humans, because knowledge empowered. They could never allow humans to wield power over them. Another reason bubbled under the surface. She couldn't get her fingers around a bubble without breaking it. No matter, she knew all she needed to know.

The guardians of the hairy hominids would never stop looking for them.

T HEY SLEPT IN SHIFTS, TWO HOURS APIECE, FIRST KATY AND RICK, THEN WARNER. While she and Rick dozed, Warner guarded the entrance. When Warner slept, she and Rick guarded, though Rick tried convincing her to go back to sleep. Not that they got much sleep. Anything was better than nothing.

At 5:45, in the predawn darkness, they sneaked out of the cave. Katy ushered them around the hill to where Rick had stashed her pack. They found it. Ripped apart.

The perpetrator had strewn her spare clothes across a ten-foot area, shredded the pack itself, and destroyed anything else he found. Her slingshot was broken in three pieces, driven into the dirt inside a hairy hominid footprint. The cardboard box housing the tray of ammo was in shreds at the base of a tree. Katy found the tray face-down in the dirt, empty. The shells lay scattered in a four-foot radius around the tray, some crushed, others buried in the dirt so snugly she couldn't excavate them. She salvaged six rounds, dusting them off on her jeans, and loaded them into the cylinder.

Voices hissed over the hill. The threesome belly-crawled to the summit to peek down, between saplings, at the cave entrance. The ground chilled Katy through her clothes. She clamped her jaw shut to quell the chattering of her teeth.

Silhouettes ducked into the cave. The creatures coming home.

When the last of them entered the cave, Katy rose. She searched the horizon for the craft but saw no lights. They must've called off the search.

For now.

Something beeped behind her. She turned around to find Warner punching buttons on his—on Rick's GPS radio. Warner frowned at the unit. As he tapped another button, his frown curved upward.

"I have found our way home," he said.

Katy huffed. "It took us two days to get here. They won't give us two days to get back. Tonight they'll search again, maybe during the day too. Don't you get it? We know too much. *They can't let us leave the woods.*"

"What do we do," Rick said, "give up?"

Warner stomped down the hillside. "We must try."

They started toward home with Warner leading them, guided by the GPS. The skin-crawly sensation of eyes fixated on her lingered even as the sun nudged its head above the horizon a few minutes before 8:00. At the stream they refilled the canteen she had salvaged. Without the decontaminating tablets they might contract any number of diseases from the water. Odds were they would catch nothing but, given a choice between death now from dehydration or death later, she'd pick later.

At nine, they stopped for a rest. Seated around a birch tree, they exchanged bloodshot glances.

Katy rubbed her neck. Her eyelids kept closing on their own, her eyes burned, and her stomach gurgled. They had no time for food gathering, though, no time for anything except praying they made it home before the craft returned. Before the hairy hominids returned.

They knew too much, like she'd told Rick and Warner. The guardians would pursue them forever unless they made themselves impossible to kill. They needed more information. They must know enough that the guardians in the orb craft couldn't afford to kill them. Somehow, they must become a threat—and not just while they lived. They must become a threat if dead. The guardians would have to let them live if killing them exposed the creatures, the truth about human history, everything the guardians wanted hidden.

Become a threat to people who possessed technology which, for the civilization she knew, existed only in the minds of science fiction writers. Make herself dangerous to people who cared more for hairy monsters than humans. Gain more power than the society that built prefab caves for the hairy hominids.

No problem.

If they knew what the creatures were, how they fit into the hominid family tree, they might have a chance—a slim one, but a chance nonetheless. She'd latch onto any grain of hope she could glean from the sands. While she theorized the creatures evolved from *erectus* and the heidelbergs, she needed a method of proving it.

She twirled a lock of hair around her finger. A strand snapped. She let it drift down onto the ground.

Hair. That was it! Hair contained DNA. If she got a sample of hair from one of the creatures, the DNA might prove her theory.

Nope, it wouldn't help. Researchers had obtained hair, even fecal, samples from the creatures and analyzed them. The results came back inconclusive, some kind of primate no one had seen before. Now if she had some *erectus* DNA…

Last time she checked, Wal-Mart didn't carry *erectus* DNA samples.

Elbows propped on her thighs, she cradled her face in her hands. She slouched her shoulders forward.

A hand massaged her shoulder.

"You've been thinking," Rick said. "You're supposed to be resting."

"I have to figure a way out of this mess I got us into."

"It's not your fault."

She dropped her hands and bowed her head. "I shot the creatures, I nosed around, I ticked them off until they told their guardians about us. I got your father sucked into a spaceship. For all we know, he's dead."

"Dad sacrificed himself for us." He kissed the top of her head. "We have to make it home, for him."

"Then what?" She stood, shaking a cramp out of her calf. "They won't let us be simply because we got to my cabin. We have to become a threat. We have to make it too dangerous for them to kill us."

Rick yawned. "Dammit, Katy, I'm too tired to scheme."

"We have to. If we could prove what the creatures are, and figure out how to hide the information in such a way that it's automatically released to the public if we die, then they couldn't kill us. Hopefully."

"That's your big plan?"

Warner, sitting against the birch's trunk, looked up at Katy. "You are right, it is our one chance. What do you propose?"

"I think the creatures are the true descendents of the *Homo* line, from *erectus* down through *heidelbergensis* and ending with the hairy hominids. Which would make them the real *Homo sapiens*. If I had DNA samples from a hairy hominid and an *erectus* or a heidelberg—"

"Hold on," Rick said, waving his hands. "You're saying they're the same species as us?"

"No. I'm saying they are *Homo sapiens*. We are not."

"So what are we?"

"Beats me, a species not descended from the ancient hominids. That's another question. Right now we need to concentrate on how to get DNA from a species that hasn't walked the planet in a hundred thousand years."

No one responded. Katy ambled a few yards away, stretching out the knots in her legs, and wandered back to the men. Still no one spoke. Rick raked his hands through his hair, his gaze focused on a leaf by his foot, his lips twisted. Warner reclined against the birch with closed eyes.

Bones or teeth were the sole remains of the ancient hominids. An ancient bone would yield mtDNA, most likely, a type with questionable reliability. Biologists used mtDNA to "prove" their theories about evolution without acknowledging the flaws inherent in such analysis. She was not attempting to prove where the ancient hominids hailed from, only whether they bore any relationship to modern humans. As yet, biologists had tested one species alone for the link. Neanderthals.

Several tests had studied DNA from specimens including the famous Neander Valley find, which lent its name to the species. The results appeared to disprove the theory Neanderthals and modern humans were related.

With the human lineage tests the main problem was that the biologists used modern DNA, employing it as a telescope to peer across the expanse of time. By hunting for the equivalent of an ant in the Amazon rain forest, the scientists concluded the variations in modern DNA pinpointed humanity's origins in Africa. The scientists examined modern DNA instead of ancient DNA because, to date, no one had isolated hominid DNA older than 100,000 years—and plenty of biologists believed no one ever would. While two researchers claimed they isolated 1.8-million-year-old DNA from a stone tool found in the Sterkfontein Caves of South Africa, the claim was unverified. The researchers had extracted the supposed DNA from traces of blood on the tool. No one knew for certain the blood hadn't belonged to an ape or other animal. Most importantly, no one could prove the tests or the blood itself hadn't been contaminated. After nearly two million years of African heat, could the original DNA have survived intact?

Any sample she might obtain posed the same dilemmas. She must try.

Katy gazed into the woods surrounding them. Before she worried about getting *erectus* DNA, she needed a specimen from the hairy hominids. Their namesake—hair—would do fine. If she could get a lock.

She looked past the vegetation, turning in a semicircle. From behind a pine tree, masked by its boughs, a pair of eyes observed her. She crept forward. Now she made out the shape of a head, shoulders, an arm. A tree hid half the creature from view. Shadows obscured the remainder. She slipped her hand inside the fanny pack to curl her fingers around the Taurus.

The creature moved, fluid as a phantasm, out from behind the tree. He advanced on her in silence. When he stepped out of the shadows, she let out the breath she'd held.

Garfield grumbled. All evidence of the wounds from Ivan's gunshots was gone.

"Rick," she said, keeping her gaze on Garfield. "Get over here."

Rick hurried to her side. Noticing Garfield, he planted himself between her and the creature.

She pushed him aside. "He won't hurt us."

Garfield said, "Oogah."

"He's warning us," she said. "Try talking to him in ancient Egyptian."

Rick grumbled, a sound quite similar to Garfield's noises. Katy suppressed a laugh. Men were men no matter what their species.

"What was the spaceman's name?" Rick asked her.

"Intef. But he's not a spaceman."

Rick spoke a phrase to Garfield. Katy recognized a solitary word: Intef.

Garfield said, "Soo-noo."

"*Sunu* means physician," Rick said. "I asked if Intef healed him, I think. He must mean they took him to a doctor."

Garfield grunted a series of syllables.

Rick screwed up his mouth. "It's hard to understand him. I think he said they're looking for us now."

A gust rattled the few leaves that persevered in the treetops. Garfield, stooping on one knee, scribbled in the dirt with a stick. Rick crouched in front of him and contemplated the scribbles.

Katy dropped onto her knees. Garfield had drawn a symbol, upside-down from his perspective, right-side-up from theirs. The symbol looked like a cross with a loop at the top.

She recognized the sign as an *ankh*, the most famous of the Egyptian hieroglyphs, the symbol for life. Garfield pointed at the *ankh*. He gestured at Katy, Rick, and Warner.

Garfield swept his hand over the earth, obliterating the symbol. He drew a new symbol. A side view of a recumbent mummy.

"Dead," Rick translated.

"Ask him for a lock of his hair."

"Why don't I explain the theory of relativity too? I'm not that good with ancient Egyptian."

"Try."

A frown warped Rick's features. He spoke to Garfield, who murmured in response. Rick stretched a hand out to Garfield's arm. He grasped a lock of hair in his fingers and reached into his pocket for his knife. When he flipped the blade open, Garfield jerked his arm away.

"Let me try," Katy said.

Rick handed her the knife. She took a lock of her own hair and lopped it off with the knife. Garfield grunted. She took hold of a long tuft on his arm. As she lowered the knife to the tuft, he widened his yellow eyes. She smiled. He looked away.

She sawed off the hair. Tucking the lock in her pocket, she handed Rick the knife.

Katy strolled toward Warner. "Now we need *erectus* DNA."

"Sure," Rick said, "got some in my pocket."

Warner concentrated on his boots. "I know a way."

"What way?" Katy asked.

He gripped his knees. "I have a specimen which may yield DNA."

"You have a *Homo erectus* specimen."

"I fund many scientific expeditions. Six months ago I went along on a dig in the UK. We found a *Homo heidelbergensis* preserved by an ancient bog. Two graduate students uncovered it while excavating the bog."

"A mummified heidelberg."

"Yes."

"I never heard about that. You'd think it would've made headlines everywhere."

"No one knows of it. I made certain only one archaeologist was present when we uncovered the specimen, and we excavated late at night. The students who discovered the specimen are completing their degrees in South America, thanks to grants from my corporation. The archaeologist accepted a substantial donation to his university in exchange for his silence. I also gave other incentives for maintaining his silence."

"Fates worse than death."

Warner knotted his gaze to hers. "I brought the specimen back to America on my private jet. Dollars greased the journey."

"Where is the mummy now?"

"In the basement of my museum, inside a vault only I Can open."

"This is the secret Ivan and Diane knew. You illegally excavated a mummy and snuck it back here. Stealing artifacts is serious stuff. Smuggling them into the States is worse."

"I know."

Hope swelled inside her, until another thought occurred to her. "Maybe we can get a sample from your mummy, but we have no way of processing it."

"At my museum I employ a geneticist who will perform the tests. He can be trusted."

"How do you know? Once he realizes what we're doing he might start seeing dollar signs. Imagine what the tabloids might pay for the story, not to mention the mainstream media."

"No one betrays me," Warner said. "Twice."

"I'm sure."

Warner could get the sample and have the DNA tests done. Rick could translate the hieroglyphs. Which left one problem.

How the hell to get home.

Rick had moved behind her. She caught him scrutinizing the ground where Garfield drew the mummy symbol. He squatted there with his hand hovering over the dirt, swishing it left to right as if following a line of text. She kneeled beside him. Hieroglyphs formed a line in the dirt.

"Your buddy drew these," Rick said.

"What's it say?"

"The gods see you."

Katy checked the sky. The sun hung low. A few stratus clouds wisped across the horizon, ablaze in pink, gold, and red. She swiveled her head left and saw the sun again. No. The craft.

Within five seconds the orb swelled to three times the size of the sun. Her skin prickled.

"Time to go," she said. "*Fast.*"

22

THEY TREKKED IN A NEAR TROT TOWARD HOME. NONE OF THE TREES, THE clearings, the vegetation looked familiar. Rick struggled along behind Katy, last in the group, forcing himself to walk without limping. The pain in his knee had subsided into a constant ache accompanied by a twinge when he bent it too far or twisted it.

Katy kept glancing back at him and smiling. Encouraging him, he guessed. He didn't need encouragement. Whenever he checked the sky he noticed the craft a ways behind them, larger than the sun, closer than he liked. Several times his hair tingled and he caught the craft looming closer. It always fell back. On purpose or because the spacemen had lost them?

They weren't spacemen, Katy said. Since he had no idea what they were or what to call them, spacemen seemed as good as anything. They flew a craft that looked a heck of a lot like a UFO. Most people said UFOs came from space. So he called them spacemen.

He knew as well as Katy did they hadn't come from outer space. Not even near space. They were as human, as earthly, as he and Katy were. While some people might question Warner's humanity, no one could doubt Intef and his buddies came from good old Earth. They dressed ancient Egyptian and spoke the ancient language, plus another tongue that sounded like a mix of French, Hebrew, and Russian.

They took his father, probably killed him. Maybe not, though, since Intef said Dad could prove useful. How his father could prove useful to people with technology eclipsing the "modern" world baffled him. Dad knew history. If Intef's people wanted information on the Roman legions or Hannibal's expedition across the Alps, they could ask Professor Bergren. Spacemen had no use for that kind of information.

Katy halted. She hissed "psst" to stop Warner. When he complied, she approached a birch tree several feet away. Rick and Warner watched as she pared the bark from the tree in big strips.

After removing the bark, she peeled spaghetti-like strings from the inside of the bark. The cambium, if he remembered his tree science. How many mornings had he listened to his father's lectures on trees while he ate Cheerios and got ready for school. How many weekends and springs breaks and summer vacations had they spent hiking through the woods, collecting insect specimens, making a game of identifying trees by their leaves. Dad taught him a lot. He remembered most of it.

A fire smoldered in his gut. He wished he remembered all of it, because he couldn't call up his father for the answer next time he saw a bird outside his apartment window and labored to recall its name.

Katy handed him a fistful of stringy bark. "Eat it."

"Not hungry."

"Injured people need more nutrition." She stuffed a wad of cambium into his pocket. "Keep nibbling on it. No time for hunting, and this'll keep us going for awhile."

She stared at him until he slipped a string in his mouth and munched on it. The taste wasn't half bad, so he chewed some more.

With a string hanging out of her mouth as she gnawed on it, Katy peeled more strings off the bark. She stuffed them in her pockets but avoided the pocket where she stowed the sample of Garfield's hair. Warner stripped bark from the tree, peeled off his own strings, and—his pockets overflowing with the stuff—headed out again. A string of bark dangled from his lips.

Minutes blended into hours.

Rick lifted his cuff to check his watch. It wasn't there. Katy ordered him to take it off and remove the battery. Overhead the sun, the real sun, poised midway through its path. Must be about noon. His stomach gurgled. He stuffed another bark string in his mouth.

The craft hovered west of the real sun.

The spacemen must know where the three of them would go. Home. In their craft the spacemen could zip ahead to wait at Katy's cabin or the parking lot at the state park. They could be invisible. Instead they made sure anybody within fifty miles would see the strange light in the sky over the woods of Anameka. Were the spacemen doing it to scare them? If they were, it was wasted energy.

He worried more about what Katy might do once they got home. DNA from a mummified *Homo* whatever. DNA from Garfield's hair. Do a test and see if the two matched. What if they did?

What if they didn't?

Katy might have a nervous breakdown if the test disproved her theory. She'd invested too much in her quest for truth. Evolution had problems, he understood that now, but you didn't throw out a theory because of problems. You solved them. You investigated, reinterpreted, kept *trying*. His whole life he believed in evolution. Maybe he should give up his devotion to the idea, but that would be like cutting out half his brain.

Supposedly, a person could live with half a brain.

He was thinking like an anthropologist. They refused to consider the evidence Katy talked about because it meant abandoning an idea entrenched in their mental makeup, abandoning a part of themselves. They could no more forget evolution than they could forget how to breathe. Katy was right, the truth was scary. If he wanted to understand the world—the real one, not the one dreamed up by archaeologists and anthropologists—and if he wanted to understand Katy, he must let go of evolution. He must let go of the orthodox.

Let go and fall into the abyss.

The truth would catch him. Wouldn't it?

THE TINGLING HAD BECOME A PERMANENT SENSATION, LIKE THE WIND TICKLING her cheeks or the cold numbing her nose. Sweat dribbled down her spine, yet her nose stayed frigid. She cupped her palm over her nose to deflect the warmth of her breath onto it. The second she pulled her hand away, the chill returned.

"Ah!"

She snared Rick's arm as his knee buckled. He'd tripped in a depression, wrenching his injured knee. She helped him right himself.

"Is it the knee or the whole leg?" she asked.

"The knee."

He rubbed his knee. If they could wrap it, the extra support might improve his range of motion and stability. They might get home quicker. Just needed fabric for wrapping the injury. Although she packed duct tape in her backpack for that purpose, among others, the creatures had either stolen it or ripped it into confetti for their we-killed-the-humans party. A party they'd have to cancel.

"Are you wearing an undershirt?" she asked.

"No. Why?"

She asked Warner, "You?"

"Yes."

"Take it off."

He shed his jacket and unbuttoned his shirt.

Rick scrunched his brow. "Suddenly you have to see a man shirtless?"

Warner peeled off his undershirt, tossing it at her. While Warner dressed, she shoved her hand into Rick's pocket, where she had seen him stash his knife.

Rick smirked. "Least I know you still like me."

She pulled out the knife. Flipping the blade open, she sliced a couple inches up the shirt's seam. With her hand she ripped the shirt crosswise, slowly to avoid tearing the strip away from the shirt, until she had one long strip. A bandage.

Bending down in front of Rick, she wrapped the bandage around his knee and pants leg. When she finished, she stood.

"Give it a try," she said.

He lifted his foot, then settled it on the ground as if steel spikes protruded from the dirt. He took another step. And another. With each step his walk became less hobble, more stride.

After traversing a yard, he announced, "Feels better."

"Good, because we need to step up the pace." To Warner, she said, "How close are we to the state park?"

"Not close enough." He punched a button on the GPS. "Eleven miles. Assuming we follow a straight route."

Eleven miles. She'd hoped they traveled more than a few miles since 6:00 this morning. They strolled instead of hurried because of Rick's injury and because they wanted to stay under the cover of trees. If the guardians couldn't see them, they might give up the chase.

Yeah right.

The world she knew had invented technology, like infrared, capable of tracking people through vegetation, walls, and dirt. The technology of the guardians surpassed anything her world devised. The guardians could probably hear her pulse through a six-inch steel door.

Clack.

Katy froze. She knew that sound.

Clack.

The first clack had issued from the left, the second from the right.

A third clack came from straight ahead.

The sound penetrated right to her atoms. She whipped out the Taurus. Gripping it in both hands, she sighted the muzzle on the woods from where the third clack issued.

Clack! The noise rapped from behind. Next came four clacks in a row—left, right, ahead, behind. They were surrounded.

She swept the Taurus left to right. A few feet away Warner held his Glock in his right hand, bracing it with his left hand, his gaze fixated on the woods ahead of him. Rick opted for a position beside her, without a gun because he'd dropped his father's rifle back in the clearing and the .45, which had run out of ammo, was inside her fanny pack.

Katy scanned the trees. She asked Warner, "How much ammo you got?"

He glanced at her but said nothing. Like a Ferrari on the Autobahn, her pulse accelerated.

Rick eyed the Taurus in her hand and the Glock in Warner's. He snatched a stick off the ground. Two feet long, thick as a thumb, the stick might prove a good weapon. If they were fighting leprechauns.

Clack!

Closer and to the right. The clacks discharged in succession—left, ahead, right, behind— getting nearer with each round. Pinpoints of red glistened in the shadows between the trees.

Six bullets in her Taurus. The same or less in Warner's Glock. And Rick's stick. "Ready for action?" she asked.

Rick raised the stick in both hands. "Can't just stand here."

When she glanced at Warner, he indicated assent with a twitch of his lips.

"Okay," she said. "Run!"

The clacks quickened into a cacophony.

Katy bolted straight ahead. With no time for looking back, she counted on the crashing behind her to indicate Rick and Warner were following. She sped past a creature hiding between two pine trees, rock in hand. He barked at her, sounding more stunned than angry.

A shriek echoed through the woods. Rocks clacked close behind. She chanced a look back and found Rick two paces behind her with Warner practically stepping on his boot heels. Past Warner, a mass of hairy bodies hurtled after them.

Grunts, shrieks, and growls merged into a sound so alien she half expected the creatures to morph into bug-eyed slime demons.

She charged through a stand of brush. Branches pricked at her.

Boots clomped. Bare feet slapped on dirt. Breaths panted.

She broke through into a little clearing and hop-stopped. Rick collided with her. Warner ran a few feet past them, where he halted with a yelp.

Six creatures fringed the clearing.

They blocked every direction. A yard or two separated each of the creatures. With their long arms, they could snag anyone who dodged between them.

Heart hammering, breaths gasping out of her, Katy queried her brain for an answer. Her mind lacked a neat search function. She could ask for the information—hell, she could scream and wail for it—but her brain relinquished facts when it pleased. And it didn't please right now.

Rick thumped the stick on his palm. Warner tapped the trigger of his Glock.

Her skin tingled. Her hairs prickled. Peripherally, she noticed a light approaching from the west. The guardians hung back to guide the creatures to her, Rick, and Warner. The creatures wove a net around them as they marched forward believing themselves safe, or at least out of reach.

They had not lost Diane, given Charlie over to the guardians, and gone without food or decent sleep only to get caught.

Nets had holes. She must find one and rip it open.

The creatures each raised a hand. They gripped stone implements with edges sharp enough to slice flesh. And nick bone. They gripped Acheulian handaxes.

Twigs crunched behind her. She looked back. More creatures had closed the net from behind.

Katy tromped into the center of the clearing. When she crooked her index finger, Rick trudged up beside her. Warner hesitated before following.

Growls hummed over the rhythm of soft grunts.

The craft drifted toward the clearing, large as five suns.

Katy roared. She flapped her arms, stomped her feet, bared her teeth, and roared once more.

Rick and Warner squinted at her.

She sputtered apelike grunts while jumping up and down. The creatures squinted at her too, their song silenced.

Rick stomped his feet as he growled and roared. After a few seconds, Warner lifted his arms over his head and shrieked in imitation of the creatures' screams. Rick bellowed, thumping his chest. Katy, still roaring, watched the creatures' reactions.

They exchanged glances, shrugging their great brows. Some shuffled backward. Others ambled forward a pace or two, lowering their handaxes.

Katy aimed the Taurus at the ground and fired.

The shot fractured the air. Dirt spewed upward.

Several creatures dropped the handaxes. The ones who had backed off spun around and fled. The ones who stayed launched into a chorus of bellowing.

The departure of the four creatures had opened a gap in the line.

Katy took off toward the gap. Glancing back, she saw Rick and Warner behind her. The creatures shrieked. They stormed after the humans.

Katy tripped in a hole. Rick thrust his arms under hers and hoisted her onto her feet. She stumbled a few steps and sprinted onward.

Branches. Brush. Twigs. Leaves scattered into the air as she plowed through a pile. She ran past a boulder seated inside a gap in the trees.

She stopped. Spinning around, she hurried back to the rock.

Rick and Warner shot past her.

She shouted, "Wait!"

Behind the rock, hidden from view where few animals would trip into it, was a trap door. The creatures had opened their hatches. They needed an escape route once they killed the humans.

Rick and Warner joined her.

Between pants, Rick said, "What is it?"

Footfalls crashed back the way they'd come. Grunts beat out a bass drum rhythm.

"A trap door," she said. "We can hide in here."

"Are you insane?"

"Yes."

A creature howled.

She jumped through the hole.

Her feet hit the ground six feet later. She leaped aside.

With a grumble-shout, Rick leaped into the hole. When he hit the ground his knee buckled and he collapsed onto his side, rolling out of the way as Warner bounded through the trap door.

Warner landed flat on his soles.

Katy helped Rick stand. The trio backed away from the trap door into the darkness of the tunnel. From here they had a good view of the sunlight beaming through the trap door.

The ceiling trembled. Shadows flitted across the trap door. The footfalls receded into the distance. The tremors in the ceiling abated.

Katy let out her breath. For another minute, they waited. When no sounds came, Warner inched toward the trap door. The square of light looked shorter. Must be the angle. Warner skulked closer.

The shadow humped into the sunlight, then withdrew.

She seized Warner's sleeve. He froze. She could imagine the look on his face, though she couldn't see it. She tugged his sleeve. He crept backward. When he got near enough, she leaned close to his ear.

"Someone's up there," she said.

He raised his gun.

She laid a hand on its barrel. Her lips still close to his ear, she said, "If we shoot, they'll hear."

He lowered the Glock and slunk past her. While keeping in the shadows, he sneaked around the left side of the trap door. She discerned his shape when he moved, but the second he stopped she lost him.

A wind teased the treetops. Line shadows snaked across the light and retreated with the crests and troughs of the wind. Clouds dimmed the sun.

What remained of the light vanished as a shadow overtook the opening.

Warner shifted position. She glimpsed his silhouette.

The creature hopped through the trap door. Sniffing, he lumbered toward Katy.

Warner lunged out of the shadows. He clinched his arms around the creature's neck, choking off its cry. The beast grabbed at Warner's arms. Light glanced.

Katy winced. Warner had a knife in his hand.

The creature punched Warner in the jaw. Warner stabbed the knife into the creature's throat.

The hominid heaved himself backward into the wall, slamming Warner backward into the hard earth. Warner's arms slackened. He slid down the wall until his buttocks met the floor. The creature clawed at the knife in its throat, at the blood dribbling out around the blade. Red soaked the creature's hands. He stumbled toward Katy, fell onto his knees, gurgled.

He toppled forward onto his belly. The knife bumped the floor. It wedged deeper into the creature's throat, angling his head sideways. The creature's eyes were open. His chest sank with one final exhalation.

Warner lay slumped against the far wall.

Katy raced toward him. When she jammed two fingers into his neck, his pulse throbbed against them. She sat back on her heels.

Rick crouched beside her. "Dead?"

"Still ticking."

Warner groaned.

A snowflake wafted through the trap door. It lighted on Rick's boot and melted. More flakes spiraled down into the tunnel.

Warner pushed into a sitting position. "We must go."

Katy hooked a thumb at the trap door. "I'll need a boost to get up there."

Rick linked his hands, like a stirrup, near her feet. She settled her left foot into his hands and he lifted. Her head cleared the opening. She grasped the edge, dragging herself out of the hole. Back on her feet, she moved aside.

Warner popped up next. He wobbled on his feet, lurched toward her. She grabbed his arm to steady him. After a few seconds, he shook off her hand.

Rick's fingers crawled over the edge of the opening. He grappled with the ground and finally heaved himself through the trap door. Once on his feet, he wiped the dirt off his hands.

He escorted them away from the trap door.

Monday, October 21

THEY SLEPT IN A SHELTER BUILT WITH PINE SHOOTS, ERECTED INSIDE A STAND of closely packed trees. Warner guarded while Katy and Rick slept and, once again, Rick tried convincing her to sleep while he guarded.

She had enough trouble sleeping when Warner guarded.

No moon. No stars. If not for the snowflakes glittering in the dark, she would've felt she crawled back into the caves. Rick stooped near the opening of the shelter. Katy huddled behind him, popping her head up every few minutes to peek over his shoulder. If any creatures tried sneaking up on them, the snow would illuminate their dark bodies against its whiteness. Unless they surrounded the shelter from behind and jumped on top of it.

She looked at the roof. Nobody there. She rested a hand on Rick's back.

They had forgone a fire. While they could've masked its smoke, the smell and the light even from a small fire might draw the creatures to them. Despite their stench, the hairy hominids seemed to have a sense of smell as keen as a dog's. How they smelled anything less pungent than a lake of sulfur through their own odor perplexed her. Her nose plugged up every time one of them walked past.

Rick stiffened. She touched his arm.

Scooting away from the opening, he pointed at the sky. She leaned nearer the opening and bent her head back. The moon shimmered in front of the clouds.

She recognized it wasn't the moon, yet it resembled the moon so much that her mind wanted to create that fiction. For a second she let it. Then she ducked back into the shelter.

Rick looked at her and she looked at him. Either the snow reflected its whiteness on their features or they both had gone pale.

Wasn't enough light to reflect.

In silence they gathered what few possessions they had, mainly the weapons and the bandage for Rick's leg. As he wound the fabric around his knee, Katy shook Warner's shoulder. He roused and, seeing her, sprang into a sitting position. He reached for his Glock, which lay beside him.

They left the shelter and jogged into the night.

The light hovered behind them, always the same size.

SHORTLY BEFORE DAWN THE LIGHT VANISHED. THEY DIDN'T DISCUSS IT. AS daylight embraced the landscape, they slowed from a jog into a fast walk. Katy's legs ached, grit blurred her vision, and sweat ran down her spine and over her chest. Whenever she passed a little hollow or a patch that had as yet escaped the deepening snowfall, she resisted the urge to flop down there and pass out. The snow kept falling. The air stayed frigid, the sky gray.

At midday they munched their cambium strings in transit.

Warner stopped.

Katy trudged up alongside him. He was punching keys on the GPS unit with a frown that accentuated the dark semicircles under his eyes. He shoved the unit in his pocket, slumping his shoulders.

"Dead batteries," he said.

"How close were we last time you checked?"

"Ten minutes ago we were six miles out."

Six miles. It felt like a thousand.

Warner straightened, inhaled, and marched forward. Katy followed.

Her watch read 2:00 when Warner halted again. She opened her mouth, but he raised his hand to silence her question. He nodded toward the trees to the left.

She squinted at the vegetation, unable to see past it.

Snap!

A shape tousled the foliage. Instead of jerking her head to look at it, she cupped a hand over her ear as she canted her head in that direction and opened her mouth. Shuffling. A murmur, as of breathing. Or a breeze. Except the wind had abated overnight.

Ka-chunk.

Her heart thudded. The *ka*-chunk of a round being chambered into a rifle.

She slipped the Taurus out of her fanny pack.

Warner dropped into a crouch. She did the same, and Rick kneeled beside her. They stared into the trees where the movement had occurred. Katy leveled the Taurus at the spot.

Rick grabbed a stick. He turned it over several times, with a sour look on his face, before he clamped his fist around the stick.

The shooshing resumed, accompanied by the dervish dance of the treetops. Within the mesh of branches and sapling trunks, metal glinted.

Katy fired.

A man shouted. Figures jumped. She fired again. Two men thrashed out of the trees, one clutching a shotgun, the other cradling a rifle in his left arm and waving his right at her.

"We surrender, lady," he said, his voice shrill. "We surrender!"

The man with the shotgun sported a sweatshirt emblazoned with an image of an eight-point buck and a rifle above the words "the buck stops here." He wore no coat, thin knit gloves covered his hands, and Nikes protected his feet. A baseball cap perched on his head, backwards. He looked about twenty-two. His buddy—probably ten years older—donned a T-shirt, sweatpants, and mud boots. He wore a rain poncho with the hood pulled over his head. No gloves.

Katy aimed the Taurus at the ground.

Warner leveled his Glock at the duo's heads. Eyes half closed, he clenched his jaw.

"What are you doing way out here?" Katy asked.

The baseball-hat guy answered. "Denny and me like to go where nobody else hunts. Catch us some government beef."

"Deer shot out of season? That's a crime."

Denny sniggered. "Don't see no wildlife rangers. How 'bout you, Ted?"

Katy said, "You walk all the way from the state park?"

"Naw," Ted said, "we drove. My Jeep'll go anywhere. Took out a few baby trees but, heck, there's too many trees anyhow."

Hope fluttered in her stomach. "How far to your Jeep?"

He hooked a thumb over his shoulder. "A mile thataway."

"You're giving us a lift to the state park." When he objected, she swung her arm up until the Taurus was level with his nose. "You are."

Rick, his voice deep and soft, said, "Better do what she wants, she shot a guy's fingers off once."

Ted switched his gaze between Rick's face and Katy's gun. "Sure, no problem."

He plodded in the direction he had indicated. Denny scuffled after him with Warner right behind, the Glock brushing against Denny's poncho. Rick motioned for Katy to go next.

She said to him, "I shot the beer bottle, not his fingers. How'd you know about it anyway?"

"Dad told me."

They both glanced at the clouds. Swallowing, Rick forced a smile.

"I used to think Dad liked talking about you because you two were…" He shrugged. "Now I figure it was a sales pitch."

Turning away from him, she started after Warner.

Softly, Rick said, "Didn't need to sell me."

A warmth spread through her despite the cold. A blush fired up on her cheeks. She subdued a grin and concentrated on the back of Warner's head.

THE JEEP'S TIRES SQUEALED AS TED SWERVED AROUND THE CORNER INTO THE parking lot at Lake Anameka State Park. He angled across parking spaces, zooming toward Warner's Land Rover. The tires squealed again when he slammed on the brakes to stop beside the vehicle.

The momentum flung Katy forward against the seatbelt, which she'd strapped on despite Denny's assurances "only candy-asses need seatbelts." The belt cut into her neck. When the Jeep ceased rocking, she unclipped the belt and peeled it off her body.

She sat squished between Warner and Rick in the backseat. Rick yanked the door handle, kicked the door open, hopped out, and planted himself beside the door. She clambered out after him. Warner exited on the other side. They reunited alongside Warner's Land Rover.

Ted spun the tires on his Jeep. Smoke curled up from them. He released the brake and the Jeep rocketed out of the parking lot.

Warner bent down, feeling under the Land Rover's bumper. He extracted a plastic box the size of a candy bar. He slid out the lid to reveal keys fastened onto a keychain. A remote control was clipped to the chain as well. After plucking the keys from the box, which he discarded on the ground, Warner punched a button on the remote. The door locks clunked.

They loaded into the Land Rover. Warner drove out of the parking lot toward Katy's cabin. They arrived ten minutes later.

Her Ford truck was parked in the driveway where she'd left it. The house looked the same. Until this moment she wondered, in the recesses of her mind, if her home would've changed as her perceptions of the world had. As she had. She no longer pondered the nature of humanity in the abstract. She needed to know. To stay alive.

The spare key was still in the woodshed, taped to the back of an old saw she'd hung on the wall beside the door. Once she unlocked the door they hurried inside, up the stairs into the living room. Rick lit a fire in the wood stove. Katy cooked dinner.

Bacon, eggs, and toast tasted as sumptuous as filet mignon. Milk became champagne with which they toasted their survival. Celebration felt strange, with so much unfinished, yet they needed to enjoy whatever victories they could muster. After the meal Katy hunched over the sink washing the dishes.

We might die tonight. Why bother cleaning up? *Because it feels normal.* She deposited the last plate in the drainer. With her fingers under the warm water, she closed her eyes.

"It is set," Warner said.

She shut off the water and faced the living room. Rick balanced on a stool across the bar from her. Warner had just clomped up the stairs from the basement, where he used the phone in the laundry room because he needed "privacy." Practically skipping into the living room, he smiled the first real smile—not a smirk—she'd witnessed on his face.

"We have reservations on the eight o'clock flight to Chicago," he said. "There we will collect your DNA sample from the mummy. A friend will conduct the tests."

Katy feigned a pout. "No private jet?"

"They are all engaged." He plopped onto the sofa. "However, by the time we arrive in Chicago a jet will have returned from Venezuela."

She wanted to ask why Venezuela. The answer would do nothing for her except satisfy her curiosity. She settled for another question. "How does that help us?"

"We must go to Canada, British Columbia." The smile faded. "There is another discovery you should see."

"Don't suppose you'll tell me what it is."

"It's better you see for yourself. You would not believe me."

She was too tired to argue.

Rick was staring at his hands. She walked around the bar to him. "Now what's wrong?"

"We'll never know what those hieroglyphs said."

"We will once you decipher them."

"They destroyed the camera."

She grinned. Slipping her hand under her shirt, she extricated the memory card from her bra. She wiggled it in his face. "But not the memory card."

"You need software to access it, don't you?"

"Charlie left his thingy here." In response to the men's hunched eyebrows, she said, "It looks like a floppy disk but you stick the memory card in it and it downloads the pictures to your computer. I loaded the software onto my computer so I could download the images straight from the memory card for use on the website. Ivan's camera used the same kind of memory card as Charlie's so the thingy might work."

A smile inched across Rick's face. He threw his arms around her waist, pulling her close. "You *are* amazing."

He kissed her.

Warner groaned. When Rick released her, she traipsed to the corner at the head of the stairs and her computer waiting there. She tapped the power button. Once the computer booted up, she opened the file manager to create a folder for the photos.

She gasped. All her files had been deleted.

The My Documents directory housed a single text file. She double-clicked on the file name, "readme.txt." It opened. The file contained one line of text.

We are watching you.

23

THE WEBSITE WAS GONE. THE BROWSER, INSTEAD OF LOADING THE HOME page of the Human Origins Project, displayed a "page not found" error. She typed in the URL for another page on the site. The same message appeared.

She logged into the site using an FTP program, software for transferring files to and from the server. The main directory was empty. She checked the special directory for CGI programs. Empty. These people knew about websites. They must, because the CGI directory wasn't visible from the main directory. They knew how to find it.

Intef's voice echoed in her mind. When he said *cam-er-a* he sounded out the word like someone who had read the word but never spoken it before. And he'd warned she would die "by the fire" instead of "by gunfire" or "by the gun" as most people would say. Though he and his cohorts exploited advanced technology, they didn't understand the lowly technology of her world. They might not know about websites.

Charlie knew.

Her throat constricted. Charlie hated messing with the website, and only bothered with it when he couldn't reach her, however he had learned to use the FTP program and access the CGI directory. If the guardians, or whatever they called themselves, knew as little about modern culture as it seemed they did, Charlie must've shown them what to do. Willingly? Under coercion?

Katy shunted the questions to the back of her mind. She said, "Those UFO-flying scumbags deleted our website."

Rick and Warner huddled on either side of her. Both leaned around her to look at the computer screen.

"Why," Rick said, "would they erase your website?"

"A demonstration of power," she said. "They want us to know what they can do."

Warner backed away. "Download the images. We have one hour until we must leave for the airport."

Rick, his hand resting on the table, stared at the computer. The last time she used her computer, the day before they left on their expedition into hairy hominid country, Rick had watched over her shoulder. How many years elapsed since then.

It happened five days ago. *Five days.*

Katy inspected Rick's clothes. Mud caked on his jeans, around the ankles, and on his boots. While some chipped off as he'd walked around the cabin, those areas free of mud bore dirt stains. Mud had also congealed in his hair. His shirt, wrinkled and dirt stained too, was unraveling along the hem. Threads fringed the edges. Sometime during the journey home He had scratched his forehead, bruised his hand, and acquired a blood stain on his thigh. Probably hairy hominid blood.

Taking in her own attire, she crinkled her nose. Mud caked on her boots. A dark stain marred her left boot, apparently blood that dripped off one of the creatures she killed. The cuts on her face had scabbed over, but they tightened whenever she smiled or grimaced or moved her muscles one millimeter. Her shirt was ripped under one arm and streaked with dirt. Her hair had metamorphosed into a bird's nest. Her muscles ached. Her eyes burned.

Warner's clothes, although dirty and wrinkled, looked passable. He had no scratches, no blood stains, and—of course—no hair crisis.

She fingered the hem of Rick's shirt where it had unraveled. "I think we both need an acid shower."

"Clothes seem kind of unimportant these days."

"The last thing we need is to draw attention to ourselves with our filth."

"Sorry, your clothes won't fit me."

Banging erupted at the front door.

She bolted out of the chair, sending it cartwheeling across the living room. Rick grabbed for the holster still clipped onto his belt, but the .45 wasn't there. She had returned the pistol to its wooden box in her closet.

Warner opened the door.

With sunset impending, the sun had dipped low in the sky. Shadows riddled the porch. The man who hunched beyond the doorway appeared as a silhouette rather than a body. Shorter than Warner, and stockier, the man spoke in a voice that whined like a jet engine.

"Got the stuff you wanted, boss."

The man handed Warner two suitcases. Warner set one down inside the doorway. The second he set down and pushed with his foot. The suitcase skated across the wood floor toward Rick, skidding into his boots.

Rick said, "That's my suitcase."

"I had my man retrieve it," Warner said. "from your father's home. If you need anything, write it down and my man will get it for you."

Rick looked at Katy. She shrugged. Pulling open a drawer on her desk, she procured a spiral notebook and a pen. She held them out to Rick.

In a voice low enough Warner couldn't hear, she said, "If you need anything for deciphering the hieroglyphs, ask for it. Might as well use the resources at hand."

"Use him, you mean."

"Why not? He's using us."

Rick took the pen and paper. To Warner, he said, "Gimme a minute."

After a whisper to his "man," Warner clapped the door shut. Katy slanted sideways until she could see through the window into the porch. The man plunked down in a chair at the table. He thrummed his fingers on the tabletop, gaze directed out the front window of the porch.

Across the room, Warner picked up his suitcase. He strode into the bathroom and shut the door.

Katy turned back to the computer. From a drawer she retrieved Charlie's "thingy," the device for downloading images from a memory card. The card was the size of a 35mm negative, and almost as thin. It fit into a slot in the card reader. She plugged the reader's USB cable into a port on the front of her computer, then opened the file manager. She dragged-and-dropped the images onto her hard drive. While the computer downloaded the photos, she trotted upstairs to change clothes.

When she came back ten minutes later, Rick handed her the notepad and pen.

"Your turn," he said. "Maybe you should ask for a Jaguar convertible and a six-hundred-acre ranch."

"Don't forget a million dollars."

She scanned his entries on the list. He had scribbled, underneath the word "books," a list of titles that all featured the word Egypt or hieroglyph in them. Katy added her own requests to the list—a laptop computer with wireless Internet connection and a digital camera. Done, she gave Rick the list.

"Give it to Warner when he gets out of the bathroom."

Rick, list in hand, walked to the sofa. He plopped onto it. Eyes closed, he rested his head against the sofa's back.

The computer had finished downloading the images. Katy popped the camera's memory card out of the reader, tucking the card in her bra again. She got two blank CDs out of the drawer, one of which she inserted in the computer's CD drive. She burned the images onto the first CD, exchanged it for the blank one, and burned another copy. The duplicate CD she stashed in the basement, under the washing machine.

The moment she hopped up the stairs into the living room, Rick opened his eyes. He rotated his head toward her without lifting it from the sofa.

"What were you doing down there?" he asked.

"Buying insurance." She tugged on his sleeve. "Better change. We leave soon."

He blinked at her. A question engraved lines across his forehead. He didn't ask it, but pushed off the sofa onto his feet instead. He slipped his hand around the suitcase handle, hefting it up, and climbed the stairs to her bedroom loft.

She watched him shamble into the walk-in closet, out of view.

Later, she would give Rick one of the CDs so he could decipher the hieroglyphs from the pictures she'd taken. Counting that disk and the one under the washing machine, plus the memory card in her bra, she had bought insurance times three.

Was it enough?

O'Hare International Airport
Chicago, Illinois

A MAN PUSHING A WHEELED SUITCASE MET THEM AT THE GATE. HE HAD A computer carrying bag slung over one shoulder. His square jaw and thick brow ridge, coupled with bushy eyebrows and a beard, made him look like Garfield's cousin. The man's gray eyes, small as a bird's, darted back and forth as he talked.

With a Chicago inflection, he said, "Got the computer. The books and camera are in the suitcase."

Warner said nothing when the man escorted them through the terminals, out a door to the curb, where a limousine waited. After they boarded the limo, the man handed Warner the computer bag. The underling stashed the suitcase in the trunk and ambled back into the airport.

"Who was he?" Katy asked as the limo rolled down the road.

Warner gazed out the window. "No one you need to know."

"Where's he going?"

In lieu of an answer, he passed her the bag. She unzipped it. A laptop computer was inside.

"Equipped with a wireless card," he said. "You can connect to the Internet with it."

She brought out the laptop and flipped it open. Punching the power button, she said, "Don't you want to know what I plan on doing with this?"

"No."

Rick, seated beside Katy, said, "I'd like to know."

"Later," she said.

When the computer had powered up, she opened Notepad. They needed a backup plan, in case the DNA test didn't work or wasn't enough. She had an idea, but no clue if it would work. She had to try.

The limo slowed, turning left.

She typed furiously.

THE MUSEUM OF PREHISTORY OCCUPIED A FIVE-ACRE SITE ON THE OUTSKIRTS of Chicago. Nearby a factory smokestack belched fumes. Little else inhabited the neighborhood.

The museum, a three-story building constructed in the Gothic style, loomed like a haunted house in the sulfurous glow of the street lights. The main doors, eight feet tall and six feet wide, stood closed. A sign at the doorway announced the museum's hours: 10-4 weekdays, 10-7 weekends.

It was 10:15 on a Monday night.

Warner fished a key chain out of his pocket. Unlocking the left-hand door, he swung it inward. A single lamp, seated on the information desk fifteen feet inside the doorway, lit the lobby.

Rick walked through the door. Katy entered after him. Warner, close behind her, shut and locked the door.

The museum smelled of dust and floor wax. The lobby opened onto a cavernous space where pale yellow bulbs cast cones of light in the darkness. To the left, the lobby ended at a gift shop's entrance. A wire mesh barrier closed off the shop. To the right, rows of wire stands and wood racks held brochures, maps, and postcards for sale.

Warner steered them into the cavern. The area housed a gallery of exhibits three stories tall, with an atrium in the center. Balconies encircled the atrium. A skylight would've brightened the gallery in the daytime. At this time of night it offered a view of the sky, with the stars blotted out by the city glow.

When they entered the gallery, Katy looked up at the exhibits that dwelled in the balconies above. A banner hanging from the second floor railing declared "Ancient Ancestors: The Birth of The Human Family." She surveyed the exhibits set into the walls around her, dioramas of ancient hominids.

Here an Australopithecus couple strolled the African savanna. There a male Homo erectus squatted by a fire, flaking bits off a stone to fashion a handaxe.

Along the length of the gallery, in the center island that filled the atrium, glass cases housed the skeletal remains of ancient hominids. As she examined the exhibits on the second level—a diorama of saber-toothed cats, the skeleton of a mammoth—her thoughts drifted back to the paintings in the hairy hominid caves. In the meeting hall she recognized images of extinct creatures, including *Macrauchenia*. But another image returned to her now, the eel-like creature with a mouth gaping three times its body width.

She had seen it before. Perhaps in a museum such as this one.

They stopped at the far end of the gallery, under the balcony. Double doors barred their path.

Waiting for Warner to find the right key, Katy asked, "Are there exhibits of ancient sea life in here?"

"Yes." Unlocking the doors, he pushed them open. "Go."

Rick went.

Katy tilted her head back until her throat muscles stretched taut. She squinted at the two floors of exhibits above her. "I want to see those exhibits."

Rick leaned through the doorway. "We don't have time."

"It's important."

He sighed. Warner waved her through the doorway, shut and locked it behind them, and swerved left. He led them to an elevator.

A minute later they stepped out onto the third floor. Warner gestured at the exhibits on the right side of the atrium. The skylight created a false horizon overhead. The moon had set, leaving a blankness where the sky should've shimmered. An oblivion. Katy shivered.

She jogged down the balcony, perusing the exhibits as she walked. Five minutes later, she trotted back to the elevator bay where Rick and Warner waited.

"It's not here," she said.

"What's not here?" Rick asked.

"The—never mind." She straightened her shoulders. "Let's get our DNA."

THE VAULT NESTLED IN THE BACK WALL OF A STORAGE ROOM ON THE THIRD floor. The steel door was equipped with a keypad and a steel handle below the pad.

Katy strolled up to the door alongside Warner. All around them metal shelves rose toward the ceiling. Boxes, bins, and crates crammed the shelves. Warner curved his hand over the keypad to obstruct her view. She exhaled. Clouds roiled away from her mouth.

Rubbing her hands together for warmth, she said, "You'll show me your treasure but you don't want me to see the combination. What do you think I'd do if I knew it? Steal the rotting corpse hidden in there?"

"Dr. Oberman will arrive soon," he said. "He will extract the DNA and perform the tests."

The door lock thunked. Warner twisted the handle. Easing the door inward enough to admit one person, he squeezed through into the dark vault. Click! The lights came on inside. He must've flicked a switch. Katy tucked through the doorway with Rick behind her.

The vault was ten feet wide and eight feet long. Fluorescent lights buzzed overhead. The walls were painted beige, the floor hewn from granite. The air felt cool, though warmer than outside, and dry. Humidity and temperature controlled, no doubt, to protect the treasure.

In the room's center, a metal coffin rested atop a dais. Another keypad adorned the coffin lid. Warner stepped onto the dais and punched in his code. A lock clicked. The lid popped up an inch. He pushed the lid open.

Katy trotted to the dais. She jumped onto the platform. Inside the box, the mummy lay within a Styrofoam bed molded to fit its shape.

She gasped.

The mummy—a *Homo heidelbergensis*, a supposed ancestor of modern humans—would've stood six feet tall in life. He had a pronounced brow ridge, massive legs and shoulders, and no arches in his feet. Yet those features hadn't paralyzed her heart and exhausted the oxygen in her lungs. No, her reaction stemmed from what covered his body from head to toe.

A coat of thick brown hair.

Dr. victor oberman had taken one step across the threshold when he stumbled over his own sudden stop. His jaw gaped. His eyes watered, because he stopped blinking. He gasped as if the room had become a vacuum.

"Holy cow, Warner," he said. "How long have you had this?"

"Two years." Warner hopped off the dais. He told Katy, "This is the geneticist I mentioned to you."

"Paleopathologist," Oberman said. "Warner forgets the lingo, on purpose I think. We scientists aren't as cool as his mercenary friends."

Warner kept his gaze on the sarcophagus. "How fast can you perform the tests?"

"My assistant can start the—"

"No." Warner's voice thickened. "No one must see this. No one must know of the tests. Only you."

"If I work after hours so no one sees, I can have the results for you Friday morning."

Warner ground his teeth.

"Sorry," Oberman said, "it's the best I can do. I've got daytime duties here too and, if I rush it, the results might get contaminated."

"What if you take the days off?"

"If I work all tonight and tomorrow night, I could have the results Wednesday morning."

"Do it. I will authorize vacation time for you."

The paleopathologist bounded onto the dais.

Katy gawked at the mummy, at his head identical to the heads of the creatures she had called hairy hominids because their hair distinguished them from other hominids. So she had thought. She needed a new name for the creatures.

Try *Homo sapiens.*

Her skin itched at the thought. For a long time she believed evolution was a fantasy, and accepted modern humans had existed for millions of years. Despite her beliefs, she felt a mental allergic reaction to the realization humans resembled the ancient hominids as much as pigs resembled dogs. If the creatures were the true descendants of the *Homo* line, if modern humans never shared an ancestry with apes and *erectus* because they predated both species, then what were humans? Where did we come from?

The guardians knew.

Guardians. Guardians was an incongruous label for people who tried to kill her. When Rick deciphered the opening section of the hieroglyphs, he translated a name. It had referred to the people who assembled the hieroglyph room. She searched her brain for the phrase.

The Planners seal this place in the name of Osiris.

Fine, she would call them the Planners. Whatever that meant. At least it didn't make them sound benevolent.

Oberman tiptoed toward the mummy. He had pulled latex gloves over his hands. A surgical mask shielded his mouth. He wore green surgical garb, complete with booties over his shoes. While Katy went comatose from her own thoughts, he had wheeled in a metal cart full of surgical tools, including an endoscope with a device on the end for ensnaring tissue samples.

The mummy's fingers were stubby, his hands hairy on top and bare on the palms. She followed the arms up to the shoulders. Wider than a man's, the shoulders sloped down from the head where a neck should've been. Next she took in the face. Hairy except for a band extending under the eyes and over the nose. The eyelids were closed, the skin shrunken from the process of natural mummification. *Homo erectus* must've been hairy too.

If an anthropologist had found the mummy, would the specimen have disappeared like so many other artifacts of anomalous nature?

If she were an anthropologist who spent a lifetime studying the conventional theories of evolution, who planted the roots of her career in evolution's soil, how might she react?

So it has hair. Either it's not a heidelberg or heidelbergs aren't related to us like we thought. Could be fake too. So its DNA matches the Bigfoot DNA. Doesn't mean Bigfoot's descended from the known hominids. Must be another hominid we haven't discovered yet who evolved into us.

Katy shut her eyes. Even if the heidelberg DNA matched the hairy hominid DNA, a hole gaped in her theory because she'd failed to prove whether heidelbergs had any relation to *erectus*. Only if she proved the line—*erectus* to heidelberg to the creatures—could she prove her theory. Even then she needed proof modern humans were not related to those hominids.

She searched the ceiling tiles for a solution as Oberman inserted the endoscope into the mummy.

An hour later Oberman exclaimed, "Got it!"

The endoscope lay on the cart. Oberman clutched a pair of tweezers and, between the pincers, a fragment of tissue. In his other hand he held a glass vial. He placed the tissue in the vial and capped it. Yanking his mask down, he grinned.

"Pretty cool, huh?" he said.

Katy looked at Oberman for the first time. He stood two inches taller than her. His hair was gray, and his eyes were hazel. Wrinkles splayed out from his eyes when he smiled. His smile, the kind that stretched his wide lips so far they seemed about to snap, revealed a missing tooth one space over from his front teeth. The bulb of his nose was red. If she had to guess she'd put him in his middle fifties, older than Warner. Maybe his age explained why Warner failed to intimidate him.

Oberman set the vial on the cart. "Now, to be double sure I get useable DNA, I'm going to extract a tooth. Other paleopathologists have had good luck with teeth."

He chewed his lip, tilting his head. "Course nobody's tried it with a mummy this old. This puppy must be 150,000 years old."

Bending over the mummy's head, Oberman whistled "Joy to the World." With calipers he prized the jaws apart. He grabbed a tool from the cart. Pliers.

Oberman winked at Katy and Rick. "Craftsman tools are the best."

"Do all paleopathologists shop at Sears?" she asked.

He ducked his head inside the coffin. "Can't do better than a lifetime replacement guarantee."

Oberman inserted the pliers in the mummy's mouth. He clamped the pliers around a tooth.

Katy twirled her hair with her finger. They needed *erectus* DNA. Modern DNA too, just to make their new ground as solid as possible. She wound her hair around her finger. Yes, her own hair could provide the modern DNA. But what of the *erectus* variety?

Oberman dropped a tooth into a vial. He pushed the cart toward the doorway.

"Wait," Katy said. "We need some *Homo erectus* DNA or this test is worthless."

Oberman sucked on his lower lip. He sounded like a baby sucking its thumb. After a pause, he said, "We've got *erectus* fossils in the hominid gallery. They've been treated for preservation but I might get a sample out of them. It's not unprecedented."

Warner lowered the coffin lid with a thunk. "You will make it work."

Hands on his hips, the paleopathologist straightened. "I will *try*, Warner. You think somebody else can do better, go blackmail them into doing the test for you."

Oberman rolled the cart out the door.

They followed him through the storage room, down a corridor, to the elevator. A minute later they convened before the double doors to the gallery. Warner unlocked the doors. They entered the gallery, leaving the doors unlocked.

Oberman, pushing the cart, trotted to the center island where glass cases sheltered arm and leg bones, fragments of skulls, photos of the sites where anthropologists found the fossils. He stopped at a case labeled "*Homo erectus*:

The First World Traveler." The title referred to the theory *erectus* had evolved in Africa before spreading outward into Europe and Asia. Some anthropologists, however, believed the species evolved simultaneously throughout the world.

Warner unlocked the case. Oberman, his hands clad in latex, cradled a leg bone in both hands. He lifted the bone out of the case. Warner secured the case lid.

Oberman said, "I'll start the tests right away."

Katy yanked several strands of hair from her head. Her scalp burned. She offered the hairs to Oberman. "Test modern DNA too."

He set the bone on the cart and accepted the hairs, which he sealed inside a vial. He gripped the cart with both hands, heading toward the double doors.

Katy looked into the case beside the *erectus* fossils. It held Neanderthal specimens, including a shin bone. A plaque under the shin bone listed its place of origin as Dusseldorf, Germany, its discoverer as—

Ivan Thaw.

She slapped a hand on the glass. "Is this the bone Ivan faked?"

Oberman paused to glance over his shoulder at her. "Still a valid fossil. He faked the DNA, not the bone itself. Unfortunately, we have to give him credit for discovering it. That part, at least, was legitimate."

Once Oberman left the gallery, Warner jogged to the doors. He locked them.

From the skylight two stories above, the moon smiled down at her. She turned back to the hominid bones.

Her skin tingled. *The moon set hours ago.*

She jerked her head back. The light hovered in the center of the skylight, glaring down at her. The occupants inside the craft observed her actions, monitoring her progress. Like a tortoise tagged with a radio transmitter, she continued her life under the scrutiny of her keepers. These keepers tracked her not out of concern for her safety but so they could know precisely when to eliminate her. Maybe they were using her as a test subject to see how much the dumb humans could learn about their true history on their own, with their own technology and brainpower.

Want to know what we can do? I'll show you.

Warner finished locking the doors behind Oberman.

"We have to hurry," Katy said, indicating the skylight. "They're too close for my comfort."

Guiding Katy and Rick out of the museum, Warner said, "We must go to Canada. What awaits us there could become more important than the DNA, where solving the mystery of our past is concerned. My jet will take us their quickly."

Katy glanced at the sky. The light had moved directly overhead.

"Not fast enough," she said.

Inside the limo, Katy sidled up close to Rick. He slipped his arm around her shoulders. Warner sat on the seat facing them. At a wave of his hand the limo rolled forward out of the parking lot. He jerked a finger at the ceiling and the driver raised a partition between the passenger area and the front seat. When the partition had shut, Warner dug a hand into his pocket. He pulled it out, his hand fisted around an object.

"This," he said, "is part of what we seek in Canada. The rest I left *in situ* for safekeeping."

He uncurled his hand. The object was an oval stone, polished to a sheen, its gray color dark enough that it appeared black until the light struck it. He tossed the stone to her. Its surface felt smooth, almost glassy. She flipped it over. Her pulse jumped. On the back of the stone someone had carved an ibis, the sacred bird of ancient Egypt. The sculptor had rendered an intricate though stylized image of the bird standing. Above the bird, the sculptor had carved an eye with a line extending down from the center. A second line started from the endpoint, curving toward the side to terminate in an upward spiral.

Rick touched the carving. "The Eye of Horus. Probably the most important symbol in ancient Egypt."

Warner flopped back against the seat. "There is more where I found the stone. Much more. I made a timely donation to the Canadian government and they approved my request to shut down the quarry where I discovered the stone. No one has entered the area in six months."

"You bribed the Canadians."

"I can bribe anyone." He smiled. "That is free enterprise."

"The Canadians know what you found."

"No."

Katy squinted through the twilight of the limo at Warner. His smile segued into a smirk. She had to admire a guy who could bribe an entire country into doing what he wanted without telling them why or what he was protecting.

"If Egyptians discovered the Americas," Katy said, "this stone must be thousands of years old."

"You misunderstand. I didn't find the stone lying on the surface or buried in a sediment layer dating to dynastic times." He leaned toward her. "I found it in the mountains of British Columbia. In a formation called the Burgess Shale."

"That's impossible."

Rick oscillated his gaze between Katy and Warner. "The Burgess what?"

"Burgess Shale," Katy said. She took a deep breath. "It's a paleontological treasure trove because it holds some of the oldest fossils ever found, sea creatures from the Cambrian Period. It's so valuable because soft tissues were preserved. You can see what the creatures looked like in life."

With her finger she traced the outlines of the ibis, the eye symbol, the rock itself. The hand of a human carved the stone. The hand of an ancient Egyptian. The hand of a Planner? Perhaps.

She must know.

To Warner, she said, "What else did you find?"

"You must see it for yourself."

"Yeah, you said that before. I'm starting to think you enjoy being mysterious and ambiguous. You should've been a fortune teller."

Rick plucked the stone from her hand. He ran his finger over the etchings. "How old do you think it is?"

"The Burgess Shale," she said, "is over half a billion years old."

24

Tuesday, October 22

I NEED SHOCK THERAPY," RICK SAID. HE RUBBED HIS FOREHEAD, SUQEEZING his eyes shut for a second. "Or maybe a lobotomy."

"Why's that?" Katy asked. She fingered the Burgess Shale stone as she watched out the window of Warner's private jet, a Gulfstream G550.

Rick and Katy sat side-by-side in two of four chairs positioned around a conference table, with two chairs on each side of the table. Rick's reflection stared back at him from the tabletop. Even through the dark polish of the wood he spotted the circles under his eyes, the crinkle across his forehead. He looked away.

Past a doorway behind them lay the galley, lavatory, and luggage compartment. In the rest of the cabin Rick counted two groupings of single seats, one abutting the conference grouping, the other adjacent to the cockpit. Two sofas, one for each grouping, faced the single seats. Warner sprawled out on the closest sofa.

Despite the glare from the reading light he'd aimed at the books on his lap, Rick could pick out the stars outside the window. He looked at Warner. The man had his eyes closed, hands clasped over his belly. His chest rippled up and down, in and out.

Rick sighed. He wished he could relax like that. Being chased by spacemen who kidnapped his father, translating a roomful of hieroglyphs in a few hours, it all made him feel like a match inside a propane tank.

Katy waved her hand in his face. "You awake? Why do you need shock therapy?"

He nodded at Warner snoozing. "Because I'm starting to like him."

"Me too. Frightening, isn't it?" She half rose from her chair. "Afraid I have to wake Sleeping Beauty, though."

"What for?"

She smiled, patted his head, and strolled toward Warner. She tapped the man's shoulder to wake him. Rick turned back to the books on his lap. Underneath the books was a spiral notebook with transliterations scrawled on it.

He gnawed the end of his pen. He'd set the laptop computer on the conference table in front of him, a photo of the hieroglyphs on the screen, enlarged to let him read the individual signs. He scrolled down to the symbol that had eluded him for ten minutes, a bird.

The ancient Egyptians had used a number of bird symbols, many of them similar in appearance. Goose, he'd thought, but the translation made no sense with the goose sign. Thumbing through the book on his lap, he found a table listing the hieroglyphs in sections broken down by size and type. The book listed four types—three for signs depicting people, animals, and natural elements like water, plus a group for miscellaneous signs. He located the goose right above another, nearly identical sign. The second sign was labeled pintail duck.

He bent his head down to squint at the two signs. Practically the same. A slight difference in the tails.

He zoomed in on the sign in the photo. Definitely the duck. Finally the translation made sense.

The murmuring of voices interrupted his thoughts, drawing his attention to the sofa where Warner reclined. Katy leaned over him whispering. Warner narrowed his eyes. She gestured with her hand to emphasize whatever she'd said. He nodded.

Katy reclaimed her seat.

"What was that about?" Rick asked.

"More insurance."

"Didn't know Warner sold life insurance."

"Not life insurance," she said. "That's for after you die. Health insurance, designed to keep us alive."

He considered asking her what she meant by insurance, why she kept having to buy them more. She would ignore the question, or smile and pat him on the head again. He'd gotten used to mysteries, especially those that germinated in Katy.

The hieroglyphs on the screen taunted him. He thrummed his fingers on the laptop's edge.

"Tell me," Katy said, "why didn't you become an Egyptologist?"

"Why didn't you become an anthropologist?"

"I would've gotten kicked out of grad school for arguing with professors."

"Beating them up is more like it." He doodled on the notepad. "Or shooting them."

"You're avoiding my question."

The scents of her wafted over him. The fabric softener sheets she used on her clothes. He'd seen them in her basement. The shampoo that smelled like kiwi fruit. No perfume, though. In her bathroom he noticed all sorts of scented items, from baby oil to hairspray, but no perfume.

"Are you allergic to perfume?" he asked.

She exhaled through her nose. The sound reminded him of a dragon spewing fire. He glanced at her sideways. Katy, arms crossed over her chest, puckered her lips.

Rick sank back into the seat, slanting his head toward her. "I didn't want to disappoint my father."

"By becoming an Egyptologist?"

"Yeah."

"Charlie's a historian," she said. "He would've loved it if you studied Egyptology."

Rick shifted his gaze to the darkness outside the window. "If I failed..."

"I don't get it." She relaxed back into her seat. "How does becoming an accountant prevent failure?"

"I thought I could never fail at something so boring. I was wrong."

"You haven't failed."

Rick pretended to read the book on his lap. He felt her staring at him, those green eyes bright with curiosity. After a moment she laid her hand on his arm.

He tapped his pen on the book. Tick-tick-tick.

"Yoo-hoo," she said.

Tick-tick-tick.

"If you don't talk," she said, "I'll go over there and tell Warner you like him."

"Don't have to get nasty." He inhaled slowly. "I quit my job two weeks ago. It was either that or punch out my boss."

He should've punched out Mitch Atkins. *Pad the bill a little, kid, our clients won't know the difference. I'll cut you in.*

Katy would've punched him. Rick restrained a smile. Yeah, he could picture her slugging the creep. She'd go for the stomach. A solid gut blow.

"He'd only been my boss for six months," Rick said. "Kept wanting me to cook the books so his bank account would be well done."

She squeezed his arm. "That's his failure, sweetie, not yours."

"Maybe." He hesitated. "Funny thing is, it doesn't bother me anymore."

"You have a calling now, just like me."

He patted the book on his lap. "One I'm not qualified for. No doctorate, no classes in Made-Up Theories about the Ancient World."

"You don't need a degree."

Rick rolled his pen across the book's page.

Katy said, "Since no mainstream scientists will believe us, what do you need a degree for?"

He twirled the pen.

The last five days had transformed his worldview from blind belief into a need for knowledge. The ideas the educational establishment pushed on him his entire life, the way he swallowed them like vitamins, disturbed him now. If the ancient Egyptians still existed, if they had advanced technology back in dynastic times, then everything he thought he knew about their culture was wrong.

What did he need a degree for? He wanted to know the truth. Grad school wouldn't lead him to the truth he sought. If he followed Katy, he might find it.

Not follow. Go with her. He'd told her they were a team and he meant it. For as long as she let him hang around.

Katy kissed his cheek. "If nothing else, you're *my* Egyptologist."

He sat up in the seat. The pen tight in his hand, he pulled out the notebook. He scribbled the transliteration of the duck sign on the page.

O UTSIDE THE WINDOW, FAR BELOW, THE UNITES STATES WHIZZED PAST. SOON they would arrive at the Calgary International Airport in Alberta, Canada. Warner had arranged for a rental car at the airport. A long drive would take them to Yoho National Park, where a longer hike would take them up the slopes of the Continental Divide and back in time 530 million years. If she believed Warner, those mountains harbored proof of a human presence during the Cambrian Period.

So far, everything he told her had proved right.

Now if her plan would just work…

Her plan depended on one assumption. She assumed the Planners knew little of current technology in the "real" world. If they hid their knowledge, or feigned ignorance to trick her, the plan was screwed. And so was she.

Take chances early. She adhered to the advice about tracking when she first saw Warner. The time for early risks had raced past her in a blur. She had no choice but to take a late risk.

The jet punched through a patch of clouds. The stars reappeared. The moon hung low against the cloud bank beneath, staying centered in the windowpane as the jet rocketed toward Canada. The Planners were out there. Although she'd expected them to follow, she also expected them to disguise their presence.

Nope. They wanted her to see them. They wanted her to feel trapped. To hell with them.

She rested her head on Rick's shoulder. Listening to the rhythm of his breaths, she closed her eyes. Amazingly, she fell asleep.

The jet flew over southwestern Alberta, approaching the airport in Calgary. Warner had stopped by a few minutes earlier to say they would touch down soon. Rick didn't ask how many people Warner bribed or threatened or both to get them into Canada without passports. If he'd asked, Warner might've pulled a Katy and simply smiled. Warner wouldn't pat him on the head, though.

Rick flipped back through the notebook to the first page of the translation, where the transliteration symbols segued into English. He'd crammed the books back into the suitcase on the floor beside his seat. The digital camera, which Katy had asked for but not yet used, sat on the table beside the laptop. He shut down the computer, snapping its lid closed.

The translation went quicker than he'd hoped. The more he translated, the easier it became. He recognized phrases that repeated, memorized common signs. It helped that the text stuck to a straightforward syntax. Maybe the Planners wrote the text plainly because they worried the hairy hominids might misinterpret the meaning otherwise. Whatever their reasoning, the style simplified his task.

He dubbed the text "The Tale of the Revered Ones" after the group to whom the offerings were dedicated. Like most ancient Egyptian texts, the Tale dated events based on a pharaoh's reign, in this case a king named Imsety. After the opening lines—an offering from the god Osiris to the Revered Ones—the text gave a clue about the dates.

On the last day of harvest, in Year 10 of the king of Upper and Lower Egypt, lord of the Two Lands, Sahor-Imsety. The royal scribe records what transpired when the great god Osiris lay over Giza.

Many Egyptologists believed the ancients viewed the constellation of Orion as the embodiment of Osiris. If they were right, the text claimed Osiris lay over Giza during the time when the Tale took place. Researchers determined Orion last hovered directly above Giza around 10,500 BC. If the text meant the constellation. If he'd translated it correctly.

He had.

Somewhere in the middle of translating the text he realized the Revered Ones it kept mentioning were the hairy hominids. The Planners revered the creatures. *For they of the covered bodies*, the Tale declared, *are the children of Amun-Ra.* Despite believing the creatures spawned from the king of the gods himself, the Planners treated them like children rather than objects of worship. The Tale also mentioned humans.

The text described how, in ancient times, two types of humans shared the planet. The Planners kept the advanced technology and the Low Ones, as the text called them, struggled to catch their meals with spears or bows and arrows. During the reigns of many pharaohs, the Planners conscripted the Low Ones as laborers. Whenever the gods needed a new temple erected as tribute, to secure the king's passage into the afterlife or ensure a good harvest, the Planners drafted Low Ones to erect the building. With the Planners' technology, the laborers easily quarried a 200-ton block of granite at Aswan in southern Egypt and transported it to Karnak, where they hoisted it eighteen feet above the ground to place it as a lintel above a temple doorway.

The text omitted how the laborers accomplished their feats, except to imply they used machinery provided by the Planners. None of the scenes depicted the machinery. The text would state the laborers used "that which raises great weights, provided by the Planners" or "that which quarries with ease, provided by the Planners."

For years the system worked. The Planners ruled. Low Ones labored in the fields, at the construction sites, and at any tasks requiring menial labor.

Until one day in Year 9 of the pharaoh Imsety.

On the tenth day of inundation—the season when the Nile flooded, ending labor in the fields and initiating the season of monument building—something happened. The Low Ones rebelled. According to the Planners, the workers grew lazy and greedy. Since the Planners despised Low Ones, considered them beasts of burden, their version of what happened seemed suspect. But Rick had no other information to go on.

Whoever was to the blame for it, the rebellion lasted fifteen days. When it ended, tens of thousands of Low Ones lay dead. Those who survived went into hiding.

Desperate for laborers, the Planners turned to the hairy hominids.

The Planners had interacted with the Revered Ones for as long as the creatures existed. They knew of the creatures' enormous strength. The Planners even taught them to speak, read, and write the hieroglyphic language.

Just one problem. Amun-Ra had declared no man should bring harm to a hairy hominid, for they were the children of Earth, the true heirs of the planet, objects of reverence.

The Planners, however, found a loophole in the god's declaration. They wouldn't harm the creatures. They would employ them as laborers, treating them with respect, providing physicians and servants to care for them, giving them "everything good and pure on which a god lives." Problem solved.

The Planners built caves for the creatures to live in under the Giza Plateau. They constructed a village aboveground where Planners baked bread and brewed beer for the creatures, where physicians treated their wounds. At the paws of the Sphinx, in a temple once dedicated to Osiris, they initiated a cult of the Revered Ones to honor the creatures. With their strength added onto the Planners' technology, the creatures built more monuments faster than any Low Ones had managed.

Once again, though, fate intervened.

The Planners detected "the hand of Amun-Ra" about to smite them. Beside the section of text about the hand of Amun-Ra, a drawing portrayed a volcano shooting a spire of ash into the heavens. The Planners realized the volcano, despite erupting far from Egypt, wielded the power to decimate the planet. The ash would blot out the sun and choke the air. Crops would fail. Their people would starve. Their advanced technology could not stop the catastrophe. The Planners had one choice.

They must leave Egypt.

But they couldn't desert the Revered Ones. If the eruption killed humans, it would surely kill the creatures too—and Amun-Ra warned no harm must come to the Revered Ones. Knowing they must protect the creatures, the Planners devised a scheme to send the creatures far away, to scatter them throughout the globe, to ensure their survival by creating isolated populations. At least some of them might survive.

The Planners chose forests around the globe, from North America to Australia. In each location the Planners dug caves, lined them with rock, and cut ventilation shafts. They also left a guardian with each group of creatures, a volunteer charged with keeping the Revered Ones in their caves until they acclimated to their new life. In Michigan, the guardian was a priest named Ranefer.

There the Tale of the Revered Ones ended. With Imsety and his people gone, no one was left to record the aftermath of the eruption or what became of Ranefer. The Planners retreated into a place the text called "the Domain of Osiris." The god Osiris lived, according to mythology, in the underworld.

Rick flipped the page. He had started a new sheet when he switched to translating the stela. The standing stone contained the end of the story, recorded untold years after the Planners vacated Egypt and went...somewhere. This text included no king's name.

Black lines behind the hieroglyphs showed where the scribes had painted outlines of the symbols before carving them into the rock. The black lines deviated from the carved symbols. Red lines, painted over the black but still under the carvings, didn't match the carvings either. The scribes had messed up. Twice. The Planners who returned to the caves had forgotten the old language.

Rick rubbed his eyes. His ears popped. Must be descending.

He skimmed his translation of the stela. A surprise awaited the Planners in the caves. Shortly after the relocation of the hairy hominids, Ranefer had died of a fever. The creatures buried him in imitation of the burial rites of the Planners. They lacked the tools for building a sarcophagus, lacked the artistry to create wall reliefs, and knew nothing of mummification. The headstone Katy found, inscribed with ill-formed hieroglyphs, evidenced their attempt.

Meanwhile, during the time when the Planners had fled the eruption, the Low Ones emerged from hiding. With volcanic winter setting in, they sought shelter. In Michigan, the humans found caves. Within those caves, they discovered the hairy hominids.

The creatures had developed a relationship with the Low Ones. The humans taught them to use spears and bows and arrows. They instructed the creatures in cave painting. The two groups hunted, ate, and lived together.

Disgusted that the creatures had consorted with Low Ones, afraid the alliance might turn the creatures against them, the Planners devised a method of both terminating the current peace and destroying the trust between humans and hairy hominids. Two events helped them realize their scheme.

First, a plague had recently swept through the Michigan caves. Although the disease killed hairy hominid and human alike, it affected children far more than adults. Nearly all the children died.

Second, shortly before the disease arrived a hairy hominid gave birth to a red-haired baby. To the ancient Egyptians, and the Planners, red signified chaos. Chaos meant evil. Since the creatures shared the Planners' beliefs, they deemed the birth a bad omen.

The Planners exploited the coincidence of the red-haired baby and the subsequent epidemic to poison the creatures against the humans. The humans caused the plague through black magic, they told the creatures. A Planner calling himself the Son of Amun-Ra had delivered the speech that terminated the peace.

Does not the red child signify the presence of evil, said the Son of Amun-Ra. Did not we, the Planners, descend from the heavens as gods? Behold, we sent the child to warn you of the Low Ones' evil. You have ignored our message. To stop the evil, to save your children, you must destroy those who have cursed you. Amun-Ra has decreed it.

The creatures believed the Planners. They believed their gods.

Here the massacre painting and the stela text converged. The creatures had slaughtered the humans.

Except for one. The creatures took one man as their prisoner, for the Planners had also decreed one human must be sacrificed to placate the gods. The sacrifice, they said, must take place on the night the star Sirius rose from its winter nap, signaling the start of the Nile flood.

The man remained a prisoner for weeks, awaiting the rising of Sirius. The creatures locked him inside the burial chamber of Ranefer. Maybe they hoped their dead guardian could protect them from the human's evil. The prisoner had painted the massacre scenes on the walls.

One spring night, when Sirius emerged from the underworld, the creatures sacrificed their prisoner to the Planners. There the text ended.

Rick figured out the rest himself. Later on, after the Planners left the second time, the creatures dug up Ranefer's remains. To ward off evil, namely the Low Ones, the creatures enshrined Ranefer's bones outside their front door like a talisman.

As for the paintings in the meeting hall, the ones illustrating extinct animals and animals from other continents, the creatures had created those paintings. Since the stela text said the Low Ones taught the hairy hominids how to paint, the creatures knew how to produce such artwork. Because the Planners had transported them around the globe, the creatures knew about animals native to Africa, Asia, and South America. Their travels explained why they painted a giraffe.

Rick shut the notebook. The Planners built the hieroglyph room because they believed Osiris commanded its creation, as an offering to the Revered Ones. They believed Osiris wanted the creatures to massacre the humans.

So that he may give a voice offering of truth, of blood and ka, of everything good and pure which the Low Ones took.

The phrase Low Ones tripped him up him at first. Once he deciphered it, he understood the full meaning of the offering.

Katy, dozing with her head on his shoulder, murmured.

The Planners needed to protect their secrets. The secret of the hairy hominids, and the secret of their own existence. They killed anyone who threatened to expose them. Like his father had said, the Planners cared about the creatures, not other humans.

Katy stirred. A lock of hair fell over her face. Rick tucked the hair behind her ear. He clenched his jaw. He wouldn't let the Planners sacrifice her to Osiris. He'd slaughter every last Revered One first.

❧

KATY WOKE WITH A JERK. HEART POUNDING, MIND SWIRLING IN A HAZE OF dreams, she sprang upright and glanced out the window. The moon-shaped light was gone. She checked her watch. Two hours had elapsed.

The light racing toward the airplane. Surrounding her. Swallowing her. The image faded into the mist where half-forgotten dreams linger.

Was it a dream?

She asked Rick, "Was I here the whole time?"

"What do you mean?"

"Was I sleeping in this chair for two hours." She felt the static electricity tingling over her. "Or was I dreaming."

"You were here the whole time."

"You're positive."

"I was awake and you were here, I'm sure. You okay?"

She sagged against the seat. The dream had felt real. The warmth of the light, the twinge as it blinded her.

She said, "I'm fine."

"Good, because I finished."

She twisted toward him. "Tell me."

He told her the story. When he finished, she faced forward. She sat in silence until her brain mustered the energy to form thoughts.

"At least we know for sure," she said. "They would kill us rather than risk exposure. Our lives mean as much to them as the lives of flies."

Rick tapped his pen on his notebook.

Katy mashed her nose against the window. Although she saw nothing, she knew the Planners loitered out there. Watching. Waiting. Why not shoot down the plane? Kill her, Rick, and Warner before they learned more about the Planners? If they wanted to stop her from exposing the creatures or showing the evidence she and Rick had found, they should act now. It was the logical thing to do.

The Planners did not act logically. Maybe their logic operated differently from the logic of Low Ones. To them, logic might dictate they observe her, Rick, and Warner to see how far they took their search, what they uncovered, how they dealt with what they found.

Or else Charlie convinced them the solution lay not in murder, but elsewhere.

Unless the Planners had gotten rid of Charlie.

Rick clasped her hand. "Dad's alive."

"We don't know that."

"I do."

She pulled her knees up to her chest, wrapping her arms around them. "Who's this pharaoh Imsety? The one mentioned in the text."

"Never heard of him."

"Obviously, the ancient Egyptian culture started way before the accepted date."

"Yep."

"You know what Egyptologists will say."

He snorted.

She leaned against Rick. He slid his arm around her shoulders.

"If the ancient Egyptians were Planners," she said, "why didn't they have high technology during dynastic times? I don't remember Ramses mentioning the vacations he took in his UFOs."

Rick said, "I think the original Egyptian culture was the Planners. Later on the Low Ones—people like us—adopted the religion, customs, and even the language of their gods. The ancient Egyptians we know about did call their language the Words of the Gods. They believed the gods gave them the language."

She chewed her lip. Charlie had said the creatures regarded the Planners as their gods. The Low Ones might've learned the language from the creatures. The massacre illustrated in the cave painting and related in the Tale of the Revered Ones involved the Low Ones of Michigan. The text said nothing about the Low Ones elsewhere on Earth.

Perhaps the humans in Egypt were friendly with the creatures and picked up the hieroglyphic language from them. The humans adopted the culture of the hairy hominids, which the creatures had absorbed from the Planners. The humans developed a mythology about the Planners to explain their advanced technology. The pyramids and their associated temples—assembled too accurately from stones too massive for primitive implements to duplicate the feat—required an explanation as well.

Enter the gods.

Many temples and a few pyramids featured hieroglyphs inscribed in them that named a certain pharaoh as the owner of the monument. However, pharaohs practiced a tradition of usurping old monuments. The cartouche of Sneferu didn't mean Sneferu actually built the pyramid. After all, the Egyptians of the dynastic era never mentioned, in any inscription or papyrus scroll, how they built the pyramids or the valley temples accompanying them. The biggest and most impressive pyramids, such as the Giza pyramids, had no inscriptions of any kind.

"What I don't get," Rick said, "is why we didn't see any hominid children. The plague must've happened thousands of years ago. Where are the kids?"

Katy leaned back in her seat. She tapped a fingernail on her leg. No children.

She sat forward. "They hide them."

"What do you mean?"

"Think about it. Believing humans are evil has become a part of their culture. The plague story is their version of Sodom and Gomorrah, a parable about the dangers of mixing with evildoers."

"But they trust the Planners."

She patted his hand. "Really, Rick, you ought to know better by now. The Planners are gods, not humans."

"Right. I keep forgetting."

Warner leaped off the sofa. He marched into the cockpit.

Katy stared at the cockpit door.

When Warner returned a minute later, he said, "We will land momentarily."

Rick stashed the laptop in its carrying case. He slid the case under his seat.

Katy looked out the window. The creatures weren't the only ones who believed the Planners were gods. The Planners believed it too.

Calgary International Airport
Calgary, Alberta
Canada

A MAN IN SHIRTSLEEVES AND GRAY SLACKS TROTTED UP THE STAIRS, THROUGH the open doorway into the jet. In one hand he grasped a clipboard with papers bulging under its clamp. A chain bound a silver pen to the clipboard. The man halted inside the doorway three feet from Warner.

Katy and Rick lingered near the chairs they had occupied during the flight.

The man proffered a hand to Warner. "Good to see you again, Mr. Warner."

"Frank," Warner said, shaking the man's hand, "it's been awhile."

"Anything to declare?"

"No."

"How long will you be staying with us?"

"Three days."

"Business or pleasure?"

"Business."

Frank scribbled on his clipboard.

Rick placed his hand on Katy's back. She rested her arm on the nearest chair.

Frank paced the length of the jet. Passing Rick and Katy, he said, "First trip to Canada?"

"Yes," Rick said.

Katy nodded. Her heart thumped against her rib cage.

Frank walked back to Warner. The men shook hands again. Katy glimpsed folded bills in Warner's hand as he reached for Frank's. When Warner retracted his hand, the bills were gone.

Twisting around to duck out the door, Frank said, "Welcome to Canada."

He exited the plane.

Katy exhaled.

Warner watched out the doorway until long after Frank's footsteps faded. Finally he strode to the furthest sofa. Kneeling, he shoved a finger into the space between the arm of the sofa and the cushion. A mechanism clicked. A panel on the front of the sofa popped out an inch. Warner pulled the panel away from the sofa to reveal a cavity inside it. A briefcase sat inside the cavity.

Warner brought out the briefcase. He unlatched it and flipped up the lid. The briefcase held three weapons, Glock 9mm handguns.

Taking a commercial flight to Chicago forced them to abandon their weapons in Michigan. Warner had given his Glock to the squat man who had banged on Katy's door, who Warner said would "drive it home."

Warner tossed one Glock to Rick, another to Katy. The third he stashed in a holster concealed under his pants leg. The guy had a thing for Glocks.

They retrieved backpacks from the luggage compartment.

On their way out of the airplane, Katy checked the sky for a false moon. She saw none.

But she felt them watching.

Burgess Pass
Yoho National Park
British Columbia

THE SUN HAD CRESTED AND BEGUN ITS DESCENT BY THE TIME THEY REACHED the pass. Some eighteen inches of snow cloaked the earth. The sky gleamed a deep blue.

Katy dropped onto her butt in the snow, her body protected by the clothes Warner bought her before they left Chicago. In the town of Field, inside Yoho National Park, they bought food and water for the expedition. They each wore a new backpack. Katy's contained nothing—yet—excluding the digital camera.

Rick stood beside her with his fingers touching her hat. Warner had stopped further ahead with his GPS unit in his hand. She heard the beeps every time he punched keys.

The wind whipped the snow into mists that swirled across the mountainside. Indirectly, she saw movement. When she looked in that direction, she spied nothing except the snow.

She patted her coat to feel the hard outline of the Glock 9mm in its belt holster.

"This way," Warner said.

"How can you be sure?" she asked. "Everything's covered in snow."

"I noted the GPS coordinates last time I was here."

Katy moved to get up. Her left foot sank into the snow. Rick pulled her out by her arm. They tromped after Warner.

They passed the quarry where Charles Walcott discovered the first fossils in the Burgess Shale for the Smithsonian Institution. The jagged peak of Mount Wapta pierced the sky off to the right. Ahead, Warner marched around a curve and vanished. Katy and Rick hurried after him.

They found him standing near a cliff face which in summer might've risen five feet over their heads. The snow, now drifted against the cliffs, cut its height by several feet.

Warner shrugged off his backpack. "This is it."

Getting the shovel out of his backpack and unfolding it, he commenced digging. After twenty minutes Rick relieved him. About fifteen minutes later they had cleared an area fifteen feet long and three feet wide, its length skirting the cliff base. The exposed shale was gray. Near the spot where Warner had started digging, planks of shale leaned against the cliff.

Warner hurled one of the planks aside.

Rick helped him remove the other planks. Finished, they stepped back a few feet. Both men stared at the area as if it contained the face of God.

Katy rushed toward them. The men blocked her view.

"I covered it before I left," Warner said. "To protect it from the elements as well as human eyes."

Katy shoved herself between the men. Rick shifted sideways to let her squeeze in front of him. By removing the shale planks they had uncovered an indentation in the ground, two feet long and eighteen inches wide. The planks had been stripped from the ground to create the indentation, and to uncover a fossil in the shale.

The bones of a human foot.

Katy crouched beside the fossil. A faint impression beneath the bones resembled the outline of a sandal. The metatarsal bones disappeared under the shale, where perhaps the rest of the skeleton waited.

A small, round hole beside the print appeared to have held an object. She pulled the Egyptian stone from her pocket. When she set the stone inside the hole, it fit. She plucked up the stone, dumping it into her pocket, and rose.

Warner said, "I stopped excavations when I found this. But I'm certain there is more to be found."

He motioned for them to step back. They obeyed. With the shovel's tip, he splintered off leaves of shale to the left of the foot. When he reached the layer containing the foot, he hesitated.

Katy said, "What is it?"

He jammed the shovel under the shale beside the area he had cleared and peeled away another layer. Ten minutes later Rick offered to take over for him. In response, Warner wedged the shovel into the shale. Teeth clamped shut, gaze locked on the ground, fists tight around the shovel's handle, he excavated the entire length of the snow-cleared area. When he had leveled the shale in the area to the layer of the foot, he tossed the shovel aside.

Katy trotted forward. Embedded in the shale, preserved by the massive landslide that formed the Burgess Shale back in the Cambrian, lay a complete skeleton of a human being. With her gaze she traced the foot to the ankle, through the leg into the hip, straight across the rib cage into the neck and skull. The right leg was bent at the knee, the foot lodged against the left knee, some of the toes missing or possibly buried in the shale under the left leg. The skull was crushed, but the fragments maintained the contour of a head. Even with the skull in pieces, she recognized its brow ridge as human.

More evidence might lay buried under the cliff or under the snow they had left in place. They should excavate more. But the sun was low. They had no time.

From inside her backpack, Katy retrieved the camera. Setting the shovel beside the bones for scale, she snapped pictures of the skeleton, including close-ups of the individual bones. When she snapped a picture of the sandal-clad foot, she noticed an impression in the shale. Leaning closer, she recognized the ribbed pattern and oval shape of a trilobite. The marine creature was fossilized inside the sandal impression, its body crossing over the toe bones. The trilobite must've landed on top of the human's foot, fossilizing there. The placement of the trilobite proved the human body got embedded in the shale at the same time as the trilobite.

They must take the skeleton with them. If they left it here, the Planners would destroy it. Although they'd kept her pack empty for stashing their finds inside it, the skeleton was too big.

To the west, a light pulsed.

Katy jumped up. She transferred the memory card from the camera into the plastic sandwich bag in her pocket, which also protected the card from Ivan's camera. The camera dangled from its strap, draped around her neck.

The light surged closer. The hairs on her neck bristled.

Warner and Rick glanced at the light. Warner cursed softly and tramped down the slope. The light cruised closer. A throbbing echoed in the distance.

Her pulse thundered in her ears. Rick slapped his hand around her arm and dragged her away from the skeleton, away from the one piece of evidence she'd uncovered that unequivocally established the presence of modern humans millions of years ago. The evidence that proved her theories. She must save it.

She yanked her arm free. Her foot plunged into the snow. She tripped, landing flat on her belly. Her face smacked into the snow. Hands seized her shoulders, lifted her up, deposited her on her feet. Rick brushed his hand across her cheek, then pushed her ahead of him. With a final glance at the skeleton, she jogged after Warner with Rick nudging her onward.

The throbbing transitioned into thumping. When she glanced back, the light had gained on them. It spotlighted the pass behind them. Soon it would expose them.

She poked Warner's back. He burst into a sprint. Katy and Rick galloped after him.

The thumping intensified until it drowned out the clamoring of her heart. A gale whipped up around them. Katy looked backward.

A helicopter hovered above the pass fifty yards behind them. Its light sliced through the twilight. The helicopter swooped by them. It touched down right in their path.

They halted. Katy searched the pass for an escape route or fortress. They could run back to the shale deposits, but what then?

The helicopter's rotors slowed and stopped. The door of the helicopter opened. Two men hopped out of the craft.

The duo, dressed in black suits with black shirts and black ties, wore shiny loafers that slipped on the snow as they advanced on Katy, Rick and Warner. Although the swirling snow blurred her vision, she glimpsed the pistols in the men's hands. The men stopped several yards away.

They were the park rangers from Texas.

Warner had slid his Glock out of its holster. When she reached inside her coat for hers, the pseudo-rangers shouted "Stop!" in unison. The taller one, an ebony-haired muscleman, waggled his gun at her.

"Toss the gun nice and slow," he said.

His pal, a slender brunette, aimed his gun at Warner. "You too, pal. And your towering friend."

Both men had shed their Texas drawls along with their ranger uniforms.

Gritting his teeth, Warner lobbed his Glock at the men. Katy chucked hers beside Warner's. Rick threw his own weapon onto the pile.

"The camera too," Muscleman said.

Katy flung the camera at him. It smacked into his chest. He caught the camera with a grunt, casting a molten-steel glance at her, and popped open the side panel that concealed the memory card. Blowing steam out his nose, he tossed the camera to his pal.

"The memory card," Muscleman said. "Give it to me now, Miss Gallagher."

She didn't move. Muscleman aimed his gun at her forehead. Rick mouthed, *Give it to him*. She glared down the barrel of Muscleman's gun. Rick cleared his throat. He jerked his head toward Muscleman. She pulled the bag out of her pocket and pitched onto the pile with the Glocks.

Muscleman plucked the bag from the pile. He looked at the cliff where they excavated the skeleton.

"We know what you found," he said, "and we've got orders to confiscate it."

"Orders from whom?" Katy asked.

"The Planners, of course. Don't play dumb, Miss Gallagher, we know you know. You must've translated the hieroglyphs by now."

She stifled a retort, loathe to admit he knew anything about her that she hadn't told him. Having strangers know her movements before she made them, it twanged her nerves.

"Then why let us find the skeleton?" she asked.

"We can't let evidence like this lie around. Somebody else might find it." He tucked the bag in his pocket. "Somebody credible, I mean."

Katy stifled the retort rising in her throat.

"You needed us to find the skeleton for you," she said. "Guess you're not omnipotent after all."

Muscleman glanced at his watch. "Almost time for that tragic landslide to hit."

"What landslide?"

He looked straight at her. "The one that kills three hikers."

25

KATY SWALLOWED HARD. A TRAGIC LANDSLIDE, ENGINEERED BY MUSCLEMAN and his buddy, would destroy the skeleton and get rid of the three of them. The Planners had schemed their way out of another quandary.

Not this time.

"If you kill us," she said, smoothing the nervous ripples out of her vocal chords before the words escaped, "the world will find out about the Planners."

Muscleman rolled his eyes. His pal goose-stepped toward the helicopter, forced to raise his feet high to keep from bogging down in the snow.

Muscleman stomped on the three Glocks heaped near his feet. The guns submerged deep into the snow. Raising his foot, he kicked snow into the hole.

Warner and Rick fisted their hands, tensed their bodies. They looked at each other, then the spot where the Glocks were buried.

"Oh no," Muscleman scolded. "You don't want to do that."

He whistled. On either side of the pass, snow shivered and swelled. Two mounds transmuted into masses of hair and sinew. The creatures' dark eyes stood out against their pale skin and white hair, like black olives in sour cream. They shook themselves, showering snow all around. The creatures plodded toward them.

Warner and Rick opened their fists. They slackened their muscles.

"I created a computer program," Katy told Muscleman. "It'll send e-mails to every anthropologist, archaeologist, and paleontologist in the world if I'm not there to enter the password every twenty-four hours. The e-mail details everything we found and gives GPS coordinates to where the Revered Ones live."

She paused to let the words seep through Muscleman's skull. "There are millions of scientists around the world. Assume only one percent believe the e-mail and investigate further. That's ten thousand scientists for every million out there. All traipsing into the woods of Northern Michigan, straight to the Revered Ones."

Muscleman glanced over his shoulder at his pal, who was unloading a cardboard box from the helicopter.

"Imagine," she said, "how much a type specimen would be worth."

"You can't really do that."

You're right, she thought but kept it to herself. She had told the truth, mostly. She wrote a program designed to send e-mails to every scientist in the world—*designed to* being the key phrase. She had no idea if the program would work. She had no time for testing it and, anyway, she found less than a dozen names of scientists before turning the computer over to Rick for translating the hieroglyphs. While technically possible, the program was unfeasible.

If her assumption proved right, she needn't worry about feasibility.

"We erased your computer," Muscleman said, "we can do it again."

"It's not on my computer. It's someplace you'll never find it."

In reality, she had stored the program on a server based in India that offered free web pages. Since signing up required an e-mail address, she used a free e-mail account from a company in Brazil. If the Planners relied on Charlie to explain the technology of the Low Ones to them, she was safe. He knew as much about the Internet as she knew about operating an offshore oil rig.

Mentally, she crossed her fingers.

Muscleman's pal approached him. He dropped the box onto the snow.

"That's not all," Katy said. "Warner, tell them about your end."

"If I should die, my people will release evidence which proves humans didn't evolve from the ancient hominids." Warner waved at the creatures. "They did."

Muscleman opened his mouth but said nothing.

"The mummy," Katy said. "I'm sure you know about it. While you and the Planners were busy following us, Warner's people took the mummy. They've hidden it, but if anything happens to us they will stage the biggest press conference you've ever seen. And they'll have a prominent scientist there to back them up."

Whether Warner had convinced Victor Oberman to go along with the plan, she didn't know. She suspected Oberman had agreed. He seemed genuinely interested in the mummy and its implications.

Oberman's comment about Warner's "mercenary friends" gave her the idea. Surely mercenaries could hide a mummy from the Planners—especially if, as she suspected, the Planners focused their energies on her.

From Muscleman's frown, she figured she'd suspected right.

With a smirk and a twitch of his gun, Muscleman said, "I'll kill your boyfriend then. Unless you hand over the program and the mummy."

Katy flashed a vicious smile. "Nice try, moron. Kill him and I have no reason to give you anything. And if I give you the stuff to save his life, you'll kill us anyway."

"I have orders to kill you."

"Orders from the Planners." She canted her head. "You're a Low One, aren't you?"

He licked his lips.

"They'd just as soon kill you as me. Help us and maybe we can stop the Planners from manipulating our world. That's what they do, isn't it? Keep us from learning too much. Beat us down like bread dough so we don't rise up too high."

A sourness infiltrated her voice. "We have to fight them. Look what they did to us before, to our ancestors back in Egypt. Who knows how many times they've slaughtered us to keep us down. Maybe they invented the Black Death and Ebola and every other plague, to keep us in our place."

Muscleman stared at her so intently she dared hope her argument had broken through the barrier, woven of ignorance and arrogance, that kept him from acknowledging the truth.

After a moment, he averted his gaze. He raised the gun.

"I have orders to kill you," he said. "That's what I have to do."

His buddy trained his gun on them.

Warner and Rick lunged at the men. Warner tackled Muscleman, knocking the gun out of his grasp with a chop of his hand. The other man cried out as Rick punched him in the gut and the jaw. Rick tore the gun out of the man's hand. He whacked the pistol into the man's forehead.

Muscleman slugged Warner in the chest. Warner's foot jerked, kicking the gun toward Katy.

She nabbed it.

The creatures shrieked. They barreled toward her.

She fired at one of the creatures. The bullet lodged in the snow near his feet. She fired again, again. Blood darkened the creature's chest. He fell onto his knees.

Hairy arms swooped around her waist from behind. The creature squeezed. The breath exploded out of her. Her hand slackened, the gun slipped, but the trigger snagged on her fingertip. She couldn't breathe. Darkness encroached on the edges of her vision.

She clasped the gun. Pointing it over her shoulder, she yanked the trigger. The jolt wrenched the gun out of her hand.

The creature howled.

She winced.

The creature's grip loosened.

She kicked his shin and she drove her elbow backward into his gut. He wailed, releasing her. She stumbled forward. Her feet plunged into a deep patch. She fell onto her left hip. The gun landed muzzle-first a foot away, with its grip sticking out of the snow.

Katy grabbed the gun. She fired at the creature's head. He slumped backward.

Warner kneeled beside the unconscious Muscleman, whose companion lay crumpled a few yards away. Rick strode toward her, grasped her arms, and hoisted her out of the snow. The other creature, still on his knees, howled. Other voices answered from the mountainsides.

Muscleman stirred.

Katy shoved the gun in her pocket. "Let's get the hell out of here."

They ran as fast as the snow allowed.

The sun had dipped low, raining flames on the mountain slopes, heating Mount Wapta's peak into a fire-reddened iron. Clouds from an approaching storm front ignited red and orange against the northern sky. Snow billowed along the ground in the wake of the each gust yet failed to douse the solar conflagration.

Katy glanced back. The men had roused. One carried the box up the pass toward the cliff where the skeleton was buried. The other brandished their remaining gun. He jerked his head left and right. Hominid calls echoed around them.

Katy froze. Pale figures swarmed down the pass from the north.

Rick dragged her forward.

Five minutes elapsed as they slogged through the snow. Warner sank into a drift up to his chest. Hauling him out took both Rick and Katy straining against the hardening snow. Free again, Warner trudged onward. He swiped snow from his clothing, grumbling in German.

Katy swiveled her torso to look back down the pass.

The men were stumbling toward their helicopter. They'd abandoned their box. The pale figures had vanished. Perhaps the creatures gave up.

Rick tugged her sleeve. She hurried alongside him.

Helicopter rotors thumped. The thumping accelerated into whirring.

An explosion split the air. The ground trembled. A roar followed, the sound reminiscent of a distant waterfall.

Half a minute later, the silence returned.

Anameka, Michigan
Wednesday, October 23

Warner had ordered one of his men to drop off Katy and Rick at her cabin. She fumbled with the spare key, knocking the old saw off the wall. She unlocked the downstairs door. With a week's worth of newspapers that she'd retrieved from the front porch tucked under her arm, she swung the door inward. They shuffled into the house, up the stairs, into the living room.

Rick collapsed onto the sofa. Katy shambled into the kitchen for a drink of water. She set the newspapers on the bar. Outside, the remnants of sunset painted hues of red and yellow behind the trees at the summit of the hill behind her cabin. The snowfall had deepened since her departure for Chicago. Eighteen inches of white stuff covered the ground.

"I didn't know a human being could get so tired," Rick said.

Katy fanned through the newspapers.

She grabbed the top one, today's edition. The headline read "Freak Landslide Hits Historic Site in Canada." The photo showed the Burgess Pass. An entire side of the mountain had collapsed into the pass. She read the first paragraph of the article.

"Listen to this," she said. "A freak landslide hit the historic Burgess Pass of southwestern British Columbia last night. The slide destroyed a significant portion of the Burgess Shale formation, home to some of the oldest fossils ever found. Geologists say a minor earthquake may have triggered the slide."

"Earthquake," Rick muttered.

She slapped the paper on the counter. "The official denial goes on. The Planners win again."

"Not really. We're still alive."

"We lost the skeleton."

"Guess I'll have to stick around until we find another one."

"Only until then?"

"Since the odds are it'll never happen, that's a lifetime commitment."

She wanted to race across the room, jump onto his lap, and kiss him. Her legs felt like wet sponges. Climbing onto a stool, she settled for smiling at him.

The phone warbled. She waited for the machine to answer.

After the spiel and the beep, a weary voice said, "Katy, this is Victor Oberman. I've got those results—"

She ripped the receiver from its cradle. "I'm here."

"Good." He paused. "I would've finished sooner but I couldn't believe the results. I took another sample from the mummy because I was sure I'd contaminated the testing. The results were identical the second time."

"And?"

"First, you should be aware that DNA tests aren't as conclusive as you might think, especially with DNA this old. You get fragments and mostly what you can trace is the mitochondrial DNA, which is inherited from the mother. There's debate over the accuracy of mtDNA studies but…I'm confident about the results from the mummy. Mummified tissue preserves DNA better than bone. The *erectus* sample is open to interpretation."

Katy curled her fingers over the edge of the bar. She dug her nails into the underside. "What are your results?"

"At best, we and the heidelbergs are extremely distant cousins. I'd put the relationship more like the difference between humans and chimpanzees. We share DNA, but we won't be inviting them to the family reunion. There is no way we evolved from *Homo heidelbergensis*."

He coughed and a slurp hinted he'd taken a drink. "As for the creatures, the hair sample you brought gave me a great sequence. Once again, the relationship to us is distant at best. However, between the creatures and *heidelbergensis*, the relationship is clear. They belong to the same evolutionary lineage."

"What about *Homo erectus*?"

"As I said, DNA this ancient is questionable. Still, I see no way on earth we evolved from *erectus*. The creatures show strong connections with the *erectus*

DNA. I'd have to conclude they evolved from the ancient hominids, not us. In essence, those creatures are *Homo sapiens*."

Though his voice remained steady when he spoke the final phrase, Katy sensed a discomfort emanating through the phone line from him. Maybe her own discomfort colored her perspective. Oberman's next words cleared up the matter.

"My God," he said, "what are we?"

"We may never know for sure."

Katy thanked him. They said goodbye and she hung up the phone.

"What's the verdict?" Rick asked.

"We need a new name for the human species."

She strolled to the sink where the windows offered a view of the trees at the base of the hill. The snow-covered hill gleamed. Flakes fluttered downward to join their mates.

Her stomach growled. She opened the refrigerator.

Outside the window above the sink, a shape moved. She froze. Her hand on the refrigerator door, she stared into the twilight.

Crunch. The sound of boots on snow. She slammed the refrigerator shut and trotted to the windows in the dining area at the end of the kitchen. She leaned across the table. The light from the living room lamp, reflected on the glass, obscured her view.

She hissed, "Shut off the light."

With a click Rick doused the light. His boots clapped on the wood floor as he trotted up behind her. She scurried back to the sink. Hands planted on the sink's lip, she pushed up onto her tiptoes to look out the window.

"There it is!" Rick said.

From the left, a shape darted toward the back of the house.

Katy got a flashlight from under the sink and dashed for the back door. Rick pushed past her, tore the door open, and sprinted outside. He halted so abruptly that she bumped her face into his shoulder. About fifteen feet up the hillside, a manlike figure seemed to glow silver.

She clicked on the flashlight. Stepping up beside Rick, she shined the light at the figure. The stranger wore a silver suit, matching boots and gloves, and a spherical, reflective helmet with black eyeholes shaped like almonds. The stranger cupped the helmet in both hands, twisted, and popped off the helmet.

Charlie wiped sweat from his forehead. "This getup is like a portable sauna."

He tucked the helmet under one arm, waiting as if he stopped by for dinner and wanted an invitation to come inside.

"Dad?" Rick said. "What…"

"They want me to clarify the situation," Charlie said. "So you understand how it's going to be."

"How what's going to be?" Katy asked.

"Think of it as our own little Cold War. Both sides have weapons they threaten to use but don't."

"You are their weapon."

"Not as bad as it sounds. They treat me decently. They're even teaching me about their history, and I'm teaching them about ours." His tone became somber. "I wish I could convince you to forget about them and me. It would be better for all of us."

The flashlight wavered in Katy's hand. Forget about Charlie? Forget the Planners held him hostage? Trust them not to kill him? Impossible.

One option remained for her. She must learn the truth about the Planners, dig up evidence of their true nature as well as her own, excavate the weakness capable of destroying them. It existed somewhere. If she searched long enough, if she dug deep enough, she might unearth it. The search might take the rest of her life.

What else did she have to do? She'd concluded one mission by discovering the truth about hairy hominids. Now she must concentrate on another.

Learning the truth about humanity's origins.

The Planners detained Charlie to serve as their Cold War weapon of destruction, a human nuclear warhead meant to dissuade her from using her own warhead—the heidelberg mummy and its DNA evidence. They must know about Victor Oberman's tests. And it scared them.

"I won't forget," she said. "Tell them as long as they keep their end of the bargain, we'll keep ours. We won't use the evidence we found."

"Good."

"We'll need occasional proof you're still alive."

"Will the odd visit do?" When she nodded, he said, "Twice a year is all they can allow."

"Fine."

Rick pointed at his father's attire. "Why are you dressed like that?"

Charlie patted the silvery fabric. "They wanted you to see the suit. They haven't worn these in years but they wanted you to know they used to."

"Why?"

"Think about cave paintings, Katy."

She thought about them. The blood vacated her face. "You're saying that the depictions of men in suits like yours, in European cave paintings and even the Nazca geoglyphs in Peru, are based on the Planners? They've been manipulating us for thousands of years?"

"Millions, actually."

"Last time I saw the Planners," Katy said, "they dressed like the pharaoh's priests."

"Oh that was for your benefit. They actually dress a lot like us. They wanted to make sure you'd recognize them."

"As ancient Egyptians."

"Yes," Charlie said. "You see, they stopped wearing tunics and sandals about ten thousand years ago. Not terribly practical for the bot—for where they live most of the time."

His flub clanged a bell in her mind. He had almost confided where the Planners lived. The start of the word—*bot*—buzzed in her brain, a mental bee searching for its hive. Something, more a feeling than a notion, told her she had the hive. She need only wait for the bee to locate it.

Charlie thumped his helmet. "Gotta go now."

"You don't have to go back," Rick said. "Stay here. What can they do? We've got the mummy."

Lowering the helmet over his head, twisting it into place, Charlie turned away. He moseyed up the hill, over the summit, out of sight. Katy and Rick stood there staring after him, both mired in a confusion that sucked them down toward oblivion. Katy grasped Rick's hand, hoping the action would free her from the emotional muck.

Over the hill, a light flashed.

A moon-shaped light behind the trees dwarfed the pines and birches and engulfed the hillside in whiteness. Slowly, the light ascended. Up, up, up. She tilted her head back until the muscles in her throat ached. The light rose higher. Up, up to the heavens, a fallen sun climbing back into its slot in the sky. The light leveled off.

It shot sideways. The brilliance shrank into a pinpoint and winked out.

Rick slipped his arm around her shoulders. She leaned against him. In her hand, the flashlight still illuminated the spot where Charlie had stood. The light cast shadows into the boot prints he made when he scaled the hill. The snow glittered. Inside the prints he made while talking to her and Rick, a piece of paper flapped in the breeze. He must've been standing on it.

Shrugging off Rick's arm, she trotted to the spot to pick up the paper. The warmth of her fingers melted the snow dusting its corner. She blew off the rest of the snow. Charlie's handwriting scrawled across the page. *Kids*, the note began, as if he were writing to a herd of young goats. The word might've annoyed her before. When she read the word a second time, a wire tightened around her heart.

Kids, whatever I just said, ignore it. Keep searching, but do it together. Make a network. Even if the more isn't the merrier, the more is the safer for sure.

He signed the note "Dad."

She handed Rick the note. After reading it, he crumpled it and strode into the cabin. He opened the wood stove's door and chucked the note inside. The paper blackened, dissolving into ash.

He shut the stove's door.

Katy hugged him fiercely.

EPILOGUE

Monday, December 23

F AT SNOWFLAKES DRIFTED DOWN FROM THE CLOUDS. KATY BALANCED ON A stool at the bar, pondering the view from the dining area windows. She thrummed her fingers on the bar. Her left heel she rapped on the second rung of the stool. A bowl of oatmeal, one spoonful eaten, sat on the bar beside a full glass of milk. The steam had long gone from the cereal, and the milk had lost its chill. Condensation ringed the glass's base.

Trees blocked her view of the road beyond her driveway.

A car emerged from the trees. It rolled toward her driveway.

She leaped off the stool. The car drove past her driveway.

Shoulders slumped, she climbed back onto the stool. Although more than a month had passed since Victor Oberman completed the DNA tests, it wasn't the results that had her stiff as a crow on a high-tension power line. A week ago Rick drove Charlie's Dodge Ram to Boston to box up his belongings and return the key to his apartment. After leaving Boston two days ago, he called last night to say he would arrive sometime in the morning.

The clock in the living room read 11:30. He had thirty minutes.

Although she wanted to see him, more than that she worried the Planners had gotten a hold of him. Driving alone from Boston to Anameka. Down lonely, dark stretches of highway. No witnesses. A bright light in the sky.

She gulped down a mouthful of milk.

A black pickup stopped at her driveway.

Was it a Ram? She couldn't tell, they all looked the same. She bounded off the stool. It clattered onto the floor behind her as she threw open the front door, crossed the porch in one step, flung open the outer door, and jumped over the steps onto the ground. Halfway down the driveway she halted.

She had spotted the pink cheeks and white beard of her mailman inside the pickup. The truck was a Ford, not a Dodge, and dark blue instead of black. The mailman stuffed envelopes into her mailbox and shut its door.

"How ya doing?" he called, waving. "Like my new truck?"

She waved. "Nice."

"Merry Christmas."

Her voice sounded forlorn even to her ears when she said, "Merry Christmas."

The mailman drove away. Katy got the mail and headed back to the cabin. She dropped the mail on the bar beside the oatmeal. After righting the stool, she meandered onto the back porch. Within the shadows between the trees, a figure moved. Tall and dark, the figure was too narrow for a bear yet too tall for a man.

One arm tucked behind his back, Garfield clomped out of the trees down the hillside to her. He stopped halfway down the hill, wriggling his nostrils. The breeze undulated his hair. He grunted twice, the sound more questioning than menacing.

She held up a hand, palm out. He mimicked the gesture.

"I know some women like hairy chests, but this is ridiculous."

At the sound of Rick's voice, Garfield grunted. Katy spun around. She bounced up and flung her arms around his neck. He caught her, supporting her with his arms around her waist, her feet a few inches off the ground. After a long kiss, he set her down.

"I leave for a week," he said, "and you take up with some other guy."

"It's not serious. He's too inarticulate for me."

Garfield grunted syllables. Though Katy recognized them as words, she could not decipher them.

She asked Rick, "Did you understand him?"

"Yep, I'm getting better at the caveman version of ancient Egyptian. He said he's protecting Isis."

"He thinks I'm Isis?"

Rick locked his arms around her waist from behind, his face near hers. "You made up a name for him. Looks like he made up one for you."

Garfield's features matched the heidelberg mummy—his hairy face, the skin exposed around his eyes and nose, his wide mouth. He fixed his yellow eyes on her, curving his lips up at the corners. He repeated the phrase while gesturing at her.

Rick spoke to Garfield in the language of the pharaohs. Afterward he whispered in Katy's ear, "Told him I can handle it from here."

Garfield spoke to Rick but focused on Katy's face. Once he'd completed his speech, he swung his arm out from behind his back. He grasped a Remington .30-06 rifle. Charlie's rifle.

Rick interpreted Garfield's words for her. "He found it in the woods and remembered it belonged to Dad. He wants you to have it."

Katy accepted the rifle from Garfield. The creature looked at his feet. She clasped his hand briefly before returning to Rick's side.

Garfield muttered. He ambled up the hill. At the summit, where he listed forward to descend the other side, his figure melded with the shadows.

"What did he say?" she asked. "Right before he left."

"The gods are leaving but they will return."

"The Planners are leaving?"

You see they stopped wearing tunics and sandals about 10,000 years ago. Not terribly practical for the bot—for where they live most of the time.

Charlie's words from over a month ago echoed in her mind, the half-spoken word *bot* sticking in her brain like a kid's tongue to a frozen metal post. The painting from the meeting hall of an eel-like creature popped into her mind. *They're connected.*

The thought seemed ludicrous. She couldn't get rid of the wriggly feeling in her gut that warned she better find the connection. Fast.

Katy bolted into the cabin, to her computer in the corner. Rick hurried after her sputtering questions she half heard. She propped the rifle against the wall. At the computer, she logged onto the Internet and navigated to a search engine. Her fingers hovered over the keys as she wondered what phrase to search for, since she had no idea what to call the strange creature depicted in the painting.

She typed "big mouthed eel-like creature with a whip tail."

When she hit the search button, the results appeared a few seconds later. The first five results had nothing to do with eels. The sixth result had a title that sounded like Latin. *Eurypharynx pelecanoides.*

She clicked the link. The browser loaded the page, which resided on a science website. The header loaded first, with a picture unfurling beneath it as the page loaded. The first line of text announced "*Eurypharynx pelecanoides*: The Umbrellamouth Gulper."

The photo unveiled a creature identical to the one the hairy hominids had memorialized in their meeting hall. In the photo the creature's mouth gaped wide. Its orange-red skin appeared almost incandescent, though the effect most likely stemmed from the lighting used to illuminate the creature. According to the text under the photo, *Eurypharynx* lived in the deepest parts of the oceans where no light penetrated. In the abyss.

Katy sank into the chair. She hissed the breath out of her lungs.

Rick crouched beside her. "Looks like the painting in the caves."

"Yes. I think your father is living at the bottom of the ocean."

They said nothing for several minutes. Katy closed the web browser. She logged off the Internet and walked into the living room. She sat on the sofa. Rick settled in beside her. They stared into kitchen for several more minutes.

"Okay," Rick said, sitting up straight. "When do we start our network?"

"When we have a couple million dollars to invest in research. Not much good having a network if you can't do anything. Doing takes money."

"We could find investors."

"To invest in researching UFO people who live at the bottom of the ocean and look after Bigfoot?"

"Right." Jumping up, Rick paced between the bar and the sofa. "Sounds crazy, doesn't it? And we can't prove any of it because we have to protect the hairy hominids."

"You mean *Homo sapiens*."

"Yeah."

He tramped toward the bar. Halting, he picked up an envelope from her pile of mail. He marched to the sofa with the envelope held out to her. She took it.

"A scintillating credit card offer?" she said, slipping the envelope around to read the return address.

Warner Industries.

Katy ripped the envelope open, yanking out a letter. As she unfolded the letter, a rectangular slip of paper fell onto her lap. She grabbed it but read the letter first. While her brain sorted out the words, her mouth became a desert, her tongue a sand dune. She felt dizzy for a second, until she looked at Rick.

She picked up the other piece of paper. A check.

"According to the letter," she said, "this check is the first installment of our lifetime grant from the Warner Industries Fund for Ancient Studies. We will receive a similar check at the start of each fiscal year."

"How—how much?"

She read the amount on the check. She blinked to be sure her eyes hadn't fooled her. The numbers stayed the same. "One million dollars."

Rick thudded onto the sofa. It rocked backward into the wall.

Katy showed him the check.

"Warner's giving us a million dollars a year?" Rick said. "For life?"

"He is a gazillionaire."

Rick held one corner of the check while she held the other. They scrutinized it for a long moment. When her vision blurred and grit assaulted her eyes, Katy slipped the check into the envelope with the letter. Didn't want to lose it.

She leaned forward. Her heel thumped an object under the sofa. She'd forgotten about that.

Withdrawing the wooden box, she proffered it to Rick. "Merry Christmas."

"I didn't get you anything yet."

"That's okay."

"You should keep this until Christmas."

She thrust the box toward him. "Take the damn thing already."

He took the damn thing and, unlatching it, flipped up the lid. "I broke it, eh?"

Lifting the .45 from its velvet pillow, which she'd made herself to fit the oak box, he hefted it in his hand. A blush rose on her cheeks.

She spoke quickly, afraid the words might stick in her throat if she drew them out at a normal pace. "No, it belonged to my father and I want you to have it now and if you say you can't accept it I'll throttle you."

"I *can't* accept it."

"You damn well better." She waited for her breathing to slow. "Consider it a trade. Garfield wanted me to have Charlie's rifle and I want you to have my father's handgun."

"Okay. Thanks." He replaced the gun in its case. "Guess we can start our network now."

"Looks like."

"So, if the hairy hominids are *Homo sapiens*, what does that make us?"

Children of the gods? Or slaves of the children of the gods? She might search her whole life without finding the answer, but she'd have lived one hell of a life when she got through.

She sneaked a look at Rick. He flashed a smile at her.

Katy jumped to her feet. "Let's get started."

Rick saluted. Seizing her hands, he pulled her down onto the sofa and kissed her. Oh well. The search could start tomorrow.

Continue the adventure!

with the next book in

THE HUMAN ORIGINS SERIES
by
LISA A. SHIEL

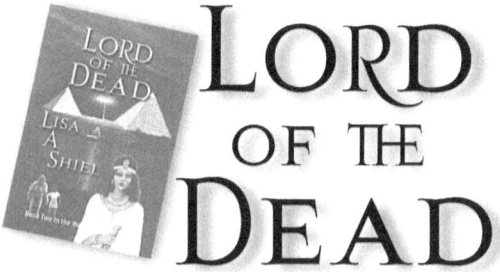

LORD
OF THE
DEAD

KATY AND RICK'S QUEST FOR THE TRUTH ABOUT HUMAN ORIGINS RACES forward! The Planners up the ante by threatening to kill Rick's father if Katy and Rick fail to find the Book. The Planners have erased their own history—the key to locating the Book—in their zeal to cover up the truth about human origins. The quest draws Katy and Rick from Michigan to the Egyptian desert as they battle an old enemy and join forces with a mysterious woman who knows more than she should about ancient history. As they unearth the tomb of a god, they realize their mission has expanded beyond just saving Rick's father. Now, they must save the human race itself from annihilation.

> "[This book has] believable characters, a fast-paced plot, and a fantastic premise at its heart."
> —Nick Redfern, author of *Body Snatchers in the Desert*

> "Incredible high adventure."
> —Bob Spear, Heartland Reviews

available from
your local bookstore, Amazon.com, BarnesAndNoble.com
or
www.SlipdownMountain.com

About the Author

L ISA A. SHIEL RESEARCHES AND WRITES ABOUT EVERYTHING STRANGE, FROM Bigfoot and UFOs to alternative history and science. She has been interviewed for big-city newspapers, national magazines, drive-time talk radio shows, and TV news. Lisa has a master's degree in library science and was previously president of the Upper Peninsula Publishers & Authors Association. As a fiction writer, Lisa developed the Human Origins Series—which includes the novels *The Hunt for Bigfoot* and *Lord of the Dead*. Lisa's nonfiction books include *Backyard Bigfoot, Strange Michigan, Forgotten Tales of Michigan's Upper Peninsula*, and *The Evolution Conspiracy.*

www.LisaShiel.com